THE FREEDOM FIGHTERS

It was all so disorganized. Things happened by chance. It was an unbusinesslike way to run a cause. But what was he trying to accomplish? Ben had traveled to England not six months ago with Dr. Franklin of Philadelphia aboard one of the Rutledge cargo vessels. They had sixteen weeks to plot and plan and exchange views. A lot of the gentleman's philosophy had rubbed off on Rutledge. Now, in 1770, Ben knew for sure that the colonies had only one way to go—they must strive for total independence from England. There wasn't one man in a thousand in the colonies who would take such an extreme stand.

He realized that few men even in Boston were thinking about total freedom from England. Most were still glad to be Englishmen, and loyal to King George III.

But freedom would come. He gave them four years at the most to put everything in perspective. He would wait, make his selections and perhaps make some converts. He looked at a small coin in his pocket. It was a gold piece stamped on both sides. One face said "Freedom Fighters," and on the reverse was lettered "Freedom or Death."

We will send you a free catalog on request. Any titles not in your local bookstore can be purchased by mail. Send the price of the book plus 50¢ shipping charge to Tower Books, P.O. Box 511, Murray Hill Station, New York, N.Y. 10156-0511.

Titles currently in print are available for industrial and sales promotion at reduced rates. Address inquiries to Tower Publications, Inc., Two Park Avenue, New York, N.Y. 10016, Attention: Premium Sales Department.

THE PATRIOTS

Chet Cunningham

TOWER BOOKS  NEW YORK CITY

This book is lovingly dedicated to Merle Cunningham and Hazel Cunningham in Forest Grove, Oregon, without whose help it would not have been possible.

A TOWER BOOK

Published by

Tower Publications, Inc.
Two Park Avenue
New York, N.Y. 10016

BOOK ONE

Chapter One
BOSTON'S STREET-BRAWL MARTYRS

March 5, 1770

As often happened these days in Boston, a gang of hecklers had gathered near the Customs House, and began throwing insults and jeers at a twelve man contingent of English Redcoat troopers who stood guard. Not a day went by that the members of the Twenty-Ninth regimental guard didn't take their share of abuse from the colonials. The soldiers had first arrived in Boston in September of Sixty-Eight, after the Board of Custom Commissioners sent wild and untrue stories to London about riots, plunder and anarchy that put their very lives in jeopardy.

During the winter snowballs and insults were the lot of the guards, but after eighteen months they had grown used to it. Today the snowballs came in larger sizes and the crowd of ruffians at the corner had grown to two dozen. It appeared not only to be saucy boys there, but mulattoes and jeering lowborn as well pelting snowballs at the soldiers. The usual ranks were swelled by a few negroes, Irish Teagues, known troublemakers and outlandish Jack-tars. The troups were avoiding the snowballs the best they could when their commanding officer, Captain Preston, came around the corner on his usual inspection tour.

The snowball that soared high over the crowd was packed hard with slush from the Boston street where the warm March sun was melting the snow. The ice ball slammed hard into the face of a Redcoat private, jolting him off his feet and breaking his jaw. He slumped into the snowy slush in surprise, with a cry of pain and alarm.

A young negro ran forward from the now jeering crowd and threw a bottle at the formation. He was joined by others who advanced into easy range and launched a shower of ice balls, sticks, bottles and small stones at the Lobsterbacks. One soldier caught a bottle and threw it back at the crowd. The action brought a swift and stinging rebuke from his sergeant.

The hecklers heard it and hooted.

"Don't be nasty, Redcoat, you pay attention to your nice sergeant," a jeering call came from the throng.

Now dozens of snowballs and sticks flew at the troopers who tried to dodge them, but quiet orders were given to stand fast, and they held their formation.

"Hey, a bottle of rum says I can hit the bloody captain there in three tries," one of the Jack-tars called. The sailor's first ice ball fell short of its mark, splattering at the officer's feet. The second went wide, and the British officer bristled.

"Take firing positions...Move!" The command shrilled through the suddenly quiet March air. The

6

twelve soldiers glanced at their officer in momentary surprise, then six stepped into a front rank, knelt on one foot, rifles ready, with the other five men forming behind them standing at port arms. No order had been given to take aim.

Ben Rutledge looked over the back of the fine black pulling his one horse chaise, and saw the crowd ahead. Sure enough it was near the Customs House. He and many other of the fifteen thousand inhabitants of Boston had grown to hate the very sight of the building. There was often a crowd of sassy youth around the building poking fun at the Englishmen on guard duty. It was good sport and never got out of hand. But now the crowd looked larger than usual, and he could hear the catcalling and screeching of insults from Yankee throats.

Making life uncomfortable, miserable if possible, for the soldiers had been a continuing form of amusement for some of the colonists since the Redcoats arrived eighteen months ago to act as special guards for the Customs commissioners.

Rutledge had heard the lies the commissioners had written to Parliament to urge them to send the troops. It was a total waste of manpower, the guards simply weren't needed. Ben Rutledge had his own battle to do with the Board of Customs commissioners, dealing with them almost daily as he must since he operated ships between Boston harbor and England. It was common knowledge that the commissioners were thieves and robbers, playing their devious tricks and making every shipper and importer fair game for their charges. No one knew what type of game they were playing or what petty changes they would make in the enforcement of the laws to trap the shippers.

This crowd seemed larger, and Ben Rutledge pulled his black to a stop well in back of the corner, hoping the men would tire of their games and he could get on home. A smile played at the corners of Rutledge's thin lips as he watched. Many times he wished he could take some kind of direct action against the plague of the Board of Customs Commissioners. Thieves, that's all they were, official cheats and swindlers, all with the blessing of Parliament.

Ben Rutledge was about five feet eight inches tall, and given to a few too many pounds at 165. He was in his thirty-fifth year and carried himself with vigor and energy. He had a full head of dark brown hair which was often covered with one of half a dozen or more of his expensive wigs, but today sported only a tall beaver hat. He wore a fancy brocaded waistcoat with silver buttons, and a large blue lace cravat at this throat. His purple plush breeches ended just below the knee where white cotton stockings took over. Ben's shoes were black leather with large silver buckles on each toe. His face was round, full cheeked with large green eyes that missed nothing and remembered everything. He was owner and sole proprietor of Rutledge and Rutledge, a hundred and ten year old importing and exporting firm with its own fleet of a score of ocean-going sailing ships and a lively trade with England and the West Indies.

Ben, from his high position, could see over the taunters and their snowballs and watch the British troopers near the Customs House. He was surprised when they dropped into the classic British up-and-down firing position of the Redcoats. He had heard about it from his militia days. Ben wished the troops would lower their arms and laugh off the taunts, so life could get back to normal. Whenever a musket was pointed there was the chance it might be fired. He tried to relax, but tension seemed to surge through everyone in the area. These pranks usually lasted only a few minutes. The whole thing would be over soon.

Another barrage of snowballs and sticks showered down on the soldiers and a man fell, shook his head and resumed his position. They were experienced troops, and would hold their fire. They wouldn't want to report that they let a bunch of ruffians provoke them into a fight. Firing into such a crowd would be a tragedy. In eighteen months of pressure by the Redcoats and taunting by the Boston Yankees, not a single shot had been fired. Ben doubted that one ever would.

The attackers grew bolder, running as close as ten yards before hurling their missiles, which now included some pieces of the street paving stones. The Lobsterbacks, frozen in their positions by military orders, took more and more direct hits. Ben saw that the captain was suffering his share of the attack, and seemed to be losing both his military bearing and his patience.

"Take aim!" The captain's voice rang out clearly and for a moment all was quiet in the street. Eleven muskets lifted and aimed at the now hooting and laughing hecklers, some of them less than ten yards away.

Above the troopers on the second floor of the

Customs House, Jeffrey Trout, senior commissioner on the Board of Customs, and not yet three months out of London, frowned down at the confrontation. His worst fears were coming true. The mob down there was about to storm the Customs House. Well, by God, he'd see to it that they were met with ball and powder! And if they broke into the building...he hefted the heavy Kentucky Flintlock pistol. It was exactly as he had heard it would be in letters to Parliament from the first board members: imminent danger of riots and anarchy, potential plundering by the colonials. More balls of snow and ice hit the troopers, who watched their officer out of one eye, and aimed their muskets with the other. Sweat beaded Trout's forehead. Why didn't Captain Preston order his men to fire and stop the whole thing? A few dead rioters would certainly discourage this kind of outrage both now and in the future.

Jeffrey Trout scowled at the mob. He was a commissioner in the service of the Crown and his Royal Majesty King George III. He was a gentleman of breeding and position. He did not have to suffer this type of outrage. He had not come to these God-forsaken colonies across the interminable expanse of water just to be hounded by young toughs and even shouldered off the street. He demanded respect. And by God he would have it!

In another two years he could finish his service for the Crown and retire, sail home and establish a comfortable house in London, somewhere near the park. It would make over thirty years of service, thirty years that had been good to him as well as to his purse. Here he would complete building his personal fortune. The port was busy, and the need for strict management and careful interpretation of His Majesty's new laws was obvious. He should be able to complete his goal here within a relatively short time, perhaps well under the two years he had promised his wife. This time she had refused to come with him on his trek and was waiting in their London house.

Trout was a large man, almost six feet, with a wide girth proving his station in life and his ability to eat well. He wore an enormous powdered wig that had a dozen colored ribbons woven into it, the whole thing draping a foot down his back. Wigs were a social necessity in London, and most popular here among the gentry. This was such a confusing place. There was no way to establish the rank of these people except by wealth, and Trout absolutely rebelled at that qualification as being totally unacceptable. If one were low born, one stayed low born. Trout shrugged. He would simply have to put up with it.

The commissioner opened the window slightly so he could see better and hear the captain, who was now talking quietly with his men, reassuring them. Trout raised the heavy flintlock pistol and rested it on the window sill.

Another flurry of snowballs came, but Preston held his men fast, letting some of the missiles hit him, brushing others aside as he stared defiantly at the jeering two dozen pranksters, confident that they would tire of their effrontery before long and leave.

Commissioner Trout was far from being so patient. He saw some of the troopers turn and look at their captain, waiting for the order to fire or port arms. Trout leveled the flintlock over the window sill, aiming it at the closest of the troublemakers, and fired.

Below, a second later, six muskets roared. The sergeant darted a look at Captain Preston, then lifted his own musket and fired. He had heard no command to open the battle. The first volley from the muskets had taken the pranksters totally by surprise. They turned and fled in terror, some screaming. A few pounded across the street and into shops. One man lay in the icy slush where he had fallen, a large red stain already showing in the snow.

Five seconds after the first volley, the rear file fired. The Lobsterbacks were in total control of the situation now. They were in action, on familiar ground. They knew exactly how to act. The front rank reloaded as the rear rank had fired over their heads. Again the Bostonians were shocked and surprised—and some died. Two more men fell, one jolted rearward, a heavy rifle ball through his chest, his back a wet blob of red as he fell dead.

"Cease fire! Cease fire!" Captain Preston roared. He looked over the ranks, fury distorting his face. "Who was the idiot who fired that first...Who was the..." He stopped. "Stand fast!" he bellowed and looked out at the street. By God, the lowborn rabble had asked for it, even if he hadn't given the order to fire. He thought he had heard a single shot before the others, but he couldn't be sure where it came from. None of his men had been injured in the firing, since there had been no return shots.

At the first volley of shots Ben Rutledge's mare shied. It took him a moment to pull her to a standstill, then he tied her as the second round of shots sounded. He ran for the corner. What lunacy! Firing into a crowd of unarmed civilians! The officer would surely be courtmartialed for this, drummed out of the service. At the corner men rushed toward him, fleeing the instant hot-lead death from Redcoat muskets. Ben brushed past two men, one holding his shoulder that billowed with red blood. He ran forward, intent on chastising the regimental officer for his unspeakable stupidity.

When Ben reached the corner, the street was nearly deserted. The soldiers still held their muskets, but had stopped firing.

Ben saw a man lying in the street, trying to drag himself through the slushy snow and icy water away from the Redcoats. Ben ran to help him, and saw that the man was unable to move any more from where he lay in the melted snow. One of his hands clamped over his flowered waistcoat at the chest where a red tide seeped around his fingers. His fancy breeches were muddy, and soaked with ice slush. The linen trousers were much too light for this weather. His blue eyes blinked as he stared up at Ben.

"Oh, sir, it hurts!" His eyes closed and his whole body shook. When his lids opened again his eyes looked misted. "Sir, they've killed me for sure!" Ben sat in the snow and lifted the boy's head and shoulders, holding the lad on his knees. The young eyes wavered, then cleared.

"I'll get you to a physician. You'll be all right."

The youth, who looked about eighteen, shook his head.

"No, no need, sir. I...I was on an errand for my father, when I saw the sport. Jeering at the Lobsterbacks. We've done it before and not..." The talk tired him.

Ben looked for help. Nobody else had ventured into the street. A few stared out at them from the shops.

The boy looked at his hand on his chest, picked it up and saw the swelling stain. He coughed harshly and made a sour face.

"If it's a blood letting your doctor orders, we've well beat him to that." The pain swept through him again, and his body stiffened. "Save your physician, sir. I've too big a Redcoat ball in me." He coughed once more, and this time a gout of blood flew from his mouth, splotching the snow red.

A few curious people had approached, staring at the two in the icy slush. A woman covered her face at the sight of the blood and stepped back. The boy saw her through filmed eyes.

"Indeed, Madam. I am sorry that I have caused you any distress." The boy shuddered and screamed, his face faded to a chalky pallor and his eyes rolled up until only the whites showed. He slumped down dead in Ben Rutledge's arms.

Ben felt for some sign of heartbeat in the boy's chest, found none and closed the eyelids. His hand came away slowly and he stared in hatred at the Redcoats near the Customs House, a growing outrage building in his eyes. He picked up the dead youth, unmindful of the blood that stained his

14

striped waistcoat and fine linen breeches, then carried him three rods to his chaise, where he put the boy in the seat. Ben looked at the five or six who had followed him.

"Do any of you know this lad, or where he lived?"

A small boy of about ten with a fancy waistcoat and silver buckles on his shoes and an expensive wig on his head stepped forward.

"Yes, sir. I do, sir. He is Malcom Tait. Mr. Tait the printer is his father."

Ben knew of the establishment. He swung up, untied the reins and began his sad journey.

Across the intersection behind the second floor window drapes of the Customs House, Jeffrey Trout bit his lip in anger as he saw the familiar figure of Ben Rutledge lift the scalawag rioter from the street and carry him to his chaise. These infuriating ruffians were bad enough, but to have one of the richest men in Boston picking up a dead one from the street...Trout worried about what the townspeople would say. Not that he cared for himself, but the talk must not stand in the way of his Royal function here or his own private operations either.

Trout watched the last of the wounded and dead being removed from the street. He must send words of congratulations to Captain Preston. The big man edged into a chair behind his desk and sat, his hand reaching for a dish of hard candy. Yes, he would have to invite Preston to dinner. It was the least he could do. Now Parliament would have a factual report that the Board of Customs Chief commissioner was not exaggerating when he wrote of danger to persons and property.

He had the report of a captain of the regiment, an actual confrontation, armed intervention, a full scale riot, weapons fired and deaths rendered, and wounds and injuries sustained by the regimental troops. As he sat there, Trout quickly cleaned the flintlock pistol and reloaded it, replacing it in his desk drawer. He opened the windows wide for a moment to let the smell of gunpowder and the smoke out of the room, then signalled for Captain Preston to come upstairs.

One had to watch out for oneself, and in this barbaric land that meant being armed at all times. Trout longed for the day when he could return to his beloved London and search for a new, more expensive, fashionable town house.

Even as he thought of it a small smile played across his face. Today he had shown them, had given the blighters a taste of formal English justice. It would be many a long day before the colonists forgot what had happened there in Boston.

It took Ben Rutledge almost an hour at the Tait printing shop. He explained in detail what happened at the Customs House, assured Mr. Tait that his son had died a hero's death and that his name would be on every lip in Boston by morning. It was a sad mission and Ben was relieved when at last he got back into his rig and headed home. He arrived at his mansion drained, physically and emotionally. His mind was a curious jumble of dates and facts and injustice after injustice, now topped by a massacre in the very heart of Boston town. At first it seemed as if it might be a planned campaign of retribution by Parliament, some gigantic conspiracy to drive the colonies to their knees and beg forgiveness for the right to continue their years as dutiful colonies of Mother England.

Ben drove the chaise to the rear of the house and stopped near the stable, gave the reins to their groom, Harry, a rawboned lad from Pennsylvania, and went up to the side door.

Ben loved this house. He had drawn up the plans and supervised the building of it himself. It was two-storied, fashioned of wood and native stone, with four dormer windows on the slant front roof, two-story columns on each side of the front door, and two ornamentally shuttered windows on each side of the columns on both floors. A truly elegant house outside and in, and Ben knew it would last for two hundred years.

His wife, Sandra, met him in the hall.

"God in Heaven, you're wounded!" she cried running to him.

He held up both hands. "Woman, stop. I'm fine, fit and hearty, only sad of soul. I'll explain while I change into something dry." He had felt the chill of his wet clothing all the way home in the brisk March wind.

A half-hour later he was still trying to get warm in front of a roaring wood fire in the big dining room fireplace. He had shooed away his wife and the maid and had the room to himself. At first he paced in front of the fire, then stood there, turning slowly like a weaner pig on a spit over a bed of hot coals.

His thoughts were still with the dying boy Tait. He may have gone from a brash young taunter to an heroic martyr without meaning to. Ben had realized the political importance of the shootings at once, but only now did he think how the story would spread throughout the whole thirteen colonies, how it would grow in the telling, and how it would hurt the cause of Parliament. The "massacre" could be well used by any group promoting freedom for the colonies.

But for the Tait boy, it was a mortal tragedy, and for the Tait family. The father, Archibald Tait, had been stiff-lipped during Ben's visit. He helped carry his son into the building and laid him on a cot in the printing shop, but a gleam of defiance had shown through the bravery. Tait would be a good man to consider when a printer was needed. Yes, he would be more than willing.

For a moment Ben wondered at the thoughts that were churning through his mind. Two years ago he wouldn't have considered such events remotely possible, but much can happen in two years. British troops, for instance. He sighed and turned, toasting his backside.

Seven years ago he had been elected to the Massachusetts Assembly, and he had been reelected every year since then. In that time he had risen to a position of responsibility. He had even gone to the Stamp Act Congress back in 1765. There he became a dedicated supporter of the rights of the colonies. The Stamp Act Congress had been the first time in one hundred and fifty years that the thirteen separate colonies had banded together and agreed on anything. They had told Parliament that the Stamp Act was wrong, bad for the colonies and for England as well, that it simply would not work, that the colonies would not allow it.

A combination of factors forced England to rescind the Act. The stamped paper was soon withdrawn and life eased back into its familiar pattern of eddy and surge like the tides in Boston harbor. But the action had sparked a faint stirring in many of the hearts of the men at the meeting. It was united action that the colonies had taken. A first move toward unity and the understanding that in such a unity lay greater strength and greater bargaining power than any colony had individually.

The Stamp Act also gave birth to the Sons of Liberty, an action-slanted organization that soon had members in every colony, was intent on smashing the Stamp Act any way possible, through violence, arson, theft, even killing if necessary. After the Stamp Act was rescinded the Sons of Liberty lost their primary cause and faded away.

Ben turned to warm his other side and stared into the blaze. The Stamp Act was only the start of Parliament's drive for more and more control and taxation of the colonies, and the great debate grew whether Parliament had the right to force either internal or external taxation upon the colonies, which were not represented in the decision making machinery in Parliament. This led to a tightening of the Navigation Act laws and establishment of the Board of Customs Commissioners to enforce the tougher new laws and to collect the port charges, bonding and tariffs. A short time later troops were dispatched to Boston—four regiments, to protect the commissioners. The whole thing was ridiculous.

Now this massacre. Ben didn't know what the historians would call it: a battle, a confrontation, a riot, the hecklers' doom, or a massacre, but whatever the name, March 5, 1770 would be a day long remembered in Massachusetts history. It could even be a landmark for the colonies in this fight for equality under English law. Ben wished he knew where it all would lead. To strong local rule? To more control by Parliament? To ten thousand British troops in the colonies to "protect" them?

Ben wished he had his pipe and some of that Burley tobacco he had found in Virginia. But it was in the den, and he wanted to stay warm by the snapping log fire.

The more Ben thought about the politics of the situation, the more he realized that the American colonies were unique in the British Colonial empire. Nowhere else did any colonial government have the self-rule that the Americans had. Before September of 1768 it was almost impossible to find an English soldier in America. The only representatives of the Mother country were the Royal governors appointed by the King, and a few judges.

Each colony had its own elected Assembly. The Massachusetts Assembly and the twelve others made their own laws for the colonies, levied taxes, mounted colonial militia to defend against the Indians, the French and all enemies. The assemblies

20

even paid from taxes the salaries of the governors and judges. There was almost no direction or control from England.

Literally the only English law the colonies had to obey was the Navigation Act, which in effect instructed the colonies to send their raw materials to England and in return to buy almost all their manufactured goods from the mother country. This was natural, since about ninety percent of all colonial Americans lived on farms or in rural areas. This was an agrarian society dependent upon the mother country for manufactured goods.

Ben sat in the big maple rocker now in front of the fire, his boots stretched to the hearth, and wondered if England had given her colonists too much freedom. Now a few minor edicts came down from Parliament, and American hackles were rising, and like angry watchdogs they were all barking their displeasure.

He had seen it growing with each session of the Massachusetts Assembly. In seven years he had seen tremendous changes. He'd heard tales that there was a movement to revive the Sons of Liberty. It had been a rowdy, undisciplined bunch, nearly a mob, hell-bent on taking the law into its own hands. More than one British sympathizer had found himself staring down a musket in those days. It had been a flash-fire organization but one with many members. Ben doubted if anyone could rekindle that white-hot fire that had birthed them. Ben knew as well as anyone. He had been a member of the Sons long ago.

Ever since that first Stamp Act Congress, Ben had been writing and talking with many men in other colonies. They were considering the next logical step. In the first conference they had shown that the colonies could act in concert. Why not present a united front in all matters disputed with Parliament? But progress was slow. Now Ben had little more than a list of those sympathetic with such an idea.

It was all so disorganized. Things happened by chance. It was an unbusinesslike way to run a cause. But what was he trying to accomplish? Ben had traveled to England not six months ago with Dr. Franklin of Philadelphia aboard one of the Rutledge cargo vessels. They had sixteen weeks to plot and plan and exchange views. A lot of the old gentleman's philosophy had rubbed off on Rutledge. Now, in 1770, Ben knew for sure that the colonies had only one way to go—they must strive for total independence from England. There wasn't one man in a thousand in the colonies who would take such an extreme stand.

He realized that few men even in Boston were thinking about total freedom from England. Most were still glad to be Englishmen, and loyal to King George III.

But freedom would come. He gave them four years at the most to put everything in perspective. He would wait, make his selections and perhaps make some converts. He looked at a small coin in his pocket. It was a gold piece stamped on both sides. One face said "Freedom Fighters," and on the reverse was lettered "Freedom or Death."

Ben stared at the coin for a long time. Few men in Boston had even heard about the coins, still fewer owned one. Soon there would be more. After

22

the massacre today their numbers would grow. And it would not be a riotous gang, but rather a carefully honed band of experts willing to risk their reputations, their fortunes, and their very lives for a free America.

The door burst open and two thirteen year old boys roared into the room. The boys were sword-fighting with wooden staves. One gasped, turned, tripped and dramatically fell mortally wounded on his father's lap. Ben knew there would be no more serious thinking for a while.

Sandra rushed into the room after them. "Robert, David, don't disturb your...father." She smiled. "I'm afraid you're already disturbed."

Ben smiled at her. He had never raised his voice to this woman and was sure he never would. He caught both boys and sat them down in front of him. "All right you two jenny runners, come and tell me what you did all day. What have you learned?"

The identical twins laughed, knowing he was teasing them. They both talked at once, asking him to tell them about the massacre, to tell them what had happened.

At first Ben hesitated, then he began. The boys were old enough to face facts. He told them the story exactly as he had witnessed it.

Chapter Two
THE UPSTAIRS ROOM

Promptly at 7:30 that evening Benjamin Rutledge entered the Old Boston Book Shop and paused beside a table with a dozen expensive leather bound volumes. They were beautifully put together and the work of the proprietor. This was one of the oldest book shops in Boston and had a fine stock of Standard English prose, considerable poetry and a few volumes of Shakespeare.

Ben nodded politely at the owner, a Mr. Jonathan Clark.

"We'll be closing in five minutes, sir," Clark said to Ben, with a slight lowering of his head. A British Grenadier with lieutenant's epaulets was reading at a nearby table reserved for browsing. A moment later the soldier rose, paid for a small volume of poetry, and left the shop.

Mr. Clark watched at the door for a minute until he was certain the customer was out of sight, then he threw the bolt, pulled the shade, blew out one of the two bull's-eye lamps and carried the other toward a small room at the rear of the combination book shop and dwelling. Ben chuckled.

"Thought for sure we had a spy there, Jonathan. He had the looks of a sneaky tiger to me."

The proprietor of the store laughed. "I worried some, but then I knew he was all right. No self-respecting Tory spy could stomach that much Marlowe at one sitting. He'd been there for more than half an hour." They both laughed, went through a curtain-hung door and up steep steps to the third floor. At the back of the landing a door opened into a windowless room twelve feet square. It held only a long table, six chairs, and a piece of slate and chalk. A tall, slender man sat at the far end of the table. Near him was a young woman, not more than twenty, and across from her a rough-looking chap with a patch over his left eye. They had been talking, and looked up.

Ben was serious as he moved up and shook hands with each of them, holding the young lady's hand a bit longer than the others.

"I was wondering if the musket fire this afternoon had cooled any of your rebellious spirits," Ben said.

The man with one eye snorted and slammed his brawny fist down on the wooden table rattling a small serving dish.

"That wasn't fair fighting! That was a massacre, shooting those poor lads like pigs in a pen. A ruddy mistake, I'll wager, is what it was. Talk is that nobody heard the bloody captain give the order to fire. Least that's what I hear. A fight? Lordy, sir. I'm more than ready any time, day or night. You just call on me, and I'm first in line."

Ben smiled. He knew Lewis Lynch would be oak-solid. He was a former British Royal Marine, mustered out here two years ago off a ship when he lost an eye in a set-to. Now he was one of

Ben's most trusted workers. Lynch headed up their action group, but so far there had been precious little for him to do.

The man at the end of the table was Dr. Joseph Warren, a fast rising power in Whig political circles, and already a mainstay in influence with the Massachusetts Colonial Assembly. He had long been a friend of Ben's and was his direct tie into the upper echelons of the colony's ruling body. Warren was a medical doctor, a physician, and one of the best in the colony. He was tall, lean and fair, with light blue eyes that evaluated everything and everyone with a remarkable critical exactness. He smiled and gave a gentle nod, his long-fingered hands folded in front of him.

"Good everning, Mr. Rutledge. It's good to see you in such a slightly angry mood after the tragedy we suffered today. Is this the fuse you've been talking about, that one direct action needed to set off the keg of black powder? Is this massacre going to be the petard to launch our war of independence?"

Ben sat down shaking his head. "No, Dr. Warren, I don't think so, or else the explosions would still be sounding. No, we're not ready yet, the population isn't angry enough. This will be a popular uprising, a war of the people when it comes, and come it must—come it shall!"

"But the British troops fired the first shots, sir. Is that still a requirement for your detonator?" the doctor asked.

"Yes, I certainly believe so. For the most part every colony will need to be pushed into the war." All five of them were seated now, and all held one

27

hand on top of the table, fist closed. One by one they opened their hands, palm up. Lying in each was a small gold coin.

"Freedom or Death," they all said together. Then the coins vanished into special, secret spots in their clothing and the meeting began.

Ben looked at each in turn. "It seems the only item we can talk about now is the Customs House shootings. Do we have any first-hand reports?"

"I treated one of the lads," Dr. Warren said. "He was hit in the shoulder, producing a lot of blood but not much damage. He'll be sore for some time, but no permanent harm was done. As I bound him up, I asked him about it, suggesting he was a member of some radical group of troublemakers. He wasn't eighteen yet, he said. But now he'd love to find a musket and do some firing at the Redcoats. He told me they weren't trying to hurt the troopers at all, they were only having sport with them. He was close when the guns went off, and he said he would swear that a weapon was fired from the second-story window of the Customs House first, and then the Redcoats fired."

Ben lifted his brows at this information. It was very possible. They discussed the point for a few minutes, then Ben moved them on. Seated beside Dr. Warren was Mrs. Sadie Wythe, a pretty, small woman of twenty, a seamstress and milliner by trade who lived in a flat on Front Street and who had been widowed less than a year ago by the pox. She wore her blonde hair long about her shoulders, not in the usual braids coiled over her ears. Her eyes were green and her nose turned up just a bit over a small, full-lipped mouth. She smiled often, saying that it cost no more to smile than to frown.

"As we all know," Ben said, "the story of the massacre will flash through the colonies as fast as hooves and sail can take it. It's my suggestion that we help matters along somewhat." Briefly he explained his own near-involvement, and with the report from Dr. Warren, they composed a letter. It contained much speculation, first hand "eyewitness" accounts without names, and roundly castigated the soldiers and their captain for such a foul and dastardly deed. It was soon composed, and Jonathan Clark hurried to bring more paper, quills and ink.

"My plan is to have each of us write the letter as one of us reads from the original. Then we'll have six copies and one good man on a strong horse can head south to New York and on to Philadelphia, leaving copies of this document with as many printing firms and newspapers as he can find along the way who will give it a sympathetic publishing."

All agreed and they started copying it. As the others worked, Lynch got up and put on his coat.

"Since I'm not so good at letter writing, I'll be off to me digs to pick up some heavier clothes, a blanket roll and find that strong horse. Looks like I'm the lad named to do the riding."

Ben paused, his quill in the air. "Thank you, Lewis. Volunteers are always welcome. I'm glad to see you on this mission."

Lynch was back in half an hour, ready to ride. He hid the packet of letters deep inside his black stuff coat. For a hat he wore a three-cornered affair which he could pull down to ward off any spring rain.

Ben took his hand when he was ready to leave. "Lynch, you ride hard but safely. Do you have a weapon?"

"An old Kentucky pistol, but she works."

"Deliver those letters as far as you can, then rest before coming back."

"Aye, I'll do that, sir. And no squabbles with the Lobsterbacks here before I show up, hear? I don't want to miss my share of the fight!"

He turned and went down the steps.

Ben watched the others. "Well, that's a fine move, a good start. It will repay us a hundredfold. Now, back to business. Sadie, what have you to report?"

She had now taken off her calash hood and let her pretty hair hang free. Her eyes sparkled with excitement and anger. "In my 'Journal of Outrage' I will surely include Mr. Rutledge's narration of the Boston massacre which took place this Monday, March 5, 1770. Besides this there is an increasing annoyance on the part of many Boston residents over the billeting of troops in our houses. Almost all consider this an unlevied tax, and I've logged several individual complaints about the increased cost, the inconvenience, and in two cases, enlisted troopers have made improper advances toward young girls living in their own homes. Both cases were quickly handled by the men's commanding officers and the soldiers banished to heatless tents near the harbor."

Sadie saw the discomfort on Dr. Warren's face, knew she had embarrassed him with such frank talk and hurried on, her fingers turning a page in a bound book where she had written various information and records.

"Certain small merchants and farmers are complaining almost daily about the Board of Customs Commissioners and their extravagant, flagrant fees, their duties and bonding for small vessels moving non-commercial goods from one point to another. A stern letter is recommended to be sent to the Massachusetts Assembly urging it to take up this matter with the Governor." She finished and looked at Ben.

"Thank you, Sadie," Ben said. "We all appreciate your fine work in getting this recorded for us. If something important happens that you hear of that you think I might not know about, please send word to me at my office."

"Yes, of course," she said, a spot of color showing in her cheeks.

Ben turned to Dr. Warren, who responded.

"Well, Ben, as you know, our dialogue in the Assembly goes on. Members there are painfully aware of the billeting outrages and the problems with the customs thieves. It's the continuing argument over the right of Parliament to levy any type of tax or revenue upon us, the unrepresented colonies. Virginia was the first to push hard on this idea. Last year they passed resolutions saying that their House of Burgess had the sole and exclusive authority to levy taxes and revenues in Virginia. They went a step further and said it was a violation of their rights to subject American colonies to a Parliamentary statute. Their resolutions were the pattern for those of our own Assembly. The Townshend Acts are wishful thinking by Parliament, and now it looks as if the new leadership of Lord North as First Minister will generally move toward their repeal. My last message from London said we might expect repeal of 'almost all' of the Townshend duties by the end of March.''

Jonathan Clark looked up, his black eyes curious. "And, sir, what will that do to our ban on imports from England? If they leave even two products on duty, will we all hold out?"

"Yes, that is a problem. My source there says they may drop all duties except the one on tea, to make themselves look good. If they do that I'm afraid our merchants will be strongly tempted to begin imports again from England, and ruin the embargo. If one colony falls this way, all will tumble downhill after them in rapid fashion."

"So it looks like we may be winning on the import duty question," Ben said. "It would be a relief for the ship owners and merchants."

"The logical conclusion from all this, ladies and gentlemen, is that we could be headed not for more confrontation with Mother England, but far, far less," Dr. Warren said. "Remember last summer when half of the troops sent here to enforce the Customs Commissioners orders were sent home? That left only two regiments, and you could almost feel the tensions relax."

"But, Dr. Warren. I think it's good that the taxes are going to be repealed by England. That will mean the colonies will again be almost completely home ruled. Isn't that right?" Sadie said.

They murmured their approval. Ben was constantly surprised by this intelligent, vivacious young woman. She thought as clearly as any man he knew. She would be a match for Sam Adams himself.

"The only trouble is, I also agree with Dr. Warren," Sadie went on. "Unless Parliament comes to us with some new harassment, we're in for a time of increasing calm and prosperity."

"Which won't help our cause at all," said the bookseller. "I'm still in favor of an active campaign of retribution and small sniping, biting attacks against the Redcoats. I've made myself clear on this point in the past, and surely it would help intimidate the regiments, and keep them off balance."

"Make them fire some more shots?" asked Ben.

"If need be. The more shots they fire, the better I like it, because that's moving us closer to the day the colonies will unite and take up arms in a public outrage and chase those damn Lobsterbacks right into the bay. Pardon my language, Mrs. Wythe."

"But, my dear Clark. Only if we can't gain our freedom in any other way should we do this," Dr. Warren said. "The less American blood spilled the better. I understand the Twenty-Ninth Regiment has moved with the other troops back into Castle William on the island in the harbor where they have the British Men-o-War for protection."

Clark scowled. "And I say we missed our golden chance! As soon as we heard of the massacre, we should have mounted a company of militia and stormed the Customs House, overrun it, taking captives and burning the place down. We could have scored a proud victory for freedom before the rest of the regiment could have been alerted."

Ben rubbed his chin. He had thought the same as he picked up the dead Tait boy in the street and carried him to the chaise. But the boy's congealing blood had cooled Ben's temper. Not yet. They were not ready for any more bloodshed just yet. It was difficult to decide, but Ben had. Now he told Clark and the others about his involvement and his feelings.

"So we must wait and watch. We will record these tragedies and outrages and illegal acts as they come, and surely more will come. Then, when we are stronger, when the public temper has risen to the right point, when the British soldiers make the wrong move and fire those next shots killing more Americans, then will be the time to strike, and to strike with the whole power of the thirteen colonies behind us!"

Dr. Warren agreed. "Right. We will be ready to fight if we have to, but only in case we have no other option. Ben is right on that score. We aren't afraid to fight, but we can't go off half mad with blood in our eyes, either. That's why the Sons of Liberty fell apart so quickly five years ago. They were founded on the idea of immediate violence to gain their ends. It didn't work then, and it won't work now. We must be smarter than that, we must use our heads, prepare carefully and then at just the right moment, we strike!"

Jonathan fired up a new pipeful and waved the other hand. "I surrender. I'm a good enough soldier to know how to follow orders. As always, I'll stand by the council's decision. Last time we met we talked about expanding our membership. We have a total of fifteen now. We suggested recruit-

34

ing twenty new men a month until we got up to a hundred. Is that still the plan?"

"I'm for it," Sadie said. "If we had wanted a hundred men this afternoon on ten minutes' notice, we couldn't have raised them. Now, if we are moving into a period of quiet, let's get our men ready and trained."

"Sadie Wythe, you continue to amaze me," Dr. Warren said. He reached over and patted her hand. "Your strategy is correct, as usual. Now is the ideal time to build up our striking force so we are ready."

"Then it's done," Ben said. "Each of us should bring in the names of five good men within the next week. Make no promises. When their names and sympathies have been examined, then we'll talk to each one and ask for his secret help. Agreed?"

They all nodded and went on into other matters of organization and emergency assembly. As the meeting came to a close, Dr. Warren stood and walked around the table.

"My friends, as you know, I'll report to Sam Adams what we accomplished here. He's the only non-member who is even faintly aware of our existence, and shall remain the only one."

They broke up then and after chatting a few minutes, Dr. Warren left with Mrs. Wythe, seeing her home from the meeting as he always did. Ben had a tankard of ale with the bookseller in his bachelor quarters below as they usually did, talking over the progress of the group. When they parted it was in good spirits. The Freedom Fighters had taken a giant step forward.

Ben drove his chaise along the Boston streets slowly, thinking about it. He was sure they were on the right path, patient, thoughtful in developing, but moving quickly enough to be potent and ready when needed. Yes, it would work.

He parked his rig in an alley, walked down half a block to the end of the passage, went through a narrow gate and up to a back door which he unlatched and stepped through. There was no light but he knew the way. First a small woodshed, then a dark stairway. At the top a dark kitchen, then toward a room where a thin sliver of light seeped under a doorway.

He knocked and at once opened the door. A girl stood before a mirror arranging a filmy silk gown that covered all of her, yet hid nothing. She smiled at him.

"Ben, darling, you're late."

He stepped in quickly, closed and bolted the door, then went to her and took her delicious young body in his arms and kissed her slightly pouting lips. His hand caught her breast and caressed it through the silk. He felt its warmth, knowing the nipple was filling with blood and standing tall.

He kissed her again, hungrily, then picked her up.

"Sadie Wythe, I got away as quickly as I could. You know very well how careful we must be."

She gave him a little cry of delight, passion and love and clung to him. "You're here, Ben. That's the important part. Oh, Ben, I love you so much!"

On March 6, 1770, dawn broke cold and blustery, a brisk wind whipping the waters of Boston bay into whitecaps and whistling through the empty masts of the tall ships at the docks. Kaleb Nelson came on deck flailing his arms, trying to pound some warmth into them. The port was just beginning to stir, but for an hour he had pushed the last watch making the ship ready to lift anchor. With the first tide at seven, he'd be gone.

His eye caught a group of men moving toward his ship. There was one civilian trailed by a six-man squad of Lobsterbacks of the Twenty-ninth. Whenever the troopers pounded the dock planks, it meant trouble for a captain. He hoped it wasn't his turn: it would hold up his sailing. A moment later he recognized the man as an official from the Customs House. It was as he thought, some damned minor problem with their infernal regulations. When Customs House men came, it always was trouble. But it was too late to get his lines cast off and under way. Even if he did, it would cause problems on his return trip.

Soon it was evident the party was bound for his ship. Captain Nelson swore a muttered stream of invectives questioning the parentage of all customs men as he made his way across the deck to the raw-lumber gangplank. The official party checked the name of the ship, then walked up the cleats of the plank and stepped on board the *Liberty*.

Nelson knew the man only as Granville, a tall portly man in his fifties, who obviously ate too much and exercised too little. He had a bulldog face and a clipped, and now irritating, Cockney accent.

"Captain Nelson, isn't it?" Granville said, tightening his hold on a sheaf of papers.

Captain Nelson nodded. He had never thought of this man's accent before as being annoying. He shrugged. His family had been rooted in the colonies for a century and a half. It made a big difference.

"And this is the sailing vessel *Liberty*?"

"You know she is, Granville. What blithering skullduggery are you up to this time?"

"Skullduggery, is it? You're the one doing the foul deed. You ported here six days ago with twenty-five casks of wine from Madeira. At that time you paid a duty on them. Is this not the case, Captain Nelson?"

"Aye, you know it."

"And thereafter you loaded a great quantity of whale oil and tar and now you make provisions to cast off, outbound."

"Indeed we were, until you slowed us down."

"And where might be the clearance papers showing that you have paid the required Customs House bond on your new cargo?"

Captain Nelson was a thick-set man who weighed two hundred pounds. He had been the victor in seamen's brawls all over the world. Now he stared in frustrated hatred at the representative of the Crown, but he held his anger in check.

"It has been the usual practice for two years to pay the bonding at the time of the outward passage, *Mr.* Granville, as you most certainly know. You've collected from me dozens of times on that exact basis, and 'tis fair to do so again."

"Captain Nelson, you know the law. The statute

38

clearly states that all goods being shipped must be bonded for at the time of loading or no more than twelve hours thereafter. In truth you finished loading three days ago."

"Damn your hide, Granville! I've heard you whipsawing small shippers this way. But you can't get away with it now. This is the Rutledge line, Goddamnit! You can't touch us!"

"By that outburst, sir, I assume you have not posted your bond?"

"You know damn well I haven't, you ugly old bastard!"

Granville's face reddened under the insult. He lifted the papers and selected one.

"Captain Nelson. This is to notify you officially that the Crown, his Royal Highness King George III, the sovereign of England, does now officially find you in violation of the Navigation Act, as enforced by the American Board of Customs Commissioners, and thereby we are empowered to seize your vessel and its cargo, both to be disposed of at such time and place as the Crown shall decree, in repayment for such fees and duties or bonds and fines as are at that time owing."

Nelson charged at Granville, ready to tear his head from his body, to smash that sneering, lying face. But two hefty Redcoats leaped in front of Granville, their bayonets mounted and gleaming on the ends of their muskets, and both were pointing directly at Captain Nelson. He slid to a stop, almost falling.

Granville laughed. "Never make a threat you can't back up, Nelson. You now have one hour to leave this Royal British Vessel with all of your crew and your personal gear. The men and yourself will be inspected as you depart, as well as anything they try to take away." He looked up at the tall, trim masts. "Yes, she's a fine ship, should bring forty to fifty thousand pounds at auction." Granville chuckled at Captain Nelson's expression and walked down the gangplank.

The Captain stood watching, not quite sure what he could do, or what he should do. As soon as these bilge rats left he'd sail out of here, that was for sure, clearance or no clearance. But as he watched, he realized the six Redcoats had no intention of leaving. One went to the bow, another positioned himself at the stern. A third stood near the captain and two more guarded the gangplank. There wasn't a damn thing he could do to prevent the loss of his ship!

A few hundred yards down the dock another Rutledge ship was boarded by an official party. This time the three Redcoats remained on the dock.

A smallish, gray-haired man asked a crewman to bring the Captain. When he came, the man stared at him a moment. "Captain Victor, your cargo menifests for inspection, please," he said. The Customs House man wore a stiff black waistcoat and had a white ruffled shirt billowing at his throat. His wig was long and heavily greased so it would hold the white powder. His name was McWhirter, and he'd been with the Commission for the entire two years of its existence here. He knew all the shippers and most of the captains, and liked them.

Captain Victor was a smart man, and fo'c'sle tough. He had come up through the ranks and knew every trick and sham the Customs Commissioners could pull. He watched McWhirter closely, and saw a different man. His easy smile was missing, his lips were now pursed, his eyes hooded and unhappy. Victor knew something was afoot. He had to play the game carefully, as he always did with the English authorities on the docks. Maybe McWhirter was looking for a few pounds of gentle bribery, but before he had always been one of the easiest customs men to work with.

Victor sent a man for the third mate and the papers, his eyes never leaving the small Commissioner.

"McWhirter, is this a mistake? You just checked the manifests yesterday when we put in from London."

The Commissioner's face sagged. He tried to stand straighter so he would be taller, but managed only to frown. "Quite so, Captain, but I must have overlooked something."

"Yesterday you said it was all proper and correct, that you seldom saw papers in such good order. I don't understand..."

The mate came with the papers, and McWhirter looked through them quickly. The penmanship was large, bold, and easy to read.

"Yes, I thought so. Twelve casks of rum. They don't show here, yet I saw them plainly yesterday among your cargo."

Captain Victor laughed. "So that's all it is. That's Captain's stores. I've got to eat and drink on these long voyages. That's me year's supply. You mentioned it yesterday, McWhirter. You joked about my capacity for rum."

The Customs man frowned harder. "The law is the law, Captain. I must demand the usual bond and the penalty, twenty-seven pounds in this case, or I'll have to take your ship."

Captain Victor couldn't believe it. He stared at the smaller man for a deadly minute as his hand came down over the dirk he wore in plain sight. His eyes never flinched, but the Commissioner lowered his gaze and stepped back.

"Come, come. I have more work to do. Twenty-seven pounds, or I'll have to impound your vessel. Which shall it be?"

Captain Victor nodded to the mate who scurried into his cabin and brought back the money in English silver in a small leather pouch. McWhirter took it, didn't bother to count it, and walked toward the gangplank. A look of contrition edged onto his face, then it was gone. Captain Victor walked with him and just as they reached the rail, McWhirter stumbled over one of the captain's outstretched boots. Victor then seemed to try to catch the commissioner but instead somehow unbalanced him even further. The small man tumbled over the low ship's rail and splashed into Boston harbor between the ship and pier.

At once the three Redcoats on the dock rushed to help the commissioner. He had not cried out when he fell. He came to the surface clutching at his wig, which had washed off. He still held the bag of coins, and kicked to a piling and a rough ladder. He climbed slowly back to the dock. He stood there for a moment, wringing water from his clothes, facing away from the ship. A sergeant of the Twenty-Ninth argued with him, pointing back at the sailing craft. But the small man would not yield. A moment later McWhirter walked away, the Redcoats marching along behind him, obviously angry at the disrespect shown for the Crown.

A short distance farther south, two tidesmen, minor Customs House officials, marched brusquely aboard the *Lydia*, another of the Rutledge ships, and quickly moved below decks, where they began inspecting cargo. The captain was not on board, still lying abed in his Charlestown home. The second mate heard the loud voices and went below deck to discover the problem. The two tidesmen stood at the side of the hold, one with a marline-spike, the other with a piece of wood as a weapon.

"Sir, these two 'Tory-rats have no right down here," one of the sailors screeched.

"We're from the Customs Commission," one of them began. The closest seaman saw his chance, darted under the long iron spike, and caught the customs man by the waist, slamming him back against the bulkhead so hard he dropped his weapon. The other tidesman swung his board, missed and was bodily picked off his feet by the other seaman and carried topside where he was dumped on the deck.

"Sir, you have no right below decks on this ship without proper written orders of the commission," the second mate roared. "Now get off this ship until you're authorized to do your dirty work!"

They left sulking. Once on the dock the spokes-man turned, his face boiling with anger. "You've not heard the last of this, I warn ye. I'll have a criminal action lodged against you and Rutledge before the sun sets, you see if I don't! It's a crimi-nal act of assault and disturbing us in our lawful duties. You'll rot in London tower before I'm through with you!"

The crew lined the rail now, laughing at the ti-desmen and hooting them down.

Two days later, Ben Rutledge was served with an official proceedings naming him and his ship's second mate and two seamen on a charge of "criminal non-compliance with the Navigation Act, and the abuse, harassment and physical as-sault on two of the commissions workers."

The same day Ben received notice of the charges, he had other worries. Two of his three-masted sailing ships had been seized by the Cus-toms Board of Commissioners for irregularities in customs duties. He had tried in vain with Gover-nor Francis Bernard to have the ships returned to him. They were being scheduled for sale the fol-lowing day. His good friend John Hancock, a pow-erful man in Whig politics as well as being the largest marine shipper in the new world, said he would also try to have the ship sale put off.

In the past three days every ship that Rutledge owned and in port had been boarded and fined or seized or quarantined for some real or imagined breach of the Navigation Act. Many minor laws and rules usually not enforced were strictly applied. Others, by long agreement handled one way, were at once changed or interpreted differently and enforced strictly.

Ben had been buffeted from every side, and at first he didn't know why. John Hancock was much more prominent in local political action than he was.

Now, as he stared at the message from Sam Adams, he knew what the cause was. Ben had long admired Sam. For a man who had failed in one business venture after another, he was now doing very well. He was the acknowledged leader in political thought and action in Massachusetts. Ben was sure Mr. Adams had done it again. He read the report, which was penned in Sam's own strange hand.

"Ben: I am now in possession of sworn statements of three well-known patriots who affirm that one Jeffrey Trout, Ranking British Customs Commissioner, was seen at the open window over the front door of the Boston Customs House on the afternoon of March 5, and that said Mr. Trout did extend a short-barreled weapon, believed to be a pistol, out the window and fired a round of shot at the men and boys jeering the soldiers below. This took place *before* any firing came from the Redcoats. After the shot from above, the soldiers fired two volleys before stopped by Captain Preston. Jeffrey Trout caused, launched and began the Boston Massacre. He then almost certainly did see you, Ben, administer aid and comfort to the Tait youngster and afterwards remove the body to your chaise and thus to his family."

Ben stroked his chin, then puffed on his pipe. It

was obvious what he should do. He remembered his days in the Sons of Liberty, and knew well and for certain that if this had happened in 1765 and the Sons of Liberty had had this type of evidence, Mr. Trout would have been ambushed and summarily executed for his part in the crime. But now, with maturity, his own temper and his own hot blood had cooled considerably. The new organization was much stronger in terms of intelligence, in motivation, and in its ability to get information and to sway important persons.

He looked down at his desk where the oak top was covered by a two-sheet list of offenses the Crown had claimed by his ships in the past few days. Every vessel he owned floating in the harbor had been fined or seized. The two impounded clippers represented a fortune. They had to be saved from the auction block. He would appeal again to Governor Bernard.

The fines alone had come to over four hundred pounds. That was a small fortune to any man. In Boston those days a bachelor could live quite comfortably on twenty-five pounds a year. The infuriating part of the fines was that most of the money went directly to the thieves at the Customs House. They had twisted the laws to their own satisfaction, and profit, and had the troops to back them up.

But now the letter from the ever-vigilant Sam Adams had shown the real cause of his problems. His ships were harrassed for one reason only, a vendetta against Ben Rutledge for going to the assistance of a dying boy. It was personal vengeance.

Ben tamped the tobacco down in his pipe and

46

relit it, then stared out his window across the ships in Boston harbor. He felt the old itchings, the urgings, the real need for some vengeance of his own—not the extreme variety of the Sons of Liberty. But something, something else. He kept thinking about it. Slowly an idea began to gather in his mind. He let it form, let it sprout and burst into the sunlight, then to grow, to rise up, develop a stem and leaf, then to bud and slowly flower.

Ben walked around his office drinking a hot cup of tea. Then at last he settled down in his comfortable chair. A smile spread across his face and showed that he had come to the perfect solution, a unique type of retribution against Commissioner Trout. And done in a way that no one could tell who did it. Indeed, there could not be the least suspicion of Ben Rutledge, since he would be in New York at the time on one of his ships. Yes, it would be a just and delicious revenge!

Chapter Three
THE TORY'S SOLITARY MARCH

Ben Rutledge tousled the heads of his twin sons, pushed them aside and held a quick boxing lesson with each, then picked up both and dumped them on a couch. He bent and kissed the cheek of his daughter Harriet, and then touched his wife's shoulder.

"I can't imagine why all of you are so interested in my little trip all of a sudden," Ben said. "I've sailed to New York and Philadelphia a dozen times, and I've never had a send-off like this one. What's so special this time?"

He was dressed in one of his better pair of blue breeches and a plain blue waistcoat with a ruffled white shirt front. Since he was going on board of one of his own ships he did not wear a wig, only a finely made three-cornered hat.

Sandra kissed his cheek impulsively. They seldom showed much affection in front of the children, and she blushed.

"Now don't you worry so about business. I'm sure the ships will come back to us. They can't simply take them for no reason. Your claim with the attorney general will surely be upheld."

He didn't often talk over business troubles with

Sandra, but this time he had been extremely concerned. Sandra was a good woman. She had been a fine wife to him, strong and upstanding, and in her own way attractive. He turned deliberately and strode to the door.

"Now, enough of this. I must be going. I'll be back home safe and sound about mid-day three days from now. Boys, you mind your mother and do exactly as she says, or you'll hear from me when I return."

"Yes, Father," Robert said, his eyes serious.

David only nodded and grinned. Sometimes Ben thought David Lewis Rutledge was far too wise for his age, as if he were a man in a boy's body that hadn't completed its physical growth.

Ben left, stepping into his chaise with Harry, their groom, driving. The gray was ready and waiting at the front door. They drove directly to the docks where Ben took out his one piece of baggage, a leather valise which came together on the top with a leather hasp and a handle. He carried it toward the water where one of his two-masters for coastwise freight lay at anchor. The *Freedom* pulled gently at its lines, almost ready to catch the morning breeze. Ben walked up the gangplank, talked briefly with the first mate, and then went below and stretched out in the captain's cabin.

An hour later a small boat left the side of the *Freedom*. She was well inside the hook of Noodles Island when the boat cleared her and made for the shore. A man with a patch over his left eye rowed the boat, and in the stern sat Ben Rutledge. His fancy clothes were carefully stored in his valise in the Captain's cabin on board the New York-bound

Freedom. He wore old breeches, a shirt he had once discarded, a rough coat and a stocking cap to keep off the brisk wind. The rowboat only paused at Noodles Island, then swung around the hook and angled toward the far reaches of Boston town.

Lewis Lynch looked up from his rowing. "I'll say it's good to be taking the fight to the bloody Redcoats. You did promise me a go at them, didn't you, sir?"

Ben chuckled at the raw anger under the ex-marine's words. "It will be tame compared to what you're expecting, Lynch, but maybe enough to whet your appetite for more. Remember, I am now on board that ship heading for New York. Everything that happens during the next two days is officially a secret between you and me."

"Aye, sir, that I ken. I'm busting to know exactly what we're going to be at. A hint, sir?"

As Lynch powered the small boat through the now calm waters of Boston bay, Ben outlined what he had in mind, and Lynch began to grin, at last to roar in delight.

"Right-o, sir! Oh, yes. That's why you had me make those arrangements yesterday. I can see your thoughts behind it all, sir. It will surely work, just like those letters I took south. 'Twas the news they wanted. I got a grand welcome at every stop. Food and drink they treated me to. The first three towns I waited while they copied down the letter so I could get to more places." He laughed. "You really think we can take care of the Commissioner this way?"

"With your help, Lewis, I know we can."

Later they pulled the rowboat into a deserted

51

stretch of Boston beach and walked quickly away. Ben's stocking cap was low on his head, his collar up against the fresh breeze. They walked toward Lynch's one-room lodging in back of a hardgoods merchant.

"You have everything we need?" asked Ben.

Lynch nodded. "Sure, all ready and waiting, just like you asked." They each took cloth sacks from the ex-marine's quarters and walked on toward the center of town. Ben marveled at the way the tiny community of Boston had grown in recent years. Now more than fifteen thousand souls called it home.

Soon they came to the alley in back of the Customs House. Ben moved ahead casually. There was no one in sight. Lynch was lookout from the far end of the alley, but Ben would have to be on the watch for himself at the near end. He found the chaise he wanted, saw that the horse had been moved for the day to some stable. He double-checked to make sure it was the rig belonging to Commissioner Trout. Quickly he went to the left-hand wheel. The usual axle inside rub plate was there, then the wooden wheel hub held in place by an outside collar device and a wooden pin driven through a hole bored in the axle. If that pin were out and the collar moved outward enough...

From the cloth sack Ben took a large wooden mallet and checked the alley again. No one was in sight. He struck the wooden retaining pin sharply with the mallet. Nothing gave. He hit the pin from the other end and felt movement. Three more hard strokes and the pin loosened enough to be worked out by hand. Ben put the mallet back in the cloth sack, threw the wooden pin over a fence and worked the wheel collar outward an inch. Now there was little holding the wheel on the axle but the loose collar and friction. He rose, took the sack and walked silently back to the street.

Lynch and Ben sat in a small tavern just up the street from the Custom House and waited. All was ready. When the big sundial in the square showed that it was nearing six o'clock, they saw the Commissioner's rig driving out the alley mouth. The well-fed black turned the corner smartly and pranced up the street. Ben watched the left wheel work outward on the corner but hold on the axle.

The Commissioner sat nodding behind the reins. His boot was on the footboard to steady himself and the top was extended up full to ward off any sunshine or rain. The black stepped out briskly, knowing where home was and that his feed bag would be waiting as soon as he finished his day's duty. Before the rig had passed the first block, Commissioner Jeffrey Trout was snoring.

Ben and Lewis walked after him, not trying to keep up, but to stay in sight as long as possible. Lewis had placed friends at strategic spots along the six-block route. It was on the second corner, a swing to the right, that the wheel worked its way off the axle. As the chaise turned, the left wheel spun off and kept rolling straight ahead. There was a sudden jolting drop on the left side of the rig, tumbling Commissioner Trout to his left. If he'd been awake he could have held on, but waking up fast, he couldn't find his bearings and spilled from the still moving chaise. He hit on one elbow and his forehead, skidding on the paving blocks for three feet before he stopped. The black, sensing the dragging axle and tilted left shaft, reacted in panic and galloped down the street as fast as he could go.

Commissioner Trout lay on the stones screaming. There were no soldiers in sight. He sat up, still spouting invective against his horse and chaise. Then he saw the four-foot-high wheel with its wooden hub and yellow painted wooden spokes with a pounded iron rim on the outside, come rolling toward him. Two boys in their teens rolled the heavy wheel like a hoop, shouting and laughing.

"You young whelps! Bring back my wheel!" Trout screamed.

The boys heard him, and changed the angle of the huge hoop until it rolled directly at the fallen commissioner. He reached up to grab it, but realized it weighed several stone and let it rumble past him. Beyond where he lay, two more boys caught up with the wheel and kept it rolling directly toward the waterfront. The commissioner had at last gained his feet when he saw the yellow-spoked wheel bounce over a tie down davit and splash into the bay.

Trout screeched, calling for aid, cursing everyone he saw, and when no Redcoats came to his assistance, he began a slow walk toward his lodgings. He showed considerable restraint by permitting only a slight limp. Trout held his lace-bordered silk handkerchief to his head to stop the flow of blood from his badly scraped skin. He was furious. His dignity had been badly tarnished. He would discover why the wheel came off and if it were that wheelwright's fault, the man would be severely punished.

A block behind the commissioner and well out of sight, Ben Rutledge and Lewis guffawed. Tears came to Ben's eyes because he was laughing so hard. The two men watched the struggling commissioner out of sight, then walked into a tavern to lift a tankard in victory.

When the ale was gone they stayed and ate a meal of stew and hard rolls topped off with a mug of rum. Ben was still in disguise, and so was Lynch. No one paid them any heed and they ate quietly, waiting for darkness.

There was no moon that Monday night, March 12, 1770. Scudding clouds heavy with rain sped over Boston, drenching everyone and everything not under cover. About midnight the two men walked through the night, not even trying to stay out of the rain, intent only on reaching their target.

When they came to the alley behind the Customs House they moved stealthily from one shadow to the next, like the Indian fighters did in the untamed frontier beyond the Appalachian mountains. Slowly they worked their way up the alley to the rear door of the Customs House. Sometimes a guard stood there day and night, but now no Redcoat was in evidence. They looked in all the possible places a soldier might be huddled out of the rain, but found no one.

Lynch examined the lock and took several skeleton keys from a ring in his pocket, but none worked. He tried an iron pry bar they carried, and on the second effort the door sprung open and they stepped inside the back room of the Customs House, their clothes dripping puddles on the floor.

Ben took over. He had been in the building many times, posting bond or having papers signed. He went through two doors, then came to the part he wanted, the first floor, just in back of the public office area. Here was where the permanent records were stored, and where all current fines and charges were posted. These were the documents that could hurt the shippers, and which the crown would find impossible to replace.

He made sure he stayed away from the racks of records showing the usual payments of regular fees and normal bonding.

From bags slung under their heavy coats, both men took out bottles of sulphuric acid. They poured the contents over the drawers of records, watching the hungry acid eat up the paperwork of two years. Ben finished the last container of acid and shook his head. The papers weren't destroyed.

"We've got to burn them, Lynch. Did you bring those pitch sticks?"

Lynch pulled a dozen half-inch square split sticks from his pocket. Each one was dark brown with pine pitch. Ben took one and went into the front of the building but found no fireplace. On the second floor he saw one in the commissioner's office. The fire had been carefully banked with a round oak log on it to smolder all night. Ben blew one end of a pitch stick into a blaze and ran back downstairs with it.

"I'll light these. You move toward the back where the guards are quartered. Get something burning there, but do it quietly. When it's set and flaming good, we both go out the same door we came in and over the fence."

Lynch, who had been lighting two pitch sticks from the blazing one Ben held, nodded that he understood and hurried to the back of the room and through the door.

Ben piled handfuls of papers on the bottom of the wooden drawers and pulled out several more. Then he began lighting each of the critical stacks of papers so they would burn, catch other sections above them and multiply the flames a dozen-fold. It was his hope that the blaze would be found and put out but only after the harmful records were burned. They were starting the other fire near the troops so the men would be alerted.

Ben fed his last two pitch sticks into the burning drawer marked "fines and seizures" to make sure it burned well, then ran for the back door. He opened it and waited. A moment later he heard footsteps and Lynch came out of the gloom.

"Let's shove off, mate, she's all a-burning!"

They left, closed the door and climbed the fence, then made their way through a house's rain-sodden side yard and into the street. They walked around the block twice, but still had to wait in a doorway across the street and down from the Customs House for what Ben guessed was half an hour before they heard noises from the far end of the block-long structure. Men poured out doors and windows. A call for the fire brigade went out and was passed from one house to the next.

Someone stormed out the front door of the Customs House and yelled that it was on fire. Within half an hour, the lines of men passing buckets of water into the building had put out the fire. Many of the papers had smoldered, charring them and making a lot of smoke without much flames. Ben and Lynch stayed out of the fire-fighting.

They grinned at each other and ambled away from the site and the small crowd which had gathered despite the falling rain. Both men were soaked through to their skins. They parted, agreeing to meet the following morning in the Black Horse Tavern near the edge of town.

Ben made his way through the streets, paused at each intersection to be sure no one was watching or following him, and a short time later lifted the latch on the gate off an alley and went into a woodshed, then up the stairs and into the Widow Wythe's kitchen. She was not expecting him. He walked quietly to the bedroom and saw this time there was no light under the door. He opened it silently and stepped inside. The darkness was total here. He felt his way to the bed, leaned over it and at once caught the unmistakable clean, fresh scent of Sadie Wythe. His gentle hands found her body, then her face, and he kissed her sleeping lips. She didn't waken, only murmured and stirred.

Quickly he pulled off the sodden clothing and dropped it in a pile. He was shivering before he was through. He slid between the blankets beside her, his naked legs twining with hers, his hands finding her breasts. This time he kissed her hard and she moaned in delight, her hands moving over his body. When his lips eased off hers, she giggled.

"I was having the most wonderful dream," she said. Then she yelped. "Ben?"

He laughed.

"Oh, my! I had no idea you were coming. Ben, why didn't you tell me!"

"I couldn't, Sadie. Couldn't possibly have told you. You see, right now I'm on a ship halfway to New York!"

They woke early, just before dawn, he guessed. It was bitingly cold in the unheated bedroom. They shivered a moment under the stack of comforters, then his hand touched her and he pulled her toward him. They made love slowly, softly, then lay watching the first dawn brighten the room.

"I'm so confused," Sadie said, her pretty face twisted with doubts, eyes glistening with unshed tears. "I've heard for so many years about wicked women who love other women's husbands, who sin out of wedlock. It was evil and wanton. It was unthinkable, so terrible, so shameful that a nice girl didn't even think about it. Making love was for married people, and that was all. We were even told about the bad women in the Bible. It was shameful scandalous, outrageous!" She reached up and kissed his cheek. "But when I'm here with you, when I can still breathe in the scent of you, I feel absolutely marvelous. I come alive, I feel like I'm a truly whole person again. I was so lost and empty after Karl died. But now I'm alive again, and I want to be with you as much as I can be. Why, darling? Am I so wicked? Why do I feel simply marvelous when I know I should be hiding my face in shame?"

He kissed her slightly tipped-up nose. "My little green-eyed pixie. You must never hide your beautiful face. It's a marvel to behold. For that matter don't hide any part of your delicious little body from me. Sadie, my secret love, it's your absolute *right* to be happy. If I can in some way make your life easier, fuller, then I have a right to do that, and a responsibility." He kissed her lips. "As for our secret, it's only prudent and wise. We don't want to hurt your reputation in any way. Can't you see that your joy isn't one-sided? I have just as much delight and satisfaction and pleasure from our being together as you. This is one place I can feel totally at peace. We both gain so much." He watched her, bent under the covers, and kissed both her breasts. He lifted up and stared at her. "I love you, you snip of a girl. I love you so much it makes me cry out in alarm sometimes. But I love my wife and children as well. We've talked about it, and I think you do understand."

"Yes, Ben, I do. I loved once so deeply, so well, and I knew it could never happen again. I could never feel that way about anyone else. Then he was taken away from me and I found a new love and I do understand, because I too love two persons. Karl will never really die as long as I love and remember him. So I do understand, and I'm so grateful and proud that you care for me."

Sadie sat up on the bed, letting the comforter fall away from her breasts, her nipples still standing tall. He caught a breast in each hand, and she sighed, then pushed away from him and began to dress in the chilly air.

He had told her about the previous night's mischief.

"You're determined to pay Commissioner Trout one more call, and humiliate him totally? There's no way I can talk you out of this?"

"No. I've suffered enough at his hand, and under his orders. I have a right to do this."

"But the group has cautioned us against violence."

He hushed her with a look. "I'm the injured party. This is not connected in any way with the Freedom Fighters, it's personal. You are not to mention a word of this to anyone."

She stood, pulling on more clothes, watching him. "Then you'll be staying here again tonight?" She glanced at him. "Oh, please come back tonight!"

He stood, naked, and kissed her. She hugged his warm body to hers, then let him go.

"Get some clothes on or you'll die of the consumption, for sure." Sadie turned and hurried into the kitchen to get a cooking fire going from a carefully tended closed container of live coals.

They breakfasted on hard rolls, with a touch of strawberry jam and hot tea.

"Do you realize that we've never had breakfast together before?" he asked, with a slow smile.

"Yes, I've thought about it." Her expression was secretive now. "This is nice, but tomorrow morning I'll be better prepared."

She left soon after that to go to the millinery shop on First Street where she worked with two others making bonnets, fancy hats and bags of all kinds. He huddled near the small cooking fire to keep his hands warm, and thought over his plans.

After much work the week before he had come up with the master framework: rid Boston of Commissioner Jeffrey Trout for good. Ben hadn't finalized everything then, and told Lynch just enough so he could lay the preliminary plans. Noon would be the best time, when there were the most people on the streets.

English sympathizers, the Tories and royalists in Boston were often used as informants against the unsuspecting Yankees in times of stress. There had been much spying and selling of information to the commissioners during the past two years, since the board had come to Boston. The troops brought more informers. Ben knew of several men along the waterfront whom he suspected of making their living by informing on ship owners and captains who were violating some small part of the Navigation Act. The spy was usually given two shillings on the spot and a quick boot out the back door of the Customs House. Then the commissioners or their lackeys would swoop down on the violators.

Since Lynch with his eye patch could easily be identified, it fell to Ben to make the report. He worked it up fat enough that it seemed a ship's captain was flagrantly violating the Act and his ship could be impounded. That would call for Commissioner Trout himself to do the dirty work, since he then would benefit the most from the seizure.

Ben and Lynch met in the Black Horse Tavern that morning and set the details of the plans. They had a tankard, then went their separate ways. Now Ben hitched along as if he had a game leg up the alley at the rear of the Customs House.

He wore another set of old clothes with a ragged muffler wrapped around most of his face, hiding all except his eyes. A black seaman's stocking cap covered his hair and forehead.

Earlier, when he passed a sundial in the street, he saw that by sun time it was just after 11:30 a.m. Perfect. It took Ben two minutes of pounding on the back door to raise anyone.

"Go away, wharf rat!" a Redcoat said when he at last cracked the door.

"Oh, no, sir. Please! I have information the commissioners will be glad to get! A bad thing the captain has done."

The soldier cocked his head, frowned, then sighed and at last motioned Ben inside. Ben hunched against the side of the wall.

"Scum. Stay there, and don't steal anything. I'll be back in a moment."

Five minutes went by before a clerk came in. He had on a fancy waistcoat, ruffled shirt sleeves and lace at his throat. He wore a long powdered wig, and was trying to look as official as he could.

He only glanced at Ben, not wanting to lower himself by speaking to such an obvious lowborn.

"Sir, sir!" Ben began. "The Commissioner General himself said to me, if I see anything important to come. I have."

"Tell me and I'll see if it's important."

"No. I'll tell only the General Commissioner. It has to do with hidden wine. Much smuggled Madeira wine!"

The clerk rubbed his smooth-shaven chin, then turned and stalked away. Ten minutes passed before the commissioner himself came. Trout had a large bandage over his forehead and he walked with a decided limp. His face was puffed and he glared dangerously.

"Well, well, spit it out, you lout! What have you?"

Quickly Ben gave him a slightly confusing story about thirty large casks of fine Madeira wine. It had been sunken in the bilges on the *Mary Jane,* a three-master owned by Hancock. Now the wine was out of the bilges in the main hold ready for off-loading. So the commissioner would have to hurry to catch them.

Trout glared at Ben, but his eyes were filled with profit. He thrust four shillings into Ben's hand and pushed him out the door. Ben hobbled part of the way down the alley, then walked faster. When he turned the corner he was running. He untied a borrowed horse and rode fast for the docks where the *Mary Jane* was moored.

They had plotted it carefully, and figured the commissioner would come by the fastest route, which led through a narrow street just across the way from the dock. There it would be easy to push several carts or wagons together, to block the street and give them an opportunity to capture him.

Ben tied his horse half a block away and walked to the spot where Lynch already had one heavy wagon halfway across the street. The wagon was placed just past a slight bend so the blockage would not be noticed until it was too late for the victim to stop or turn.

A man waved, and Ben saw it was Lynch, with a muffler covering most of his face. Behind him were four more men, all about the same size, with scarves shielding their faces. The weather had turned bright, but a brisk wind still whistled through the buildings. Back the way Ben had come, a man ran into the street and waved both hands.

"Aye, sir. That's the signal. Trout is coming. He got himself a new wheel for his chaise. Look sharp now!"

They all moved back into the shadows to await the critical time to thrust the second wagon forward.

Ben heard the clopping of the horse's hooves on the paving stones, then a rig whirled around the corner, Commissioner Trout himself flicking a whip over the horse's head.

"Now, lads!" Lynch ordered, and a wagon loaded with boxes rolled forward, blocking the street.

For a moment Commissioner Trout's chaise rolled on. Ben wondered if the man didn't see the blocked street. Then Trout shouted at the horse and jerked back on the reins. The frightened animal reared his front feet high, but he stopped just before crashing into the wagon. When the horse went up, he lifted the stiff shafts of the chaise with him until Trout almost rolled out the back of the small two-wheeled rig. He got the horse under control and at once a man stepped out and took the bridle. Another man stood at each side of the chaise.

"Out of the way at once. I'm a British official on important business!" Trout thundered.

Neither man moved.

"Come now, lads, I must get to the docks,"

Trout said, a little more reasonably. He seemed to realize this meant trouble.

"Get out of the chaise, Trout," a voice boomed from behind him. Ben had lowered his normal voice to make it impossible to recognize.

"Out? I say, this is going too far!"

The man beside the rig reached in and grabbed Trout's arm, dragging the commissioner out of the contrivance and standing him beside it. Another man came and they hustled Trout into a deserted building that had recently been a tannery. As soon as Trout was inside, the wagons were moved and his chaise driven down the block.

Inside the tannery, two men went to work methodically. Lynch slapped Trout hard across the face and jerked the bandage off his scraped forehead. Then Ben growled in a hard-to-recognize voice.

"Trout, you have ten seconds to start taking your clothes off. If you don't, we'll rip them off you."

"Now see here, sir. Do you know who I am? Yes, I see that you do. This is treason, kidnapping, assault. I'll see you swinging at the gallows for this! You realize that, don't you?"

Lynch had worked around behind the commissioner and suddenly yanked the heavy powdered wig from Trout's head. Lynch threw it on the floor and listened to the cry of surprise.

"Really, now!"

Lynch's knife began slicing buttons off the waistcoat. Trout held up his hand.

"Enough. I'll disrobe. But why?"

"You'll find out, Trout."

He proceeded slowly, until Lynch's knife point hurried him. When he had his long knit underwear off and stood naked, Lynch painted on his back the words: "Town Idiot."

The chaise came around to the door and they hustled Trout into it, with Ben and Lynch on each side. They drove within four blocks of the Customs House, where the offices and stores brought a noon-time throng of shoppers. Both men got out and pulled Trout with them. Each had a cat-o-nine-tails and popped Trout lightly on the back. He howled in pain.

"Start walking, Trout, right up the street. You'll get encouragement all the way. Please bow and say hello to all the ladies we meet."

Trout stared at him, killing hatred boiling from his eyes. The cat clawed his back lightly, and Trout groaned, then began walking forward.

A woman came out of a market, screamed at the sight of a naked man in the street, and darted back into the shop. Ben searched the way ahead. There was no sign of any Redcoats. As usual, they were having their big noontime meal.

"Keep walking, Trout. Don't run or we'll lay the cat on you."

Trout walked, head down. Two small boys hooted at him and joined the group behind the victim.

A shipper recognized Trout and roared in delight. "Give him ten lashes for me, boys!" he called.

Ahead in the street at hundred-yard intervals stood three men with wrappers over their faces. As the group moved, it picked up dozens of young boys, all screaming and taunting Trout. Men hooted at the commissioner, two women fainted when they met him almost face to face. Young girls tittered, rushed into shops and peered out through the windows.

"I'll see you all hang for this!" Trout screamed.

A moment later two women openly laughed at him. Down the street a dozen men poured from the Bull and Bear Tavern. They all knew Trout and offered the herders tankards of ale.

Ben dropped out of the procession as a new man took his place prodding Trout and laying the cat on his back, this time drawing blood to smear the painted black words. Trout screamed. Ben faded to the side of the street, but kept near the group. He spotted a Lobsterback coming from one of the shops. The soldier looked at the crowd and laughed, then recognized Trout and began to run toward them, reaching for his sword. Ben's boot tripped the soldier neatly and as he fell Ben fell too, tangling arms and legs so it took them several seconds to get to their feet.

The soldier jumped up at last, swearing at Ben, and ran on. Ten yards ahead Lynch had seen the tangle and tripped the Redcoat again as he passed. When Lynch helped the Lobsterback to his feet, his knife point was inside the opening of the heavy coat and pressing through the soldier's shirt pricking his chest.

"Stand there and watch the sport like a good little English subject, or this knife will play tag with your insides. You understand that good, Redcoat?"

The soldier nodded, watched the spectacle pass and looked away. When the parade came abreast of the Customs House there were thirty in the heckling group, and when Trout bolted for the sanctuary, they hurled him back and held him in a circle of tormentors which marched him forward away from his safe house.

As Ben had expected, the Customs House officers had seen the trouble, and before the march had moved half a block, a dozen Redcoats with fixed bayonets poured from the side door into the street and formed a wall of steel across the passage. Trout ran ahead, making a mad dash toward the shining steel blades. Two soldiers lifted their weapons for him to run under, then lowered them and began marching ahead at the pranksters. The men and boys screamed in delight, dancing a yard away from the steel, but moving back, dispersing, and shouting insults at the enforcers.

Trout took a long coat from one of the soldiers to cover himself, then walked with as much dignity as he could muster into the side door of the Customs House.

The men who helped in the naked march had faded into the crowd. Five minutes after the street had cleared, Lynch and Ben lifted tankards of buttered rum in the Black Horse Tavern and gave a small cheer. No one paid any attention to them. It was a happy moment for both. They had seen the detested Customs House Commissioner spanked and shamed and stripped of his clothes and his dignity. There was no possible way the man could exert any authority or leadership in Boston now. He would be off on the first sailing ship headed for London.

Ben fingered the small coin in his pocket, the

gold piece with "Freedom Fighters" stamped on one side.

This was not a victory for the cause. It was a small and, he realized, petty bit of personal vengeance. But to him it was one of those steps that had to be taken, an act of defiance that must be made. It had been a satisfying two days of work. After some ale and a shank of lamb, the two men went into the street, found a vacant spot in the sun next to the tavern, and sat watching the street. Everywhere people were talking about the march of the naked Tory. Ben sat and let the sun soak into his bones. It had been a long time since he had merely sat idle on a weekday. It felt delicious. But what of the cause? How could he further the principles of the Freedom Fighters? He had lost two tall ships. It was a thundering blow financially. Each merchant ship was worth at least fifty thousand pounds, and that in an economy where a single man could live comfortably in Boston on twenty-five pounds a year. He would have to scramble to cover his losses and stay on his feet.

For the moment he put his worries aside, said goodbye to Lynch and stood. There was a delightful blonde young lady waiting for him. For a few hours his own private revolution was suspended. He would indulge himself this afternoon and tonight. Then early tomorrow he and Lynch would row back to Noodles Island where the *Freedom* would pick him up at noon.

Chapter Four
A TORY IS A TORY IS A TORY

Edmund Cunliffe whacked the naked girl across the buttocks and sent her sprawling on the featherbed. She rolled over, giggling.

"That was a good one, luv. Do it again."

Instead Edmund dropped on top of her and began chewing one large brown-tipped breast.

"Come on, luv, whack me backside again. I like it."

He slapped her face and she howled in delight.

"Now you've got it! Hit me anywhere, I like it. Gets me churn a'moving. Say now, you ready for another little romp?"

The girl was about twenty, on the heavy side, with huge breasts sagging from their own bulk. Her hair fell long and unwashed in matted strings down her back. Green eyes assessed this man of the night. She knew he was rich, but she had no idea just how rich or who he was. If she could only get him drunk enough before she passed out herself, she would get most of what was in his purse. She'd learned never to clean out a man, but leave a little so it wouldn't look like he'd been taken. Maude reached for the whiskey bottle and sipped it, then passed it to Edmund.

"Drink up, luv. It gives you twice as much wiggle and bounce."

He slammed the bottle aside.

"I don't let my slaves drink slop like that," he said, his voice sarcastic and snobbish. He slapped her again. "You're a slut, Maude, you know that? A common whore, a good piece of ass, but an ugly bitch with lice in your head, you know that, Maude?"

"Yes, luv, anything you say, luv." She reached for his crotch.

Edmund slapped her again, feeling a surge of raw, sharp emotion he had never experienced before. Sex and violence, together—they triggered some deep emotional reaction in him. He slapped her again, this time hitting one big breast. She wailed, not in pain, but in delight. He felt his own hot blood stirring, jolting through his veins. Fantastic! He hit her breast again and she grinned as she yelped.

"More, luv, more!"

"Don't talk, bitch!" He hit her again, rolled her over. "Up on your knees and show me that doggie teaser way you know that the French count taught you. Show me!"

Maude giggled. She might be everything he said she was, but she could make any man stop, drop his pants and beg for more. She had a way with her, she did. Everybody said so. And before the night was over, she'd have half of his poke, and he'd be glad to let her take it. He'd expect it. Half was the usual. If she could drink him into unconsciousness first, he'd expect it. This was one Tory she damn wouldn't forget. Not a rich one like him.

She rolled over, got on her knees and groaned when he slapped her fat buttocks.

Three hours later Edmund Cunliffe staggered out of the Staghorn tavern's back door and found his chaise. It was the best one along the street, anyone could tell that. He was still drunk, totally drained, and ready for sleep. But first he had to get home. Christ, but that whore had loved his tool. He thought she was going to bite it off a dozen times. Edmund grinned, stumbled into the chaise and slapped the reins on the back of the bay. It was a damn good thing his horse knew the way home.

Twenty minutes later he left the horse still hitched to the rig behind his big house. Lot would put them both away. Cunliffe got to the back door and inside just as his house slave, Lot, came awake from a chair where he had been waiting.

"Damn nigger, you're supposed to meet me at the door!"

"Yes, suh."

Edmund pointed toward the chaise and the slave hurried on to take care of the horse. Lot was thirty-five, and had been with the Cunliffe family for ten years. He considered himself lucky not to be still in Virginia working a cotton or tobacco field. Mr. Cunliffe, senior, had come through Virginia one day and picked him right out of the field and bought him on the spot. Then they both came back up here into the cold land of Boston. It had probably saved his life, Lot knew. A man could stand just so much, and before Mr. Cunliffe came, Lot had been in two fights with the lead boy on the tobacco plantation. After each fight he had

73

been horse-whipped. The next time, he swore he'd kill the lead boy, and the white overseer too. That would have meant his own slow, painful death.

Lot unhitched the bay, put her into a stall, hung up the harness and went back into the house. He found Mr. Cunliffe flopped on his bed, unconscious. Lot began undressing the man and got whacked twice for his efforts. Edmund Cunliffe was beyond knowing what he was doing. Lot persisted and soon had the man rolled between the thick comforters. When Lot was sure his master was sleeping, the slave arranged Cunliffe's clothes on a chair, folding them neatly. At the same time he extracted a five-pound note from the master's purse and carried it to his quarters in the basement of the mansion. There he pried up one corner of a wall board and slid the note behind it, adding it to the small fold of bills. He had over a hundred pounds put away there! That was a fortune. A freeman could live on fifteen pounds a year if he was careful. A poke like that would be enough for Lot to make it for three or four years. Mr. Edmund never knew the difference. When he went out whoring and drinking he couldn't remember how much he spent and how much the whores stole from him. Lot laughed. He didn't plan on being a house slave forever. He'd seen freemen right there in Boston blacker than he was. He guessed there weren't no more than two hundred house niggers in all of Buston and maybe ten, fifteen freeman. One of them had a pretty little wife and kids. Lot's black eyes sparkled as he thought about it. Mr. Cunliffe had decided Lot shouldn't marry nor breed with any other slave.

74

But mighty soon now, he'd take off. Lot realized he had to go west, into Kentucky probably. Wild, untamed Kentucky! The very thought of the word sent shivers through Lot. He'd need a last name as a freeman. They'd call him a runaway slave, but nobody cared much, out in Kentucky, as long as a man could shoot a musket or one of them new flintlocks he'd heard about. A man who could shoot straight was a man, top man, no matter what color his skin was. Kentucky! What a dream it was. After he got set up on a farm or working for someone, he'd find himself a nice little black girl and live with her. Kentucky!

The next morning before ten, Edmund Cunliffe sat in Commissioner Trout's office in the Customs House. There had been a note waiting for Edmund when he arrived at the Cunliffe Carriage Works just after nine o'clock.

Edmund nodded. "Yes, Commissioner, I agree. Your treatment by those criminals is outrageous, scandalous. I'm sure the Crown will bring charges against every one of the low-born scum before long. I've mentioned the fact to two of our superior court judges now, three times."

"Good, good, Cunliffe. I appreciate that. And I'm a man who stands by his friends." His face darkened just thinking about the horrendous experience two weeks ago when he had been paraded through the street. He shook it off.

"Now to another matter, Cunliffe. It's about the new chaise you have ready for me. I believe that we took care of the monetary consideration yesterday. When can I have delivery?"

"Mr. Commissioner, if it isn't too early, what about right now? I drove your new chaise over myself, and one of your men is exchanging our horses. Here, look out the window."

The commissioner moved as quickly as his size and still sore leg would allow, and peered through the opening. The chaise was magnificent, with a retractable top that could extend well beyond where most stopped; a handsome leather cushioned seat to ride on and wheels with spokes painted in alternate silver and blue. There were other silver adornments around the inside of the carriage and Commissioner Trout knew even from a distance that they were pure silver as he had ordered. It was a masterpiece. He wanted to run downstairs and use it immediately, but the grooms were still changing the horses.

"Oh, Commissioner, was this the window where you saw the toughs throwing rocks at our soldiers?"

"Yes, yes, right here. Our men were taking an awful pounding. I saw a rock hit one trooper and break his jaw. I was surprised how long they were restrained before they fired the warning shots in self-defense."

"Warning shots?"

"Why, yes. Two volleys is a warning. Anything more and it would have been a serious confrontation, almost an action."

"I see."

"Yes, and right here was where I saw that bounder Rutledge rush up and comfort one of the villains who had been stoning our men. The lad

76

had been hit in the warning fire. Now low-born, Jack-tars and mulattos you can expect to be brawlers. But to have one of the rich men of our city get down in the street and comfort one of the outlaws, and then remove him—well, it was just more than any gentleman should have to put up with. Unfortunately there was no way I could bring charges against this man Rutledge."

"Yes. Mr. Rutledge is well liked in this city, though I can't see why."

"Well, he's a troublemaker, I can tell you that, Cunliffe. The man will take a lot of watching. If this Rutledge steps out of the strait and narrow, I'll bring the Crown down on him fast. He'll come to no good in the end, I'll bargain that."

"Hasn't he got in trouble already by smuggling?"

"Aye, indeed he has, sir. Two of his ships have been impounded until he pays the forty thousand pound fine upon them. His captains were caught openly defying standard orders and regulations. Seizure was the only recourse by the Crown, else these ne'er-do-wells walk all over their betters."

Cunliffe rubbed one hand over his chin, as he was wont to do when thinking hard. "Commissioner Trout, I just may be able to be of some small assistance to you in this Rutledge matter. In fact, I've been thinking of doing some shipping myself soon, and if I had a way to obtain ships without a ridiculous outlay of hard cash money..."

He left it hanging there, and Commissioner Trout smiled. He often had overtures such as this when a vessel worth fifty thousand pounds was going on the block. He looked up at Cunliffe and liked what he saw. The young man was rich, of a good English family. He had even gone to school in London, and he definitely had the right political opinions and contacts.

"Cunliffe, I might be able to help arrange something for you. Every auction must have a public notice, you realize. However, there can be certain delays and postponements—a dozen perhaps."

"Until only a few show up at the auction."

"Precisely. You spoke of some help you might be to me in this matter of Mr. Rutledge."

"Yes, yes, I did. These setbacks, the fines, the impounding of cargo and the seizure of ships has put our Mr. Rutledge in quite a serious financial bind, if I am to read rightly what I hear in the taverns and coffee houses. At such a time when Mr. Rutledge is in serious financial strain, any kind of distraction or personal problem would only cause him more trouble and mental anguish, leaving him that much less able to handle his financial matters."

They had moved back to the commissioner's desk, where both finished sipping cups of tea.

"Commissioner, what I have in mind is the seventeen-year-old daughter in the Rutledge household. She's of an age when men court her. Men will even be approaching her in public. It could be a most interesting chase, and it would provide you with exactly the diversion you need to make a flanking move and ruin the Rutledge business dynasty for good. I could almost guarantee you an unending series of confrontations and embarrassments for our mutual friend, Benjamin Rutledge. Do you follow me, Commissioner?"

The big man had reached for a dish of hard candy and popped two chunks into his mouth. A small twitch bothered his right eye for a moment, then ceased.

"Indeed I do follow your thoughts, young man." His eyes twinkled. "And if you did bed the wench in the bargain, you wouldn't mind the sport a bit yourself, now would you, Mr. Cunliffe? I've heard of your reputation with the women in our town."

Edmund bowed carefully. "I only wish it were half earned, then I would have a smile all of the time." He smiled. "But, Commissioner, I must say, one ugly woman in your bed is certainly worth three or four beauties in a church pew."

They both laughed and shook hands, and Cunliffe knew he was half launched into the shipping business. It would be a good adjunct to his other interests. He could buy a tall ship for commerce, but why do that at normal price levels when he could obtain one legally for five or six hundred pounds, perhaps a thousand? The price of the ship at auction would all go directly to the custom commissioner, Edmund was certain. Two or three ships would bulge the stuffy commissioner's bank account nicely.

The commissioner nodded toward the door. "Pardon me, my dear sir, for being impatient, but I simply must go to look at my new chaise. It's truly magnificent, and the Crown and myself both appreciate the remarkably low price you placed upon it."

Edmund smiled. His business manager would frown at the price, since it was almost fifty pounds less than the costs of the materials alone. But Edmund deemed it well spent. He could mark it down as a good-will gesture. Already it had borne great fruits.

He followed the limping commissioner down the stairs and out to the front of the building. The horses had been exchanged and the commissioner took a quick trip around the block, then stopped for Edmund, who went for a short ride with him. By the time they were back at the customs house, Edmund had asked the commissioner to come to dinner that evening.

"We'll have entertainment, of course," Edmund said. "I think you will enjoy it."

Commissioner Trout's eyes glowed. "Will this be entertainment such as I've heard you sometimes provide guests?"

"Whatever you wish, Commissioner."

"I understand you sometimes offer white, black or Chinese."

It was Edmund who laughed. "Commissioner, I had some other form of amusement planned. However, the change is no problem. I can offer any of those you suggest."

The big man smiled, rubbed his aching right knee and turned to Edmund. "I should like one of each, please—three—and all on the smallish side, but well-rounded and extremely willing."

Edmund congratulated himself. "A pleasure." After tonight, his new shipping venture was assured.

That afternoon, sitting at his big desk at the carriage works, Edmund began planning his campaign against Rutledge. The shipper's most vulnerable spot was the enticing daughter. Edmund well knew how protective most fathers were of their daughters, especially an only daughter. He smiled. He had been in delicate negotiations with a few irate fathers before, but here he had a special case. What was called for was just enough bravado and attention, without provoking the man to violence. The girl, yes—he didn't even know her name, but a promise was a bond.

He would find out her name, try to meet her quite casually and very properly with one of her parents there, then he would work his charm on her. He would be bold, then draw back, harass, then pull back, but never would he go so far as to anger Mr. Rutledge into demanding satisfaction. Some fathers would fight at the hint of a scandal about their daughters. And Rutledge was not a low-born. He was class, he was breeding, he was...money. Edmund settled it quickly and simply. He would do nothing that might make Ben Rutledge even consider a duel. Edmund did not like dueling. He had been in two, the first on a lark with a good friend in joint conspiracy. It had been carried out to the letter of the formal dueling code. Each had a second. Each presented weapons. One chose the type of weapon, the other made his choice of the pistols. Then they walked off ten paces from the back-to-back position, turned, and fired. But each fired in the air. Then they ran and embraced each other and went for a drink.

His second duel was serious. It had been over the affections of a young girl. An older man claimed Edmund had stolen the girl away from him, and in truth he had, purposefully, with malice and on a bet with a friend. The other man was middle-aged, fat and ugly. It had been no contest. After Edmund bedded the wench he dumped her on her doorstep.

The gauntlet was dropped, the time arranged. Edmund had practiced with a pistol, but he was a miserable shot. All day he had fired, and at sunup the following morning had come to the field of honor with two hours' sleep. When he saw the bleak woods, the pistols and the furious older man, Edmund wanted to run, but he couldn't. He was afraid he would vomit.

The time came, and everything was ready. They selected pistols, paced off the ten steps, turned and both fired at almost the same time. By then Edmund wanted desperately to kill the man, but he missed. The other man's ball slashed through Edmund's left calf, tearing the muscle, disabling him for a month, but it left no permanent damage. Ever since that moment Edmund had permitted no possibility that he would become involved in a duel. He would take an insult and walk away. He would hire someone to rough up a person he had a grievance against. He used his wealth to get done for him what he would not do. In truth, he thought he might faint if he ever had to stare at the end of a dueling pistol again.

He would play this new game, but he would be careful, extremely careful, and of course, he would win.

Back at his desk, Edmund smiled, satisfied with the day's work. The business ran itself these days. He hired the best managers in each field and paid them well. Then he checked on them often and carefully, and he kept them honest. Anyone found cheating or stealing was promptly prosecuted to the fullest extent of Massachusetts law.

The huge business had been built by his father, who suffered an early death when his heart stopped one day. He had been forty-five. Edmund came home from England, where he had been working for an advanced degree at Oxford, to take over the business. He had learned the details quickly and made some vital changes to increase profits. Then he expanded. He moved into similar businesses and also bought as much property and as many downtown lots and buildings as he could. The country could only grow, and he would be in a commanding position. Look how London and its surrounding areas were built up. Some day, Boston would have as many people in it and surrounding it as London.

Now he was going into another business, shipping and importing. He would get his basic stock at a steal, and grease the palm of the customs commissioner at the same time. Yes, it had been a good day. All in exchange for the harassment of a citizen through his most attractive daughter. He tried to recall the girl. He was sure he had seen her with the family somewhere recently. Then he remembered, just last Sunday, coming out of church. She was taller than her mother, with long brown hair touched by hints of red. Her eyes were blue, as he remembered, and he had been at once attracted to her pinched-in waist and full bosom. That would be one to undress slowly, savoring her ripe figure as he progressed.

He could remember nothing more of her face. His eyes had found a more attractive feature. Edmund laughed. This would not be a hard task at all. In fact, he might even enjoy the chase, as short and inconclusive as it by necessity must be. He tried to remember more, but could only guess at the long slender legs that must hide under all those skirts. What he would give to strip away those skirts and see her legs unsheathed!

Edmund Cunliffe lived alone in a big mansion on the hill with a staff of six servants. They kept the three floors and thirty-two rooms spotlessly clean and ready for use at any time.

It was not unusual for there to be guests, three or four ladies, staying overnight, and sometimes a gentleman or two. Life was never dull at Cunliffe Mansion and Edmund made no restrictions on the servants and their chatter with friends. Three of his servants were slaves, Lot, and two maids, Esther and Ruth.

Two years ago his mother had moved out and left her pride and joy to her son. She said she could no longer stand to see him abusing her cherished home. He laughed at her and doubled her allowance. As the sole heir, the entire Cunliffe estate went to Edmund, and his mother was at his mercy for her keep.

Edmund put his feet on the polished mahogany desk and read a newspaper. It was the *Loyalist*, and contained one of Edmund's own articles under the pen name of "Locust." He read it now in print with a swell of pride.

"There comes a time in the course of every English colony when the citizens of that domain must realize that they are inseparably bound to Mother England, and that to contemplate disobeying the legal commands and laws of our king, and of Parliament, is irresponsible and unthinking. As it has been shown time and time again, the common people, the peasants, are unwilling, uninterested and certainly incapable of governing themselves. It is obvious that in our form of a republic, the gifted, the landed, the wealthy and the intellectuals must retain the responsibility of running the machinery of government to protect the common man from his own worst habits."

Edmund nodded. He couldn't agree more! Brilliant chap. The run-of-the-mill man on the streets of Boston was totally incapable of self-government. Any such idea was a snare and an illusion, and all men in Massachusetts must be reminded again and again of this fact.

As long as the colonists were under the wing of Mother England, the French and Spanish would stay away. It was so logical, so wise, so practical, and so supported by over two hundred years of colonial empire building, that Edmund became increasingly short-tempered with anyone who did not understand the simple truth.

During the rest of the morning Edmund worked at writing another of his essays for the *Loyalist*.

The following day Edmund stayed in his office most of the morning awaiting some word from his messenger. He had posted a man on horseback not far from the Rutledge mansion to report any movement of the mother and daughter. Yesterday had not been productive, but perhaps today. It was just after noon when a messenger came in and made his report. Edmund dismissed him, then put on his striped waistcoat and adjusted his white powdered wig. He walked briskly out of his office and two blocks down, then made a right turn and continued two more blocks.

When `he entered the Johnson Music company, he noticed there were several customers in the store. He couldn't remember being inside it before. He wasn't musically inclined. Edmund looked at a fine pump organ, then touched two violins and moved on. He waved a clerk away, then around a display case he saw her. Harriet May Rutledge was looking at some expensive hand-copied music scores. He walked toward her and saw she was with her mother, as he expected. Near the older woman he paused.

"Mrs. Rutledge, isn't it?" he said looking directly at her eyes.

Sandra Rutledge glanced up. The man did look familiar, but she wasn't sure. Then she remembered.

"Yes, that's right. And you're Mr. Cunliffe. I've seen you at church. I didn't know you were a musician."

He moved a step closer. "Well, I'm not much of one, but there's an organ in my house that hasn't been used for years, and someone wanted to play it."

"So you needed some music."

"Why, yes."

"Well, Mr. Cunliffe, you can't go wrong with Bach. I much prefer Bach to any of the contemporary composers."

"Bach. Yes, ma'am." He turned toward Harriet. "This can't be your daughter? Why, I remember when she was..." He stopped and laughed. "No, that is not the right thing to say to a beautiful young lady."

Sandra Rutledge felt a stab of apprehension as she watched the man staring at Harriet. True, she was beautiful, her young face flawless, such clear skin. Mrs. Rutledge swept into the conversation lag.

"Yes, Mr. Cunliffe, this is my daughter Harriet. Harriet, this is Mr. Edmund Cunliffe."

Harriet had frozen. She stared at him, nodded and turned. "Mother, I'm not feeling at all well. Could we please go home?"

"Yes, dear. Yes, of course." She looked at Cunliffe. "I think Harriet has some illness. She's been sickly all morning. Please excuse us."

Sandra Rutledge put her arm around her daughter's shoulders and helped Harriet toward the door. Sandra had been flabbergasted at the deliberate frankness of the man. Edmund Cunliffe had stared at Harriet as if he were disrobing her. Sandra knew those looks. He couldn't take his eyes off her bosom. Harriet had a beautiful figure, but a gentleman simply did not stare that way. It was unforgiveable! She turned and watched the man still looking at them as they moved toward the door. Thank goodness Harriet had had the grace to ignore him.

They went down the steps, across the walk and into the carriage that waited for them. She ordered the drive to take them home at once, and turned to her daughter.

Harriet's surprise and shock were gone now. She spat out her anger in one expressive word. "Ohhh, Mother did you see how he stared at me? He watched me as though he knew how I looked with my clothes off. I was never so mortified in all my life! Mother, he kept staring right at my bosom, he never even glanced at my face but once, and then he kept looking at my chest. I wanted to die!"

"Yes, dear, I saw him. He's terrible. I didn't know what to say. But you certainly handled it well, just beautifully." She took a deep breath. "Well, I can assure you, Harriet May, that I will speak with your father about this man, and he will talk to him severely. The man has no manners, no common courtesy—he simply is not a gentleman. I'll make certain, Harriet, that you never have to look at him again."

Harriet smiled and patted her mother's arm. "Oh, that's all right, Mama. He didn't touch me. He didn't hurt me. He just stared." She was quiet for a moment as the carriage bounced over the rutted dirt street, creaking and groaning. "Mama, is that the way father looks at you when you're...intimate?"

Mrs. Rutledge glanced out the side of the carriage quickly. "Now, girl, that is nothing you need to know about. After you're married is plenty of time for that, and then you'll be finding out for yourself. Now hush with that kind of talk. A nice girl doesn't even *think* about things like that."

Harriet Rutledge smiled, watching her mother's averted head, and knowing she was embarrassed.

"Land sakes, then, Mama, I must be just grievous evil, because I've been thinking a lot lately about that kind of thing. Like what it would be like for a boy to put his hands on me, and touch me...touch my...my chest."

"Harriet May Rutledge! Now you just stop talking like that. This isn't the kind of thing nice girls mention. I mean it. You just forget about that or you don't go to the next church picnic. You act like a lady, and then men won't think they have the right to stare at your bosom."

"Effie says men stare at her. She says they look at every girl who's got a big front, married men as well as single men."

"Now hush!" said Sandra, her face flushing. "You just hush, Harriet May. You be quiet now and I won't have to tell your father what you've been saying. It'll be hard enough telling him what that terrible Mr. Cunliffe did today. You know how your father's been worried about his business."

At home, ten minutes later, Harriet ran to her room and began at once thinking about Edmund Cunliffe. He *was* a handsome man, and old—he must be twenty-five, at least! Idly she wondered what her father would say when he heard about the way the man had ogled her breasts.

That night, after the maid had cleared away the dishes and Harriet left to go to the music room to practice on the organ, Sandra told her husband about the flagrant ungentlemanly acts of Edmund Cunliffe. Ben listened to it all, then sat back.

"Cunliffe is a Tory, that explains a lot," Ben said, his brow creasing. "He's a bachelor and a rake, and he had his way with numerous women, most of them wenches and bad women." Ben stoked at his pipe. "Of course, there could be some deeper purpose."

Sandra looked up. "Some political motive, since you're not a Loyalist? You think he might be trying to use an affront to our little girl against you?"

"It's possible. These days, a person has to expect almost anything from the Tories." He smiled. "Sandra, I didn't know you were so interested in politics. When did this take place?"

"Since you became so involved. I've been reading your newspapers, and some of the booklets. With the Crown so bothersome about your ships and business, it's just natural that I become interested."

"Sandra, you're a good woman and a fine mother."

She looked up, love lighting up her face. He was her man, the only one she had ever known, the only one she ever would. He would always be her man. Ben stood up and stretched.

"I'll be sure to make a point of talking to Cunliffe the first chance I get. Not tomorrow. There's more trouble with the ships and the bonds. Do you realize that Rutledge ships have been accounting for over half of all the fines at the port? And our two ships have been the only ones seized here in the past two years?"

"Ben, does that mean the commissioners are punishing you for your political stand?"

"It may be. But John Hancock is not a Tory, and he's been relatively untouched. Sam Adams wrote me a note saying that Jeffrey Trout, the head commissioner, did in fact stand at the window the day of the massacre, and did fire his pistol through the open window. The man almost certainly saw me there trying to help the lad who was killed. None of my troubles began until *after* that date, until *after* the Boston Massacre. It does make you stop and think, doesn't it?"

"There is no appeal to a higher authority, the courts?"

"Sandra, it's an English judge sitting on our bench. It's the English system, in an English colony, where the Parliament in London tells us what to do, taxes us without representation, forces guards and soldiers upon us to billet free in our homes, sends trade commissioners to steal from us, and passes laws so we can import goods only from Mother England. No, there is no court on this earth to appeal to, only the one good, gracious and never failing higher court of God."

"I'm afraid I'm not that patient, Ben," she said smiling.

Ben chuckled, and they moved into the living room where the lamps were lit.

"Neither am I that patient, Sandra. Neither am I. And we are trying to do something about it, but on a very limited scale."

"Your letters to the other colonies?"

"Yes, partly. Now, don't get yourself embroiled in politics. You have your hands full with our boys, and with this alluring young lady you have raised up in my house."

Sandra smiled and sat near him on the couch, moving her leg so it touched his. "Your daughter is very beautiful, isn't she? She's taller than me, and larger in other places, as well. She's a rather remarkable young lady, your daughter, sir."

"It's probably because she takes after her

mother, Mrs. Rutledge. Yes, that's the cause of it all, I'm sure."

Sandra would have blushed at the thought, but she was having those very feelings her daughter had asked her to explain that afternoon. She caught his hand and squeezed it.

"Tonight, Ben Rutledge, I think we should get to bed early and..you know...catch up on our sleep."

Ben looked up from his newspaper and winked.

Chapter Five
ATTACK FROM THE REAR

Ben Rutledge paced the narrow confines of his sparsely furnished office, then stared out the small window at one of his tall ships at the wharf. It seemed indeed that trouble was his middle name these days. This morning word came that another of his clipper ships had been seized for smuggling, the crew dismissed and the tall ship towed to a dock leased by the customs commissioners where it was under a twenty-four-hour Redcoat guard. It was the third vessel to fall to the commissioners in less than three weeks.

The craft had just arrived in port for the first time since the tightening of controls—if that was what the current rash of fines and seizures could rightly be called. The captain had no idea what was happening or how to react. He had been caught in some minor infraction, exactly what Ben didn't even know yet, and his ship had been taken at gunpoint. Ben paced the floor again. It was a conspiracy, a vendetta by Commissioner Trout, there was no doubt about that now. The man should be removed from an office of trust—shot would be better. If only the colonies were in a state of war with England it would be a simple matter, but Ben had no real stomach for murder. He shunned it as strongly as he had denounced the massacre by the English Lobsterbacks. The infuriating part was that all of this had come down on Ben's head for a simple act of kindness by one human being toward another.

Oh, for the luxury of an easy conscience! Then he could simply order the man waylaid, shot and disposed of, and Ben's own troubles would come quickly to an end.

Ben stared at his ships and sighed. He had to do something quickly if he were to survive as a viable business venture. But what? Strong friends? They would have to be Tory to have influence with Trout, and Ben wasn't going to stoop to such means. That would cost his conscience just as much as murder. Powerful friends in other areas? What about Hancock? The largest ship owner in Boston had been little affected so far by the commissioner's crackdown. A long talk with Mr. Hancock might be worthwhile. Hancock had been most friendly at their last meeting. True, they were business competitors, but they were not enemies. Perhaps Hancock had some procedures, some methods of arranging bonds or manifests, something that would ease Ben's problems. He went to his desk, resolved to write a letter to Hancock, but at once dismissed the idea. It was too slow, and too apt to be misinterpreted. No, he must see the man—today, this morning, right now!

Half an hour later Ben sat in John Hancock's handsome office. It was twenty feet square, immaculately furnished in the style of a gentleman's den. A large teakwood desk stood in one corner.

Across from it was a fireplace with a fire laid and around the room were grouped leather-covered overstuffed chairs and a couch. The walls were of a dark wood paneling, one decorated with a preserved swordfish ten feet long. A cabinet to one side contined a silver tea service and china cups, as well as a wine and liquor section below. On another wall hung matched dueling pistols and along one whole wall was a series of pull-down charts of every ocean and many seas and bays of the world.

Hancock himself was a big man, well built and taller than Ben by five inches. His face was slightly pinched under a high brow and thinning hair. His eyes were close-set and gave him a constantly harrassed look. Now he was smiling as he handed Ben a cup of tea in a fragile blue china cup.

"Lemon or cream?" he asked.

Ben shook his head.

"Well, Ben, I'm glad you came. We have a lot of things to talk about. You're in the Assembly, of course, and you were also at the Stamp Congress back in Sixty-five, weren't you?"

Ben said he had been.

"Well, good. That congress was a fine start, the first time our thirteen colonies have ever agreed on anything. You must be in your eighth term in the Assembly." He smiled and sipped his tea. "Ben, I understand also that you have been a consistent worker for more cooperation between the colonies, especially a much stronger stand against Parliament and its attempts at taxation on the colonies of any kind."

"Yes, Mr. Hancock—"

"Please, it's John. Call me John. 'Mr.' is for my

employees. I'd appreciate it."

"Yes, of course. And you're right. I believe strongly that our colonies must fight every type of taxation by parliament since we have no representation."

"I agree, Ben, absolutely. And if we can work together, all thirteen colonies...this whole customs house operation is repugnant to everyone, not just the shippers. But before we get to that, may I assume that when Mr. Adams told me that you have certain other functions beside those which are visible, that he was not leading me astray?"

Ben laughed softly. "John, I have never known Mr. Adams to tell an untruth knowingly. I don't understand what purpose he may have had in telling you this, but if Mr. Adams told me a similar story about you, sir, I would believe it."

"Good, good. The old Sons of Liberty group is sputtering around again, but it was always a disorganized, overzealous, unthinking mob. We don't need a mob, we need something better, more efficient, more intelligently operated. Let's talk more about this later."

"John, I'd consider it a rare privilege," Ben said, sipping his tea.

"Now, from what Adams tells me, you helped a boy who was shot in the massacre three weeks ago, and Commissioner Trout saw you. Since that day he's been hitting you with every violation of the Navigation Act he can think of, and making up a few as he goes along. I understand he has seized two of your ships."

"Now the count is up to three. Another one was taken early this morning."

John Hancock slammed his open hand down on his polished desk, making a resounding bang.

"I've had only a handful of violations, and just two fines. This is devilish, outrageous, supremely unfair." He walked to a large six-panel window and looked out over the city from the second-floor advantage. Hancock massaged the back of his neck and slowly turned.

"Ben, together we control nearly seventy-five percent of the shipping that comes in and out of Boston harbor. Would you say that's about right?"

"Yes."

"And we should have some power, some influence, even the potential of a serious threat, if we chose to use that power. Together we could strangle this town, put merchants out of business, and cause some real problems for the English troops."

"Yes, we could. We might agree not to bring in any goods from England. The two of us declare an embargo against all English made goods. Now that would raise one hell of a mess and cause Parliament a great deal of trouble."

"Indeed it would," said John, his eyes glowing. "And we shall remember such an idea. But that won't solve your immediate problem. What can we do now to help you get free of the economic vice-grip the commissioners have you in?"

"The three ships they impounded are the biggest problem from a money standpoint. They put a forty thousand pound fine and a minimum bid on each one of them."

Hancock whistled. "That's a hundred and twenty thousand pounds. The thieves! Everybody knows all of the money, or most of it anyway, goes straight into the commissioner's bank accounts. It's ridiculous making you buy back your own property. There must be some way around it, some way to stop their illegal actions."

"All I've come up with so far are some direct kinds of action, and none of them seemed practical."

Hancock poured more tea into their cups. "Something like marching Trout through the streets naked?"

Ben had to grin. "That was an interesting experiment. When I heard about it I did give a cheer. However, it didn't produce any lasting results, I'm afraid."

"More tea?" Hancock asked, his own smile broadening. Then he sobered. "Ben, I'm in complete sympathy with your situation, and what you're trying to do for all of us. If there is anything I can do, at any time, please let me know. As far as your situation with your three ships, I'm going to do some talking with the superior court judge. There may be legal recourse. And I'm going to try to work out an answer to your problem within the next two days. Has a date been set up for the auction?"

"Yes, April 27."

"Almost a month yet, so we've got some time. We should have a sure-fire system before then."

Ben stood up, pleased with his visit, feeling that he had made a real friend who could be helpful with his business problems, and perhaps a friend for the Freedom Fighters.

"John, thanks for your help. My only thought right now is to post a guard at the outer harbor and meet each of my ships as they come into port and warn them about what is happening, and to be sure that they follow precisely the letter of the law of the Navigation Act. That way I shouldn't have any more seizures. I'll be working on some other plans of my own, but I'll sure welcome any suggestions you may have."

They shook hands and Ben left the plush office.

Back in his own dingy, small, cluttered room, Ben laid out the list of charges, the fines paid, and the value of the tall ships that had been seized. In total it was not enough to ruin him outright, but nearly so. He would have to tread carefully if he did lose the big ships. It was absolutely vital that he devise some plan to save them.

Ben studied the lists again. Fines of over a thousand pounds. Incredible. He had paid less than forty pounds in fines in the previous two years. Briefly he figured what he should have to do if there was no way legally of reclaiming the three ships.

One plan was to seize each of the clippers in the blackest night and sail them to New York for a quick sale to the highest bidder. There would be a tremendous risk factor to all men in the crews. It was not a practical plan. The warships would send out their fastest gunship after the three and probably overtake them before they could reach another port.

A second plan was to attempt to buy his own ships at the time of the auction. Possible. But why should he be forced to bid on his own property?

A third plan was to challenge the legality of the seizure in the courts. This he was already doing, but his lawyer friend who began the action said there was almost no chance that a judge would even hear the case, claiming that Parliamentary law superseded colonial courts, and therefore neither the judge nor his court had any jurisdiction.

The fourth plan was to have someone else buy the ships for him, but again it held the chance of a large sum of money being spent to buy back his own property.

Ben checked the papers that ordered his craft taken. They stipulated that the sale must be held no earlier than forty-five days from the time of seizure, and no later than sixty days. This gave the shipper adequate time for legal recourse and for appeals.

Ben laid down the papers and began filling his pipe. There had to be a solution, something he hadn't thought of before. How could he assist in the work of the Freedom Fighters if he had no economic base from which to function? It was imperative that he remain solvent. But how?

Ben was puzzled about the continued presence of commissioner Trout. How had he overcome the shame of his public naked march and remained in his position? Slowly Ben realized that there was no superior here to order Trout home. Trout could order any of the lesser commissioners out of the colonies, but he was the leading man. And since he was a representative of Parliament, not even the governor, who was appointed by the King, could order the commissioner to leave. Ben pulled at the just-lit pipe and scowled. He must harass the commissioner continually, force him to go back to England. And it should be done soon. Ben went home a little after four o'clock. He checked his pocket watch. One day he had made a count in the city of fifteen thousand souls, and he could locate only five other mechanical timepieces. Most shop owners opened their businesses by the sun or by mutual consent. The big sundial in Boston Commons was the only community standard for time.

It was just about 7:30 p.m. when Ben entered the Old Boston Bookshop and said hello to the proprietor.

"Mr. Jonathan Clark? I'm looking for something on the origins of English justice."

"Right. Ain't we all, Ben," Jonathan said. There was no one else in the shop. Others of the committee were already upstairs.

"I'm not sure we'll find anything like justice for a good long time," Clark said. He turned over his "closed" sign on the door and extinguished one of the lamps in his bookshop and carried the other into the back room, then up the stairs to the secret room.

Everyone else was there including a guest.

As soon as Ben came into the room, he saw Sam Adams. Adams' short pudgy body and round pink face were a familiar sight to everyone in Boston. Sam Adams had been the conscience of Boston, its liberal leader, its scream for justice. Ben knew him from casual acquaintance in the Assembly, and in some Boston town hall political matters. They had never been close friends, but now Sam Adams hurried over to Ben.

"Ah, Rutledge, it's good to see you. Dr. Warren has indicated that you are the mainspring."

Ben took the offered hand and gripped it firmly.

"Mr. Adams, we're pleased you could accept our invitation to come to inspect us, to see how we function, and if you wish, to offer us some advice. We quite simply, sir, are at your service."

Samual Adams smiled. "My friend Rutledge. I have seen your fine work in the Assembly, and have heard about your efforts for six months now from Dr. Warren. But I am here tonight only as an observer, to educate myself, and perhaps to be of some help to what I understand is a rock-solid organization with sound direction, positive leadership, and outstanding purpose, as well as having teeth to back up any barking you might do."

Ben took his place at the head of the table, nodded to Lewis Lynch who puffed on a corncob pipe, and to Sadie Wythe and Dr. Warren. Mr. Adams was sitting beside Ben. When they were ready, all except Mr. Adams put one hand on the table, palm closed, then opened the hand. Lying in each was the Freedom Fighter's gold coin.

"Freedom or death," they all said together, then the coins vanished into hiding places in their clothing.

Ben turned to the man beside him. "Mr. Adams, we are honored to have you with us tonight. Dr. Warren has been our informal link with you, and it's good to show you directly what we have accomplished, and what we're planning. I think our first order of business should be a report on our recruitment drive."

There followed a brief statement by each of the five regarding the enlistment of followers. When the total was put together, the Freedom Fighters numbered forty men.

"We're in no rush, but we want good men, who can shoot and who can be counted on. This will in no way interfere with a man's militia duty. If he is called, that takes priority. But we feel there will be much important work for us to do before any of the militia is called out!"

Sadie gave a summary of her *Journal of Outrage.*

"Since our last report there have been three more cases of wrathful fathers complaining to the captain of the guard concerning conduct of the troops billeted in their homes. All were for improper advances to the young ladies in the homes. The *Boston Gazette* has told of two attacks on women in the street by off-duty English soldiers. Both men have been jailed and are being prosecuted by the superior court.

"There is a growing list of homeowners complaining about thefts from homes by soldiers billeted there, and increasing anger about the gunships and the way they prey on the small and large shippers around the port, bay and rivers. The Redcoats claim smuggling, which is untrue. We demand the harassment end.

"Almost daily we hear reports and receive post from points long distances from us concerning the massacre here on March 5, and the shock and anger of the citizens. We believe part of this correspondence is due to the way we sent out messages and letters and had Mr. Lynch spread the word the day after the massacre.

"Our weekly roll of Freedom Fighters now stands at forty."

All around the table they murmured approval, and Ben took over.

"Ladies and gentlemen, Mr. Adams arrived tonight. I have been trying to reorder and condense my thinking about our movement. I for one have a firm commitment to freedom, liberty from the ties with England, as my long range goal. But perhaps we need to set down in some kind of written form, exactly when and where we should move to help further this cause of total freedom. A set of specifics concerning where we will take armed action, or secret action, in order to promote liberty."

Ben called on Dr. Warren, then Jonathan, and soon each one had agreed and the group determined that it should set down some basic principles and operating procedures. Dr. Warren was asked to put together a short document.

Then they talked about organization and procedures for fifteen minutes. In a lag in the conversation Lynch spoke up.

"I don't know if I should be bustin' in here, but I'm in favor of each of our members having a weapon at his command. I'd like each man to have a flintlock rifle and a pistol. What think ye of this plan?"

They talked about it for almost ten minutes, heard from Mr. Adams, and in the end decided that each volunteer should own a rifle, powder horn and the various devices to make the weapon fire, as well as a quantity of powder and ball good for 100 shots.

Lynch beamed. "Yes, I can see we're making progress. I have ten men in my group now. Would it be approved to call them the start of a company? If so, I'd like to hold a turkey shoot with my men as soon as possible to train them in the use of their weapons and sharpen their aim. Ain't nothing worse than a batch of untrained men trying to shoot flintlocks."

Again Lynch's suggestions were approved and it was determined that each of the "companies" should employ some discreet means of holding shooting matches to train the men in the use of their weapons.

Ben turned toward their guest. "Mr. Adams, you've seen something of our operation, know much of our expectations and our dreams of liberty. Are there any comments you'd care to make?"

Ben had a profound respect for Samuel Adams. He had graduated from Harvard in 1740 and three years later won a Master of Arts degree. He had been born into a prosperous family and began his career in a business his father wet up for him, but he failed miserably. His inheritance melted away from previous claims on it and he soon began taking minor government jobs with the city of Boston. At last he became a tax collector, and in those hard times built up a deficit of eight thousand pounds. In the early 1760's he joined the patriot party and soon became one of the best-known political figures in the state, taking part in the Stamp Act turmoil. In 1768, he was elected to the Massachusetts Assembly, and was off and moving in the political sphere.

Now Sam Adams shifted his rotund body and

looked at each of them from dark eyes. His face seemed rounder than ever when he smiled, which he did now.

"Comments, yes. Encouragement, yes. I'm distinctly proud of each one of you. Mrs. Wythe, I understand you're a most valuable member of this group. More power to you. Sometimes I think our women are tragically wasted. They could do so much if only we would let them. I also hear that you're still the best marksman in the lot." He beamed. "Now, as you know, I am a proponent of total independence from England. We're Americans. Let's have our own nation. Not many people think this way yet, I know. I know many today are solid English loyalists, and have been for the past two centuries. But our numbers are growing. More and more men are realizing that we can never be truly free under the yoke of the English Parliament. We must be patient. We must prepare, and we must train. We must also harass and disrupt in a casual manner that very system that grinds us down. We must speak out for our own rights, and we must fight every form of taxation that Parliament tries to impose upon us as if it were a giant net that would surely capture us and hold us prisoners.

"Eventually our people, the men and women in the streets, will know and understand that it must be liberty—or slavery. Then, and only then, will we be ready for open conflict, because it will be a popular uprising, a war of the people, and that's the kind of battle that no imperial nation three thousand miles away can fight and hope to win.

"To work toward this goal we don't need a mob,

we need an organized, highly trained and responsible group of men and women who know how to fight for liberty."

Adams smiled and shook his head. "Well, now. I didn't mean to make a speech, but you are very special friends of mine. Here I can say anything I want to and know it will stop within these walls. I do caution you that we must be judicious in the use of arms. We aren't ready for any major confrontation. An armed episode now would bring more troops, even bombardment from the English men-of-war riding in our harbor with their cannon, which would mean wholesale slaughter of women and children. We can't have that. And remember, our militia is strong. For twenty years every able-bodied man in the colony has taken his turn in the citizen army. What the English do not seem to realize is that this fighting force can do battle with English Redcoats just as easily as it has fought French and Indians. It goes without saying that I am with you fully. I can't officially join, since my legs can't stand up to any of your sudden mobilizations, but I'm with you. We'll keep in close contact through Dr. Warren, and if there's anything each of us can do for the other, let's talk about it at length and at once."

Ben had been watching Sadie as the leader of the freedom movement in the colonies talked. She was attentive, nodding in agreement, her small face set in determination. Ben marveled that she could love him. He felt a stirring deep in his loins but suppressed it.

The meeting broke up soon after that. Ben had a quick ale with Jonathan, then drove to Sadie's flat. She was in the kitchen, where she sat with a cup of tea. As soon as Ben came in, she looked up, troubled.

"Ben, will I have to kill anyone?"

He laughed gently and bent, kissing her worried, trembling lips. Then he lifted her to her feet and pulled her slender body hard against him. He kissed Sadie's upturned face and only then felt some of the tension ease from her. She cuddled against him, her breasts pushing firmly on his chest.

"Ben, I worry so. When shooting at a target or a squirrel I have no trouble. But could I deliberately sight in and fire at another human being? I don't know."

Ben's hand found her breast and began rubbing it gently, then slid inside her dress top.

"Sadie, Sadie, you're so tense. You need to relax, to stop thinking about it for a minute. When you're at war, it becomes morally acceptable to kill, and if you're ever in a situation where someone else is trying to kill you, the decision to try to end your enemy's life will be far less theoretical than it seems right now."

"Ben?"

"Yes."

"Please kiss me again."

Ben held her close, kissed her open mouth and felt her straining against him. Gradually she relaxed and he lifted her in his arms and carried her toward the bedroom.

"My tough little soldier, you're about as rough and mean right now as a feather pillow."

She smiled and unbuttoned his shirt front.

"Sometimes I feel so strong, able to do anything . . ." She sensed the tears coming and didn't know why. Was it because she loved this man so deeply, yet had to sneak around in darkness and behind lies just to feel his hands on her, to moan in pleasure as his swollen staff plunged delightfully into her willing body? Was it because she didn't feel evil or wicked, because she was a woman in love who wanted her man holding her and lying on top of her, crushing her into the bedding and making love to her so gently, so tenderly, so wonderfully, that she would cry from the pure beauty of the union?

He laid her on the bed and took off his shoes.

"Darling, don't undress. I couldn't stand to wait that long!" She pulled up her skirts and tore down her underthings. "Quickly, sweetheart, right now, or I think I shall start screaming and burst!"

The next day, before the family was up and around, Ben heard a knocking on the rear door. Harry, the driver, got up and took the message. He came to Ben's bedroom and rapped quietly.

"Sir, Captain Teague on the *Land of Hope* sent a message that he would appreciate you coming to the dock right away. It's something about the bonding."

Ben scowled. "Yes, thank you, Harry. I'll get right down there. Hitch up the chaise for me. You don't need to come. You get the other rig ready and take the family to church, and explain about my early call." Ben closed the door and dressed.

Behind him Sandra sat up. "More trouble with

the ships?"

He explained what he knew, kissed her soft mouth and told her to enjoy the service. He was sure he wouldn't have the problem worked out in time to get home and change.

Sandra pouted a moment, then shrugged. That was part of the price of having responsibilities. She was sure some of the newer parishioners must wonder if she were a widow.

It was five minutes to ten when the Rutledges arrived for services at the Christ Congregational Church. This was the largest church in town but since it was not the Church of England it was not attended by the wealthy, the Tories or the English officers. The powerful men of the English tradition and government were members of the Church of England. Ben had long realized that the Congregationalist ministers were some of the strongest voices in the colonies against England, against taxation, and against what the ministers considered the equally evil forces of the Anglican bishops and the Pope himself.

Sandra Rutledge, followed closely by her daughter Harriet and sons Robert and David, moved to the family pew just four rows from the front on the lectern side, and settled down.

Harriet wore an exquisite new dress with a tight bodice that molded her figure delightfully and nearly swept the floor. She had seen two young men watching her as she came down the aisle, and it prompted a pinkness at her temples and cheeks which gave her a radiant glow. She sat beside her mother, ready for a boring, tedious and dry two-hour service. Harriet wasn't feeling at all religious.

She was more concerned with the party her mother had promised her on her eighteenth birthday. Her mother called it a coming-out ball. There would be flowers, music, dancing, lots of boys her own age, and for the first time she would be permitted to have a glass of champagne.

Harriet thought she heard a whisper. The church vibrated with a pre-service buzz as worshippers found their seats, exchanged muted greetings and shuffled their feet.

The whisper came again, and Harriet felt her mother grip her arm.

"Harriet, don't turn around, simply ignore the person behind you," Mrs. Rutledge commanded.

"Who is it?" asked Harriet.

"Never mind!"

"Good morning, Miss Rutledge," the voice said again, not more than a foot behind her ear.

She turned, saw the amused eyes and half-open mouth and snapped her head back quickly. It was *him!* That awful Mr. Cunliffe. The one who had stared at her chest until her breasts had simply burned. Was he some kind of monster? Harriet sat ramrod straight, without moving, her eyes forward, and a new frown on her face. But inside she was remembering how she had felt when he had so brazenly stared at her and made her feel undressed. It had been a warm glow, a kind of knee-wobbling weakness that streamed through her veins. Yes, that was it, a weakness, a warmth, a sudden hunger, and a sudden ache far, far down between her legs. She would never tell that to another living soul, but it was the truth. She often wondered what it would feel like to be with a man, to have his hands on her bare flesh, on her breasts.

Her mother touched her arm, and held up the prayer book—or was it a hymnal? Harriet couldn't tell. Her eyes wouldn't focus and again she felt that ache far, far down.

It was a full two-hour service that Sunday morning, and when Harriet rose to leave with her family, she purposefully avoided looking in the row behind her. But he was still there. He stood at the aisle letting others go out ahead of him. Harriet hesitated. Her brothers were already ten feet beyond her going down the aisle. She moved past Mr. Cunliffe, and saw to her surprise that he stepped directly behind her, between her and her mother. The aisle was filled again, jammed tight, and Harriet stood almost touching her brother Robert. He turned and grinned and she patted his shoulder.

Suddenly she was aware that the person behind her was extremely close to her.

"Oh, pardon me," a man said, and something brushed against her bottom. It was Cunliffe. She knew his voice. He was disgusting. Then he touched her lower part again and before she could move his hand pushed against her buttocks, tried to wedge between them, and then stroked slowly upward.

"Oh!" she said softly as the hand pulled away. Robert turned and made a silly face, but she couldn't laugh. The line moved ahead and she walked with it, tried to stand sideways, but when she stopped, Cunliffe bumped against her. They were jammed shoulder to shoulder in a crush of many people in the aisle. There was no way anyone could see below a person's waist. She felt Cunliffe slide in closer behind her. His hand snaked between the closely packed bodies, pushed below her buttocks and tried to pry her legs apart. She wanted to turn and slap him, to scream and tell everyone what he was doing, but she couldn't. No one had ever touched her there, ever! She couldn't move. She kept her legs tightly together as his hand rubbed and rubbed. It was a jolting thrill, a shock, a sensation she had never known before. Then her brother stepped forward, and he was shaking hands with the minister. She went behind him automatically, taking the minister's hand, smiling, nodding, and then she was outside. She stood between her brothers and saw her mother come up quickly, frowning. Before Mrs. Rutledge could say a word, Edmund Cunliffe walked up and bowed.

"A pleasure, Mrs. Rutledge, to see you again. I must report that I bought some of the Bach music and it was perfect. And this is your lovely daughter, Harriet."

Harriet stared past him, unblinking. What kind of man would do what he did and then come up brazenly and say hello? His kind—the Mr. Cunliffe kind.

"Good day, Mr. Cunliffe. I don't want you speaking to my children." She stepped in front of Cunliffe, between him and Harriet, so close she stepped on one of his feet, and he backed away quickly. He laughed, moved around, and approached the girl from the other side.

"You're looking extremely beautiful as always, Miss Rutledge," he said.

Sandra caught Harriet's hand and pulled her down the street away from the man. He followed. He talked to them all the way to their carriage, and even helped the ladies into the seat.

Sandra looked down at him scornfully. "Mr. Cunliffe, if you ever approach me or my daughter again, or try to talk to us in the street, I'll have you arrested and charged with assault. Good day!"

The carriage jolted away and Edmund Cunliffe stood watching, a small smile rimming his handsome features.

Later that same evening, Sandra told Ben about the confrontation with Edmund Cunliffe. Ben was puzzled. The man had all the woman he wanted. Why would he suddenly become smitten with an inexperienced seventeen-year-old girl? And why with a daughter of a known sympathizer for colonial causes against the Crown? Ben worried for a moment, then cast it aside. There would probably be no more contact. If there were, Ben would make a personal call on Cunliffe and order him to stop bothering the family. That would do it. Cunliffe was not known for his bravery. He usually ran from any physical confrontation.

Ben told Sandra his decision and she seemed satisfied. He settled back to read the latest edition of the *Boston Gazette*. It was filled with important political maneuverings.

A moment later Martha brought a sailor into

the study, his round hat in his hands, pitch odor ripe on his pants and an expression of fear and awe on his rough face.

"Begging your pardon, Mr. Rutledge, sir. But Captain Nelson says you should come right down to his ship."

Ben lifted his brows. "Why, man?"

The sailor turned around and found only Mrs. Rutledge listening.

"I wasn't supposed to say unless I had to, sir. But Captain Nelson, he done shot one of them customs commissioners."

Chapter Six
TALL SHIPS ON THE BLOCK

Ben and the seaman drove to the docks as fast as their horses could charge through the streets. On the way Ben found out from the messenger that no physician had been summoned. Ben sent him riding toward Dr. Warren's house and office with an urgent message for the doctor to come at once—and with no questions asked.

When Ben's rig pulled up at the dock, he leaped down and ran up the crude gangplank to the deck of the sailing ship *Liberty*. Captain Nelson met his employer, his wind-and sun-weathered face ashen, drawn now in frustration and anger.

"I couldn't help it, sir. It was an accident, I swear!"

Ben watched Nelson for a moment in deepest sympathy, then motioned for him to lead the way to the low ranked customs commissioner who had been put in the captain's cabin.

A seaman there with a dirty rag pressed it against the wounded man's chest. Ben made sure he was not Commissioner Trout. There was little blood on the shirt front. He lifted the man and looked at his back. The pistol ball had come out just under his shoulder, leaving a terrible wound.

"Stop the bleeding!" Ben ordered sharply. He checked the path of the ball and guessed it could have penetrated through the man without harming any vital organ. It had entered the man's upper left breast, probably smashed a rib and carried through above the lung.

"Feed him all the grog he'll drink," Ben commanded. Captain Nelson produced a bottle of rum and one of brandy. Only the seaman in the cabin and the messenger seemed to be on board. That was lucky. Ben told the sailor to make the commissioner drink, then motioned the captain outside. They stood on deck, looking at the last few lights burning in Boston town.

Ben turned to Nelson who explained.

"He came on board in a surly mood. Angry he was and a little drunk maybe. Said he was the only one who hadn't impounded a ship yet. Told me flat out he would find ten violations on the *Liberty* and she'd be Crown property within an hour. Now, sir. I've been in this since the start, and I know how they work. I've followed the law to the letter. This commissioner Burke-White got abusive, threatened to impound your ship for no cause at all.

"I said that was illegal. He told me that hadn't bothered them before, with the other ships. He began telling me all the violations he was charging me with. Sir, I'm a fair man. I can't abide a cheat or a swindler. So when he told me if I gave him a hundred pounds he'd keep quiet about the violations, I knew he came on board just for the bribe, 'cause he brought no redcoats with him. I pulled my pistol out of my bunk and cocked it. It was

118

fresh primed and ready. He kept telling me the new charges and how his price had gone up. He laughed and held out his hand.

" 'Nothing else you can do, Nelson, and you know it,' he said, sounding much more sober. It had all been a trick. I swore at him and charged, ready to knock him down. I swear I forgot I had the weapon in my hand. When I fisted my right fingers the pistol went off, and there he is."

Dr. Warren puffed up the gangplank, saw Ben and went into the captain's cabin with him. The doctor looked at the wound, nodded as the man drank more brandy, then cleaned the injury and applied a dressing to stop the bleeding.

"He'll live, worse luck. I'll get him patched up here, but then what should we do with him?"

Ben looked at Dr. Warren and called his carriage. "Dr. Warren, do you know any of the girls in the brothels who owe you a favor? Maybe some medical work they couldn't pay for?"

Dr. Warren nodded. "About a dozen of them. How can they pay a doctor?"

"Good, good. Pick the one with the most willpower and one that is intensely loyal to the cause of liberty. She must also be something of a playactor, able to keep her mouth shut and say only what she's told to say. At the same time she can earn ten pounds."

A half-hour later they were ready to go. The victim had been roused again and again and forced to drink brandy until the bottle was empty. He was falling down drunk. They carried him to the dock and loaded him on board Ben's carriage.

Ten minutes later they were inside one of the

cribs on First street. Burke-White had been sprawled on the floor, the fired pistol nearby.

Ruthie stared down at him, a curious smile on her full face. She was a strong, earthy girl who had made her own way in life since she was thirteen and big enough to attract men. She had been eager to help out.

"A bit of play-acting is it? To help out Doc Warren? Sure I'll do it, I owe him. And if I can spit in the eye of them fancy English fops, so much the better!"

Ben and the seaman left and for fifteen minutes Ruthie and Dr. Warren went over and over her story until she had it just right. Then a banging came on the door and it swung open. A pair of redcoats came in, with Commissioner Trout right behind them.

"Honest, guv'nor, I didn't know it was loaded. I've had to use it a dozen times with some blokes what won't do what I tell 'em. But I swear it was never loaded before. Somebody done played a trick on me. He was roaring drunk, he was, when he come in and I did my bit for him and he wanted something more. Something I'd be too delicate even to mention. I don't go in for all that fancy French stuff, so I pushed him away. He came at me even after I got the sot dressed, mind you, and then the blamed thing done went off with a roar. I was more 'sprised than 'e was, guv."

Commissioner Trout watched the girl, who was a little on the heavy side, one huge breast peeking out from her thin blouse. The nipple was dark brown and had risen with excitement. Trout nodded at her and looked at the man on the floor. It

120

was Burke-White, just as the messenger had said. Trout didn't know he fooled around with the doxies. The man on the floor tried to say something that came out "ship...damned ship."

Ruthie stood, letting the breast swing free from her half-opened blouse and stared down at the commissioner.

"Yeah, he's been talking about some ship he's supposed to go out and inspect. Been mumbling about it on and off ever since he came in. Said something about going to find a batch of violations, whatever the hell that means."

Trout started to push her away, then moved his hand to cover her breast, and felt the girl tremble as he did. Dr. Warren wasn't looking at them. He might just stay on here awhile.

"Can he be moved, Dr. Warren?"

"Oh, yes, he's well enough to be taken to the customs house or his home. He should be in bed then. I'll change the dressing every three days. Nothing vital seems damaged."

The two redcoats came on command and lifted the commissioner carefully and carried him to the buggy.

"Easy, easy!" Dr. Warren cautioned.

Commissioner Trout stared at the physician.

"Dr. Warren, there is no sense making any record of this. He's just a spirited lad who got a bit—out of hand—shall we say. And the young woman seems innocent of any wrongdoing, simply defending herself. It was an accident. We'll put it down that Burke-White was wounded in the line of duty. No reason anyone else should know about this. Is that clearly understood?"

121

"Just see that I get paid for my services, and it's forgotten as far as I'm concerned," Dr. Warren said.

Trout dug into his pocket, brought out a five-pound note and handed it to the doctor. "That should take care of tonight, and your subsequent dressings. Correct?"

"Yes. Yes, indeed. Well, I had better be going." Outside, Dr. Warren climbed into his chaise and drove away. The other rig with the injured commissioner was also gone, and Trout was alone with the girl. He closed the door and watched her.

Ruthie had her back to him and when she turned toward him she had dropped her blouse. Her large breasts wobbled and bounced as she took two steps toward him.

"Now, you, guv, you're the kind of gent I like. A girl would do just about anything to help you get your jollies. You 'ave a few minutes? I mean, you're strong and big and I like 'em big." She loosened the top button on her skirt.

Commissioner Trout couldn't take his eyes off her breasts. He'd never seen bare breasts so big. His wife looked like a child in comparison. He growled, locked the door and turned toward her, both his hands stretched out, fingers grasping.

Two days later, Ben Rutledge sat in his office watching the westerly punishing the remains of the early morning fog that clung to the Boston harbor. It would be a bright end-of-March day, Ben knew. If only his own future looked half so bright.

At first he had been cautious about the Nonimportation Agreement that colony after colony adopted. It was a differing resolve, but the thrust of it was that the colonies should not import any taxable items listed in the Townshend Act passed by Parliament. These were glass, paper, paint and tea. The feelings ran high in most colonies with some halting all imports from England entirely. Ben found his import tonnage reduced by half, with many merchants refusing to buy much of the goods they usually did from England.

In New York the toll was even worse for merchants and shippers. In 1768 they imported goods valued at 482,000 pounds sterling from England. But the next year the total dropped to goods valued at only 74,000 pounds sterling.

Ever since May 13, 1767 when the Townshend duties went into effect, the people had been restless and patriotic by turns. There was an upsurge of homespun, and a disdaining of brocades and laces and fancy velvets imported from England.

The graduating classes of 1770 at Harvard College and at Princeton forbade fancy gowns and took their degrees in homespun. In many elegant entertainments it was fashionable to appear in homespun even for the ladies, forsaking garments which had come from England.

This was part of the dilemma that Ben faced as he stared at his columns of figures that March day in 1770. There was still strong public sentiment to avoid all English goods. The people knew the action was hurting the English merchants, and that these men were putting heavy pressure on Parliament to repeal the hated Townshend Act. But would Parliament do so? And even if it did, would this mean enough new work to keep Ben out of debt?

There were almost no buildings of any type being constructed in Boston. There were no nails, no lumber, little building materials of any kind. In many areas, the colonists were going into light manufacturing. This type of activity had been prohibited by England. They were supposed to import all the manufactured goods they needed from the mother country. By now Americans were realizing that they would have to become self-sustaining in certain manufactured goods. This was difficult, because over ninety percent of the population in all the colonies were still farmers. Ben Franklin had told Parliament in 1766 that the great majority of the colonists would undoubtedly remain farmer for centuries to come.

Rutledge dropped his quill and stared at the figures. There had to be an answer, and one better than murder. A vile vendetta, a personal campaign of ruination was waged against him, with no quarter and no rules. So why did he have to be so blasted honorable? Still, he would not order the man killed, nor would he do the deed himself. He might call Trout out in a duel, but Ben was not in favor of dueling. He had campaigned in the Assembly to have the practice outlawed in Massachusetts. Ben had never been in a duel, and he had no desire ever to be. But, if he called out Trout, it would be a quick way to settle the problem—win or lose.

Ben shook his head and looked at the columns again. The three tall ships were the key. Ben thought back to the auction he had attended two years ago. It was the first he could remember in Boston. The ship was from New York and had been sold. In fact, Ben bought her on orders from a New York firm, as their agent for the owners of the vessel. The sum had been some thirty-seven thousand pounds sterling, and he had been reimbursed the same day by the New York agent. Value of the craft had been over sixty thousand.

An idea began to form as Ben thought about it. It had several unusual and interesting aspects. He remembered all he could of the auction itself. He would make some discreet inquiries. Ben was certain there could be no law or ruling against a ship owner bidding on his own vessel. He sat thinking, his mind jolting off on tangents, related offshoots that brought a smile to his face. Yes, it might just work, if he were right in his assumptions and if he could get the cooperation he needed. Both were vital.

Ben looked back at the books on his desk. He had set up his lookout on the point and had put a pilot aboard every ship of his coming into port with strict written instructions from him to direct the captain to follow the letter of the law, to bend over backwards not to violate any aspect of the Navigation Act or to arouse the anger of any commissioner or inspector. He even authorized a ten-pound bribe if necessary to get through the normal inspections. In the last two days there had been no fines or problems with the commissioners.

Ben wondered if the shooting the previous Sunday had anything to do with it. When Commissioner Burke-White came out of his long drunk, he had probably told exactly what happened. But had they believed him? The other officials probably laughed him down, poked him in the ribs and inquired about how good the woman had been. The fact of his prowling the cathouses would surface soon. Ben had made certain by sending Lewis Lynch into the Tory hangouts and launching the story the way he wanted it. Ben was sure that in two days, half of Boston knew of Commissioner Burke-White's romp in the crib. At least there had been no official inquiries, no charges either against Ruthie or against the *Liberty*. Neither had his ships suffered a fine in the past two days.

The shooting may have made the commissioners a little cautious, but Ben knew that such luck couldn't last. They would be after him again, soon, and harder than ever. His plan had to work.

But that was a long-range operation. Trout. The one word was his whole problem. He had to set up something, a whole series of continuing "experiences" for Trout, personal jeopardy, even financial difficulties that would encourage Commissioner Trout to take an early retirement and return to London.

Ben sat there pondering.

Jennifer Bull and Harriet Rutledge had been best friends as long as either could remember. They were cousins on Harriet's mother's side, and were within four months of being the same age. Tonight Harriet had received permission to sleep at her cousin's house after Mrs. Rutledge had made sure that both of the elder Bulls would be home all evening.

126

"A perfect lady, Harriet Rutledge," her mother had said. "That's what I expect you to be while you're over at Emma's. I'll get a complete report on the two of you, so you just mind your manners. You're a grown-up lady now, and there's no time for childish pranks. You do understand, Harriet May?"

Harriet nodded, a wide grin on her face. Her mother still remembered when she and her cousin had played all sorts of pranks and tricks on visitors, including dumping a bucket of water on the new minister. But that was when they were twelve and they didn't know the man was a preacher.

"Yes, Mama, I'll promise to be good. But you did say I can tell Jennifer about my party, didn't you?"

The Rutledge handyman had driven her across town to her cousin's house. Harriet hadn't been inside the home more than five minutes when Jennifer led her upstairs to her room and fell on the big bed.

Jennifer was slightly built, with few womanly curves, a petite, attractive package topped by small breasts and a face that was a perpetual delight. Her round face sparkled with green eyes over soft natural shadows, a pert nose and a full mouth that forever curved into a grin, a smirk or a laugh. Her hair was brown and now curled in dozens of ringlets down her neck.

"Fine and dandy, Miss Harriet May. Am I angry with you!" Jennifer put on a scolding face that quickly melted into a giggle. "You have been flirting with this older man for two weeks now, and you never even told me."

"Jennifer Bull, whatever are you talking about?"

"The man, the one in church, the one at the music store. The one who stared at you. Mother didn't remember his name."

"Oh, *him.*"

"There is one then! Who is he? What does he look like? Did he touch you? Is he rich? Is he really handsome? Is he as old as Mama said?"

Harriet sat on the edge of the bed and touched Jennifer's shoulder. "Those of us who are older know about these things."

"Oh, pish-posh. You don't either know about those things. Did he stare at your breasts? Yours are big enough, he must have. How did it feel?"

Harriet sighed. "Feel? You silly goose. He only stared at me, he didn't touch me...that time."

Jennifer sat up, her eyes wide. "That time? You mean he did touch you the next time? *In church?*"

Harriet held herself a little straighter, looked away from her cousin and then back. Her chin came up just a little. "Yes, he touched me in church."

Jennifer's eyes were flashing now, sparkling with curiosity. She turned toward Harriet with one hand in an open-palmed gesture.

"Where? Where did he touch you?"

Harriet stood and looked around her cousin's room. It was a lot like her own: big bed, chifferobe, a closet and a small desk for reading or study. When Harriet sat down again beside her cousin, she practiced her most aloof, most icy stare. "Dear cousin Jennifer, I could never tell you that. Do you think I'm one of those women who...who tells?"

Jennifer giggled.

Harriet looked at her in surprise, then she too began to laugh.

"He did, didn't he? He touched you 'way down low." Jennifer moved closer to Harriet. "Make you a bargain. You tell me about what this man did, and I'll tell you what Andy Otis did to me just three weeks ago. All right?"

"Andy Otis? Isn't he that little freckle-faced lad with the wild red hair who was always chasing us home?"

"Yes, the one who was shorter than we were, with the strange brown eyes..." Jennifer smiled. "Only, you haven't seen him lately. He's six feet tall with shoulders that won't go through a door, and his hair is like burnished copper, it's so deep red, and..."

Harriet held up her hands. "Stop, stop," she said. "It's a bargain, but it has to be good, as good as what happened to me, and you go first."

They grinned in agreement, but before either could say another word, Mrs. Bull called the girls downstairs to help fix dinner. The Bulls had no cook or maid, no domestic help at all. Mr. Bull was a printer working at the firm of Edes & Gill in Dassett alley behind the state house. The Bulls managed quite well, but they were far from being rich.

Right after the dinner dishes were done, and the girls had played a game of spelling bee with Jennifer's parents and two younger sisters and brother, the girls scampered upstairs. Jennifer set a coal oil lamp on the dresser and the girls looked at each other.

"You first, Jenny."

The younger girl frowned, then shook her head. "Let's get in bed first."

Harriet agreed. They turned their backs and disrobed, slipping into chin-to-toe nightgowns. They got into the double bed and sat against the big headboard.

"So?" Harriet asked.

Jennifer hesitated. "Cross your heart and hope to die, Harriet May Rutledge, that you'll never tell another living soul?"

Harriet made the sign and swore and watched Jennifer.

"Was it really Andy Otis?"

She nodded. "Yes. Oh, yes, it was him. I think I'm in love with him. He's so big and strong. He wants to be a ship captain."

"Jenny, what did he *do?*"

"Oh, that. We were walking home from school and he said he wanted to show me something in that old store two blocks from school. It seemed funny, but I went inside with him by the back door. Soon as we were inside he turned me around, held me by both shoulders and kissed me right on the mouth."

"No!"

"Oh, yes, and I was so surprised, I didn't know what to do. So I just stood there, and then he kissed me again, with his arms around me and my...my front pressing against him."

"He actually kissed you."

"Oh, yes. I'd never really been kissed before, you know, by a boy. He kept telling me how pretty I was, and how he liked me, and that he'd

130

do just about anything for me. Then he put his hand over my breasts, right on top of my dress. I wanted to scream, but I couldn't."

"Tell me what it felt like," Harriet said. "How did you feel?"

"At first, frightened. What if somebody saw us? That was all I could think of. Then he started rubbing, and I could *feel* his hand right through my dress and my petticoat. I was all warm, just all of a sudden, and my breast felt hot and...and tender, sensitive. He rubbed it some more and then kissed me again. As he was kissing me his hand went in the top of my dress and under my petticoat and right on my bare breast!"

"Oh, lordy, Jennifer! You just let him?"

"It happened so fast, I couldn't stop him and then it felt so...I've been wishing some boy would do that so I could see how it...I've wanted to tell somebody about it, to talk about it. I know it was wrong, but...but it felt so good, so right! It didn't seem bad at all. Was it bad, Harriet?"

Harriet shook her head. "No, of course not, Jenny, it wasn't bad. It didn't hurt you, did it? I think it was kind of nice, very natural. Now, tell me exactly how you felt when his hand was...there."

Jenny leaned back and smiled. "Oh, Harriet! I can still almost feel his hand, I was warm, and happy, mellow and happy, just pure joy. It was glorious! The most remarkable feeling I've ever had. Then I knew what Mama meant when she said not to let a man go too far. I mean, Harriet May, right then I think I would have let Andy do just anything he wanted to with me."

"You don't mean he did?"

"Oh, no," said Jennifer quickly. "Land sakes, no. I guess he might have, but a team of horses went by outside in the alley and he pulled his hand back surprised. I think he was a little scared too. He kissed me once more and I felt him wiggle his hips and moan a gasp or two. Then he grinned and said it was time he was getting me home or my ma would have his scalp."

Harriet thought about it. "You've seen him since?"

"Oh, yes. We walked to a shop one day, but I wouldn't even let him hold my hand. He kissed me once, but just quickly in back of our house and I didn't let him touch me there again." Jenny smiled as if remembering that day three weeks ago. Then she giggled. "Now, Harriet May, you can't ever tell anyone, you promised. And now it's your turn to tell me about that scandalous Mr. Cunliffe. I hear he has two fancy women living at his mansion!"

Harriet told the story, from the first meeting in the music store right through his hand between her legs in church and then helping them into their coach.

"Oh, dear! And he touched you down there, *in church?* He is a rake, simply a womanizer. I've heard about him before. But now what are you going *to do* about him?"

Harriet hadn't thought about that part of it. She decided her father would speak to Cunliffe and that would end it. But what if it didn't end? What if she met him again? What if he caught her somewhere alone, and pulled *her* into an empty store?

The girls talked and talked, reliving the experiences a dozen times, then speculating what might happen.

"On solemn oath," Jennifer said. "We'll always tell each other what happens to us, in everything...even with boys. We'll never have any secrets, ever!"

They swore, kissed each other on the cheek to make it binding, and then blew out the lamp. As they lay there in the dark, each girl was thinking what it would be like actually to "go too far" with a boy, as their mothers had warned them about. Neither one could wait to find out.

The following Thursday Harriet and her mother were in the newly opened Franklin Lending Library. Harriet had wandered back between some rows of books. She was fascinated. She had had no idea so many books existed. Her father had a few in his study, but nothing like this—all of the classics, and even some humorous books.

She was at the very end of the row of stacks looking at a book she had taken off the shelf. Almost at the same time someone took two books off the other side of the shelf at eye level, and she found herself looking directly at Edmund Cunliffe. Harriet gave a quick little gasp, but somehow she couldn't move away.

The corners of his mouth turned up in a derisive grin as he saw the confusion on her face.

"Well, Harriet May, good afternoon. You liked it the other day, didn't you? Liked it when I rubbed you?" He said it in a low voice, almost a whisper.

At once she looked to see if anyone else could hear them. No one was within earshot. She looked away from him but couldn't will herself to walk.

"You might as well say you enjoyed my touching you. I sure did. In fact I'd like to do it again right now, if you'd come over here on this side."

She couldn't move either way. Harriet thought her voice had left her too, but still she wasn't sure if she wanted to just rush away. He couldn't hurt her over there. He spoke lower and watched. She leaned closer.

"Harriet, sweetheart. I've got plans for you. Big plans. I know you like me, know you're just itching to have me put my hands on those big, gorgeous breasts of yours."

She wanted to run now, really wanted to, but she was still frozen in place. His smile came back, softer now, and she turned and looked at him.

"Don't worry, I won't scare you, or hurt you. I'll just open your bodice and put my hands there and play with your two beauties. Damn, but you've got good ones! And then I'll move my hands down farther."

Harriet heard someone coming. She slammed the book back in place and looked up. It wasn't her mother. If it had been, her mother would have realized at once what had happened. Harriet moved past the woman and away from the stacks to another section of the library in a deserted spot. She pretended to read a book, and when her mother was ready to go, Harriet was almost normal again. She hadn't seen anything more of Edmund Cunliffe.

On the buggy ride home, Harriet could think of nothing else but what he had said. It was like what Jennifer had told her. She wondered what it would feel like. Harriet shook her head. She simply shouldn't be thinking that way. But Harriet went right on wondering and wondering. Some day, she thought. Some day soon.

Chapter Seven
BY COVER OF GREAT DARKNESS

Lewis Lynch moved cautiously. The time was nearly three a.m. as he settled behind a large oak tree fifty feet from the front windows of the second-story flat where Commissioner Trout lived. It was a small, sparsely furnished accommodation, but the commissioner usually did little there but sleep. He had arrived home rather late this night and Lynch waited until he was sure that the Crown's lackey was sound asleep.

Lynch lifted the sling he had made that afternoon. For two hours he had practiced with it down by the creek, getting back his old knack for the weapon. He had once been very good. Lynch came home from the creek with a pouch of inch-thick rocks and with his aim restored.

Now he placed one of the rocks in the sling's soft leather holder and twirled it around his head three times. On the fourth circuit he let go of one of the sling's straps and the rock shot forward, slamming into the commissioner's house a foot from a window. Lynch grinned and tried again. On the second try, the stone crashed through the upper window. All was quiet for a few moments, then Lynch heard a roar and saw a lamp flicker on inside the commissioner's flat.

The one-eyed man's third stone smashed the other window in the big front room of the apartment, followed by another roar and Trout's head poking out the window where the glass had been. Lynch faded behind the tree and when he peered around the oak, Trout's head had vanished inside the room again.

Lynch settled down to wait. When he guessed by the stars that it was nearing four a.m., he bombarded the upper flat again with a dozen missiles as fast as he could sling them. Some hit the unbroken window sections, others slammed against the front of the house and one or two went through the windows inside the room. Again the light came on and Lynch could imagine the commissioner in a rage getting into his clothes to come out and investigate.

Lynch rubbed the patch over his left eye, then ambled away into the darkness, walking toward his small shack where he would sleep until noon and then report to Ben that his mission was accomplished.

Sadie Wythe was also late getting to work that morning. She had been up half the night worrying over her decision. About four she had made up her mind and at once dropped off to sleep. This morning she was still firm in her resolve, and she arranged a quick meeting with Ben to let him know what she was going to do.

It began over a month ago when she kept meeting one of the English officers of the Twenty-ninth regiment. He was billeted in Mrs. Carrington's rooming house. Mrs. Carrington also owned the flat where Sadie lived. Each week Sadie went to the main house to pay her rent and each time she had seen the lieutenant. He had Mrs. Carrington introduce him and after that he had made it a point to be there whenever Sadie came. He let her know by his every word that he was interested in her. The soldier hadn't asked her out to tea or to dinner at one of the restaurants, but Sadie knew it was only a matter of time.

She had thought a lot about it. Lt. Jack Darland was a pleasant boy, not much over twenty-two. He was only a lieutenant and she guessed he was in administration somewhere. Certainly he didn't act like a field officer. She had told Ben about him right off and together they worked out a wild plan. Sadie could encourage him, get to know him better and if the chance presented itself, find out some vital bits of information about the British operation, numbers of men, movements, plans.

At first they had joked about it. But last night she had presented the idea to the Freedom Fighters' council, and members said they would back her if she decided she wanted to go through with it. Last night, after Ben had left her, she couldn't sleep, but she had decided once and for all to see if the plan would work. She must use this young man and attempt to gain some advantage in the cause of liberty.

Sadie didn't feel like a spy. Goodness knows she didn't look like a seductive woman spy prying secrets out of unwilling soldiers. It would be pure chance if she did find out a worthwhile fact. But she knew she must make the effort.

Jack Darland was only slightly taller than she was, maybe five foot four, with close cropped blond hair and a touch of a blond moustache. He was slender, presented a smart appearance in his uniform, and was soft-spoken and apologetic about being ordered to live at Mrs. Carrington's place.

The next week passed too quickly for Sadie. Three times she had been to see Mrs. Carrington in the evening, and each time Darland had been there in the sitting-room and had talked with her and even played cards once. The last two times he had asked if he might walk her back to her flat, and she said he could. She had thanked him and touched his hand with hers and felt him tremble. Then she went up to her room quickly.

Later, as she lay snugly satisfied in Ben's strong arms, she knew they would talk about it again. Ben had argued against it at the council meeting, saying the youth could not know anything important, so Sadie should not take the chance. But the Freedom Fighters' council voted him down.

He kissed her forehead just below her long blonde hair.

"I never should have let this get past the joking stage," he said, a hint of anger in his voice.

She put her fingers over his lips.

"Darling Ben. You do what you can for freedom. Is there any reason I shouldn't too? Jack may know nothing that could help us, but then again, he might. If he doesn't, I simply tell him to leave me alone and that will be the end of it."

"But if something is important. If there's something that you could find out, and risk your life getting..."

"Well, then I'll have to decide, Ben. If it is vital, or even important, it will be well worth taking a chance."

"You'd bring him here to your flat?"

"If I think it would help, if it's practical...yes."

"You would be more than...friendly with him?"

Ben sat up and watched her in the dim light of the lamp. She was so beautiful it caused a deep ache in his chest. She sat beside him, the blanket spilling down from her shoulders revealing her small, pink-nippled breasts.

"Ben, if that's the only way I can find out what I need to without his realizing it, then yes, of course I would be more than friendly. Ben, I'm not a child!" Color rose in her cheeks, flaming up her neck. "Look, a soldier uses his body to bear arms, to attack, to fight. He risks his *life*. I'm a Freedom Fighter too. I know that I have a responsibility as well to use my...my body for whatever purposes I can to help our cause. Ben—if I need to go to bed with him to get the information, I will." She reached over and put her fingers over his lips as he began to speak.

"Ben, we're not even sure if Jack Darland does know anything that could help us. He may be only in charge of the colonel's horse or the officers' kitchen." She kissed him. "Ben, the situation we're talking about will probably never come up. If it does then we'll decide for sure." She put her arms around his neck and pulled him down on top of her, covering her small body.

"Right now, darling, please make me the happiest woman in the whole world. Once more, quickly! Then you must hurry home."

Three days later, Sadie found out that Darland was assigned to the supply division servicing both regiments. It was also his duty to help coordinate and supply the men-o-war in the harbor. That night Lieutenant Darland escorted Sadie to a late evening dinner in one of the better taverns, where they had a delightful meal. It was close by and they walked there.

"That must be very difficult work, arranging for food and water and uniforms for all those men," said Sadie.

He shook his head. "Not at all. Most of it comes from England on ship, and it's off-loaded here. Much of the food and water for the ships comes from here. Of course, by billeting troops in private homes, it does cut down on our food supply problem."

Sadie felt a little giddy. She wasn't sure where this was leading, but she stumbled along.

"You mean almost everything you need comes in ships from England? What about muskets, powder, cannon balls?"

"Yes, of course, especially that. There isn't a good gunpowder manufacturing plant in the colonies. Some of them try, but the powder isn't up to our standards. I keep our supply filled and up to date. The whole powder magazine and the armory are under my control."

He said it with a touch of pride and she made some appropriate remark, hardly able to speak because now she knew for sure that she had discovered something of value.

Two days later they had confirmation. Lt. Darland was indeed the duty officer assigned and in charge of the on-shore weapons stores and the powder and shot magazines all in the customs house.

Ben kissed her quickly. "We have two men doing a little survey on their own. What we need to know is the exact location of the magazines, and what kind of guards they have on them. When we have all the details, we will decide if we should simply shoot the locks off the doors, or if we'll need keys for a quick operation."

"I can get the keys. Jack has a big ring filled with keys that he always carries with him."

Ben pushed the thought aside. "Not yet. Not unless we decide it's vital that we have the keys. You've done enough already."

The council heard the developments and began making plans. It was assumed that the magazines would be raided. Then planning had to be done: where the war prizes would be stored, how many wagons would be needed to transport the arms, and how big an escort should be used to get the munitions to their new home. Immediately Boston was ruled out as a spot for the munitions cache.

"If we hide it here, everything could be recaptured in a few minutes by the Redcoats," Dr. Warren said. "I'd recommend we start thinking about a supply base outside the city somewhere, a fortified position where we can build up a good-sized quantity of arms and stores."

Dr. Warren was picked to determine the location

and make needed arrangements with the owner of a building or farm. Lewis Lynch was to work out the gathering of six sturdy wagons and teams, and Ben agreed to pick the forty men needed for the action. He would notify the captains, who would tell the men, give them time and place assignments and tell them what weapons to bring.

Sadie sat in her chair at the square table, her Freedom Fighter's gold coin still clutched her in hand. Dr. Warren watched her, his face breaking into a grown.

"Mrs. Wythe, you can stop seeing this Lt. Darland now. We don't need to risk you any further. In fact I think it might be better if you pull back now. We don't want you to risk your...we don't want you in any more danger."

Sadie smiled and touched the doctor's hand. "What you mean is that you don't want me to risk my honor...my body. Gentlemen, I've been married, remember? I know all about sex and making love and how to seduce and be seduced. I don't consider myself a loose woman, but if it comes to that, I'll be proud to use my body for the cause of liberty. Now, let's get on with the planning."

The following evening, Sadie invited Darland up to her flat for tea. He smiled, eager and yet somewhat surprised. He was not in his uniform. Soon they were in her small kitchen. Sadie made tea as he sat at the table on a straight-backed wooden chair watching her.

"I had a girl in England a lot like you, Sadie. Oh, she was a bit shorter, I think. Same color

144

hair, beautiful she was, but not as beautiful as you are."

"Now, Jack. I'll give you tea without all the compliments." She finished making the tea, poured and gave him two small cakes she had made the night before.

After they were finished she smiled. "Want to take the grand tour of my home?"

He nodded. She led him into the small sitting-room, where she kept a framed picture of her husband. It was a drawing a friend had made after his death. She brushed past that and motioned to the closed door. "In there is my bedroom, and that's the size of my house."

He was standing close to her, and as she turned she brushed against him.

"Oh, sorry."

He reached out and took her shoulders in his hands. His face was slack, serious. "Sadie, I'm not in the least sorry. I'm happy. You don't know how pleased I am that you let me come to see you here."

Sadie knew then that he was falling in love with her. She didn't know what she could do about it. She had no feeling for him at all. She couldn't. The council had found out the keys were an absolute necessity for the raid on the magazines. She had a job to do and only she could do it.

She smiled and leaned toward him a little. His head came down and his face grew even more serious.

"Sadie, would it be all right...could I kiss you?"

She leaned further toward him and lifted her mouth to his lips. His kiss was not the cold inexperienced peck she had expected, but a strong demanding kiss. He pulled her close against his body and she felt his hips pressing against hers.

Slowly he let her go. She had her arms around his neck now, smiling at his eager grin. "Jack, would it be all right if I kissed you back?" She reached up, letting her lips part slightly and felt his tongue bore between them. A moment later she took his hand and led him into the bedroom.

Gently, slowly, she undressed him. The white neck cloth, then his frock coat, and the dark wine-colored breeches. She felt the bulging key ring in his pocket, heard it thump when it hit the floor. She gave a small sigh. The brandy—where was the brandy? Within an hour he had to be thoroughly drunk and so exhausted he would sleep.

It was past midnight when Sadie opened her kitchen door leading to the landing and found Lewis Lynch waiting. He took the ring of keys and ran down the steps on his way to a Freedom Fighter member who was also a locksmith. Since they didn't know which key fit the locks on the powder magazines, they would make duplicates of all of them.

Two days later the final preparations were made, and the raid took place. Ben led it, commanding forty Freedom Fighters. Ten men with flintlocks were set up as a covering force to handle any resistance from the ten or twelve guards positioned for the night in the far end dormitory rooms of the customs house. Ten more men handled five heavy farm wagons, one each as driver and guard. The remaining twenty Freedom Fighters were assigned the task of invading the storage areas and hauling out the loot to the wagons in the alley.

Ben and Lynch went into the customs house through the same unguarded door they had raided before. This time, one of the keys on the ring fit the door. They waited five minutes until a roving guard sauntered by. He was dropped silently with a rifle butt and his uniform stripped off him before he was tied and gagged. They moved down a corridor and found the armory and powder magazine in a half-basement just over the water line of the bay. Each door had three sturdy locks, but they opened with the keys from the ring.

Lynch grinned as he swung the doors wide. Inside were stacks of long guns, shot and powder. The men began carrying it out and loading it on the wagons. The lobsterback guard, almost naked now, was deposited in the powder room. He'd be found in the morning.

Ben watched the loading for half an hour, then checked his large, round pocket watch. It was a little after 3:30 a.m.

"Get them moving!" Ben ordered. "We've got to be out of here in fifteen minutes!"

Lynch waved and ran back to the magazine. A line of men came out, each loaded with rifles, boxes of pistols or shot. Others carried wooden boxes filled with black powder, and two rolled a five-pound cannon along the wooden floor. Men ran from the wagons, back inside for more. As each wagon was filled, it was disguised with a half-load of hay and the driver moved it slowly down the alley.

Ben looked at his time piece again. "Five more minutes," he told Lynch. "Keep them moving. Concentrate on the powder now. Let's clean out all that powder we can."

The man nodded. All were running both ways now, panting, sweating in the cool night air.

The next to the last wagon creaked out of the alley, with two extra guards riding in back.

As the last man came from the door of the customs house with the final box of powder, Lynch said they were all done. Ben laughed in delight and counted his men. All were accounted for. Ben relocked the outer door.

"I closed and locked the doors inside," Lynch said. "Them redcoats ain't gonna know anything is missing until they open it up."

Ben waved at the men, saw the last wagon move off and then led the rest of the Freedom Fighters down the alley and to the street where a dozen horses and two chaises had been left. The troops were relieved at their guard and holding positions and told to fade away and go home. Some of the men were now so tired they could hardly walk, but on every face was a grin of delight that they had actually struck back at the hated redcoats. They had made an offensive move, and they knew they had hurt the Englanders and made the start of their own great cache of arms that would be used to win their freedom.

Ben swung into his chaise and motioned Lynch up beside him.

"It was a good night's work," Ben said. "Now we have one more small task."

Lynch nodded. "I'll get it finished right away, sir."

Ben handed Lynch the full uniform that had been taken off the redcoat guard. "Good luck, Lynch. Play it out just the way we planned."

Lynch saluted by touching the tip of his three-cornered hat, and jumped down from the rig. He called to a man standing in the dark moonlight shadows and they turned down the street the opposite way. Ben was relieved he wasn't going with them.

Dr. Warren would meet the wagons at the edge of town and escort them under another ten-man guard toward Concord and the Archibald farm where the goods would be stored in secret. It was planned that everything would be well out of sight before noontime.

Ben brooded as he drove. First there had been Sadie's sacrifice and her danger. He knew this affair had hurt her more than she would ever admit. But she was strong and, more important, stubborn and independently willed. She would survive. He had argued long and hard on the subject of the young redcoat lieutenant but in the end the council had won. They had met without Sadie to argue out Darland's fate, and each of them knew what it must be. Ben knew at the time it was the only logical and secure method to thwart an inquiry. Every time Ben realized the horror of it, he remembered the young rebel dying in his arms the day of the massacre. That made it seem at least bearable.

Captain Paul Preston, of the Twenty-ninth Regimental Guards, stared in shock and surprise at the scene in front of him. When the matter was first reported to him earlier, he had ordered the area sealed off until he could get there. Not a word was to be spoken to anyone concerning it.

Now he stared at the pathetic spectacle. It was just past the docks on a sandy beach where daytime swimming took place and where families shared picnic lunches. A blanket was there, an official-issue English army blanket. Nearby were the remains of a box lunch, undoubtedly some midnight snack prepared for a price by one of the taverns.

Then there were the bottles. Two of them brandy, nearly empty, another of port wine. One bottle had been broken. On the edge of the blanket, all neatly stacked, were a woman's clothes. The dress was a fancy one, with "harlot" written in every seam. It was all there, the petticoat, underthings, and stockings. On the other side of the rumpled blanket lay a long pipe and a small glass jar containing some black substance. The captain had seen enough of Chinese opium dens to know what that was all about.

He turned now and stared at the body of Lieutenant Jack Darland, lately of His Majesty's Regimental Guard and under the captain's own command. How could it be? The body lay where the high tide had rolled it. There were no marks on the corpse and the most obvious answer was that Darland had arranged his midnight picnic and tryst with some woman, became overcome with the opium, then staggered into the surf and drowned.

Surely any woman, harlot or saint, would run away as quickly as she could from such a situation. The cribs weren't far away, and her lack of clothing wouldn't have held her back. Yes, that was the way he read it.

The medical officer, Captain Rothingham, turned the body over and made a quick examination. He shook his head at Captain Preston, indicating he could find no other cause of death than drowning.

Captain Preston glowered at the scene. Was what he saw the truth or was it what some foul, murderous colonial swine wanted him to accept as truth? It could have been staged, the officer poisoned or forcibly drowned, then dumped into the water and the right goods carefully planted on the beach. Then Preston thought about what Jack Darland had told him the day before. Darland said he had his sights on a woman, a young and pretty one, and he was determined that he was going to take her to bed soon. Just before they had parted Darland saluted Preston grandly and showed him a bottle of brandy.

"Tonight's the night, sir!" Darland had said in high spirits. Then he left the post to return to his billet.

Preston gave a sigh. He knew that Darland had never touched an opium pipe before. Why now? Sex alone would have been enough to keep Darland in surging high spirits for a month. The opium was entirely out of character. But then so was a floozy, Preston swore silently. This, and then some problem in the powder magazine. Did his troubles never end? He'd have to go back and check out what must be some shortage of shot or powder. That had been Darland's responsibility, too. And didn't he see a report about one of the guards being missing this morning?

Preston turned abruptly. He wouldn't let it pile up on him. He would turn in his report to the colonel. That was why the army had colonels. God knew they did little else. Men died in war, and this was damn close to war. Five of the colonials had died a month ago; maybe this was how they planned to even the score. At least the count was still five to one. Preston had no desire to investigate this incident any further. The captain signaled the men behind him, who gathered up everything on the beach, including the opium and the alcohol, then loaded the body onto a small cart they had brought with them. Let the damned colonel make anything out of it if he could. Captain Preston would turn in his death report on the accidental drowning of Lieutenant Jack Darland, and as far as he was concerned, the case was closed.

Sadie didn't go to work at the millinery shop that day. She sent a note that she was ill, then sat in her living room and stared at the wall. She wasn't ill. She wasn't hurt—except bruised a little in spirit. She was worried. Sadie knew the men had been talking about the planned raid on the powder magazine, knew it was set for last night, and realized that she hadn't been in on any of the planning.

She hadn't heard what happened. Sadie was

afraid to contact Ben or any of the others. She was worried and afraid about something else too. She was a good enough strategist to realize that, after a successful raid on the munitions, Jack Darland would be suspect. As soon as the theft was discovered, Jack would be brought in front of the colonel and grilled for hours. They would question him and question him and soon discover his friendship with Sadie. Then they would be able to nail down her connection with the Freedom Fighters, and they would know for certain how the keys came to be duplicated. English officers were not stupid.

So Sadie knew the day before the actual raid that Jack would be in for big trouble, and danger, too, she surmised. Then this morning she couldn't go to work. She was emotionally exhausted, and she began to think about Jack again. He hadn't hurt her as he made love two nights ago. Instead he had been a practiced and tender lover. Emotionally she had been torn in half, but that was not what bothered her now. Partly she was ashamed for deceiving him. She had never before used her body as a weapon; never, never had she made a physical union with a man she didn't love and cherish.

When she realized that Jack would be in danger from his superiors, she also tumbled to the fact that the Freedom Fighters council may have intended him harm as well. He had been used, he had served his purpose—why let him remain on the scene to tell how it had happened? It was then she knew what the council had talked about when she wasn't in the room. The council could have planned to harm Jack! Yes, that had to be it. They too would see the danger. Would they spirit him away? Kidnap him? Maybe put him on board a ship, shanghai him on a ship to South America or to the Orient around the Cape? She was sure they wouldn't cut out his tongue or anything so inhumane as that. At last she decided they would indeed kidnap him, and she was sad. Why should he suffer because of her? Then she remembered that it was for the cause of liberty, and somehow that made it all seem better.

It was nearly noon, and she could sit in the room no longer. She walked to a small market for some ripe fruit, and there she first heard about it. A redcoat had drowned last night, someone said. She pressed forward to listen more closely. The wife of the green-grocer was talking.

"And so they found him 'alf in and 'alf out of the bay, all drowned like a rat. And him with three 'alf-filled bottles back on the blanket. The floozy he was with done took off at a fast sprint, I'd say, and with not a stitch on her body since all her clothes was on the blanket." The woman laughed. "Bet that was some foot-race she ran!"

Someone asked who the redcoat was. The woman shrugged.

"Just some bloody redcoat's all I know. But he was an officer and a gentleman, mind ye. A lieutenant at that!"

Sadie stopped selecting apples and pushed away from the stand. She was sure she was going to vomit. Holding herself stiffly she walked around the corner and leaned against the building.

Drowned? Some lieutenant? That could be Jack

Darland. That *must* be Jack Darland. So that was what they were planning behind her back! Well, she never would have stood for anything like that. She didn't mind taking chances, but just to kill that poor young man! She was angry now, her sickness forgotten as she marched home. Fury marked her every step. She *still* wouldn't stand for it! She would put on a clean dress and go to see Mr. Ben Rutledge right in his office. As she changed and combed her long blonde hair, she began to understand some of it. The council knew she would not agree to killing the young man. That was why they didn't tell her. They must have decided it had to be done for security. So she wasn't considered an equal with them after all!

As she walked toward the docks and Ben's office, she saw the whole matter more clearly. It had to be done. Even she had guessed that some action would be taken against the man. But if they simply kidnapped the lieutenant, he would find his way back to Boston, and he would tell the authorities what really happened. Then she would be in danger. She might even be hanged. She would be taken to England for a trial.

The closer Sadie came to Ben's office, the slower she walked. Perhaps the council had been right after all. She tried hard to set her thinking straight. She had volunteered to do the job, she had even suggested it in the first place. Did she have the right to storm into Ben's office and demand an explanation? Was that the democratic way? It must have been a democratic vote of the remaining members of the council when they sealed Darland's fate. She saw

Ben's office ahead and at the same time saw him step out the front door and into his familiar chaise. She turned quickly so he wouldn't see her.

Ben caught up with her a block further on. He called to her sharply, and she knew it was not the first time he had spoken.

"A ride, Mrs. Wythe?" he asked.

She wanted to shake her head, to say no...but she nodded. She stepped into the chaise and sat as far as she could from him.

"Was it Jack who drowned last night?"

"Yes."

"You knew it was planned?"

"I did."

She sighed, gave him one quick wounded look and stared at the street. "I've convinced myself at last you must have been very sure that it had to be done before you went ahead. I realize you did it in part to protect me as well as the movement."

She looked at him but tears blurred her sight.

"I know you were thinking right, that I have absolutely no basis for my anger, my resentment...oh, Ben! He was so young!" A sob slipped through her defenses.

"Yes, he was young. Sometimes a good and brave deed on one person's part requires another deed by someone else to make sure our people are safe." He watched her. "Sadie. Go ahead and cry, it's all right. I'll have you home in a minute."

"No!" she almost shouted it. "No, I don't want to go home...not yet."

He flicked the reins and the horse moved. Ben guided the rig toward the edge of town, then along the coolness of the wind-swept bay. Neither of

156

them said a word. When he stopped the horse and put down the reins she held herself away from him. Then the tears came and she fell into his arms, sobbing.

He held her and let the tears stream out, knowing that this was probably the first time she had cried since learning the truth. It would be good medicine for her. When at last she stopped sobbing and looked up, he kissed her trembling lips.

"It's over. Now we must go on. Did you know that the raid was a great success? We took over two tons of fine black powder, fifty flintlock rifles and two boxes of pistols and I don't know how many fine powder horns or how many pounds of balls, as well as one good five-pound cannon."

"But it cost a man's life."

"Sadie. The Freedom Fighters are at war. In wars, people die for a better cause, a better life. Men, women and sometimes innocent children die. This man was a soldier."

"And I had just made love to him in my own bed!" She pulled at his frock coat. "Ben, will I ever be able to live in that place again? How can I ever sleep in the bed? I know I'll never be able to make love with you there again."

Ben kissed her softly, brushed back the blonde hair from her cheeks, then kissed the tip of her nose. "Yes, Sadie Wythe, you will be able to live there. Think of those five boys who were shot down in the streets just over a month ago. Their life's blood flowed out in the snow. English muskets did that, Sadie. Think of the five sorrowful families of those youth. We Freedom Fighters are the advance guard. We're at war for America, even though she doesn't know it yet. In war there are casualties. Remember that. People die. You or I might be the next one to fall. So you *will* go back to your flat. You *will* go to work tomorrow. You *will* act just as you did last week, act as if nothing has happened, so no one will suspect. And you will live in the house and make love there, because you are a soldier. And you are my own true love."

He bent and kissed her breast, blowing his hot breath on it until he felt her nipple begin to fill with blood and rise. Then he kissed her lips softly again and took the reins.

"Now, Mrs. Wythe, it's time we both get home and go on with our lives, so separate, yet so wonderfully joined together."

She leaned on his shoulder and held his big hand all the way into the edge of town where she got out of the chaise, and walked three blocks to her flat.

The first thing she must do must be to go and express her shock and sorrow to Mrs. Carrington and tell her how sorry she was about the accident. It would be expected.

Chapter Eight
TWO NOT OF A KIND

For the past six nights Lewis Lynch had been bedeviling Commissioner Trout. Three nights in succession he bombarded the flat with stones from his sling. The second day the window glass had been replaced and that night it was broken again. They left the windows broken after that. The fourth night Lynch threw a skunk through the commissioner's window. Lynch knew how to trap a skunk and keep it from spraying its perfume until he allowed it to. The commissioner stormed out of the apartment so fast he only had one leg in his breeches.

The fifth night it had been a nest of angry hornets Lynch found in the woods, captured with smoke, and then hurled through Trout's broken window. Each time Lynch began his devilment between one and three a.m. depending when the commissioner went to sleep.

The sixth night the commissioner had been driven from his flat with blasts of hurled rocks and a smoke bomb. When he came out the lower stairs, Lynch tapped him on the head with a cosh. By the time he woke up, the commissioner was stripped, and covered with a generous application of tar. The feathers followed and the British lackey was led to the square and tied to the sundial. No one found him there until some redcoats cut him loose about seven the next morning.

Ben waited two days. Still there was nothing about the commissioner returning to England. No changes had been made in the customs house procedures. Both Ben and Lynch were surprised.

"It would be enough to roust me out of the colony," Lynch said. Ben agreed. Since Lynch was often doing something for Ben or for the council, Ben had put him on the Rutledge & Rutledge payroll. When there wasn't any work to do for the council, Lynch worked as a messenger between ships, ports and the home office.

"Now we wait a few more days," said Ben. "If he still refuses to leave, we'll try something new. It wouldn't surprise me at all if he moves into the customs house. It would give him security and protection. He could get some sleep at night. He looked rather pale the last time I saw him."

They both laughed. Lynch went back to work and Ben looked again at the balance sheets. His business was struggling to survive. The Nonimportation Agreement was still cutting deeply into imports, which meant Ben had less business. A few more goods were being bought from England, but it went in surges.

At least Ben had suffered no new fines or seizures since Burke-White had been shot. That helped, but the seizure of the tall ships would be a crippling blow if it was allowed to stand. The plan he had been working on was progressing. It hinged on exactly when the ships were called up for auction. The scheme could work...but only if several elements all fell into line at the right time.

Ben closed the books and left the office. On the way home he considered the progress of the Freedom Fighters. He was pleased that everything seemed on schedule. They had nearly a hundred members now and some of the groups were having turkey shoots to sharpen up their marksmanship.

As Ben left his chaise in the back yard, his twin sons surprised him with warwhoops of an Indian attack. Suddenly he was jolted into a new realization. The boys would be fourteen on April 12. If this struggle with England didn't burst into the open for three or four years and then lasted three or four, his two sons would surely be involved in the fighting. They would have to bear arms. They'd had no training. Every farm boy learned how to shoot as soon as he was big enough to carry a musket. Ben now determined to give them both instruction in firearms and the use of a fighting knife. At least they would then be able to defend themselves.

Ben wondered how the boys would do in combat. On the surface, the identical twins looked and acted much the same, but they were poles apart in temperament.

Robert, the older by nearly an hour, was the serious one. He was solid, steady, reliable. Ask Robert to do something and it was done. He never forgot things or lost them, and Ben had an idea Robert would make a fine businessman. His only drawback was that he was a bit of a plodder, sometimes happy to slog along without thinking through a project, without asking why, not caring about the main scheme of things.

David Lewis Rutledge, on the other hand, at times seemed too wise for his age. Once in a while he would smile strangely at his father and Ben wondered if there were a reincarnated spirit in the boy of one who had been a great scholar or teacher. David was more sensitive than Robert, and also more easily wounded. At times he was brilliant in surprising and diverse fields. One day he drew a beautiful house and on another piece of paper wrote down the architectural and structural requirements for building the house. As far as Ben knew, David had never been exposed to the finer points of architecture.

Several times David had brought poetry to Ben to read, and it was quite good. Not an Edward Taylor of course , but surprisingly well structured verse, rhymed and with a spark of real truth. Both Ben and his wife had been pleased with David's work.

That same evening, before the sun went down, Ben took the boys into the woods near the Charles River and showed them his new rifle. It was a Charleville 1763 flintlock musket in a .69 caliber that fired the usual round ball. The smooth bore barrel was forty-five inches long. That, coupled with a wooden stock and the trigger mechanism area of eighteen inches made the entire weapon two inches over five feet long. The musket weighed eight and a half pounds.

Robert was awed by the long gun. "Gee, Father. Are we going to watch you shoot it?"

"Of course. Then, if you want to, you can fire it yourselves. I'll explain how to load it with black powder and the round and how to get it all ready. Would you like to try it?"

Robert nodded vigorously. David shrugged, then watched his father carefully. "Yes, Father, if you want me to. But before, you've always said we didn't need to know about guns."

Ben stopped loading the flintlock. "Yes, David, I did say that. But now I've decided that every man should know how to fire a rifle, to defend himself."

"We're going to be fighting the English soon, aren't we, Father?" David asked.

Ben lifted his eyes to the boy's, which were steady and sure.

"Yes, David. In the next three or four years we could very well be in a bloody war for our independence from England. If so, I want both of you boys to be experts with the long musket."

Ben fired at a "V" mark he had carved in a tree two dozen yards away. Ben's round came between the three-inch sides of the "V" but almost at the top. They went on loading and firing until it was almost dark. David had been a reluctant participant, but he watched closely and learned at once how to load, prime, ram and ready the flintlock for firing. On his third practice shot he tore the tip off the "V" with his ball. Neither of the other two came within two inches of the target center.

On the ride home in the chaise, Robert asked if he could drive. Ben passed the reins to him and quickly saw that the boy had a delicate touch with the leather and a kind of understanding and kinship with the animal.

At home Sandra questioned Ben about the sudden shooting match, so he explained. A cloud settled over her, darkening her face.

"You really think there might be a war? With England? How could we possibly win? They have a whole empire, thousands and thousands of troops, all the shot and powder they need. Their warships in the harbor could flatten all of Boston in a few days."

Ben watched her for a moment, not sure where to start. "You said you'd been reading some of my newspapers. There's nothing immediate, war won't come next month. It will be a gradual thing, a slow buildup of impossible demands by England, and growing tension in the colonies. I can feel it. There is a group of us who believe more and more that for America, liberty and total independence from England are our only hope. If a war began now, we would be blasted into rubble in a day, that is true. But when it finally does come, this war will be a general uprising, a rebellion by the people. Great masses of men in the streets and on the farms and in the villages will demand that we fight the British and throw off their unfair rule. When that day comes, no force on the face of the earth will be able to defeat us."

Sandra frowned. "Oh, dear, if it takes three or four years, the boys will surely be involved." She shuddered. "I think I shall have to be reading more of your newspapers."

Upstairs, David Rutledge looked at his brother across the chess board and waited patiently. Robert had been scowling and staring at the board for two minutes.

"You still want to play?"

"No, Dave, you're winning. You always win."

"I'm better than you."

"At chess."

"At lots of things. Of course, you're better than me at some things, too."

Robert looked up in surprise, his angry answer stilled. Usually when his twin brother began this way he went on and on. "Why did Father let us shoot his new flintlock?"

David rubbed his nose and his cheek twitched as it sometimes did when he was worried, thinking or angry. "Why? Because he wants us to learn how to shoot so we can be soldiers in his war. He's planning a war with England, you know."

"He is not!"

"Yes, he is. Do you ever read the newspaper he gets? It's a rebel paper put out by the Whigs. The Tories are the British sympathizers. Father is a Whig. I thought you knew that."

"No, I'm not much concerned. It was good sport, though, shooting with that long gun."

"You have to keep your eyes open when you squeeze the trigger."

"I did."

"No, Robert, you shut them. I saw you. Next time watch the sights and the target the way Father told you."

David noticed the glum expression on his brother's face. "What do you want for your birthday, Robert?"

"Oh, a boat! A real sailboat with one sail, about twenty feet long, so I can sail in the bay and pretend to be a captain."

"I rather fancied you might. I want a complete

165

set of the works of Shakespeare."

"Who?"

"William Shakespeare. He wrote plays and poetry, dramas mostly."

"You're crazy, David. You could have a horse or a boat or maybe your own rifle, and you only want some dumb books?"

"No, I'm not crazy. Because twins have to be alike so if I'm crazy, that means you're crazy, too. Right?"

"Aw...books!"

"Do you retire from the game? If you don't, you're only two moves from checkmate." David saw the anger on Robert's face. He got up and waved. "Loser returns the chessmen to the box, our rule." He sighed and stared at his twin. "And remember, Robert, we're going to be fourteen next month, not ten and still playing with toy boats."

Robert threw a pawn at David as he ran for the library door.

In his room, David lit two lamps and tried to read, but tonight not even Shakespeare could interest him. He took out paper and quill and began writing. Most of it made little sense. It wasn't poetry. He rambled on for a few words, then thought about what he had heard about the war. He knew now for sure that there would be a war. Father had said so. He had heard his parents talking earlier, and he had seen the redcoats and heard about their rules and their mischiefs. More than once he had pelted the guards at the customs house with snowballs and pebbles. He knew he had been lucky not to have been there the day of the massacre. If so, he might be one of the five lying in their graves right now.

David thought about death, but it didn't frighten him. To him it was a great mystery, a riddle that could be solved only by experiencing it. But then it would be too late to do anything about it. David was determined to try as many things in his life as he could, including girls. They were still a nagging, gnawing mystery to him. One day the year before he had burst into his sister's room to ask her something. She had been dressing and was standing there without a thing on. Surprise flooded her face and she started to reach for her dress, then she didn't and let him stare at her unclothed body. His eyes were glued on her big breasts jutting out from her chest. He was fascinated.

Harriet had laughed softly. "You've never seen a girl undressed, have you, David?" He couldn't reply. She paused for a moment longer, then slowly turned and slipped into her petticoat and shooed him out of the room.

There was so much he wanted to see and do and learn! He had talked with Dr. Franklin when the great man was in Philadelphia a few years ago, and he was fascinated by all the inventions.

David dropped down on his bed, laced his fingers behind his head and closed his eyes. He would see and do and go everywhere in the world! He would study here and go on to Harvard, and then maybe to Oxford, if there wasn't a war on. He wanted to see and do and taste and touch...everything. He would get on one of his father's ships and sail away. London, France, Germany, the south seas! It would be wonderful!

Robert stood in the library, furious with his twin brother. Furious because David had won, because he had shot the flintlock better, because he knew about Shakespeare, because he did so many things better than Robert.

But he was the oldest, Robert told himself. He knew more about the business than David ever would. He had been in and out of the offices, run errands, did many things at the docks. All the captains knew him. Some day he hoped to move in as a full-time partner with his father. For business you didn't need to go to college. He'd be ready in two years to go to work full time at the docks, on a ship or in the office!

The thought sustained him as he put away the chessmen. So he had lost—he didn't care now. He was going to win where it counted, where the money was. He would one day own Rutledge and Rutledge, and that was what was really important.

It had been fun shooting the long rifle today. Maybe the next time out he could do better, and maybe his father would let him shoot at a squirrel or a rabbit. That would be much more fun than aiming at a log. Robert looked forward to the next weapons lesson with anticipation. As for his birthday...well, maybe he should ask for a sailboat, *and* a pistol *and* a good saddle horse to ride. Yes, that would be fine!

The evening was looking much better as Robert closed the library door and carried the lamp with him as he went toward the living room. He blew out the lamp and put it on a corner table, then stood in front of the fire. It was the end of March but still brisk in the evenings, and the heat from the snapping, burning oak and maple felt good. His mother and father had stopped speaking when he came in. They smiled now and went on talking, only in quieter tones, so he could not hear what they were saying.

Commissioner Trout lay on the table as the regimental surgeon judiciously applied turpentine to the last of a hundred stubborn patches of tar that had not washed off in the hot-water shower-bath he had taken in the dormitory section of the customs house. Two roving patrol guards had found the commissioner just after seven that morning, cut him loose and carried him into the friendly territory of the building.

Once there, the regimental physician had been called. He shook his head in wonder.

"Sometimes it's hard to think of them as Englishmen, sir," he said. "Sometimes they act like savages wearing our clothes." Judson Rothingham was a round, soft-spoken man who had served all over the globe with His Majesty's forces.

The tar was tenacious, and in spots it took off patches of skin rather than release its grip. Even so, there were few burns. The tar had been melted, then cooled just enough so it could be laid on with a trowel. If it had been "brushing" hot, the tar would have burned skin and flesh alike.

"Well, now, we seem to be coming along nicely," Rothingham said. "Just a bit to go now."

"I'll have them *shot!*" Trout fumed, bellowing the last word in a surge of pain as tar came loose, pulling with it half the hairs on his lower leg. "Oh, yes, this is the final insult. I will find them, track them down, sniff them out and use my own pistol to shoot them dead with grim satisfaction. It will be a case of justifiable homicide if anyone ever proves that I did it. I will stay here now for years if I must to right this terrible wrong!"

The doctor twisted up the side of his mouth in disapproval.

"That's good for the spirit, Commissioner, but as far as your body goes, I suggest you don't set foot out of the customs house for a few months without an armed guard. You should move in here for better security, or to the fort out in the bay. No sense taking any more chances. You have only a few months left before your retirement, right, Commissioner?'

"Yes, the retirement, yes. New house in London. But move in here? Ridiculous. I can stand on my own two feet..."

"Commissioner, I don't want you out of bed for a week. No telling what additional damage I may find. So you'll be here for a week at least. It's the best hospital I've had in ten years, and I want you to use it. I'll send six men to bring your things from your flat, move you out. Now lie down and get under that blanket. Let your body rest for a few hours, man. Let it rest."

Commissioner Trout forced his body to relax, to let the anger drain out of him. He would track them down, whoever they were. He had some suspicions. He knew there was talk around about the rowdy Sons of Liberty. That had been a mob-violence, murderous organization back in the

Stamp Act days five years ago. His spies in the community told him the group was trying to get active again. The commissioner had heard they were nothing more than a riotous, undisciplined gang of thieves and killers which went around in the guise of patriots for the colonists' cause. They seemed to be only a handful of dissidents trying to stir up troubles. For a moment he wondered if the ship owner, Rutledge, had any hand in his harassment. He thought about it for a moment, then dismissed it. Rutledge was too weak, too concerned with trying to make a living and getting back his three tall ships. No, he could expect no trouble from Rutledge. The shipper had been taught a lesson he wouldn't forget. Rutledge's captains were obeying the laws when it came to the Navigation Act regulations, and that was a good sign.

Now, if he could determine who were the leaders of this Sons of Liberty gang, and punish them some way—perhaps have one or two of them meet with fatal accidents. The word would spread quicker than on a woman's tongue. He would find out. Gold had a way of opening men's mouths and helping them tell all they knew. He would have his information within a week.

Commissioner Trout settled down in his bed and let the doctor pull a blanket over his stinging, complaining body. At least now he had a plan, a method of attack. He would sleep now. God, he would sleep better than he had in seven full nights!

Captain Preston watched the doctor leave the bed and walked with him down the hallway. "The commissioner—is he going to recover?"

"Few people die of tar and feathers, especially when the tar isn't at all hot."

"Good, we've got enough trouble here already. The colonel is all over me about the theft of the munitions and weapons. I haven't a clue. Keys were used, but six or eight officers have keys. What am I to do, question each officer on my staff? Already I've replaced everything here from the ships' stores in the harbor."

Doctor Rothingham, also a captain, stopped and stared hard at the younger man. "You know, Preston, it just might be that these loud talkers are right. Maybe we should get out of here and let them go their way. Some of them seem to be working extremely hard toward that end. This is a gigantic land, it must be over a thousand miles just along the Atlantic seaboard. I've heard it's over three times that wide stretching across to the Pacific Ocean. The British Isles would be lost if we dropped it anywhere inside. Why do we think we deserve to control a territory this gigantic?"

The doctor saw Preston lift an eyebrow, and he sighed.

"I'm a physician, not a politician. I guess I should leave that up to you." He walked toward his office.

Preston watched him. The damned colonies were the *property* of England. The people here were no better than tenant farmers, serfs. There was no way they were Englishmen, and they most certainly were not equals. That was trying to stretch credibility too far. He walked toward his post, chastising the doctor, and wondering what he was going to say at the final hearing that afternoon into the death of Lieutenant Darland. The session was to be held as usual in front of the colonel. Captain Preston would be the main witness, since he had taken command of the body and the death scene. Preston shrugged. How could it go badly? The whole thing was so obvious that a child could judge what had happened. And that was what he hoped the colonel would decide.

Chapter Nine
READY, AIM, FIRE

"It just ain't right, sir," Lewis Lynch protested. "I got me near to twenty men in my company, and only six of 'em can handle a long gun proper. Six out of twenty, sir!" Lynch slumped into a chair beside Ben's private office desk. "First time I been shooting with all of 'em, sir, and they just can't do it. When we took them on they all said they'd fired a musket before, but it must have been a dozen years for some, and never, I'd guess, for the rest."

Ben was aware of the problem. It was true in all the groups. Some of his own company had demonstrated that they were not at all proficient with the long guns. He made up his mind quickly.

"Lewis, I want you to work on this. You've had the military training. Draw on that, and plan out a drill procedure on the flintlock musket. Lay down the procedure for loading a flintlock in ten easy steps. Work through them with four of your best men. Train them every night for the next week out by the Charles River until they can run through the routine smartly and without fail. We'll use your squad as a demonstration and training group for all the other companies."

"Aye, aye, sir!" Lynch said beaming. "And can we draw shot and powder from our Concord stores?"

"Yes. We'll check with the council, but I don't see any problem. Our weapons are no good if we can't fire them. When the men learn to load and shoot, then we'll get into accuracy lessons. This week, Lewis, I want those four men of yours trained and sharp by Monday night so we can put on a demonstration for the council!"

When Monday night came on that April 2, 1770, two buggies left downtown Boston and met in the woods near the Charles River. Lynch and his marksmen were already there. They wore no uniforms. One was a baker, the others a farmer, a blacksmith and a hardware merchant. Ben had alerted the members of the council that they would see a demonstration that would rival the best English redcoat regimental marksmen.

At the clearing the carriages stopped and the council members got out. Ben and Sadie rode in separate coaches. They smiled and nodded.

Lynch led them a short way into the woods to a clearing where he had set up targets fifty yards away in the edge of the brush. His four marksmen stood at attention with their long guns at their sides. One had a new Brown Bess stolen from a redcoat. Two others used regulation Brown Bess flintlocks issued from the stolen Concord supply, and the last men had a Charleville 1763 flintlock like Ben's.

Lewis turned toward the council members and no longer was he the apologetic, slightly rough, unsure man from the council meetings. Now he was a soldier, doing what he knew well, a leader of men who spoke crisply and firmly, sure of himself and his duties.

"Gentlemen, and Mrs. Wythe. This is a demonstration to show you how quickly and efficiently the musket should be utilized in modern warfare. As I'm sure most of you know, the flintlock term is descriptive of a method of delivering a spark to ignite the powder in the pan of the weapon which in turn fires the remainder of the black powder in the barrel, discharging the musket.

"Generally there has been a twenty-count procedure to get a musket ready to fire, which can often make it a one-shot piece in any close-in fighting. We have cut down on the steps and simplified it to reduce the time needed. The new system uses seven steps. We will demonstrate."

Each man had over his shoulder three straps connected to a leather pouch, a leather box, and a powder horn. In the box were paper-wrapped cartridges, in the second musket balls.

"Ready, begin. *One!*"

The men lifted the heavy weapons and brought them to halfcock.

"*Two!*"

The four men each took a paper cartridge from his supply, bit off the end and poured powder from the paper into the pan near the trigger until the pan was filled.

"The council remembers that the cocking hammer holds a piece of flint that comes glancing down on the steel cap of the pan. The pan now contains the primer powder and when the flint strikes the steel cap of the pan it sparks, setting off the primer."

He paused for a moment. *"Three!"*

The men lowered the weapons with the butt on the ground and poured the remainder of the measured papers of powder into the muzzles of the weapons.

"Four!"

The men crumpled the now empty wad of the paper that had held the black powder, so the council could see the end of it which contained a rifle ball. They inserted the wadded paper first, then the ball end into the muzzle.

"Five!"

On the next command the four men pushed the ramrod down on the ball and wadding, seating it firmly in the far end of the barrel, then tamped it down.

"Six!"

The men shouldered the weapons and cocked the firelock.

"Seven!"

The men turned, aimed at targets, and all fired in unison. The belching roar of the four flintlocks deafened everyone for a moment and sent a small black cloud of smoke into the wind.

Without orders or command, two of the four knelt and began the reloading procedure, working quickly and skillfully. When they were finished, they stood, and the other two men knelt and began loading their weapons. As soon as the second pair began loading the first pair fired. Soon the second team stood and fired as the first team knelt, ending the demonstration.

Dr. Joseph Warren clapped, his face beaming.

"Very good, Mr. Lynch. And you say we have almost a hundred men who can function in this manner?"

"No, sir. We only have five. We've been training for a week, sir. It's my opinion that we need this type of training for each of our men, give them some military precision, train each man for a week, evenings. Show them how to quick-load and then give them basic marksmanship. A dozen musket balls count for nothing, sir, unless they strike the intended target."

"And how could such training be done, Mr. Lynch?"

"Sir, we have five fully trained men now. Each of us could go, one to a company, to train four more men in a week. Those four men could each train four more men the following week and we would have the entire Freedom Fighters trained in the quick-load method with a flintlock within two weeks!"

Jonathan Clark now applauded. "Good, good. I'm in favor of doing this training at once. We can issue powder and shot from the stores for twenty rounds per man."

Sadie seconded the idea and each member of the council agreed. It was to be done. As soon as it was decided, four shots boomed into the air of the growing twilight, as one after another of the long guns went off in salute.

The five members of the Freedom Fighters council returned to Jonathan's bookstore for the rest of their meeting. They authorized Lynch to draw shot and powder as needed for the training, then set up a massive picnic on the Charles River for two weeks later, April 21, a Saturday.

"It'll be a good chance for a real shooting match between the men and companies, and we can all have a feast and get to know one another," Ben said. "I have a feeling many of our men don't know who the rest of the Freedom Fighters are. Oh, we'll call this gathering the 'Friends of Boston' in case anyone asks. We're interested in Boston's cultural and educational institutions."

Lewis set up definite times for his expert marksmen to train the men in the companies, and the meeting ended.

Later that evening, when Ben knocked on Sadie's door, he found her sitting over a cup of tea. He kissed her on the cheek and sat down at the small table across from her.

"Problems?" he asked.

She shook her head, making her long blonde hair swing. But her face told a different story. Her green eyes were touched with flecks of anger, and her chin came up.

"Maybe I should let someone else take over my company. Arnold Compton keeps telling me I shouldn't even be in the movement. Says no other women are. They're home where they belong, making pies, cooking stew and nursing their babies. Maybe he's right."

"Hey, that doesn't sound like you. Wait until you outshoot him. Have you had your own private contest with Compton yet, as I suggested?"

"No, it keeps being postponed. Usually he does the putting off. I'll wait now until he has the new training. I'm taking it, too, with the others. Then on the day of the picnic we'll have it out. The best shot in the company will be the company commander and sit on the council."

"The council may veto that idea. That way, anybody could challenge any commanding officer at any time. That doesn't make sense. We need you on the council."

She stood and went around to his chair, leaned over and kissed his lips hard. "Ben, will you sit with me on the couch and hold me very close? I don't want to go to bed with you tonight. I'm too angry. I just want you to hold me, and pet me, and whisper in my ear. Talk and talk and make me feel like I'm good for something besides making those silly little hats, baking pies and being a bad widow."

He held her. Ben knew that Compton had been sniping at Sadie, telling her she should get out. He had hoped that Sadie's natural brightness, her happy, easy way with people and her pretty face would win him over. It hadn't. Compton must be out to prove something. He'd have his hands full when he went up against Sadie in a shootout. Sadie had grown up on the frontier and learned to shoot as soon as she was big enough to hold a long pistol. She graduated to a musket and specialized in providing wild turkeys for the dinner table.

He talked to her, kissed her cheek and then her lips and told her how wonderful she was in every way. Gradually she settled down and her self-confidence returned. As her cheerfulness came back, so did her desire, and she pressed against Ben, then unbuttoned her blouse. Ben bent and kissed her throbbing breasts, then covered them and lifted her to her feet.

"Darling Sadie, I'd love to tear your clothes off and do all sorts of wild things to your lovely body, but our old enemy is after us again...time."

"Oh, *damn!*"

Ben laughed. She never cursed except when they were alone, and it still amazed him. She had learned every foul word known to the frontier backwoodsmen, and she assured Ben they not only knew them all but made up a few interesting combinations of their own.

She smiled and stood up on tiptoe to kiss his nose, then his mouth and stepped back.

"I love you, Ben Rutledge, but I refuse to do anything to harm your wonderful family, or your gracious wife. Now get your hat and get yourself home."

He kissed her at the door, wishing for the moment that things were different, simpler, but they were not. They probably never could be without inflicting a great deal of pain on innocent people. Ben nodded, said he would see her again soon, and walked down the steps to his chaise.

Edmund Cunliffe stared at the report in his hands, wondering what he should do with it. He *would* do something, he knew that. A smile slid over his face, an expression of anticipation. He could almost see Harriet Rutledge now as he peeled layer after layer of clothing off that remarkably luscious body. He beat down his sudden desire and concentrated on the plans. First he had to get her alone, and this looked like the opportunity. His observer had made it certain now, Mrs. Rutledge went to a meeting every Wednesday afternoon promptly at one. It was a Bible study class at the church. She was gone until almost four o'clock. There were only two servants in the house, a cook-maid and Harry, the driver and gardener. Harry would be gone with Mrs. Rutledge, and that would leave Harriet alone with the cook. He could figure out some way to get rid of her. He leaned back in his leather chair, noticed one of his management men waiting to talk with him, but ignored the man. This was too good, too exciting not to think through carefully. If he planned on being there just after the chaise left, he would have at least half an hour, even if Harry brought the rig right back home. If Harry did something else, or waited for Mrs. Rutledge, it could give him three hours! The very thought sent him into another fantasy.

Edmund tried to imagine what it would be like to undress Harriet May Rutledge. By God, he was going to find out very soon! What day was it? He glanced at the pad on his desk where the calendar lay.　Oh, this *was* Wednesday,　the day of Mrs. Rutledge's weekly meeting.

So he had a week to plan it. A week to invent some excuse to get the cook out of the house. A quick trip to see a sick sister? That usually worked. He motioned for the observer to come back into his office and sent him away to find the name of one or more relatives of the Rutledges' cook. Then everything would be set up and ready to go.

For an unchecked moment, Cunliffe shivered, thinking what Ben Rutledge would do if he ever found out about this. The thought of the man's terrible fatherly anger and his physical fury made Cunliffe pale. He had to be sure not to injure the girl physically, and he had to make her like what he did so much that she wouldn't dream of telling anyone. That was the clue—love her so well that she was swept off her feet. He knew she would fight him. She would yelp and scold and make those little cries, but all the time she would be panting for it, eagerly awaiting it. At last she would let him take her by force to justify her own conscience. He'd had it happen several times before with virgins. They were always the most trouble, but in the long run, the most delicious as well. Women really liked sex as much as men— why wouldn't they admit it?

The thought of a furious Ben Rutledge dampened his excitement. He had never intended to take the campaign this far. He had paid off Commissioner Trout by disrupting the Rutledge household. What more could the commissioner want? If only the little bitch hadn't let him press his hand up between her legs in church. When he rubbed her there, she had loved it! She wanted more and more, he was positive she did, no matter what she said or how uppity she acted. She would be something! He wanted desperately now to initiate her into the pleasures of love.

But the potential of violence from Rutledge was still there. Somehow the threat, even a possibility of it, not only sharpened his desire, it also made his knees weak and his forehead blossom with sweat. He would set up the seduction so carefully that no one but the girl herself would know he had

ever been there. An old coat would help, a low hat
—he would walk there so his carriage wouldn't
give him away. Yes, it would work out well. He
had nothing to fear from Rutledge, because he
never would know about it!

That was when Cunliffe remembered something
else. Rutledge had been the man in the Massachusetts Assembly who had worked long and
hard to outlaw dueling in the colony. He had
failed. Such a man would never participate in a
duel himself, much less give the challenge for one.
The thought made Cunliffe feel a lot better. He
would give his spy an extra five pounds to restock
his supply of rum and brandy, if he got the new
information that was needed about the Rutledge
cook.

Nearly two weeks later, on April 21, members of
the "Friends of Boston" met on the Charles River
at Mulligan's meadow for a picnic. It was a brisk,
unusually warm spring day, with a few wildflowers
already peeping through the greening grass. The
cows had been herded into one end of the meadow.

Groups of families arrived just after ten in the
morning, and before long games and foot races of
all kinds began. Some of the men had impromptu
horse races and the inevitable hatchet-throwing
contests took place.

Each family brought enough food to feed three
families, and all the food was spread out on a
table made of saw horses and planks covered with
bright tablecloths. The spread was a hundred feet

long and piled high with every kind of food from chicken to steamed clams and lobster, from fruit pie to layer cakes. There was enough food to sustain an army for a week.

When the dinner was over and a few naps had been taken in the brilliant and unusually warm sunshine, the men picked up their long guns and wandered off to Mulligan's bluff where they set up targets and measured off fifty yards true distance. The spent rounds would bury themselves harmlessly in the soft sandstone bluff.

The shooting matches began. The favorite target was the "V" cut Ben had used with his boys. The "V" now was smaller, with the sides no more than two inches long. A ball hitting the side of the "V" scored one point. A ball landing between the slanted "V" sides earned two points, and a ball that cut the point off the "V" brought five points.

The men quickly divided into their regular companies. Each company then organized its own contest. Sadie's group had the end position. The men were set to making their own targets from chopped up two-inch-thick, foot-long limbs. Each limb had been axed flat on one side and the "V" cut into the wood. The first man placed his target and ran back to the firing line. When all three shots had been fired, a whistle blew and the five shooters ran to the targets and each brought back his own, setting up the next man's target branch while he was there. The heavy limbs were positioned in niches cut into the sandstone and held in place with rocks. They would usually take the three shots before coming dislodged.

Competition was stiff within each company as

every one of the twenty men worked to be the best in his group and hoped to win best in the troop mark. Each man's score was tallied by the captain as he brought back his target.

As company commander, Sadie let all of her men fire before she did. After the training of the prvious two weeks, the men looked proficient in their shooting, and the marks were better than Sadie had hoped for. There was a shout when the first man recorded a five score on his target. Sadie watched her men and judged each target as it came back. There were few arguments as to whether a hit was a five or not. She settled any complaint quietly. Soon one of her men hit a five, a two and a one. He was her leader with eight points.

Arnold Compton, the huge farmer who lived just up the Charles River, was known for his fine shooting. He had adjusted the sights on his Brown Bess and was eager to fire. Sadie told him to go next and he lay down at the mark and quickly ran through the six steps of priming and loading. His first round was close to the center. He fired twice more, a grin curling around his wide mouth. When he came back with his board a shout went up. He had two clear five-pointers and a one, for a total of eleven. It was probably enough to win top honors in the whole troop.

Sadie sighed and ran her other shooters through efficiently, then took her turn at the line. The roar of the muskets continued as she primed and loaded, ramming the ball in solidly with just the right amount of pressure.

She sighted in on the "V," blinked away a drop

of moisture that rolled down from her forehead, and aimed again. Her finger tightened on the trigger, which she had adjusted for a lighter pull than normal, and the hammer fell. For a moment the smoke hazed the target but she was sure she had hit the thick limb. She quickly loaded and sighted in again. This time her finger worked more smoothly, her aim was more precise, and she knew she had scored well.

"Come on, come on. Hurry it up, Mrs. Wythe, I want to see how bad I bet you." Compton said it, a teasing smile on his face that held as much anger as jest.

She battered down a quick panic and sighted in, pretending the "V" was a tom turkey's head over a log, eyes looking to see what strange animal had made the funny turkey call. She needed the bird for dinner that night in the frontier wilds. Sadie fired.

One of the men ran to the target when the all-clear whistle came, and brought back the limb. The smile on his face was all Sadie could see as he brought the foot-long target back to her. He had turned it over so the target blaze would not show. Before she turned it over Sadie looked at the boy of eighteen years and smiled. "Is it good, William?"

"I think you'll like it, Captain Wythe," he said.

Sadie shivered. Although they decided the leaders of each company could be called "Captain" no one had ever called her by that title. Compton had talked down the idea.

She turned the log over slowly. Compton swore under his breath. A gasp went up from the men crowding around her.

Sadie wanted to cry but she knew she didn't dare. The "V" tip was gone. One of the rounds had carried it away cleanly. Another round had gone in almost the same hole, nicking the side slightly but an easy second five-pointer. The third round tore though the branch dead center between the sides of the "V." She had scored a twelve, beating Compton!

The big man shook his head. "I'll be damned. I let some woman beat me."

"No, not just *some* woman, Compton," William said. "That's Captain Wythe, the top shot in our whole damned troop."

A cheer went up and as Sadie looked out at the smiling faces, a tear slipped over the side of one eye and rolled down her cheek. She glanced at Compton. He sighed and grinned at last.

"Goddamn, I think we got us the best shot and the best captain in the whole troop. Captain Wythe, it's a pleasure to serve with you." Compton touched the tip of his hat in a salute and the men clapped and cheered.

Another errant tear slid down her cheek and the men kept right on cheering. Sadie tried her voice and found she could speak after all.

"Lieutenant Compton, it's good to serve with you." The immediate promotion of a second in command in each company had been authorized by the council but not all companies had a lieutenant. The promotion brought a continued round of shouts, cheering and slapping Compton on the back. When it died down, Sadie grinned at the new officer. "Lieutenant, please detail four men to go to our target area when the all clear is sounded and see how many of our shot can be recovered."

"Yes, ma'am!" Compton said, again flicking a salute.

Sadie returned his salute smartly. She took the paper with the report of her company's scores and walked to a small table where the council would gather.

Lynch and Ben were already there. Each had a man who had scored an eleven. "Should we have a shoot-off?" Ben asked.

"Why don't we wait until all scores are in?" said Sadie.

"What was your total score?" Ben asked her.

She spread the report out beside the others and Ben laughed.

"We don't need a shoot-off at all."

Dr. Warren brought his report and the target of one of his men. Dr. Warren had scored an eleven, but he displayed the wood for evaluation. Sadie looked at the target and saw at once there was no doubt about the two five hits. She checked the third shot for a few seconds, then looked up. "It's a clean two-pointer. The only marks on the line of the 'V' are splinters."

The others agreed and it was determined that there would be no shoot-off since men from each company were digging into the sandstone to save all the shot they could.

"As soon as the men are assembled we'll have a formation and present the co-winners with the prize, new powder horns with their names carved on them."

Lynch beamed at the whole operation. "These

men almost look like soldiers," he said. "I could take a squad of them out and really get something accomplished. They can fire, they can load quickly, and they know how to hit a target. That's good."

The others congratulated Lynch on the training. A short time later the men gathered in a crowd around the small table and Ben presented the new powder horns to Captain Lynch and Lucas Trotter, the newly-made lieutenant in Dr. Warren's company.

Back at the picnic site, the men dispersed and joined in the last of the games. The young people were having sack races, wheelbarrow contests and impromptu wrestling matches.

Sadie sat under a tree and watched Ben go to his carriage near the river. His twin sons pulled him away at once to help run a three-legged race. Sadie did not try to see Ben's wife. She had no real desire to see Mrs. Rutledge. What good would it do? The idea of meeting Ben's wife or talking to her left Sadie in a cold sweat. No, it was better to stay far, far away. For just a moment the fluttering black wings of despair touched her. Why did she have to love a married man? And why, oh why couldn't she have children? She had asked Dr. Warren about her lack of conception. She explained that she and her husband had tried very hard to have children, but they didn't. Dr. Warren told her there was so much they didn't know about reproduction that he had no idea what the trouble might be. He simply couldn't answer her question. He asked her about her sex life with her husband in some detail, but he did it in a way that didn't embarrass her. At last he said that the problem could simply be that she was barren, or that her husband could have been sterile. Either one could have caused it. She was thankful for his help. The first physician she had asked about it had been so embarrassed that he hadn't been able to talk to her at all.

She shrugged, picked a dandelion and blew away the seeds. At least she had her work at the store, and her work with the Freedom Fighters. She smiled secretly. And her love for Ben Rutledge. So what if it had to be hidden? It was just as wonderful, just as vital. At least, this way, she could have him part of the time.

Sadie got up, scolded away her dark thoughts and walked through the wagons, waved to friends and even participated in a rope-skipping game. She saw women who had been into the shop, but she hadn't connected the names with any of the Freedom Fighters. Now she could.

It had been interesting during the first part of the picnic. Men discovered that good friends were also in the movement, though for weeks each had been keeping his membership secret from the other. It was the first time the whole troop had been together.

Gradually the hundred family units began to get ready for the drive home, and wagons and every type of carriage and chaise loaded up games and picnic baskets and moved down the road toward Boston. Sadie had come with Dr. Warren and his wife, and now she saw his carriage about ready to go. She hurried over the meadow so she would not hold up his departure.

Under a tree near the river, Ben lounged on the new spring grass and talked with Captain Lynch. They had been there for ten minutes discussing the day.

"I heard yesterday about the new auction date for my three ships," Ben said, changing the subject. "I don't think I was supposed to find out, but I went to the customs house and asked a clerk who didn't know me when the next auction was set for. He went to a desk and came back with the date, saying one was set for April 27 but it had been moved to April 30.

Lynch frowned. "They postpone it, and that makes it longer for you to wait, and the more money you lose on the idle vessels."

"I'm sure that's part of their thinking. But it gives us three more days to conclude our plans."

"We'll need more men than we thought before," said Lynch. "Why not use some of the Freedom Fighters?"

"How could I do that? This is personal business."

Lynch thought for a moment. "You could ask for volunteers. And you could say that if the plan works, and you get all three ships back, you'll use one of them for council business whenever it's needed, and you'll commission one as a privateer to prey on British shipping if and when open war does break out."

Ben thought it over. It would solve the problem of manpower. Privateers would be in great demand when the shooting did start. It could be the beginning of a navy for the colonies.

Ben slapped Lynch on the back. "Lewis, I think

you've got it. You've come up with the answer to a problem that's been nagging me. Now, full speed ahead with our plans. I'll talk to Mr. Hancock as soon as I can next week."

The men stood. Lynch headed for his saddle horse and Ben moved toward his carriage. If he could weather ten more days, he had a very good chance of getting back his ships legally, and no court here or in England could deny his action!

Chapter Ten
TO CATCH A TROUT

Monday morning Ben Rutledge sat in his chaise, two blocks from his waterfront office, and watched the people milling around the Boston sidewalks, bustling about on daily tasks and errands. It was nearing noon, and the church bell would ring presently. He had made a habit of these weekly stops to watch the people. It was an attempt to keep himself up to date on the general public pulse, the atmosphere, how the people really felt about the English troops.

A pair of lobsterbacks came down the street near the shops. Ben watched the people's reactions. Two elderly women scowled and stared hard at the soldiers as they passed. Three young girls were hustled into a store by their mother until the redcoats walked on. Farther down the street three young men watched and waited for the lobster-backs' approach. The three youths were taller than the soldiers, rawboned, and probably about eighteen years old. They stood with ax handles in their fists and spaced themselves across the sidewalk.

The soldiers stopped and talked briefly, looking at the three. Neither of the military men was armed. They angled across the street, but the colonial youths moved and intercepted them. The red-coats stopped two yards from the axe-handle-armed colonists.

"Where ye bound, lobsterbacks?"

"Down the street," one of the soldiers replied.

"What if we don't want you to walk down our street?"

"Why would you say that?"

"To make you lads sweat."

"We could go get help."

"Not without turning your yellow tails and running."

The two men talked again, then marched straight ahead, arms up to ward off any blows. But none came. The colonials shouted insults at the redcoats, who continued down the street.

Ben noted it. The Massachusetts colonists were angry with the soldiers, upset by the taxes, furious over the lack of goods they had been used to, but also they were determined to hold true to the Non-importation Agreement as long as possible.

However, Ben felt the people were not yet ready to fight; not yet ready for open warfare. Ben shook his head. It would come, it had to come eventually. His latest word from one of his ship captains who just arrived from London was that it was expected that the Townshend duties would be repealed any day by Parliament. This was April 23. His ship had left London on January 25, making a quick twelve-week passage. Parliament may well have repealed the duties by now—all except one on tea as a face-saving measure. Such a move would be considered backing down by Parliament, and it would be hard, perhaps impossible, to hold the colonies firm on the non-importation pledge. Ben figured that New York merchants would be the first to vote down the agreement. If New York fell, the twelve other colonies would have to follow to protect themselves...and imports would be wide open again.

That would be fine for business, especially Ben's shipping trade, but it would lower the anger against England. It would cut the shouting and fury, and relations with the mother nation would enter a new, easier phase. That would cool off the movement toward independence and liberty.

Ben slapped the reins on the horse's back and drove to his office. He still had to see John Hancock and make final arrangements for their little surprise for Commissioner Trout's auctioneer.

By four-thirty, Ben had taken care of the matter with Mr. Hancock, and was talking with Lewis again.

"Any suggestions for our next operation, Captain Lynch?"

The one-eyed man shook his head. "No, sir. I agree on the man to do the job. A little bit of theatricals and he should have it. We also have the uniforms we need."

Ben listened, pleased. "Any suggestions for the time of day? At a busy time, or just before closing?"

"Busy. The busier the better. I'd say about eleven o'clock, when the merchants go in with the previous day's receipts."

Ben and Lynch went over the operation again, carefully checking and reviewing each step of the plan. When both were satisfied, they lifted tea cups in a toast.

"Here's to a farewell party," said Ben.

"Aye, where we won't be the ones leaving," Lynch added. But his good eye looked troubled. "Course, sir, there are some risky parts. Like if we have any trouble with the signature. It's one thing to practice it and another to get it just right with some eagle eye watching you. Then there's the off-chance that Trout himself could be out and around that day. Dare say that would be most embarrassing, sir, to run into him and his two bloody bodyguards out in public."

Ben put down his cup and made a mark on the papers in front of him. "In any action there is an element of danger, Lewis, as you well know as an ex-Royal Marine. But in this case we'll have to call it a calculated risk we must take. The odds are all on our side that it will work out well. If the prize is worth the sweat, the labor is soon forgotten, right?"

"Oh, yes, sir. Right."

They parted after setting up a meeting time of nine-thirty at the edge of town for the next day.

The following morning, when Ben arrived at the warehouse, he wondered how developments were going. He couldn't think of any mistakes they had made, or any more research or preparation they could have done. The scheme was almost ready to go and he could only hope that it would go as planned.

He stepped into the warehouse and closed the door. It was dark as the inside of a musket barrel. Ben sensed someone nearby. A second later he felt a knife blade across his throat.

"Friend or foe?" the query came.

"Rutledge, Ben Rutledge."

"Right, Captain. Good to have you on board. Captain Lynch and the rest are in the office, straight ahead.

Ben thanked the man he never saw and groped his way through the gloom to the office. He could see a slant of light coming through a crack. Inside three lamps blazed.

Commissioner Jeffrey Trout sat in a chair facing him, dressed as Ben had often seen him: golden silk neck cloth, ruffled front shirt, a vibrant purple frock coat, and breeches of slightly lighter purple tone with golden stockings. His shoes were polished black with square-cut silver buckles.

The only trouble was that it was not Commissioner Trout's face.

"Well, sir, what do you think so far?" Lynch asked. He stood beside a man who was mixing putty and some type of flesh-colored liquid.

"Fine, perfect, except for the most important part. Can he fix the face right?"

"I can, sir." The man who spoke was short, a hunchback with a craggy face. He was one of the best artists in all of Massachusetts colony.

"Mr. Whipple, good day, sir. We're depending totally on your skill to make everything perfect...to make this work."

Whipple nodded and went back to mixing the putty. The basic body was right: six feet tall, thickly set at 225 pounds. Ben took another look, checking to be sure the imposter was Arnold Compton. His heavy black hair had been dusted white and an expensive long white wig fitted into place.

199

It had a familiar look and a dozen colored ribbons woven into it that Trout always used. Ben spoke to Lt. Compton, then Whipple went to work with the soft putty molding and changing the jaw line, building up a ridge of flesh over the eyes where new brows would be fixed. Luckily the ears were covered. Trout was known to use eyeglasses and a set was produced as close to the original as possible.

Whipple sat back after half an hour and began fanning Compton, who had been ordered not to speak until given permission, so the putty would have a chance to set and harden properly.

"Now say something, Lieutenant Compton," Whipple directed.

Compton let out a series of oaths and they all laughed. Whipple examined his handiwork again and could find no cracks or problems. He began brushing on a faintly pinkish fluid paint that soon took on a flesh tone. Carefully he spotted on a mole on Compton's chin, then backgrounded the forehead and lastly pasted on a set of brows that were identical to those of the real Trout.

Ben backed across the room from Compton and stared at him. If he didn't know for sure, Ben would swear that Compton was Commissioner Jeffrey Trout.

"The face is as good as we can make it," Whipple said. "Now let's try the walk." He stood and watched the pseudo Trout walk across the room.

"No, no! You're not twenty-eight, your name is Jeffrey Trout and you're nearly sixty and you have a bad right leg with a limp, remember?" He scowled. "Try it like a tired old man."

"Sure, Compton. Just the way you walk after your fourth tumble in one night at Maude's!" someone said and everyone laughed. Compton was well known at the town's most expensive brothel.

He tried the walk, then he did it again. For half an hour they practiced the walk. Suddenly two men rushed into the room. Both were redcoats carrying Brown Bess muskets with fixed bayonets.

"Hold on, all of ye! Or you're dead where you stand!" one of the redcoats shouted. The other man worked his way around to the far side.

"We'll rescue you from these colonial curs, sir," the second man said. He brought his weapon around and trained it on Ben. The weapon was on full cock. "No, you don't, lad. Don't move again, or I'll put a ball right through your gizzard!"

One redcoat grabbed Trout's hand. "I'll help you, sir. This way. Smartly now, out the door. We've got more lads just outside waiting for us."

The men in the room stood in stunned surprise as the redcoats ushered the fake Commissioner Trout out of the room. When they left, Whipple cursed.

"Don't just stand there, men. After them!" he shouted.

Before anyone else could say a word, the redcoats and Trout came back through the door laughing so hard they almost fell down.

"Fooled ye colonials, didn't we, sir?"

Ben looked at the redcoats closer and realized they were both men from his own company. They were the redcoats that had been dressed up for the scheme.

"Fine job, men, wonderful!" Ben said, coming

out of his shock. "I thought for certain you were real redcoats and our plans were smashed. Oh, you did fool us!"

He consulted his watch. It was ten-thirty. That left ten minutes for Compton to work on the signature. They had obtained an official signature from one of Ben's papers, and Compton had been practicing on it for over a week at home. He did a few more strokes, then took the advice of the artist who could write it perfectly.

Ben got their attention. "Time you leave. The three of you will drive in a closed carriage from here to within half a block of the Boston Land bank. Then get out and walk to it, and be careful to use that limp, a haughty expression and berate anyone and everyone you come in contact with. The touchy point may be that you don't have all of the deposit chits. You've lost most of them but you'll take the bank's word for the total amount of your deposits. These are rather poor copies we've worked out. The saving point here is that you say you'll be glad to sign a complete and total waiver releasing the bank of all liability over the lost records. We have the paper for your inside coat pocket. Use it only if you must. Try to bluff and whipsaw your way through without it. Then reluctantly bring it out only if you must. Questions?"

"Yes. Will I want paper notes, silver, or what?" Compton asked.

"Gold, you deal only in gold—any equal amount of gold coin or bars will do quite nicely. Also tell them you have your own guard to help you take it back to the customs house."

There were no more questions. If the ruse failed,

it was every man for himself. The three knew this, and each carried a flintlock pistol loaded and ready to fire in his belt under his clothing. The barrels had been cut off four inches for easier hiding. The three got into the carriage at the back of the building and drove away.

Lynch rode away on his horse. He had to set up a protective screen of six Freedom Fighters with flintlocks high on rooftops near the front of the bank. If worst came to worst, his men could lay down covering fire as the three players tried to flee the stage.

Ben carried his pistol primed and ready to fire, as did several others, who now positioned themselves as inconspicuously as possible half a block from the bank, between it and the company of redcoats at the customs house two blocks away.

As Ben watched, the carriage came to a stop some forty feet from the Boston Land bank, and the imitation Trout and his two redcoat guards left the rig. It all looked normal to Bostonians. They hadn't seen much of the chief commissioner lately, since his tar bath, but since then he had always been with his pair of tough-looking lobster-back guards.

Trout motioned one of them ahead of him, and the other behind, and they began a slow walk into the bank. A small boy tried to spit on the commissioner, but he whacked the boy on the shins with the cane he had taken to using. A woman screeched at him for being cruel to a child. Trout merely flicked his cane toward her and continued with his dragging half-step toward the bank. At the door he waited while the redcoat opened it and he entered first. Then the guards came in quickly and followed Trout as the commissioner walked past a line of customers and through a small swinging gate until he stood before the desk of the bank's vice-president. The man looked up, at once jumped to his feet, and asked Trout to be seated.

"Sir, I have come to withdraw my entire account from your bank. As you know, I have a considerable amount with you. I wish to remove it now, in gold of course, and I'll sign the proper papers and receipts for it."

The banker stared at him for a long moment, then pushed a withdrawal form to him and asked him to fill in the amount and sign it.

Compton signed Trout's name with a flourish and using the long turkey quill wrote across the section for the amount: "Entire balance, closing out account."

The vice-president, named Furham, didn't understand the procedure, and liked it even less.

"Sir, you don't know the amount?"

"My bookkeepers aren't as good as yours. Just get me the balance. My time is limited."

"But surely you have your deposit records, your..."

Trout surged out of his chair, turned and stalked to the door marked "President" and barged inside. Two men sat in front of the president's desk. Furham shot into the office, right in back of Trout.

"I'm sure we can work this out, Commissioner, there's no reason we should trouble Mr. Jacobson..."

The president looked up, anger in his eyes, but

when he saw the chief commissioner, his ire faded.

"I'm not in the habit of dealing with incompetents, sir," Compton said in the best imitation of Trout's voice. He motioned to Furham. "This lackey of yours is brash, insulting and totally incompetent to do his job. I suggest you discharge him at once."

"Commissioner Trout, these gentlemen will wait in the other office for me. Why don't you sit down and let me handle this for you. I'm sure we can work it out."

"I want you to know, sir, that I have no argument with your bank, or its accounting. It's just this infuriating man..."

Jacobson took the withdrawal form from Furham and waved him out of the room. "Well, I see nothing wrong with the document. There's no reason a man of your stature must remember the balance in his account, is there? Mr. Furham, proceed to close out this account and bring the entire amount in gold to Mr. Trout. It's obvious that he's been called home to assume a more important position elsewhere in the British empire. Hurry, hurry!" The president of the Boston Land bank smiled at Commissioner Trout and began to make small talk, when the commissioner stood.

"Sir, my leg. I'm afraid I can't sit very long at a time. Neither does walking please the blasted leg. My carriage is the only place I'm half comfortable."

Trout walked stiffly into the lobby and paced, sat in a chair and nodded when Furham himself pushed up a footstool for the aching leg.

"Can't you rush, man? My boat is set to sail for

London this afternoon, and I have much to do. If I don't get on board in time, and they leave, I'll have you scalped!"

"We are going as fast as possible, Commissioner," Furham said. "That's a large amount of coin to count."

"Yes, and you count it right. If I'm a pound short I'll have you all in prison, understand? Now, you go and help them do it faster. Move!"

He watched the man leave. "Oh, when I get back to London I'll simply buy my own doctor and keep him at my house."

Outside, Ben and the others could do nothing but act unconcerned to cover up their gnawing desire to know how it was going. Ben paced past the bank once, glanced in and saw nothing amiss, so kept going. The six musketmen positioned on rooftops nearby kept out of sight, with only a random peek over the false fronts of the buildings. Time wore on.

Inside the bank, the two redcoat guards had been pressed into service to help carry the chests. There would be three small chests filled with gold coin. Another short delay resulted when a messenger had to go to another bank for a loan of gold coin to complete the large sum required. One of the redcoat guards went to the street and drove the carriage in front of the bank. He loaded two of the chests and as Commissioner Trout signed the receipts and marked the account closed and paid in full, the other chest was safely stowed aboard.

The commissioner snorted at the vice president, saluted the president, and marched out of the bank with his second redcoat guard close behind.

He got into the coach and it moved down the street at a normal rate of speed, heading for the customs house.

Just past the customs house and carriage picked up speed, wound around the edge of town, then struck out along the open spaces by the bay where it met another coach, somewhat smaller and fully enclosed.

Ben Rutledge stepped from the second rig.

"Yahoooooooo! We did it!" He shouted.

Arnold Compton leaped from the large carriage, tearing off the fancy clothes and scratching at the putty on his face.

"Damn right we did it!" he bellowed. The five men there, including the two guards still in their red coats and Lewis Lynch, danced around like a quintet of madmen. They helped Compton wash and scratch the putty and paint from his face. He and the two redcoats changed into their regular clothes Ben had brought with him, then they looked at the gold the receipt showed a total of 22,638 pounds sterling, and all in gold!

Ben let it run through his fingers, his face filled with both anger and admiration. "It's a tribute to Commissioner Trout that he was so dishonest and so villainous that he could steal this much money in so short a time."

Ben gave each of the four men twenty pounds in gold, then he subtracted the eighty pounds sterling from the total and marked it as "collection expense."

It had been planned that any money liberated would be used as a war chest for the Freedom Fighters. One third of it would be kept with the munitions in Concord; one third in Dr. Warren's safe, and the last third in Ben's safe at his office. Each chest would be double-padlocked and require two keys to open the locks. No man would hold more than one of the padlock keys.

"Lads, save the uniforms. We may want to play redcoat again one of these days," Ben said as they separated to deliver the chests and get them locked.

Later that afternoon, a basket of fruit was delivered to Commissioner Trout at the customs house. It was accompanied by a note supposedly from the president of the Boston Land bank, thanking Trout for his patronage, and wishing him a speedy and safe trip back to London. It thanked Trout for keeping his account with the Boston Land bank, and said they were sorry he had to close it out. Ben had written the note and sent the basket of fruit so that Trout would find out about his loss immediately.

Two minutes after the package was delivered, Trout let out a roar that shook his bookshelf. He screamed for his top aide and sent him quickly to the Boston Land bank to inquire what in hell that madman Jacobson was talking about. Trout said he had no plans to take a trip and he certainly had not closed out his account at the bank.

In less than five minutes, Mr. Jacobson rushed with the commissioner's aide to the customs house. Jacobson looked as though he had been hit with a falling tree. His face was flushed, his collar wet with sweat, and the wig he wore so proudly was now askew.

Not even Ben could find out everything that

took place in Trout's second-floor office. The thrust of the screaming argument came out piecemeal. Trout swore that he had not been in the Boston Land bank that morning. Jacobson swore that Trout had been there, that he had twenty witnesses who would swear the same, and that he had a valid receipt for the delivery of the total amount in Trout's account of 22,638 pounds sterling. The sum was paid in gold coin.

The battle raged. Trout swore he would break the bank, he would have it closed by the Crown, that he would ruin every director, every guarantor, every depositor.

Jacobson had not reached his position by shrinking from danger or threats. He could shout as loud as Trout, and did. He called Trout a swindler, a thief, a cheat and a shameful blight on the good name of all Englishmen. Jacobson stormed out of the room repeating his proof that Trout had indeed drawn out the money. "I myself waited on you in my office after you stormed in like a royal ass. You had your two guards along in full uniform, and you signed the receipt. And, sir, if you continue to act in this insulting and childish manner, I shall have the law on you for slander. Do you hear me, Trout?"

The commissioner slumped in his chair, and Jacobson marched out of the room, his back rigid with fury.

Two days later Commissioner Trout resigned his position, turned over his duties to his second-in-command, and quietly boarded one of the twenty-four gun frigates in the harbor which was heading back to England. He would make a complete report to the king's advisors and to Parliament. Those old men in session had no idea what kind of madmen and thieves these colonists really were.

The same day Trout left for London, Edmund Cunliffe at last put Operation Harriet into action. Twice before he had tried, but each time a guest came or some other occurrence thwarted his plans. This time he had seen the cook slip out of the house five minutes after Mrs. Rutledge and the driver left. So there was Harriet alone, waiting to be taken, a fresh young blossom needing to be plucked.

He shrugged the old coat around him, pulled the floppy hat farther down over his face, and walked the last half-block to the Rutledge mansion. He went faster the nearer he came to the house, and at last he lifted the large brass knocker. When he dropped it, the sound seemed to boom through the house, and a moment later he heard someone inside running for the door.

The panel jerked open and two panting boys stared at him.

"Hey, look, a crazy man," David Rutledge said.

"He isn't crazy, he's only poor. Give him a coin."

As the boys fumbled in their breeches for a coin, Edmund Cunliffe turned and ran. How stupid of him! The brothers! How could he have forgotten about them? And why hadn't his spy reminded him? He had emptied the house of all except the two most dangerous to him. At last he slowed his walk, made it to his chaise and drove away quickly in the opposite direction from the Rutledge house.

The auction of Ben's three tall ships had been set for ten a.m. Monday, April 30, 1770. Ben and John Hancock arrived at the auction at different times. The pier where the ships were tied up had been leased by the Crown some time ago, and had only the three seized ships tied there. It was a finger pier extending two hundred feet into the bay. At each side of the pier entrance were warehouses, with a narrow opening for freight wagons to drive onto the pier jutting into the bay.

When Ben arrived he saw two wagons pulled up near the largest of the warehouses. Sitting in the seat of the first wagon was a man with his hat pulled down over his face, apparently sleeping. Three other men stood waiting.

Ben walked out onto the pier, and a few minutes later, John Hancock came out with the Crown's auctioneer.

At the warehouse, the man with the slouch hat over his eyes watched the men go past, then pushed back his hat and gave a signal. Both wagons wheeled into place across the pier entrance, blocking it. At once the men lifted sections of an eight-foot-tall wooden fence from the wagons and nailed them in place across the end of the pier entrance from one warehouse to the next, sealing it off.

Just as they finished, a carriage pulled up, and a prosperous-looking gentleman stepped down.

"Is this the site of the ship auction?" he asked.

Lynch moved toward him. "No, sir. It was, but they moved it to the far end of the harbor. Down at the other end near Twain Street on pier four. You'll find it easily, sir."

The man swore under his breath, got back into his rig and left. Lynch grinned. "One for our side. Now bring down that small chaise in case we need it."

Two more prospective buyers came, and after some convincing, they turned around and headed for the imaginary new sales site three miles away.

Lynch wondered how it was going inside. The auctioneer would be waiting for more buyers, but would have to start the bidding when it was called for.

The next chaise was a fancy one, with scroll-work, drawn by a sleek black mare. The man driving stared down at the new wall and the men now busy hammering away for effect.

"What's going on here? Isn't there an auction on the pier today?"

"Sorry, guv, this pier's been closed for repairs. Done moved the blinkin' auction down to pier four, they did."

"Nonsense. I saw the masts of the ships as I came down the street. They all three are right out there. I can see the tips of them over the fence. I'm Edmund Cunliffe, and I demand entrance!"

"Begging your pardon, sir. Could I step in your rig for a look? Must be some other ships moved in."

Lewis took the step into the chaise and continued moving forward with a smashing right fist into Edmund Cunliffe's angry jaw. The man slumped into the seat. Lewis jumped down, motioned to one of the men who scrambled into the chaise and drove it away to a pre-selected spot in the country. Mr. Cunliffe would have a five-mile walk back to town, and then he would have to try to find his horse and rig.

At the end of the pier, the customs house auctioneer looked at Ben's watch.

"Yes, yes. I do see that it is fifteen minutes past the appointed time, but there should be more bidders. We have had a dozen inquiries in the past few days. I know of two more gentlemen for sure who are coming."

Hancock tapped his walking stick on the planking. "I, sir, don't care who else is coming. The bidding was set for ten sharp. Start it now, or I'll have the whole matter up before the judges."

The auctioneer, perspiring freely now, looked back down the dock and saw the new fence, but decided not to make an issue of it. He didn't want John Hancock as a lifetime enemy.

"Very well, gentlemen. With the power invested in me by His Majesty King George the Third, I hereby declare this auction open on the first of these three fine sailing ships. Minimum bid is 40,000 pounds sterling. What am I bid, gentlemen?"

Ben looked at the ship, back at the auctioneer, then at Hancock. Neither one said a word.

"Come, come. The first vessel is valued at just over fifty thousand pounds by an independent appraisal. Now, what is your opening bid?"

Silence again.

Hancock spoke up. "Mr. Auctioneer, as I understand it, by law the auction is now launched and must be concluded. Since there is no bid at the stipulated minimum, the field is now open for any bid at any price. This is the law of the Admiralty, am I not correct, Mr. Auctioneer?"

"Well, I suppose...I'm sure there will be other bidders here. It's late, however, I realize. And there are two independent bidders as the law requires. I know. I just can't figure out where the other men are. They said they would be here. One was absolutely sure."

"Then I suggest you continue the bidding, and this time it is open with no minimum," Ben said.

The auctioneer shrugged, wishing he had brought along at least a pair of guards with him. Then he could deny ever opening the bidding and the soldiers would have backed him up with their sworn statements and their flintlocks. He took one last look down the planks.

"Very well. The bidding is reopened with no minimum. Do I hear a bid for the first ship?"

"Two pounds sterling," Hancock said at once.

"Two pounds, sir?" the auctioneer asked, his surprise and anger mixing.

"Two pounds."

"Three pounds," Ben said.

"Four pounds."

"I bid five pounds, sir."

"If you want a battle of it, ten pounds by Hancock."

"Eleven."

"Twelve."

"Fifteen pounds, sir!"

"Sixteen and that's my tops," Ben replied, his face serious.

"Twenty pounds!" John Hancock said.

The auctioneer stared at them, shaking his head. "Gentlemen, this ship is worth fifty pounds sterling. How can you offer the Crown twenty pounds?"

"Because I bid twenty pounds," said Hancock. "And because the Crown stole the ship illegally in the first place and on a preferential technicality. Do you have a higher bid?"

Ben shook his head.

The auctioneer almost choked. "Sold for twenty pounds to Mr. John Hancock.

Five minutes later Hancock had purchased the other two ships for fifteen pounds each, paid his money in gold, signed the purchase forms and taken title to the sailing ships.

By the time the auctioneer had walked back down the pier, he stared in surprise. Where he had seen a fence only minutes before, he now found nothing. The wagons and men he had seen as well were gone. Now he knew that his eyes must be playing tricks on him. He hurried to his horse to get back to the customs house and made out his report.

He was greatly relieved to remember that Chief Commissioner Trout was gone and on his way home to London. Trout would have sacked him for sure for getting only fifty pounds for three sailing ships worth 150,000 pounds. He shuddered, mounted and rode.

Ben and Hancock watched the auctioneer ride away, then shook hands, and both laughed.

"He didn't know what to do!"

"We had him hog-tied from the start."

Hancock signed over the titles of ownership to

Ben and refused to take the fifty pounds he had spent.

"Call it a good deed for a friend," said Hancock. "I told you I'd be glad to help any time I could. I want you to remember that. I'm in this fight against the English to the very end." He paused. "Oh, I understand you have a new organization called the Friends of Boston. I heard about your picnic and shooting match. I like to take out my flintlock now and then and fire a few rounds. How do I inquire about joining this fine organization?"

There was a twinkle in Hancock's eyes over his fine silk neck cloth.

Ben smiled. "I think it would be a good idea if you do join our little group, Mr. Hancock. I'll talk with our membership selection committee very soon. But I would say you just paid your dues in full."

They shook hands again and walked out to the street where their rigs were waiting.

Chapter Eleven
NO TIME FOR TORY DOGS!

Edmund Cunliffe tipped the glass high, emptying the last of the brandy. He had recuperated the first day after his long walk back to Boston from the country. The second day he brooded over the audacious kidnapping, and its evident purpose of making him miss the ship auction. But he had memorized the face of the one-eyed man, and he wouldn't be hard to find. Edmund promised himself he would hire a spy to seek out the man, and then there would be a satisfying vengeance in watching the man beaten to a bloody stump of a human being.

The anger, fury and disappointment at not being allowed to bid on even one of the three seized tall ships, had flamed and burned itself out. That part was all but forgotten. That man, the one-eyed devil who had hit him and sent him into the country, would be the one paying the piper before long. But right now Edmund had a far more enjoyable adventure...Miss Harriet Rutledge.

Today was Wednesday. For the past two weeks he had not known how to get the Rutledge twin boys out of the house. At last he struck on a plan, and it had worked. It had been a fishing and sailing trip into the bay, and the Rutledge twins had been invited along as special guests. It had cost him ten pounds to hire the boat and arrange the trip, but it would be well worth it. The boys had left the dock just after noon, and would return at dusk. His spy reported that Mrs. Rutledge was at her Bible study class as usual and the cook would be called out by a messenger to go to see her sick cousin. It was the third time he had used the ruse of the sick relative, but it worked. Cunliffe was sure that the cook would not tell her employer the truth. She would take the half-day off gladly and not worry about the lucky mistake that made it possible.

Cunliffe drove as before in his oldest carriage and stopped three houses down from the target. He wore his ancient black coat and an old fishing hat that covered most of his face. He walked up to the door and knocked. This time there was no rushing of feet, only the door opening and the girl looking at him curiously before she frowned.

"Yes?"

"Miss Rutledge, I'd like to talk to you for a moment. Something's happened to your mother."

"What?" she said, jolted, surprised, taking a step backward.

He took advantage of her movement, stepped inside and closed the door, then took off his hat.

"Miss Rutledge, I couldn't count on a chance meeting again. I had to come to see you."

"Mr. Cunliffe!" she was shocked now, frightened, but she covered up that part well. "Get out of this house this very instant!" She reached for the door but his foot held it closed. He caught her wrist.

"Miss Rutledge, you and I are going to get to know one another a lot better this afternoon. You see, I know there is no one else in the house. Now is your chance to ask me to touch you and feel you the way I did before. You want me to, don't you?"

"Get out!" Harriet screamed, her terror showing through now, and she knew it was the wrong thing to do. She should have hit him or simply run. His hand clamped over her mouth and she could only mumble. She struggled to maintain her senses. She had to keep her wits. She would not panic.

"Now, Harriet, we can't have you screaming that way, can we?" He dragged her into the sitting room and toward the long couch across from the big fireplace.

"Yes, this looks like a good spot, since I don't even know where your bedroom is. This will work out just fine. I'll take my hands off your mouth if you promise not to scream. All right?" She nodded. He moved his hand.

"Help!" she screeched as loud as she could. He put his hand back over her mouth, and she bit him and yelled again. Cunliffe slapped her face hard. Her scream choked off. He pushed her down on the couch into a sitting position and sat in front of her.

"We'll have no more of that, understand? I'm stronger than you are, and I can keep right on slapping you until you are quiet. Is that completely understood?"

She nodded. He slid off the old coat he had worn and reached for her face. She tried to pull away but he held her head in both hands, leaned over and kissed her on the lips. She didn't respond.

"Come, now, Harriet, you can do better than that. Is that any way to kiss?" His hands followed down her cheeks, then he kissed her again, pulling her body tightly against his. Again she had no reaction whatsoever. His hands moved lower, to her chin, neck, then gripped the top of her dress and ripped it to her waist.

She gasped and tried to slap him, but he caught her hand. Tears streamed from her eyes.

"Oh, yes, that's better. Let those magnificent mounds have room to surge outward. Yes, I'm looking forward to uncovering them completely and making love just to them."

She was covered now only by the fitted top of her petticoat. Harriet tried to put her hands up, but he pushed them down. He kissed her again and for a moment she felt something new, a kind of warm glow, but it passed and was replaced by a shiver of fear and anger.

She couldn't speak, she could think of nothing more to say, all she wanted to do was cry. She should be screaming at him, telling him what her father would do to him. But she could only sit there, stare at him, and wonder what he would do next. She was both terrified and fascinated. His hand moved, touching her breasts, cupping them, rubbing them gently through the thin cloth. Again she felt a hint of a sensation she couldn't describe. It was a kind of warmth, yes—it felt warm and good.

His hand moved again, ripping her petticoat,

pulling both the front half of the petticoat and dress off her left shoulder, pushing them down to her waist, exposing one breast.

He stared at it for a long moment.

"Beautiful, simply perfect, so big and soft and *beautiful!* I knew they would be this way." His hand touched her naked breast and she shivered, then she exploded in fury. She screamed a terrible howl of torment and her hands flew at him, fingernails digging into his cheeks, clawing downward. She tried to push him off the couch, then tore at him again. She was crying and screaming both at once now. His hands struggled to catch hers, then he sprawled on top of her, pushing her flat on the couch, holding down her legs, fighting with her hands, capturing one, only to be slashed by the other. At last he caught her second hand. He panted and swore at her as he stared down. He held one hand over her head and the other at her side, his face a half inch from her pink-nippled, throbbing breast.

A roar of outrage thundered through the room as Ben Rutledge stormed toward the couch. His hands caught Cunliffe by one arm, dragged him off the couch and threw him toward the wall. Cunliffe almost got his balance, stumbled until he slammed heavily into the wall and crumpled to the floor. He struggled to his feet just as Ben charged, fists swinging viciously, his knee ramming upward but missing Cunliffe's groin. Two fists exploded on Cunliffe's head and he cried out in pain.

The blows dazed him and he stood helpless for a moment. Ben kneed him hard in the crotch and saw the man's eyes glaze in agony that he had never dreamed could be so intense, so numbing, so devastating. Cunliffe sagged and held onto Ben's shoulders, until Ben drove his fist into Cunliffe's jaw in an uppercut that jolted the carriage maker an inch off the floor, and dropped him backwards on the carpet in the middle of the room.

Ben turned to Harriet. "Are you all right?"

Her eyes were still filled with her own outrage, and she barely heard his voice. She couldn't understand the words, only remember her own anger and terror as Cunliffe clawed at her. Harriet watched as her father turned back to the helpless man. He kicked Cunliffe in the stomach, causing him to retch again and again. Ben kicked him in the chest hoping he would break some ribs, but he realized he had on his light shoes not his heavy boots. He lifted Cunliffe from the floor to a sitting position and kneed him viciously under the chin, jolting Edmund backward, slamming him to the floor.

Ben wasn't sure how much damage he was inflicting on the man, he only knew that something drove him to do more and more. Something told him to pound and beat and kick and slash at this animal in front of him until it was still and lifeless on the floor, motionless and never able again to harm another young girl.

"Daddy!"

Ben turned and looked at her. Harriet watched him from tearful eyes, half her dress still down around her waist. She stared at him, then got up and walked to her father. She put her arms around him.

222

"Daddy, please don't kill him. Please, Daddy, don't get in trouble by killing him. He didn't hurt me. He never touched me lower down. He didn't rape me."

At last the words and their meaning got through to Ben. The importance of it penetrated his hate-filled brain, smoothed out his surging blood flow and the spurting adrenalin. Slowly he unclenched his fists.

Ben patted Harriet on the back, kissed her fore-head and moved away from her. He looked at Cunliffe and shuddered. Never before had he been so furious. Never before had he honestly wanted to kill another human being. Ben pulled Harriet's dress up to cover her, then watched Cunliffe. The man was still conscious. His knees were drawn up to his chest to relieve the terrible continuing pain from his groin. His eyes were closed. Bloody lines showed on each cheek where Harriet's fingernails had clawed him deeply. His jaw hung slack and loose as if it were broken or unhinged.

Cunliffe retched again and again, but nothing came from his mouth.

"Get out of my house, Cunliffe," Ben said.

The man on the floor struggled to open his eyes. "She asked me to, she wanted me to, then she got scared."

Ben shook his head and started to kick Cunliffe again. "After your concentrated campaign of se-duction? That's a stupid thing to say, Cunliffe. Now get out of my house."

"I can't walk."

"Then crawl, you bastard! Crawl all the way to the street or I'll kick you out with my boots."

223

Cunliffe tried to get to his knees, but fell from that lofty height. He began to crawl toward the door.

Harriet watched him. He was broken. She knew that never again would he try to seduce a woman. He fell again, his cheek scraping on the hardwood floor beyond the carpet.

Ben kicked his buttocks and he yelped, surged to his hands and knees and moved another dozen feet, moaning all the way. By the time he got to the front door, it was open. He was just over the threshold when Ben put his foot on Cunliffe's side and shoved, toppling him down the six brick steps to a hard landing on the sidewalk.

Cunliffe tried to sit up, but he couldn't. "No man does this to me, Rutledge, and lives!" He said it slowly, blood dripping off his chin. "Nobody! I challenge you to a duel to the death."

Ben laughed. "I don't fight duels. You know that, Cunliffe. Besides, I don't have the time to shoot mad Tory dogs. Now get off my property or I'll get my horse and drag you off!"

Ben went back inside and watched as Cunliffe crawled to the gate. He used the fence to get to his feet, then stumbled along the white pickets toward a chaise two houses down the block. When Cunliffe made it to the rig, it took him another five minutes to get up into the seat. Then he drove away. Ben watched Harriet.

He took her gently in his arms, and as he did she began to cry. Tears flowed and she sobbed as he carried her upstairs to her bed as he had done so many times—but not for many years.

After ten minutes of weeping she sobbed her

way out of it and they talked.

"We won't tell your mother about this," said Ben. "She would only worry. Thank God she wasn't here. If any of the neighbors say anything, we'll tell them that Cunliffe and I had an argument. Now, get rid of these clothes, have a hot bath, and then take a nap." Ben paused. "You're sure he didn't hurt you? I mean..." In spite of the shock and anger she still felt, she worked up a small smile at her father's reluctance to use the word. "No, Father, he did not rape me. He only touched my breasts."

"Good, good. Now get those clothes thrown away so your mother doesn't see the damage, and have a nice long rest. This must be our secret. It's my fault. I should have had it out with Cunliffe before, when he bothered you in church. I never dreamed he would have the audacity..." He turned and left the room, closing her bedroom door securely.

The next day Harriet slept late, and when she got up she dressed simply and sat in the sun. She could only think of yesterday as a nightmare. It hardly seemed real. She had no physical marks to show for it. Cunliffe certainly did! Those marks she had put on his face would last for weeks! Perhaps she had scarred him for life. She decided she would tell Jennifer about it as soon as she could. After all, they had a pledge of honor.

Curiously, she felt fine. Attempted rape. That was a story that would be a dozen times better than Jennifer's.

The days slid past and by Monday she had forgotten the terror. She had shared her secret with her father, and he had kept it from her mother and brothers. She was happy to let it stay that way.

Ben Rutledge went directly from work to the meeting of the Freedom Fighters council above Jonathan's bookstore. He made a complete report about getting his ships back, realizing that most of them already knew, but he wanted it to be official.

"And since we did use Freedom Fighters in the operation, I pledge that one of my ships will be available for Freedom Fighters' work at any time and on call. In case of eventual armed conflict with England, one ship will be outfitted and dedicated as a privateer under command of the Freedom Fighters and for their profits, to attack British shipping in and around these united colonies."

He explained as well the raid on Commissioner Trout's private treasury, how much gold was taken and how it was being guarded and how the books were being kept by Mrs. Wythe.

All expenditures would be approved before the fact by the council. After he was finished, Sadie took the floor.

"I want to bring to the council's attention again the hard pressed small farmers and shippers around the harbor, bays and inlets. The revenue ship *Richard* has been plaguing them for months on end now. The captain of the craft is Rothan Capspree, and has been described to me as a villain, scoundrel, lecher and madman. His sailors and the troop contingent on board just last week butchered a milk cow on the Potter farm, cut down six cherry trees for firewood since they were closer than trees in the woodlot, and generally harassed the womenfolk of the farm until run off by a load of buckshot from a musket fired by the owner of the farm."

Dr. Warren thumped the floor with a walking stick.

"Aye, I'll second that message. I've heard from many about the antics and devilment of this villain. It may be time we took some positive action about Captain Capspree."

The others talked it around and the general feeling was that some action should be taken. Ben spoke quietly, but said he was of the opposite view.

"Our people in London tell us that at any moment now parliament could be rescinding the Townshend Duties. This, in effect, will be a great victory for us. I'm not sure if we should do an overt violent act at this time. However, I like the idea of striking at this vulture who is stripping our bones clean. I ask that we postpone any action for a month, and consider it again then."

The vote to postpone was unanimous.

Dr. Warren took the floor. "I think we're going to have hard times coming up." He waved one hand. "No, I don't mean that we will be in personal danger, or the movement will be in jeopardy. Rather, I am fearful that conditions will improve too much in our relations with England. The facts seem to be these: as Ben pointed out, reports from London indicate that Parliament by now has probably rescinded all the Townshend duties except that on tea. If they did it in the middle of March, we should know about it by the middle of June. If they voted on April 15, we'll get the word here by ship about July 15. And when that word comes, it will herald some distinct changes.

"You know how we've been shunning English manufactured goods, trying to get by with what we have, with what we can make ourselves here, even proclaiming homespun a fashionable item to wear to social occasions. Fine, fine. That spurs forward our desires for total independence. However, when the duties are taken off imported goods, it is going to be impossible to hold the Nonimportation Agreements in force. This is simple human nature. If one colony cracks and drops the embargo on all English goods, the rest will soon follow. What we can expect is that imports will jump back to where they were and increase, the shortages will vanish, we will be putting up new buildings again, growing, progressing, and the hatred against England is going to approach the vanishing point. So, what happens to the Freedom Fighters? We're going to have to stay ready, try to right any wrongs we can find, and hang on like a bulldog to a heifer's nose. We could be looking at two or three years of prosperity, of non-interference from England, and even with very few word battles to wage. That's our evaluation, and I want you all to be aware of it and be ready.

"Due to the expected drop in our immediate action need, I would suggest that we freeze our membership at the present level, and add men only as replacements."

His suggestion was adopted and a short time later they broke up. Ben had his usual pint with Jonathan, then bid him good night and hurried to

Sadie's apartment.

She sat reading a book and sipping tea. Ben turned over the small volume and saw it was Benjamin Franklin's *Way to Wealth*. She smiled.

"Since I'm not by any means rich, except in my friendships, I thought Dr. Franklin might have some good suggestions that I could put to use."

Ben sat across from her and poured himself tea. "I'm sorry I spoke against your plan to blast the *Richard* out of the water. It isn't quite the right time yet. Next month we'll know a lot more and can decide."

She put her cup down and went in back of his chair where she gently massaged his neck and shoulders.

"Is it going to be quiet and peaceful here soon?"

"Yes, I'm afraid it will be. All we can do is wait. Things will change. Parliament will make another mistake, a big one, and that might be enough to set off the sparks that we need.

"And what about you and me?"

"I won't stop seeing you. I can't. You've grown into a marvelous, wonderful, life-stretching habit. I think I love you more now than ever before. Is that possible, to love two fine women at the same time?"

She kissed his neck, whispered "yes" in his ear and caught his hand. Sadie led him to the bedroom and slowly, lovingly undressed him. Then she slid out of her own clothes and turned the lamp down low. She stood over him, a shadowy picture of soft curves, young firm body and long blonde hair falling around her breasts.

229

"I'll never be able to live without you, Ben Rutledge. You have become a vital element in my life, my spark, my leaven, my incentive. You are the reason I get up every morning. You are my reason for smiling. I love you."

She sat beside him, then moaned softly and reached for him. "Darling, I do love you so!"

The next morning, Ben was called downstairs to the front of his office about ten o'clock. There was some kind of disturbance, a man who would not leave until he saw Mr. Rutledge in person. Ben sighed and walked down the stairs to the desk where a dozen of his workers had gathered. One man talked earnestly to someone with his back to Ben.

"May I be of help?" Ben said firmly from behind the man.

He turned. At first Ben didn't recognize him. A heavy bandage swatched his neck and chin. Long scratch marks welted on both cheeks and his nose was broken. The man was Edmund Cunliffe. He could talk with an effort. His eyes glinted with hatred as he took two steps forward, caught his leather gloves in his right hand and slashed them across Ben's cheek.

"Sir, I challenge you on the field of honor. I will pit my life against yours, if you are not too much of a coward to meet me. Tomorrow morning at sunrise near the Charles River dueling oaks. I will be there promptly."

"Mr. Cunliffe, you know I disapprove of dueling. I have made my position quite clear on this subject. Besides, you don't seem to be in any physical condition to defend yourself. I grant you the chance to withdraw your challenge with honor, as these men will be witnesses."

"The famous Rutledge cowardice now shows plainly. I shall not withdraw my challenge." He slapped Ben again. "Rather, I redouble my efforts to shame you into accepting an honorable contest. If you, by any stretch of the imagination, are an honorable man, you will accept. Will you meet me, sir, or won't you?"

Ben stared at Cunliffe's swollen face, at the careful way he moved and at what could be a painful broken jaw.Here was a challenge presented not in private but in front of a dozen witnesses in Ben's own company. How could he laugh off such a challenge? How could he refuse it?

Ben scowled at Edmund. "Mr. Cunliffe, even though it is against my principles to settle disputes in this manner, you leave me no choice. I dislike killing even a stray, diseased animal. However, ridding Boston of such a diseased creature as yourself will be an honor and a rare privilege. I will be there tomorrow morning, promptly at sunrise, to meet you on your field of honor—or field of death, whichever it may be."

Cunliffe gasped at the insult, turned and walked quickly out the front door.

Several of the workers drifted back to their jobs. His general manager, Douglas Inshaw, stayed near.

"Is there any I can do, sir?" he asked.

Ben shook his head and slowly returned to his office. He sat in his chair and looked out over the harbor for a long time, trying to memorize each feature, each ship, dock and bit of land. He might never see that scene again after tomorrow morning.

Ben wrote a two-page letter to Sadie, trying to explain why he was doing it, why he had to meet the challenge. He was afraid to talk to her, afraid that he would lose his resolve. He must do this! Ben asked Lewis to be his second, and then went home. He would have to tell his wife. She would want to know the whole story, and he would tell her. He thought it had ended when he kicked Cunliffe down the steps. It would be a difficult task telling Sandra and he dreaded it.

Later that night he lay in his own bed, Sandra's head in the crook of his arm. She was sleeping soundly, as she always did after they made love.

He got up quietly, paced to the window and looked out over Boston. Would he ever see another sunset, another night? He had spent two hours that afternoon practicing with both of a match pair of dueling pistols from his den. They were decorations—he had never dreamed he would use them. Both were fine weapons. His aim had sharpened.

Now he watched the moonlight over the town. He had expected to be around and watch it grow, to see Boston become the most important seaport on the coast; to see the thirteen struggling colonies fight a great war with England and emerge the winner, then to form a republic, a union of the colonies functioning together, yet separately.

He had expected to live to see so much come to pass.

Now he wondered if he would.

Could he kill a man in a duel?

In a pitched battle, in a war, he could kill.

But could he sight down on a man and shoot to kill, even a man he knew had no right to live, who should be brought up on charges before a judge?

Ben paced the room a dozen times, then looked out the window. He knew he should sleep, should get all the rest he could so he would be ready to make the decision as he took those ten paces and turned. "Stand sideways, present a small target," Lynch had told him that afternoon and made him practice it, pacing off, turning and firing at a tree.

"Stand sideways and don't rush," Lynch drummed at him. "The first shot usually isn't the winner, the first well-aimed shot does the damage. To fire quickly and miss is to earn a quick grave, for then the opponent can take his time and sight in on a stationary target with an eternity of patience."

What would Cunliffe do? Ben could not remember the young man being involved in duels. Why hadn't his law passed to outlaw dueling?

Was he willing to go through with it?

How could he get out of it with honor?

What the hell good is honor when your life's blood is pouring out of a .44 caliber hole in your chest?

Ben stared at the eastern sky and realized it held the first blush of false dawn. He had to get dressed and kiss Sandra good-bye. He would not tell the children. If he came back he would tell them later. If he didn't...

Ben Rutledge pulled on his clothes, choosing a black waistcoat and breeches and dark blue shirt as Lynch had ordered to make himself a harder-to-see target. He wasn't sure yet if he could go through with it. Could he even lift the pistol? If Cunliffe fired first and missed, could he aim down on the man? More important, could Ben stand there and wait for the other flintlock pistol to send a death-producing ball slamming toward his body? Would he flinch, scream, or run for cover?

Ben sighed. There was so much left to do! Would it be finished without him? He pulled on the last of his clothes, woke Sandra and kissed her good-bye, ordering her to stay in bed and wait.

Then he walked downstairs and out to the chaise that was hitched and ready to go. He would pick up Lynch at the Tower road on the way to the oaks.

Ben stared down at the set of dueling pistols. What was it he had told Sadie? "When you're in a kill or be killed situation, it's much easier to pull the trigger, and worry about the philosophic arguments of taking a life later."

Now there was no later. Within an hour his fate would be decided. He would be dead or alive. Ben whacked the reins on the horse's back, eager now to get on with it.

BOOK TWO

Chapter One
HONOR BOUND AND BLOODIED

Boston, Massachusetts Colony
May 22, 1770

Ben Rutledge eased the one-horse chaise to a stop at the side of the muddy street, where he was supposed to meet Lewis Lynch. The black snorted as Lynch materialized from the shadows. The man was a one-eyed ex Royal British Marine, who had been discharged due to his impaired vision, and who chose to remain in the colonies. Now he was Ben's right-hand man, expert in weapons and tactics, and currently his mentor so Ben's first duel would not be his last.

Lynch waved at Ben and swung into the chaise. They had planned to take only one rig. Then, if by ill chance Ben was unable to drive home, Lewis could do the job.

"It's a fine morning, Mr. Lynch."

"A fine morning, indeed it is, sir," Lynch said, his heavy brow nestled low over his good eye as he surveyed the other man. "The coat's right, at least—black as the bottom of a sea bag, so you won't give him no good target. But, sir, remember, turn sideways at the end of the ten paces. It takes a little half step but the smaller target area makes it well worth while. And take your time aiming. A first shot means nothing if it goes wild. This is a one-shot chance you have to kill off that bit of garbage—that creature claiming to be an honest man."

"You're talking my arm off this morning, Lewis," said Ben, a hint of humor breaking through his gray mood.

"Better I talk it off than Cunliffe shoots it off."

Ben whacked the reins on the mare's back, and they moved down the road toward the Charles River marsh. It was four miles yet to the Dueling Oaks, the favorite spot for affairs of honor such as this to be settled. And settle it he would.

Ben had not asked for the duel. He had tried with all honor to allow the challenge to be withdrawn, but it was not to be. Cunliffe was ready to stake his life on his shooting hand to avenge what he considered a grievous insult complicated by injury. In the balance Ben thought that his seventeen-year-old daughter had suffered the real injury.

He would rather not think about that day when he had arrived home and found Cunliffe tearing off Harriet's clothes. Ben had surprised him and beaten him until Cunliffe couldn't walk, then Ben made him crawl to the street. That was three weeks ago. The challenge had been given in Ben's own place of business, RUTLEDGE & RUTLEDGE, an importing and shipping firm with a long history.

Cunliffe had stormed into the building and made the challenge in front of a dozen of Ben's employees. There was simply no way Ben could refuse to pick up the gauntlet. Cunliffe was a bachelor, owner of a big carriage works, wealthy, a well-known rake and drunkard who had forced his own mother out of the family mansion so she wouldn't interfere with his wild parties and his cohabitation with what was whispered about as being three or more scarlet women and local floozies.

Ben glanced at Lynch, who seemed more concerned about the duel than Ben himself was at the moment. Ben had forgotten for a second that he was facing death at the end of a dueling pistol. Thank God, the pistols never shot straight, not nearly as accurately as the flintlock long rifles. Would he ever fire his long gun again? Would he ever see another sunset? This was no formal students' affair: Cunliffe would try with all of his skill to put the ball squarely into Ben's heart. Ben now had only fifteen minutes to decide if he would shoot to kill or to wound—if he had the chance. Ben had wrestled with the decision all night, and he hadn't found the answer yet.

He had told his mistress, Sadie Wythe, that when an enemy was shooting at you in a war, and it was a kill or be killed situation, it made it much easier to pull the trigger that could take a life. He hoped the same would be true on this shabby field of honor.

The chaise came to the river road and Ben saw the oaks ahead, a stand of a dozen or so close by the river in what really was a pasture, but had become so popular as a dueling ground that the man who owned it had built a gate into the fence and a trail had been worn. Now the gate stood open and Ben saw a carriage under the oaks.

"This seems to be the right place," Ben said, glancing at Lynch, who was suddenly ever more grim-faced and tense than he had been.

"Please remember, sir," said Lynch. "There's no rush—no hurry at all. The first shot that misses doesn't hurt you. Steady down, keep sideways, and fire only when you have the aim you want."

Ben looked at the one-eyed man and smiled. Now he felt calm, his nerves were at rest, his stomach solid and steady. Ben's good nature came surging back and he knew that win or lose, he would go into it with an open mind, knowing that he was in the right. And if God were just, he would be dealt with fairly.

"Lewis, have you ever fought a duel?"

"Twice, sir, but with sabers. More fitting a marine, and besides, it makes less work for the funeral detail."

Ben chuckled at that, then guided the black through the gate over the humps and ruts to a spot under the trees. Two men, both wearing black suits, stood waiting. Another form showed through the side curtains of the carriage.

Ben knew neither of the young men in black. One held a box the right size for dueling pistols. Ben took his own velvet-lined box as he tied the reins and stepped to the ground.

Lynch plucked the box from him and held up his hand, motioning Ben to stay by the carriage. Then Lynch went out to the other seconds. Ben watched him. No weapons had been specified in the challenge, but the usual one was pistols. Lewis evidently argued that since Cunliffe had thrown down the gauntlet and there was no weapon stipulated, Mr. Rutledge should be allowed to choose which set of pistols to use. Lewis won his point and chose the Rutledge matched pair Ben had practiced with, then opened the box to show the weapons to Cunliffe's seconds. That done, the men waved at the participants to join the group.

Cunliffe walked from the carriage with difficulty. It was evident that his injuries were no better than before. His head was still wrapped in a bandage, but it was reduced so he had the use of both eyes. Revealed were long, deep scratches down both cheeks where Harriet's furious fingernails had mauled him. He walked with a decided limp of his left leg, his left hand on that leg as he moved forward. Cunliffe did not look at Ben.

"Gentlemen, this is your field of honor," the younger of the Cunliffe seconds said. "You are here to settle the challenge with pistols. If there is no objection, Mr. Cunliffe will have the first choice of Mr. Rutledge's weapons. Choose."

He held out the open gun case to Cunliffe, who lifted his hand to them. It wavered, he looked at the second, then stabbed for a pistol. He picked it up, dropped it on the box, then caught it firmly and held it in his right hand.

Ben took the second weapon.

"Participants will inspect the weapons and make sure they are both properly prepared, primed, loaded and ready to fire," said Lynch. Both did.

They were instructed to stand back and wait for the signal, then take ten steps, turn and fire. Ben had thought it through. Ten steps would be about twenty-five feet. Double that would be fifty feet. He had practiced at that distance yesterday afternoon. Each held his weapon with the muzzle pointing at the sky. Ben waited, his nerves now calm from some extra strength. He didn't yet know if he would aim to kill or to wound, or simply shoot in the air . . . if he had that much time for an option.

Edmund Cunliffe wondered why he was standing there at dawn on this summer day. His pride had demanded it, pride had won out over common sense, over the will to live, over his natural inclination toward cowardice. He admitted it, so why didn't he simply lower his weapon and walk away, shouting an apology over his shoulder? It would be better to be disgraced than dead. He had been a total failure in the militia when he took his training. At last he had bought his way out of it. He had heard that Ben Rutledge had been an officer.

Cunliffe knew he should simply turn and run.

But he could not. Pride wouldn't let his legs move. Cunliffe felt his stomach turn over, but the bile he tasted was not the real problem. His stomach churned and rolled, and then, with no warning, his bowels emptied. The stench was immediate and unmistakable. He knew a deep stain must be showing on his black breeches. A tear welled up and cascaded down his cheek. He hadn't fouled his clothes since he was three.

"Ready, set . . . walk!" The command came from Lynch, who had seen the anguish on Cunliffe's face and noticed his accident.

Ben Rutledge moved out at the order, in complete control, his strides measured, steady: one, two, three, four, five . . .

Cunliffe hesitated and was a fraction of a second behind his opponent, but at least he was moving. He would turn at ten and fire quickly, killing the bastard, sending him into hell, and then he would laugh over the body! Yes, he would laugh. Sweat popped out on Cunliffe's brow in the chill of the dawn as he took the steps . . . six, seven, eight, nine, ten, and turn.

Cunliffe spun on his toes, brought the pistol down quickly with his chest still facing his opponent, and fired at once.

Ben had turned almost at the same time as Cunliffe, pivoted on his toes, took a half step back toward the starting point with his right foot so he could hold his body with his right arm and side toward his enemy. His flintlock came down in an aiming pattern he had practiced a hundred times the day before.

Ben heard the other pistol fire, felt a whisper of air as the ball sped past him. Cunliffe had fired and missed!

Cunliffe cried out in sudden anger, then in fear and frustration, but he held his position. Missed? How could he miss? The sights were dead center on target. He had failed and now he would soon be dead. Get in the first shot, they had told him, so he had hurried. Hurried to die. Cunliffe waited, still sick to his stomach, smelling the feces in his pants, hoping now that it would be over soon, and he would be dead.

Ben knew he was safe as he realized Cunliffe had fired and his shot had gone past him. Ben refined his sight, bringing it dead center on Cunliffe's exposed chest. His pistol wavered, then he lowered his sights until he aimed precisely at the other man's crotch and fired.

Rutledge thought he could see the ball leap from the pistol barrel and slam through the air, straight for Cunliffe. At nearly the same time, Cunliffe cried out and was jolted backward by the force of the big pistol ball hitting his flesh.

Ben lowered the smoking pistol, waved at the

blue smoke pall created by the black powder and smelled the acrid odor. Cunliffe was on the ground.

Ben walked toward him, saw Cunliffe holding his crotch and screaming as if he had been mortally wounded. His movements showed he was in great pain, but he made them with vigor.

The flicker of a smile touched the corners of Ben's mouth as he stood over Cunliffe, who was still screeching. Both of his seconds were there, one frantically waving toward the deeper part of the oaks, the other trying to calm Cunliffe.

The wounded man shouted at them, using all the vile oaths and curses he knew. When he saw Ben standing over him, he quieted. His face shadowed with anger, but pain won and he began blubbering with all the desire of a man who wants to die but knows that he has not yet earned that right.

Ben looked up and saw a horse and a familiar chaise pull up near the wounded man. Dr. Joseph Warren tied the reins and jumped to the ground, then picked a small bag from his rig and came forward, a wide smile on his face. He shook hands with Ben and offered his congratulations. All the time, Cunliffe sent a steady stream of curses at the doctor's back.

When Dr. Warren turned, Cunliffe choked off his threats and the tears came again through his moans and cries. Dr. Warren viewed the patient in the dust with ambivalence. He wanted to let him lie there in pain, even bleed to death, but he knew that he could not. He had been told about the problem between Ben and this man. Lewis had asked him to be present in case Ben was injured. Now he had to fulfill his pledge to all of humanity, and be a healer.

"Well, take off his breeches and clean him up, you lunkheads!" the doctor spat at the closest of the seconds. "I can't treat him through all that fancy cloth and excrement."

The second removed Cunliffe's breeches cautiously, accompanied by much howling and cursing, then cut open the crotch of his underwear with a pocket knife and removed the foul-smelling mess.

Dr. Warren knelt by the man in the grass and examined him briefly, used some instruments from the small bag, and made quick repairs to stop the bleeding. He bandaged the genitals.

"Mr. Cunliffe, you're not going to die," Dr. Warren said. "The pistol ball you asked to have fired at you grazed one of your testicles. That's what's causing you this intense pain. The round also practically cut your penis in half. We'll probably have to remove the rest of it in my office tomorrow. You have your friends bring you in at ten a.m. Mr. Cunliffe, you'll probably never be able to have sexual intercourse again."

By the time Dr. Warren and Ben reached the chaises, Lynch was there with the recovered brace of pistols, ready to drive.

Dr. Warren held up his hand. "I would say, gentlemen, that a drink all around is in order,

246

to celebrate this recent action, and with the hope that we will see no more of this dangerous type of behavior among our council members, unless it's Lobsterback's ball we're facing."

Ben accepted the flask of medicinal brandy from the doctor's hand and pledged that never again would he be tricked, angered or shamed into fighting a duel.

A half-hour later Ben drove the chaise into the stable area behind his house and saw Sandra waiting for him on the rear porch. She lifted one hand in quick greeting, and he saw the relief spread over her face. She wiped at her eyes, then walked sedately to meet him. He could tell she was burning with questions, but she only smiled as he came to her, kissed her lips and put his arm around her as he walked up to the porch.

"All right, Sandra, it's over, it's finished, and you'll never have to worry again. My dueling career has ended."

"I'm glad," she said, emotion welling up so quickly that she could hardly get the words out. "It's been a very long two hours since you left."

"Killing a man takes time," he said.

Her eyes came up quickly and saw his smile.

"No, I didn't kill him. Instead I tried to punish him for some of his sins."

He told her then exactly what had happened from the time he picked up Lynch. When he came to the actual position of the shot, he hesitated. She laughed softly.

"Husband, I have seen a man's organ, you know. Is he ruined so he can't scare our little girl again, as he did in church?"

He told her what Dr. Warren had said. She blushed in spite of herself and held her hands over her face, then hugged her husband.

Ben had never told her about Cunliffe's attempted rape of Harriet right there in the house. Now he never would.

"Woman, quit mewing around here and get me some breakfast!"

Soon Ben was sweetening a cup of black coffee with a lump from a sugar loaf in its traditional deep blue-purple paper wrapper. He had half a dozen slices of thick bacon just cut from the cured slab, and finished breakfasting with coarse brown bread topped with honey. Before he left for the office, he had his usual tankard of hard cider.

Ben drove, as usual, toward his business, where he would try to continue putting together the fortunes of Rutledge and Rutledge after the nearly ruinous way the Customs Commissioners had dealt with him for the last three months.

His first stop was before he came to the office, however. He parked in an alley half a mile from his place of business and walked part way along the narrow passage, then went through a gate and into a small rear yard where he opened a door and quickly climbed steps to a back apartment.

Ben knocked, then opened the door slowly

and saw the lovely face of Sadie Wythe.

She had been crying. Now fresh tears burst from her eyes and she flew to him, holding him so tightly he couldn't close the door.

"You're all right, you're all right!" she said. Then more tears came, stopping her words.

He pushed her into the room, closed the door and held her tightly. She wore only a light robe. Ben smiled, knowing she preferred to sleep naked. Evidently she had risen and slid into the robe as she waited for some word from him. When she leaned back, the tears had stopped, but they left wet streaks down her soft cheeks.

Sadie, nearing her twenty-first birthday, reached five feet, one inch tall and wore her pretty blonde hair long. Her face had sensitive green eyes, a tipped-up nose and a small but full-lipped mouth. He had met her in the Old Boston Book Shop one day when he and Jonathan were discussing politics. She had been of the same mind as they, and soon she was on the very inside of the Freedom Fighters movement. Later he had found out that her husband of less than a year had been struck down by smallpox six months before.

She hugged him again and looked up. "Oh, Ben, darling, I've been sitting here just waiting and waiting. I couldn't sleep all night, dreading the sunrise, the dawn, because I knew what would be happening. Oh, darling, I'm so happy, and I love you so much!"

She stretched up and kissed him, her tongue

brushing against his lips, her small body pressing close against his.

"Darling, I couldn't go to work until I knew. I couldn't work, and then I started crying. You don't know how I would have missed you." She paused and a frown crossed her face. "What about Cunliffe? Did you shoot him?"

"Wounded, but he'll recover." He told her exactly what the pistol ball did and she sighed.

"Perfect, that's just perfect. Retribution for an over amorous Romeo. It really serves him right."

She leaned away from him, her robe opening a little. Her face was radiant, her smile glowing.

"Dear, sweet, darling Ben! You don't know how happy, how delighted I am that you weren't wounded." She pulled her robe closed and kissed him again.

"Now I've got to go on to the office. I'm a businessman. But I wanted to stop and tell you what happened."

"If you hadn't, I would have shot you myself," she giggled. "What about some breakfast?"

"Thanks, I just had some." He took a step toward the door. "I'll see you tonight at the meeting?"

She nodded.

"But I don't think afterwards—I didn't get any sleep last night, either."

"Time for some coffee?" She had picked up a tin coffee pot and put it on the small wood stove.

Ben gave up and tossed his hat on a chair and straddled another. "Yes, time for coffee. Now, how is everything coming along with your Freedom Fighters' company?"

They talked for ten minutes about the Freedom Fighters as the coffee boiled. She said she would be at the meeting that night at Jonathan Clark's bookstore.

"Dr. Warren will pick me up as usual," she said. "It seems a shame to deceive him this way."

"The good Dr. Warren would chuckle and compliment me on my fine taste in picking such a delightfully figured woman," he said, patting her small, round bottom. "Now I must be going." He kissed her cheek, her eyes, and at last her mouth. Then he went out the door and down the steps without looking back.

When Ben arrived at his second floor office in Rutledge & Rutledge, he found several problems waiting for him. They were getting more orders for shipments now than in several months, as the embargo against all English goods fell apart. There had been a mixup in the communications from England concerning the Townshend duties, which broke down their own embargo. As he now understood it, the duties on all goods except tea had been repealed on March fifth. That was the day almost three months ago when the Boston Massacre had taken place. Ben had come upon it just after it happened. He had helped one of the wounded, a young man, only to watch him die in the slushy snow of the street.

That simple act of kindness had triggered an intense campaign of retribution against Ben and his company by the Royal Customs Commissioner, Jeffrey Trout, who confiscated three of his tall merchant ships, and then levied thousands of pounds in fines on his other vessels in a hit-or-miss attack that had brought the company close to bankruptcy. But he and his good friend John Hancock, of the wealthy shipping Hancocks, worked out a scheme so Hancock could buy the ships at an exclusive auction for ten English pounds each, and give them back to Ben. Now he had a solid day's work ahead of him if he wanted to keep the many aspects of his big firm under control and moving ahead. He had two good managers, but they needed help, advice, and guidance from time to time.

By four that afternoon he had settled a wrangle on board one of his ships in the harbor, helped resolve a dispute with a big important Boston shipper, and found a missing consignment of goods. He was thinking of asking one of the many shipyards around Boston to begin plans for two more tall ships for him, but he held off for the time. He was worried about the political scene as much as anything else.

Ben went home at four that afternoon to take his twin sons on a hunting trip. The light lasted longer now, and he had promised them a chance at some birds or a rabbit or two. His twin sons, Robert and David, were as unlike as twins could be. Robert, the older by nearly an hour, was the more serious. Rob was solid, steady and reliable. He seldom forgot things or lost them, did what he was told without argument, and took responsibility readily. The twins had just turned fourteen in April. If Robert had a fault it was that he was a bit of a plodder, not given to creative thought and more willing to be led than to lead.

David Lewis Rutledge sometimes seemed much too wise for his age. At times he would smile at his father in a certain knowing way that made Ben wonder if the boy might be the reincarnation of some ancient scholar or teacher. David was far more sensitive than his brother, much more easily hurt. At times he was brilliant in interesting and divergent fields. Ben had seen David draw a house, then show the specifications and details of how to construct it, what materials to use and where the load bearing stresses would come. David had never had any training in such matters.

Once Ben saw some poetry David had written that was quite good. Already he had a natural style and a touch and feeling for words that caught Ben by surprise.

At home Ben dusted off the Charleville 1763 Flintlock musket and took the usual supply of .69 caliber round balls, powder and wadding. The gun was just over five feet long and was hard for even a grown man to fire without a front support.

Robert loved the sport of hunting. David went along because he was asked to go, and Ben thought the lad realized that he should know the basics of hunting and woodsmanship. The first time Ben had taken the boys out for target practice, David outscored both Robert and his father. He was a natural with the long gun.

David and Ben drove toward the Charles River in the chaise. Robert wanted to ride his new horse. David was content to sit in the rig and watch the sky, trees and animals. They left the horses at the edge of the woods near the river and hunted for half an hour. David shot one rabbit at fifty yards, and Ben got another. Robert missed his one chance and pouted half the way home.

They ate the rabbit that night and gave the second one to a neighbor. Fresh meat was usually shared among several families, even in a well-to-do area such as Rontout street. If one of the neighbors killed a deer, it meant meat for everyone. This was the only practical way to treat a large amount of fresh meat which otherwise would spoil in a day or two unless it was cold enough to hang the carcass outside to freeze. Most of the town homes had no smokehouse or any way to salt down meat to preserve it.

Ben left the house just before seven that night, according to his big pocket watch which he had bought on a London trip. Timepieces of any kind were scarce in Boston in the 1770's. Most of them were large and complicated and tremendously expensive. The majority of people told time by the church bells or by the sun.

Ben walked up to the Old Boston Book Shop a little after seven o'clock and browsed at the table filled with expensively bound books. All were of English printing, rebound in leather. He said good evening to the owner, Mr. Jonathan Clark, then saw that no one else was in the shop.

"Any of the others arrived yet, Jonathan?"

"Lewis is upstairs."

"I'll go on up. It's been rather a full day for me."

"Yes, so I heard." Jonathan grinned. "I hear our Mr. Cunliffe won't be entertaining the floozies for a while."

"Yes, such an unfortunate shot," said Ben, his smile broadening.

Jonathan chuckled and checked to be sure the alley door was locked. When he came back, Ben went through a curtain into the rear of the store, where the living quarters were. After going past one more curtain, Ben climbed the narrow, steep and dark stairs to the light at the top. He stepped into a room without windows, lit by two candles in holders and a Betty lamp. Lewis Lynch looked up from his work of polishing a new flintlock pistol.

"Ain't she a beauty, sir?"

Ben took it and admired the sleek cherrywood handle, the fine workmanship and the heavy barrel.

"If only they would shoot straighter," Ben said. "Some day a man will invent a gun barrel that will make the ball fly straight and true. I've thought on it, but I certainly have no idea what the principle might be. How can you improve on a perfect circle such as a musket or pistol ball?"

The two men were still talking about it ten minutes later when Dr. Warren and Sadie came into the room. Dr. Warren was his usual lean, smiling self. He was a tall man with fair skin and light hair over intense blue eyes that evaluated everything and everyone with a critical understanding. He had graduated from Harvard in 1759, studied medicine in Boston and entered practice in 1764. Dr. Warren was a fast-rising power in Whig political circles and a friend of most of the colony's ruling body. He was also the best doctor in town.

They greeted each other, and a moment later Jonathan Clark had shuttered his shop and joined them, closing and locking the door that led into the room from the stairs. They sat around a rough-hewn table in the windowless room. The Betty lamp with its hook dangling beside the handle was on the table. It was little more than a shallow iron dish with a curved upright handle which held a chain and hook. In the lamp a metal bracket pushed upright a coarse wick from the whale oil and gave off a dull, smoking and ill-smelling flame. But they were all used to the smoke and the odor.

The group sat on benches, and each extended a hand to the center of the table, fists closed. One by one they opened their hands, palms up. In each was a small gold coin.

"Freedom or death," they all said together. Then the coins with their Freedom Fighter slogans engraved on them were tucked away in secret pockets or places in clothing where they would not be soon found, and the Freedom Fighters Council meeting began.

Ben started it as the general leader. "It's good to be here and see all of you. I wasn't sure this morning if I would even have this opportunity again. But that matter is resolved, and we need not discuss it further. In fact, I would appreciate it if we did not. Mr. Lynch, I believe you should bring us up to date on the state of our manpower, our arms and our ability to put up a fight if need be."

"Yes, sir, Mr. Rutledge. Our current five companies are holding at near strength. I have nineteen men in mine, and we total ninety-five, who can be armed and available in two hours' notice. We're holding at that strength, as the council decided recently, until this present state of peace and prosperity passes. We, sir, would like to ask permission for another target practice match in a month or so, to keep the lads sharp."

Ben looked around the table. Several nodded in agreement.

"I think that's the will of the council," Ben said. "Work out a time and place, and get everyone informed."

"That's about it, sir. We're ready and waiting. Our ball is ready and our powder dry."

"Thank you, Mr. Lynch."

Ben had been pleased with the formation of the five companies, each one commanded by one member of the five-man council. They had recruited slowly and carefully, finding reliable men who believed as they did. Each man had to furnish and arm himself with a flintlock musket and pistol, and he had to become and stay proficient with the weapons. They met monthly for training and instruction. Sadie commanded a company, just as the four men did, and easily won the marksmanship contest in her group of twenty men. They had cheered her on and she named the second highest man as her lieutenant.

Ben looked over at the doctor. "Dr. Warren?"

The young physician stood and prowled the room as he spoke. "As we had heard, the Townshend duties were repealed, to our surprise, on the exact date of the Boston Massacre, March fifth. As usual, it was some time before we heard the news and got the true facts. But the duties are off now for sure, on everything except tea. I would guess that might produce some conflicts before long. If it does, we must be ready, and even assist it. For now we can settle back and reflect on our legislative victory. We have not convinced Parliament that she has no power to regulate us with laws, but we have in effect forced that same Parliament to rescind a law which the colonials found particularly repugnant.

"However, as we figured more than a month ago, such a move by the British would cause more trade, more prosperity here at home. We can again buy our nails, building materials, brocades, laces, and all those small and delicious food items we have missed recently from Mother England. All this means reduced tensions between us and Parliament, and England. There will be a more relaxed tone by the British troops still illegally quartered here, and fewer restrictions and a more lenient enforcement of the trade laws. This will be good for the people, good for those of us who consume and deal in trade and shipping. Which is a rather long-winded way to say we're in for a serious siege of peace."

The five faces around the table were set, discouraged. Ben knew he had to rally them.

"Friends, I know this is a setback for our cause, for the coming revolution, but it will pass. England will make another serious mistake, and when she does, we will be ready. All of us know that when a real revolution takes place, it must come from the hearts of the people. The general population must be of a common mind and rise up and truly rebel and throw the invaders out. It must be an honest revolution of the masses. If we talked about freedom from England right now, we would interest only a handful of our politicians and less than one percent of our population. We must work beneath the surface, and we must work effectively. Our sole importance isn't our hundred armed men and women. It's giving leadership to the forward motion of the revolution."

"But what can we do now?" asked Lynch.

"Dr. Warren, any ideas on that?" Ben followed.

The physician sat on the bench and twisted. "I have been thinking that we should send out a second report to our friends around the colonies about the state of health of those wounded during the Massacre. This would be one more barb in the hide of the English Parliament, and would help keep alive the memory of the incident, and the patriots who died there."

The council quickly approved the idea, and asked Dr. Warren to write the letters, have them copied by a public writer or printed if the quantity made it necessary. They were to be sent by the regular mail post or with known travelers who might deliver them by hand. Any expenses should be noted and reimbursement from the "Trout Treasury" would be made.

Mrs. Wythe spoke up.

"I'm more concerned than ever about the

antics of the revenue ship *Richard* that has been hounding our small farmers around the waterways and bays and on the Charles. I've mentioned this before. This Captain Capspree is little more than a pirate, a scoundrel and a villain. He kills farmers' animals, takes over homes, and has ransacked a small village. I'm in favor of some serious thoughts as to how we can punish him or at least show that we strongly disapprove of his actions."

Everyone had a say about Captain Capspree, then Ben took the floor.

"It does seem that we should now consider some action against this sea dog. Lewis, see what you can find out about the movements of the ship, the number of men on board and how they are armed, how many cannon—the usual intelligence needed for a military operation with a striking force."

"Aye, aye, sir!" Lynch said, with a grin. "It'll be a real pleasure, sir!"

Jonathan brought up the matter of quartering troops in Boston, but it was felt that little could be done about it. The British were there under Parliamentary law, even though it was a bad law. The matter was tabled for further study. The meeting ended.

It was near supper time when Sadie decided to try the emergency assembly system she had worked out for the fifth company of the Freedom Fighters. She put on a shawl, walked to the corner of her street and went into the tin goods dealer. Mr. Rausch had not yet closed. There was no one else in the store.

"Good evening, Mr. Rausch. How are you tonight?"

"Just fine, captain, and you?"

She said she was well. "Mr. Rausch, we're having an emergency assembly of our company as soon as we can near the dueling oaks. You launch the operation by contacting how many other men?"

"I get in touch with two, and they each talk to two more and each of them contacts three more. Is it a real emergency or just an exercise?" Harland Rausch's eyes glistened with excitement. Already he was taking off the heavy apron he wore to protect his clothes. He was a rangy man, strong, supple, heavily bearded. He was also the second worst shot in her company. They walked to the front door.

"An exercise? We'll both find out about that when we get to the oaks, won't we? Good day." She went out and he locked the door behind her.

Sadie walked swiftly back to her apartment and changed into the clothes she had laid out earlier. For her Freedom Fighters action work she always wore men's clothes, heavy trousers with a wide belt, sturdy shoes, a small-sized man's shirt and a loose fitting cotton work shirt over that to hide her figure. On her head sat a black and white three-cornered cap, covering all of her long blonde hair.

Sadie left her apartment by the back door, went through the alley and walked swiftly to the livery stable two blocks over, where she hurriedly saddled a small bay she had arranged to have available, and rode back to her alley. There she took a heavy flintlock musket from its hiding place in the ground-level shed, looped the powder horn over her head and fastened the leather boxes containing ball and packing to her belt.

Then she rode out.

Late afternoon strollers along the Boston streets thought nothing of what appeared to be a young man riding out of town on a summer afternoon with a flintlock musket balanced over one shoulder, on the way to do some hunting. If a family wanted fresh meat for the table, someone had to ride into the country to shoot it.

Sadie was not used to riding, and by the time she came to the oaks she was beginning to feel sore in her legs and rump, but she sat her saddle with pride as she reined in at the big trees and found six men already on hand.

At once she ordered them to hide their mounts in the deeper woods, and to set up a patrol situation where they would lie in ambush for the next of their company to arrive and capture them. The men dispersed where she indicated, hiding behind good cover and concealment of rocks, trees and bushes. Before the last man was fully concealed, they saw a pair of riders coming down the river road. Sadie slid behind a tree out of sight and waited for them. Sure enough, they turned in toward the oaks, rode to the trees and dismounted. One of the men was her second in command, Lt. Arnold Compton, the one who had challenged her for leadership of the company and lost in a shoot-out. She had promptly promoted him to second in the company.

Sadie smiled and signaled to the first man in line who raised his flintlock, aiming in the air. The word jumped along the semi-circular line around the two riders until all six weapons came up.

"Surrender and strike your weapons!" Sadie shouted, and at once the two center Freedom Fighters stood, their long guns aimed at the new pair.

Lieutenant Compton swore softly, lifting his hands. His companion did, too.

Half the men in the ambush burst out laughing at the surprise on the men's faces. Sadie shouted at them to be quiet. On her signal the closest man ran forward, stayed out of the line of fire and took the flintlocks and pistols from both men who, while surprised, relaxed when they recognized a man from their own company.

Sadie called out again, and the other ambushers came out of their positions.

Lt. Compton pushed back his small-billed

cap and grinned.

"Very neat, Captain. You took us completely by surprise."

"The point is, we shouldn't have, Lieutenant. You were riding to an assignment. You didn't know if it was a drill or a real engagement. From now on, every mission is real unless it is specified in advance as a target meet. How many of you men have loaded your flintlocks and are ready to fire?"

Two held up their hands.

"After this, whenever you are called out, be sure that your weapons are ready to fire before you get on your horses. Is that understood?"

They nodded.

"Now, Lieutenant Compton. Pick five men and take them well upstream, then turn and come back toward us as if you are on the attack. I want you to come through those woods as silent as Indians. If we see you, we'll put a musket ball into a tree over your heads, then you come on in. If we don't see you and you get within fifty yards of us, you win the two bottles of rum."

That brought a cheer from the group.

Lt. Compton selected his men and then talked to Sadie.

"Just where in the hell . . . begging your pardon, ma'am . . ."

She stopped him.

"Lieutenant Compton, I've heard more swear words, vile language and vulgar talk than you ever will. If it's natural for you to swear, you go right ahead. I really don't mind."

"I'll be damned!" he said, laughing. "Well, I wanted to know where you grew up, and where you got all this know-how about fighting."

"I grew up on the frontier, on the fringes of the wilderness, and if a person couldn't shoot straight, she didn't stay alive very long. We had frequent Indian visitors."

"And you shot your share of them?"

She stared at him coolly. "Lieutenant, that's like asking your betrothed how many different men she's made love to."

"That don't mean beans to me. I'm not even promised."

"You have your orders, Lieutenant." She turned and positioned one of her men in a new ambush position nearer the road. She had the man prime his musket but not load a ball, so the weapon would make a fierce noise but send no projectile. She sent the last man in her command a hundred yards upstream as a forward scout toward the direction from which Lt. Compton would probably be attacking them. Then she joined the ambush, her own flintlock primed and loaded with powder and packing but no ball.

As they waited in the ambush, they talked in whispers, and soon they heard the pounding of hooves on the river road from town. Three horsemen came, followed by four more. They all turned into the dueling grounds. She had given her man instructions to fire only on her command and then to aim into the air so there could be no chance of powder burns from the flash of the primers.

Sadie waited until all seven had come up to her first ambush man, then she shouted: "Fire!" Two muskets discharged in a sudden blast that sent the seven men into scattered confusion. One man was thrown from his mount. Another rider's horse bolted.

Quickly the attackers stood and identified themselves, and the men brought their animals under control and rode to where Sadie stood. She had them dismount and tie their horses, then sent her last man forward to reinforce the scout waiting for the expected attack.

She paced in front of the newly arrived seven. "How many of you have had militia training?" All but two held up their hands. "Good. Now, how many of you have your weapons ready to fire?" No hands showed.

"Gentlemen, I realize we are not at war, but this was a readiness operation, a surprise call-out to see how you reacted. So far, only two out of fourteen of you have come ready to fight— with their weapons loaded and primed. After this, on any call-out or assembly, we will assume *it is not a drill*, until told otherwise, and we will come as follows: provisions for three days, ball and powder for fifty rounds, and weapons ready to fire."

She paced again. "Lieutenant Compton is in

the process of attacking our position. We'll have to deploy you men to help repel him. Prime your pieces now, but do not load a ball. That way we'll get the effect of firing without any danger."

She watched as the men primed their weapons.

"How many of you have had combat experience against the French or the Indians?"

No one had. She sighed. "When fighting Indians, or in the hit-and-run type of operation we most probably will use, it is always best to keep yourselves spread out, dispersed. Then one lucky cannon ball can't wipe out a squad. When you're spread out you make a number of small and hard to hit targets, instead of one big, easy one. The British haven't learned this lesson. They continue their massive cadence count attacks. Summary—when in action, spread out, keep low, take advantage of any rocks, trees, walls or buildings you can for protection, and be ready to fire your weapons at all times."

She paced again. "Now, Lieutenant Compton may expect us to think he's attacking from the same direction he went upstream. He won't. He'll not be able to cross the marsh, so he'll try slanting to the right or left and hit us from one side. Brockingham, you take three men and spread out at ten-yard intervals at the very edge of the oaks to the river road. Keep your eyes open. If you spot Compton or his men, try to take them by surprise and capture them. Otherwise shoot over their heads and push them back."

When Brockingham had left, she took the last three men and covered her right flank all the way to the river. She pushed fifty yards toward Lieutenant Compton's expected location and concealed everyone.

Fifteen minutes later Compton hit both flanks at about the same time. He was surprised on each one, expecting the main body to be in the center. His men on the right flank were overpowered and legally "captured" without a shot. On the left side, Compton had been fired upon by two of the men there with primer only, and had been so surprised he forgot that he was loaded with ball and nearly returned the fire. He came into the assembly point five minutes later, smarting from the failure.

"Lieutenant Compton, that was a good move," said Sadie. "You used your head and did not try to push through a known fortified position. You tried to outflank it, and normally it would have worked, only I guessed correctly. If you had sent all your men one way, you would have outnumbered us two to one and won the fight and could have pushed on to your main objective."

It was nearly dusk. She made a final count and found she had in all sixteen men. Not bad, out of eighteen, and on a special surprise call-out.

"Are there any questions about this operation?"

"Yes. Can we make a fire?"

She said they could.

"Did you really bring some rum?" someone asked.

She had her horse brought around and took out two big jugs of rum from her saddle bags. The jugs had been waiting there for two weeks. As the fire blazed up, they passed the jugs from hand to hand, and then asked her about fighting the Indians.

For an hour she told them about life on the farm, where every farmer had his flintlock at his side as he worked the fields, where every log cabin had firing slots in it and double doors and double window shutters. She told of seeing four of their neighbors burned out by Indians, and one whole family slaughtered because they refused to fight back. That was when her father taught his whole family how to shoot, and kept them at it until all could hit a "V" target at a hundred yards.

"I was thirteen the last time the Indians attacked us. Father was in the field when he heard the first shot. He came, running low, to the house, helped us slam the last of the double doors and the double window shutters, and then we each went to our assigned shooting slots. As it turned out, there were only four savages. They were drunk on rum. We killed two of them before they realized they were up against six flintlocks. When they sobered up enough, they stole one of our horses and both rode off on it. They even lost the rifle they had stolen."

"Did you kill any Indians, Captain?" a voice asked.

"That's not really a fair question. If I say yes, you'll think of me as a braggart. If I say no, you'll think I'm lying and my stories are just so much talk. That question is the same as if I asked you if you were still a virgin."

The last word brought hoots, shouts and peals of laughter as the questioner was pummeled and jostled in his spot by the fire.

"Now," she said, when they quieted down, "are there any more questions about the operation? We must be an efficient fighting force if we are needed. We'll be hit-and-run, Indian-type fighters if we have the chance. That way more of us will live, and more of the enemy will die. At first we may only be used as a show of force, but even to do that we must be ready and willing to fight, to fire, and to do it quickly."

There were more questions—about how to keep powder dry and fresh, how to store a flint-lock, and the best way to clean and oil it. Most of them had pistols now, as well, and there were several questions about them. Sadie turned the weapons questions over to Lieutenant Compton, who was a qualified expert. He had made several pistols in a small workshop on his farm. It was his snowy-weather hobby when farming duties dropped to almost nothing. A week after Sadie had beaten him in the shooting competition, he had presented her with one of his handcrafted, numbered Compton Flintlock pistols as a gift. It was number eleven.

Shortly after the questions were over, the men brought up the horses, put out the fire, and rode as a group back toward town. They went as a cavalry unit, three horses wide in five rows, with those at the rear who would drop out first to go to surrounding farms and villages. One excited farmer riding toward them thought he had run into a British mounted patrol. Lieutenant Compton laughed at the idea and convinced him they were only a hunt club coming back to town after an outing.

Lieutenant Compton stayed by Sadie's side as she rode. Her long blonde hair was still hidden under her hat and she looked much like any of the other Freedom Fighters.

As the troops peeled off to go to their homes, Lieutenant Compton stayed with Sadie and followed her all the way to the livery stable, where he unsaddled her horse and put fresh straw in the stall.

"You really don't have to pamper me," Sadie said. "I've cleaned out my stall and taken care of horses half my life."

"Then you won't mind a little help, Captain."

She looked around for the stable hands, but they hadn't heard him. "Sadie. My name is Sadie."

He walked her to her front gate and took her hand.

"Sadie, I'd like to come calling."

"I'm a widow, Mr. Compton."

"I know."

"The fact is, I'm involved with someone else right now. I don't know how it's going to turn out. Otherwise I really would enjoy seeing you, but I'm afraid that I just can't. We can be good friends, though, and we can still make this the best damn company in the whole troop."

He sighed, slapping the reins against the broad shoulders of his horse. "Aye, Miss Sadie, we can be good friends and we will have a fine company. But I'll be waiting my chance with you as well, and I hope some day it will come." He touched his hat and mounted his horse.

For a moment he watched her, a smile softening his face, then he was gone, riding down the street.

Chapter Two
A CHILD OF LOVE

That Sunday evening late in May, Ben Rutledge sat in his parlor watching his family. Harriet dutifully stitched on some pillow covers her mother insisted she have ready and waiting in her wedding chest. Robert whittled with a new pocket knife on a soft piece of pine, trying to make the hull of a ship. David sat reading a book which looked like it came from Ben's small library. Occasionally David would stare off into space for a few moments, then continue reading.

In the chair on the far side of the room, Sandra rocked slowly back and forth. Now and then her glance rested on each of her children, and her face seemed to overflow with tenderness.

For a moment Ben wondered why he was so blessed, so fortunate to be born into a family with a head start on the rest of the world. The family company, the money had made the initial difference, but in his own defense he had made the firm grow, nearly doubled it since he took over. He had expanded dock and warehouse facilities, bought a dozen more ships, and weathered the storm of the Customs Commissioners. Now it looked like it was fair winds astern and easy sailing ahead. And this family! No one had caused him any grief or any problems. Harriet was growing into such a lovely young lady that it made him wonder what the fates might have in store for her. Such a beauty, such a figure, so slender and well-formed. Already her beauty had resulted in a few minor problems, but the cause had not been Harriet. The root of it all had been Cunliffe. Now that was over and behind him. The twins were certainly on course, growing up quickly and gracefully, with vigor and continual interest in the world around them. Already he could see that Robert would be the one to go into the business, and he should do well, eventually taking over the entire operation. David? Ben had no idea what David might do for his life's work: poet, philosopher, scholar, even a lawyer.

Ben watched Sandra working on some needlepoint—another chair cover, he decided. She was such a fine lady, a wonderful mother, a loyal and sensitive wife. There was little he would not do to keep her from harm.

The nagging doubts assailed him. How could he think that when he knew very well he *was* doing something already that would hurt this woman dreadfully if she knew? How could he face himself in the mirror to shave each morning, knowing that he had both a wife and a mistress.

Ben had battled with the dilemma often during the past nine months, and each time he had come up with the same answer. "It is possible to love two women at the same time, to hold them both in the highest esteem, to cherish and love each, and to hold no ill feelings, no jealousies, to make no comparisons and no adverse judgements about either one." His love for his wife knew no bounds, was all-consuming and endless. His desire, his passion and his love for Sadie Wythe was just as deep, as intense, and just as endless.

For most men this would be an impossible situation: ". . . thou shalt either love the one and hate the other . . ." To Ben it was exactly like the love a father and mother have for a first-born child. Their love and devotion to the baby is total, all-encompassing, forever. Then later another child comes along and again the love from the parents is total, all-encompassing and forever. The love for the second in no way lessens the love of the parents for the first child, or the third or fifth. Loving his two women seemed to him to be parallel with a parent loving all his children. It was the correct conclusion and the ideal way to operate his life—even if part of it must be lived in secret and isolation.

Ben watched the family a moment more, put down his newspaper and remembered one of the new games a captain had brought back from England with his ship. It was called dominoes.

He went to his den and came back with the box.

"I don't think any of you have ever seen this game. It's rather new, just arrived on a boat from England. It's called dominoes. No, Sandra, it's not a hood the monks used to wear. Here, let's move the small table over so we all can sit around it and I'll show you how it's played. There are several ways to score, as I understand."

They all came to look at the wooden blocks when he emptied them out of the box. They were oblong, black on one side and divided on the other with chips of ivory glued on them. Each had from one to six chips on each half, except for a few that were totally blank on one half. He spread them out and explained it the way the captain had told him.

They played for an hour, keeping track of who had the least "count" on the dominoes left in his hand when someone went out. When it was over, David had won all three games. Robert looked at him sourly and stalked off to bed.

Sandra caught the look and saw her husband frown slightly.

"Well, that's an interesting game. I enjoyed it. Congratulations, David, for picking up the idea so quickly. You're good with figures, do you know that?"

"Yes, sir. It comes easy for me."

"David, have you wondered about what you might want to do when you come into your majority?"

"No, sir, not really. A lot of things interest me."

"Like what, David?"

"Well, medicine. I'd like to spend a few days with Dr. Warren, if I could, before school starts. It's one profession I've thought about. Then, I like to write. It would be smashing to be a famous poet, only that's a sure way to starve and be in the scuppers all the time. I had thought of learning how to play an organ, but we don't have one."

"A pipe organ, such as we have in our church?"

"Yes, I'd like that."

"Well, we will certainly consider it, David. Perhaps you could practice at the church. Have you ever thought about architecture, drawing plans for houses, buildings?"

"Not as work—that's just for fun. It's a kind of a game I play to see how I can make buildings look different, yet still get the support beams in the right places so they won't fall down."

"You seem to have a talent for this also, David. It's a gift that few have, you know. You might consider architecture, as well, on your list of possibilities."

"Very well, Father, if you wish me to." He looked at his sister, and while his parents were glancing at each other, he stared at the cleavage that showed over the bodice of her dress.

Harriet saw his open gaze and she smiled.

Brother David seemed to be growing up so much faster than Robert. At least David was to the point of wondering what lay beneath her clothes.

David stood. "I hope we can play your game again some evening, Father. It was fun. I'm going up to my room now."

They watched him kiss his mother good night, dutifully peck his sister on the cheek, then shake his father's hand and run for the stairs.

The three sat there, each deep in personal thought.

Sandra watched her husband fill his pipe. Was any woman as lucky as she? She had everything any woman could want: a true and loyal husband; enough wealth to make life easy so they could afford household help; time to dabble in a charity or two, and three delightful children who were all growing up so quickly and in the very best way possible.

Oh, how she loved her man! She knew some women who didn't even like their husbands, so they were trapped. Ben was the perfect husband, father and bedmate. She felt a glow as she remembered last week when he had awakened her in the night and deliberately kissed her breast. He was so gentle, so attentive, and he could make her body want to surge into flight just by touching her in certain places. Sandra shivered, remembering.

She watched now, alert for any service she

might do for him, any small item she might get. But he had his pipe and tobacco. She had never liked the smell of a pipe, but now she was used to it and hardly noticed it. She went back to her needlepoint. Only a few more rows and the pattern would start to take shape. That was the part she loved best.

Harriet watched her parents for a moment, but they both seemed to be thinking extremely hard, or about to go to sleep, she wasn't sure which.

She wondered if they would make love tonight when they went to bed. She'd been thinking a lot about making love and how it would feel. Yes, she *was* curious—after all, she was almost eighteen. Lots of girls had two babies by this time. Now, that would be something, a baby! Yet she had no real desire to get married and have a house to take care of and right away start raising a family. Somehow it didn't appeal to her at all. There were so many places she wanted to go first: to London on one of her father's ships, then to Paris. Oh, the wonderful things she had heard about Paris!

She looked over at her mother. Did her mother make love every night? Well . . . after all, she did undress in the same room with her husband, and they must look at each other, so wouldn't that get them excited? Or perhaps they undressed at different times, or in different parts of the room. Perhaps every night would be too often. She'll have to ask her cousin Jennifer

Bull. They were almost the same age, and they were good friends. Often they spent the night at each other's homes and talked and talked until the candle burned out. Jennifer just might know.

Harriet felt a little shiver tingle along her spine as she thought about Edmund Cunliffe. He had known exactly what he wanted. Even now she wasn't sure how to describe her feelings at the time he began tearing off her clothes. He had been savage, brutal, and that had excited her. Yes, now she could admit that much. She had been sexually stimulated when he ripped off her red and white shirtwaist and touched her bare breasts. It had been like lightning striking her, and she had been so awed by it momentarily that she forgot to fight him. He didn't hurt her. Since that time she had wondered a hundred times what would have happened if her father hadn't come home just then. Cunliffe would have stripped her naked, then held her down and . . . and raped her. She gave a deep sigh and went back to stitching the hem of the pillowcase. She had embroidered a butterfly on this one, and was now finishing it with a tiny-stitched hem that looked most professional.

Maybe she would never feel what it was like to make love. Perhaps she would be an old maid, and dry up and get mean and cruel and nasty—yes, and ugly, too. She smiled as she thought about that. No, she would have no trouble finding a man to marry when she wanted to. Already she had discouraged four young swains from courting her. She simply said she wasn't ready, and her father had politely told their parents it wasn't time yet. She did enjoy the bold stares she got sometimes on the street, even when she walked with her mother. Men knew she was around, all right. But she really didn't want to think about marriage. Not yet.

She sighed, put away her sewing things in a small basket with a reed bottom and a stitched bag on top with a drawstring. She made certain the needle was secure, then pulled the string and said she was going up to her room.

"Well, it's almost bedtime anyway, dear," her mother said. "Good night, and pleasant dreams."

Her father mumbled a good night. He was concentrating on his political newspaper again, *The Speaker*. He read it most of the time he was home. Harriet looked at it once and found the writing as dull as a dusty dandelion. She didn't see how he could stand it.

In her room, Harriet lit a second candle, then pushed the small bolt locking her door and undressed. She slipped into a long, thin nightgown and put her clothes away. In the very bottom of her small dresser she saw the red and white taffeta waist. It had been ripped in half. She held it for a moment, looked at the torn cloth, and tried to revive some of the excitement of that day, but this time it wouldn't come back. She folded the waist carefully and hid it deep in the drawer. It was the one she had been wearing when Cunliffe attacked her, the one her father had told her to burn, but she had saved it. She wasn't exactly sure why.

Harriet lay on her bed. It was a warm evening, and she didn't need the thick comforter. She pulled up the sheet and lay there, staring at the ceiling, still wondering how it would feel to make love. At last she blew out the candles and went to sleep.

Monday slid by slowly for Ben as he worked at his business, accepting orders, straightening out problems, trying to load each of his ships the best way for each trip. When he arrived at the meeting room over the bookstore, he was tired and ready for a change of pace.

Lewis Lynch was full of information about the *Richard*.

"The revenue ship is constantly on the prowl. There are three such vessels along the Atlantic coast, but none is as active as the *Richard*. Her captain has levied fines of more than five thousand pounds in the last six months. The only other revenue ship to assess any fines has a total of eighty-four pounds."

"What about her captain, this Capspree?" Ben asked.

"Captain Rothan Capspree is a career naval officer, and he is absolutely outraged because he has been assigned to such a small ship with no real fighting duties. He is determined to make a name for himself anyway."

"Well, we should be able to help him along on that score," Ben said. "What about her arms?"

"She's a sixty-footer, a two-master with a normal complement of twenty men and two officers. She draws eight feet and has two four-pound cannon on board battened down, one fore and one aft. The men have Brown Bess flintlocks and a few pistols."

"Nothing sounds unreasonable so far," Dr. Warren said. "What about her schedule? Does she make regular runs?"

"That's the worst part, sir," Lynch went on. "She is strictly on call and casual. She might be in port for two days or a week, then sweep from down the bay and the Charles River the next day. No set runs, no way to tell where she might be from one day to the next."

Dr. Warren scowled, then lifted his light-colored eyebrows.

"I guess that makes our job that much harder," Dr. Warren said. "But perhaps we could make our plans, and then spring at the *Richard* when it came to a certain point, when she comes to the place we want her."

Ben listened with interest. "Lewis, you say she draws eight feet? Much of the back bay and most of the Charles isn't anywhere that deep at low tide. It does give one ideas, doesn't it?"

"Aye, sir. Ground her somewhere."

"Exactly. Is it then the will of this council that we take action against the *Richard*, with the intent of destroying the vessel, but to do so with no loss of life on either side, if possible?"

A chorus of "ayes" came from the group.

"Mr. Lynch, I'm assigning you the responsibility of establishing the council's navy. I have a craft of which I believe we can alter the appearance, to fool the revenue ship and cause it grievous harm. We'll proceed with that tomorrow morning. Now, Dr. Warren, could we have a report from you on the political and economic situation of the colony?"

Dr. Warren nodded, and stood. "Mrs. Wythe, and gentlemen. As you know, the political tenor of the colony has moderated markedly since the repeal of the Townshend duties. More people are smiling, more people are now and soon will be working again. The state of the economy of our colony is rising, and with it the contentment of the population.

"We are still under the imperial heel of England. Still have troops quartered in our buildings. We have redcoats walking our streets, 'protecting' us from heaven knows what, but most certainly backing up the authority of the Customs Commissioners and the revenue ships such as the *Richard*.

"There is much mumbling and grumbling in the assembly, but I deem nothing will come of it. We have a good number of strong English supporters in our legislature, and they hold considerable influence. This is a slack time in the fortunes of those of us who hope eventually to win our freedom from the tyrant in England. It has long been my strong belief that the English government simply is not constituted correctly to rule half the globe, as it tries to do. The politicians in Parliament are more concerned with the problems of turnpikes in Yorkshire than with taxes in the colonies.

"Most of those in Parliament, I am told by Dr. Franklin, wouldn't give a farthing for the enforcement of the navigation acts in the colonies. The whole idea of the acts was to restrict our imports of manufactured goods so we could buy them only from England. Then her merchants could line their pockets. We can also only sell our raw products to her so she can manufacture them and ship them back to us at a staggering profit.

"As you all know, the strict administration of the colonies has been left to the king, who turned it over to his Secretary of State for the Southern Department. The secretary left it up to the Board of Trade and Plantations, a sort of advisory board with little power. The Board of Trade suggests to the Secretary of State what he should do. He tells the Royal Governors who hold sway in each of our thirteen colonies. The Royal Governors then tell the colonists what they must do, and by that time the original idea is so distorted and out of touch with reality that we colonists go ahead and do as we please.

"At least the system has allowed the colonies to develop a strong measure of reliable, practical self-government. I doubt if in any other colonial settlement around the world there is the freedom for self-government that we have here. England has prepared us for our freedom by her very laxity. She has set us up with legislative bodies and a group of judges and courts. She has given us the right to vote and to elect these legislators. She has even insisted that we have our own trained and armed militia. None of these obvious preparations for total independence has been done under cover or by stealth. No, indeed, the British Lion lay lapping up our bounty and letting our pretty political entities form and develop. In fact, Mother England encouraged it, because then she didn't need to waste troops and administrators in the American colonies. It is unique in the annals of colonialism, and of course, it is a gigantic and stupid blunder which will eventually cost England her greatest prize in the world, all of the North American continent."

Dr. Warren had been pacing as he spoke. He laughed now, wiped one hand across his handsome face. "I'm sorry. I sounded as if I was before a high bench somewhere, arguing for a convicted felon, or trying to get a bill passed through the assembly. But these are my thoughts and my beliefs. We have only to watch, wait and be ready. If we are ready, we will win. There is no way under God's golden sky and green countryside we can fail."

He sat down and wiped his forehead with a kerchief. "My final suggestion: that we go ahead with the *Richard* surprise, hit her with whatever our action department says, and that we continue to watch for similar situations where we can take effective action. We must keep our powder ready at all times."

Ben stood up as Dr. Warren finished. "Thank you, Dr. Warren. It's always interesting to hear your counsel for the group on political matters. We're glad we have a contact with the highest leadership of the Whigs here in Boston, and know that you will keep us informed of any moves that we should know about affecting our situation." Ben sipped a cup of the tea which Jonathan had brought around for each of them a short time before.

"Now, Jonathan, we haven't heard from you. How is our intelligence section?"

"Lately the flow of young officers into my establishment has increased. I've managed to get the finest collection of military manuals and books available anywhere in the colonies from what I've been told.

"Some of the younger officers are astounded. As they talk I do pick up bits and pieces, but nothing so far that has any real value. There's more talk of pulling out the last two regiments of redcoats and sending them back to England, or perhaps into the Caribbean. But so far it's a wait and watch situation."

Ben looked at Sadie, and it was all he could do to keep a secret smile from breaking over his face. "Mrs. Wythe, have you any reports?"

"I'm keeping my journal of the outrages of the British upon our land and people. But they seemed to be tapering off, except for the *Richard*. Dr. Warren's letter concerning the Massacre of March fifth has been printed and thirty copies sent on their way to newspapers in all the colonies. The costs have been deducted from our Trout Treasury, and the bookkeeping duly recorded."

Ben looked around the table. "That seems to be all for tonight. Mr. Lynch and I will keep you alerted about our preparations for launching our own navy, and how and where we will plan the confrontation between these two mighty ships of war. I expect it can't happen before our next meeting since we'll need several days to get ready. The timing will then be up to Captain Capspree and his trips."

The meeting broke up then, and Ben went below with Jonathan for their usual tankard of ale. They rehashed the meeting, and got around to remembering the wild, violent days when both had been members of the Sons of Liberty. Back in 1765, it had been an experiment in vigilante action that failed mainly due to the excesses of the participants.

Five minutes later, Ben said good night and drove away. He wheeled his chaise down several streets to an alley where he often stopped, and tied the reins. Soon he was through the gate and up the stairs, pushing open the back door of Sadie's apartment.

She stood by the stove, heating water for tea. Sadie had come up the front way only a few minutes before. She had spent ten minutes in quiet conversation with Dr. Warren, explaining to him that she simply couldn't go out with him. She was still officially in mourning, and besides, there was someone else. She decided that she had been convincing, and they had parted as good friends.

She had taken the coals from a small, tightly closed, heavy tin box where she had stored several that morning after her breakfast fire. With luck there would be one or two alive and ready to burn again. By the time Ben came in she had the water boiling briskly and had just put in the tea leaves. She took the pot off the heat.

Usually she ran to him, but tonight she waited by the stove. He caught her shoulders and kissed her, then picked her up and swung her around.

"We're going to take care of your revenue ship. Aren't you pleased?"

"Yes, of course." Her arms were around his neck to hold on and she reached up and brushed her lips across his cheek. He had shaved before he came to the meeting and she detected a faint trace of soap on his skin.

Ben put her down and let her finish making the tea. He sat at the table and watched her.

She was so graceful, so trim and youthful. "I'm a very lucky man, do you realize that, Sadie Wythe?"

"Lucky? Why so? Because you have two women you can flit between whenever you wish?"

He sensed a problem, and tried to go around it. "No, darling, of course not. I'm lucky that I can be with you, know you and love you, be in the Freedom Fighters with you."

"And that you can bed me?"

"Yes, that's part of it . . ."

"Don't you get enough loving from your wife?"

Ben stood and walked to her. This was not at all like the confident, strong Sadie Wythe he knew. He put his arms around her and felt her stiffen, then she began to sob and cling to him, the pot of tea forgotten. The tears continued as he picked her up and carried her into the small bedroom. He placed her on the bed and sat beside her, then lay down and held her in his arms, kissing her tear-stained face, waiting patiently. After a few minutes of crying, the tears stopped as suddenly as they had started. She brushed them away and sat up, looking at him seriously.

"I think it's time we had an important talk, Ben Rutledge."

He lay there, put his hands behind his head and watched her. Ben had been wondering when something like this would happen. Sadie wasn't a child, she was a grown woman, influenced by the traditions of marriage-husband-home. It was bound to affect her sooner or later. He smiled, not showing his doubts.

"Talk, yes, of course. Talk about the *Richard*?"

"No, Ben, not about that, about *us*. But it's not what you might be expecting. I don't want to destroy your family life, or hurt your wife or children. Ben, I want to have your baby."

She sat watching him, her green eyes glistening with unborn tears, her long hair half over one shoulder, hands folded in her lap, her lips slightly parted, her face alert and vulnerable.

Ben sat up quickly, concern flooding his face. "Are you—expecting, Sadie?"

She smiled. "No, Ben, no, darling Ben. Not yet, but I desperately want to have *your child*."

"But how could you . . . I mean, you aren't married . . . you couldn't stay here for your confinement."

She leaned over and kissed him. "Of course not, silly. But I *am* married, I have a legal and proper married name, I'm a respectable widow. I can go to my sister's house in New York. She's most understanding and forgiving, and no one else there would know just when my husband died, so there's no problem with that. Later we can work out some kind of arrangement. I could say I was bringing back my dead sister's child, or something." She touched his cheek gently. "Darling Ben, don't you see? I don't care if people *do* talk. I want a baby to hold and to see a part of you in his face, his hands, the way he walks. I want the baby my husband couldn't give me. I'm a woman, and it's my duty, my obligation to reproduce and help fill up this beautiful new land of ours, which will soon be free. Ben, I want a son who can grow up, so I can see a part of you and me living on. Then I'll know something of immortality, because his descendants will live forever. And one small part of me can go on with him. Does that sound unreasonable?"

Ben held her in his arms. "It's not only rational and understandable, it's the most beautiful way I've ever heard it said. Sadie, I love you, you know that, and you know I love and respect my wife and my family. I'll try never to do anything to harm or shame them. But I love you, too. We talked about how that was possible, remember?"

He pushed her back, kissed her lips, then frowned. "But sweetheart, how can you suddenly decide to have a child? Why haven't you these past nine months? I'm just a man. I don't understand the mysteries of these things."

She smiled. "Darling, before my husband died I went to see a doctor because I couldn't conceive. He explained some things to me about my body, and when and how would be the best time to make love so I would have the best chance to conceive. During the past nine months I have just reversed his suggestions and the timing. Then, too, he said I might continue to have trouble conceiving because of the way part of me is shaped or tipped, or something."

Ben touched her chin, then her cheeks. She was so precious, so beautiful, so amazingly like a man at times, yet now so different, so womanly. She wanted a baby. He should have expected that. Most women did want children. It was natural, it was normal. But she didn't demand what most women would—that he leave his wife and marry her.

"Benjamin, may I bear your child?"

He kissed her and pushed her gently back onto the bed. For a moment he lay on her, pushing her into the softness of the featherbed. Then he moved to one side and kissed her demandingly.

"Little Sadie, a captain does not ask another captain if she may do something. One captain is equal in rank to all other captains, and they work out any agreement on an even and level basis of equality. Darling Sadie, I would be proud to have you bear me a son or a daughter."

She threw her arms around him. "Oh, sweetheart, thank you, thank you!" Then her brows tightened. "Now, we must get started. I did some figuring, and from what the doctor said, I should be the most ready for you during the next four or five days. Is there some way you can get away from work on Tuesday and Wednesday? I'll have a sick headache and stay home. Then if you could come here Thursday night . . ."

"Four days in a row?"

"Yes, it's a theory this doctor was working on. He wasn't sure, of course, but he thought it would give me a better chance if we made love once a day these four days. Oh, he said one time each twenty-four hours would be best for a full month, but he said not many men could stand up to that for very long." She giggled. "I don't think I'd mind trying it, thought."

"Shame, Sadie. That's no way for a lady to talk."

"Tonight I don't want to feel like a lady, I'd rather feel like a wicked courtesan, or a naughty woman, one who desperately wants to have a child."

"Let me begin to see what I can do about helping." His hands went to her face and he held her head as his lips closed over hers, and Sadie sighed, wondering if the miracle of conception would take place that night.

Ben Rutledge and Lynch sat on Wentworth's Wharf and studied the boat tied there. It was twenty feet long and flat-bottomed; it drew no more than twelve to fourteen inches of water. It had been specially made to skim over the marshes and to work the flood channels at low tide for shellfish. The mast was lightweight and shorter than most, so it would not tip over the boat. Usually it carried weights for stability. The only problem was that it *looked* like a shallow draft boat. It hadn't been used for almost a year and had developed some leaks. Ben and Lynch decided it would do, so Ben hunted up the owner and bought the craft for thirty pounds.

The two men bailed for an hour, then rigged her lone sail and with great difficulty worked her out of the slip and slowly northward just past Lee's shipyard to the long wharf of Rutledge & Rutledge.

For two days Ben had a crew of men working over the scow, giving her a new coat of paint, a new name—the *Avenger*—and putting on new canvas. They added a short jib forward for more speed, then hoisted her out of the water for a quick patch job on her flat-bottomed hull. All the work was done behind one of Ben's big three-masters, and while it was not a secret, Ben did not advertise what he was doing.

On the third day his ship's carpenters went to work and built a thin wooden hull around the outside of the ship that would make her look like any other twenty-footer with a deep hull running low in the water, drawing four to six feet. The false work on the front and sides extended a foot below the surface of the bay, which should be adequate. By nightfall of the second day the false work was done and the boat looked exactly like what she was not. Pasteboard boxes were put on board so she seemed to be loaded heavily. As many of the boxes were stacked on deck as practical.

While shipwrights worked on the hull, Lewis had been on the far reaches of the Charles River in a small sailboat investigating. The Charles to the west of Boston emptied into Back Bay, a huge salt marsh which was dry at low tide. Lynch had found an ideal spot well beyond the Boston Neck toward Roxbury where the Charles became a river again. The plan was to have scouts watching for the revenue ship to go up the Charles on one of its patrol runs during high tide. As soon as it came upriver, someone would ride and notify the Freedom Fighters, who would swing into action.

Lynch's company would be called out to report to a spot near Roxbury under command of its lieutenant, Wallace Rice. Lewis would get the *Avenger* under sail from Berry's shipyard on the far northern tip of Boston near Barton's Point, and sail up the Back Bay toward Roxbury. Once there he would wait for the *Richard* to come into view out of the Charles, and he would pretend to try to outrun the heavier ship.

That was the rough plan, and it was all ready to be put into operation the following day with the *Avenger* on site and waiting in Berry's shipyard. However, it was nearly two weeks before they had a chance to try the plan. The *Richard* hadn't been seen at all near Roxbury for that time, but this day she did work up the channel of the tide-swollen Charles nearly to Roxbury, then turned up the other channel to the right and wound around Cambridge town.

Lewis sailed his *Avenger* to Roxbury well before the other vessel came back down the river. He worked out of the village to the point where he wanted to be, and waited. He saw no one on the Roxbury side of shore, but knew for certain that there were fifteen flintlocks there, primed, loaded and waiting. They would be on Bounty Point, an arm of land sticking well into the boggy marsh along the Back Bay shore.

When the *Richard* drifted back down the Charles, someone on board spotted the *Avenger*, which had put up sail now and moved away from the patrol craft. Capspree put on more canvas and with a following wind soon cut the distance to the new boat in half. Lynch couldn't seem to make good time even though the tide was with him and starting to move out quickly. Lewis steered closer to shore and saw the larger ship following him. They were both still well in the deep-water channel.

When the voice from the *Richard* hailed Lewis from two hundred yards and demanded that he come about, Lewis lifted the jib and pulled away, only to have the forward cannon boom at him from the patrol craft. The shot flew well over the *Avenger*. Now Lewis angled slightly more for shore, aiming for the point of land, which he knew at this time would be scarcely two feet under water. If the larger ship saw him navigate across the point successfully, it would believe that it could go through as well. That was the crux of the whole scheme.

Lewis looked down as he slid over the submerged ridge of land barely eighteen inches under the surface, and kept moving straight ahead.

Lynch could almost see Captain Capspree counting his fines as the faster revenue ship quickly closed on him. The cannon fired once more, again shooting over his head, trying to slow him down and make him stop.

Lynch watched the *Richard*. No one threw a lead line to test the depth, so they had no idea the land would slant up so suddenly here. Lynch turned more inland to get out of the direct angle of fire of the forward cannon. He watched the bigger ship and softly said, "Now."

There was a grating as wood struck the underwater ridge. Then Lynch heard a shot and another cry. The forward force of the ship drove it well onto the underground ridge and stopped it. Then the ship wavered in the light wind and at last tilted toward shore and hung there at a 45-degree angle, not yet permanently grounded, but in a dangerous position.

Men scrambled on the tilted deck. Lynch turned the *Avenger* directly for shore toward a stand of small pine trees. Less than a minute after the *Richard* grounded, the first rounds of musket fire came from the shore, a hundred yards away. Lewis could see the musket balls striking the revenuer, splintering decking, poking holes in the sails, sending the sailors scurrying for cover.

Lewis looked at the sky. The sun had two hours of life yet, so it wouldn't be dark for three hours. Plenty of time. He felt the suck of the tide stronger now as it hurried out of the flatness of the Charles River marsh. In another hour the water around the *Richard* would be less than a foot deep and the craft would be finished.

On shore Lewis' second-in-command, Lieutenant Rice, followed his orders perfectly. He fired a fifteen-shot initial volley and gave explicit instructions not to hit anyone on deck. The first fire had driven the crew below decks, and Lieutenant Rice had seen only one man since, probably the captain. A round was fired into the tilted deck every thirty seconds now, as they waited for the tide to take care of the final tilting of the ship.

Sadie Wythe and Ben stood to one side, watching the operation. A few moments later Lewis Lynch beached his craft and waded through knee-deep water to shore. He grinned and saluted Ben.

"Looks like it worked, sir," Lewis said, shaking Ben's hand.

"Indeed it does, Mr. Lynch. The tide should be out in about another hour. We've had no return fire except one musket shot. We never did hear the ball."

They watched the water vanishing toward the far end of the marsh-like Back Bay.

"Mr. Lynch, fire fifteen rounds at them, one at a time, at two-second intervals. Then reload and repeat the mission. Try not to hit any of the men out there."

"Aye, sir." He gave the orders to his men, who blasted off the shots. Then Ben took a hailing tube he had brought in his chaise and went to the water's edge.

"Ahoy on board the *Richard*. Put down your arms and come over the side. You can wade to shore now. If there's any resistance, you will be shot down like seadogs. You have no choice. Lay down your arms, jump off this side and come to shore. You will not be harmed here."

Ben's only answer was a musket shot. The ball hit the water twenty yards in front of him.

Ben waited a few minutes, then repeated his offer. This time there was no response. Ben and Lewis conferred, agreed on a plan and went to Ben's chaise, where they took out a three-gallon cask of black powder. It was already set with a burnable fuse. They carried it to the *Avenger* and put it on board. Lewis gave new orders to Lieutenant Rice, then returned to the *Avenger*, and he and Ben pushed off. Each had his flintlock and pistol. Ben sailed the *Avenger*, working against the slight breeze toward the *Richard's* blind forward point.

As they came within fifty yards, the flintlocks on shore began to pound away at the *Richard*, laying down a covering fire, as arranged. Balls thumped into the decks and brasswork every five seconds, then two or three shots came at once, followed by a short pause. The firing was sporadic, allowing no easy movement on board. No more firing came from the *Richard*. Ben maneuvered the *Avenger* within ten yards of the revenuer and saw no danger. Then suddenly a man bolted from the forward tilted hatch, pistol in hand.

Ben grabbed his own pistol and as the man fired at Lewis, Ben aimed a shot at the man, who had gold braid on his shoulder. Lewis' right thigh felt the hot ball as it slammed past him, burning cloth and drawing blood. He was knocked down, but jumped up at once.

Ben's pistol shot had flown straight and true, smashing the man's shoulder, flopping him back to the hatchway. Ben thought the man may have been the captain.

Quickly Ben maneuvered the *Avenger* up to the now quiet side of the tilted ship. It showed half its bottom already. Lynch had fastened a length of chain around the powder cask, and now threw the end of the chain over the rail of the big ship and tied it fast. The cask of powder rested against the uptilted starboard side of the *Richard* at a point which would be well below the waterline if she were on an even keel.

Lynch checked the fuse, then held his pistol so the flash of the primer in the pan would ignite the bomb fuse. He fired the pistol. The ball slammed off the side of the *Richard*, but the primer flash ignited the petard's fuse as well.

Lynch pushed the *Avenger* away from the revenue ship, saw the wind catch their sail, and felt them swing toward shore. They were a hundred yards downwind toward shore when the explosion ripped into the wooden side of the *Richard*, blowing a two-foot gap in her sturdy hull planking.

Now, even waiting for high tide would not save the *Richard*. She couldn't sail again without extensive repairs.

Lynch and Ben landed near where the Freedom Fighters waited on shore. Ben ordered another fifteen-round volley, this one to be sent all at the same time. When it jolted into the *Richard*, Ben took his hailing tube and went to the edge of the water again.

"On board the *Richard*. You have two minutes to show a white flag of surrender. Otherwise we will set fire to your vessel with you on board and burn her to the waterline. The choice is yours. Leave now. Come over this side and wade to shore. You will be free to walk back to your station. You will not be harmed."

As Ben spoke, the first form appeared at the hatch, climbed through, slid down the slanted deck and jumped into the water. He hit feet first and went in up to his waist in mud, then began walking toward shore. Others followed him until soon twenty men had left. Ben could see no gold braid on any of the shoulders. Before

303

the first man got to shore, Lynch posted a guard on the horse and the two carriages. The British seamen were pointed the right direction toward Boston and told to march. Most were dazed and angry, all were wet and muddy from the slime and ooze on the bottom of the bay, but it would wash off. The shame of losing one of Her Majesty's ships might not.

Ben stopped one of the non-commissioned officers from the British ship. He had a scar on his right cheek and wore a moustache and a snarl.

"Where is your captain, sailor?"

"Still on board, sir."

"Is he coming off?"

"He said he won't be leaving until he's dead or the ship is burned out."

Ben nodded and let the man catch up with the rest of the crew. Lynch sent two men to follow the British sailors well away from the area, to make sure they kept moving and didn't come back to try for the horses.

Ben motioned to Lynch. "We have to go back out there and rout the captain and the mate. We'll each take two pistols and our long guns. If we leave now, there's still plenty of water to float the *Avenger*."

They borrowed pistols, made sure all were primed and loaded, then pushed them into their belts and got the *Avenger* underway. One of the Freedom Fighters had cut two long poles for them to use. They left the sail down and poled the flat boat through the water, coming up quietly on the blind side bottom of the *Richard*.

Lynch went up the side silently. Ben followed, tying the small boat against the big one. Just as Ben got to the slanting rail, he saw Lynch bring his pistol down hard on the top of a man's head which had just raised out of the hatch. In the process the pistol jolted and fired, sending the ball against a bulkhead.

From below they heard another pistol shot, then a groan. Lynch saw the sailor he had hit at the bottom of the ladder, holding his head. The man, the first mate of the *Richard*, looked up at the faces above him.

"Damn ye! Damn ye all! Captain Capspree has just blown his brains out. Now you've all bought the noose for sure!"

It took Ben and Lewis half an hour to transfer the body and all of the arms and powder and shot from the ship into the *Avenger*. Ben wanted to take the small cannon, but there wasn't enough time.

Lewis found a can of pine tar and some turpentine and splashed it around the decking and on the sails. He fired a shot from his other pistol so the flash of the powder in the pan would flame down onto the turpentine. It ignited the vapors and set the whole thing on fire.

It began to burn furiously. as the *Avenger* pulled away. Ben watched the flames race up the sails, devouring them like some huge cloth-eating monster. Lines burned in half and dropped on deck. The decking began to burn, flames surged along the oiled decks and were soon leaping from one end of the ship to the other. One mast burned off at the bottom and fell sizzling into the mud of the marsh, its cross-arms stabbing deep into the mire.

On one side, Ben saw three rats scurry across the slanted deck and fall into the water, where they surely drowned.

By the time the *Avenger* reached shore it was full dusk. The flames snarling their way through the revenuer attracted a group of spectators down the bay, but no one showed up near this point.

Ben put the captain's body and the wounded young first mate ashore and told him he was free to go. He stared at the dead man, then at the carriages.

"They won't help you. They have orders not to. You're on your own," Lynch snapped at him.

Ben told Sadie to drive the chaise back to town. He would go back with the *Avenger*.

Ben and Lewis poled the boat out to deeper water, caught the outgoing tide and swept past the tip of Boston at Barton's Point in half an hour. Then they sailed past the large mill pond at the north end of Boston, and soon slanted around Hudson's point and back down the harbor side of the Boston peninsula. It was full dark by the time they poled their way in through the low tide harbor to the Rutledge and

Rutledge wharf. Two night watchmen helped the men unload the *Avenger*. The goods went into a small room in the nearest Rutledge warehouse, and were tightly sealed up under lock and key.

Back on the street, both men found themselves without transportation, so they walked to the Black Horse Tavern, the same one where they had celebrated during their campaign against Customs Commissioner Trout.

They lifted a tankard of rum and drank to each other's health, then to the short, sweet life of the *Avenger*. Neither of them mentioned the death of the captain of the *Richard*. It had been by his own hand, though due to their attack. Capspree had been afraid to stand a court-martial for the loss of his ship. So be it, Ben thought. This was war, undeclared yet, but war, and in every war, men died. The Freedom Fighters' first casualties were those who had died in the Boston Massacre.

Two hours later they went back to the Rutledge wharf and found the *Avenger* was no more. Orders Ben left had been carried out. The false work on her had been stripped off by lanternlight and the boards burned. Her special paint job was left, but as she sat in flickering light, she was once again only a flat-bottomed boat ready to prowl the marshes and shallow bays for gathering shellfish. Nothing about her resembled in any way the dashing *Avenger* which surely would be diligently sought by the

British authorities before another sun had set.

The next morning Ben heard about the attack on the revenuer boat before he got to his office. He stopped at a coffee house before he went to work for a quick cup and to listen to the talk.

"I heard it was fifty men with muskets who attacked the ship in shallow water, killed the captain and drove off the crew before they burned her to the water," said one man.

Others had all sorts of stories, but they were certain that it had been some citizens who had done it, and with just cause, too. Captain Capspree was not mourned by anyone in the coffee house that morning.

At his office Ben heard that the British navy would hold an inquiry into the matter at once. They had posted an armed boat near the *Richard* to discourage looting of the remains of the ship.

The dead captain would be given a burial at sea and each crew member would be questioned about the cause of the tragedy. Word would be sent to England on the afternoon tide, requesting an official inquiry by Parliament in the colonies to find the guilty parties and to punish them promptly.

Ben sat at his desk and smiled. It was a fine uproar! People were talking about it on the streets and in stores. Now and then a small cheer would go up. The council had expected an inquiry, but they also knew it would take a long time before England could do anything about it. It would take a month for the news to reach England, and perhaps another month or two for Parliament to set up an investigatory commission. Then they would have to come by ship back to the colonies. It would be three or four months at least before anything could happen.

Ben called in Lewis Lynch and together they talked about the *Richard's* guns and powder which rested in the Rutledge warehouse.

"My suggestion, sir, is to hire a four-wheeled wagon and move the whole supply this morning out to that farm near Concord where we have been storing our supply of powder and ball which we 'borrowed' a few months ago from the Customs house."

Ben agreed. "Good plan. You might want to conceal your load in some way, such as under boxes of fish or a pile of straw, something that looks natural."

Lewis nodded and was on his way. He had funds which the council made available for his use. He simply recorded his expenses and turned in the receipts to the treasury.

As Ben sat at his desk and looked out across the wharfs, he contemplated their attack. It had been undertaken carefully, was well planned and executed. The death of the captain would complicate the official investigation, but the mate would surely testify that the captain had shot himself. What could the crew say? They were not even there. Crew and mate would have a hard time identifying anyone. It was nearly dark. Lewis would be the easiest. His black eye patch was easy to spot. Ben could send him to New York on a ship if it came to that.

Ben was satisfied that the operation had been a success. It would serve as a real irritant to the British, relieve the unjust harassment of the small shippers and farmers along the Charles and the bay, and in the end serve well in the Freedom Fighters' main purpose—liberty! Ben turned back to his desk and began the day's business.

Chapter Three
THE CURIOUS AND THE SATISFIED

Harriet Rutledge sat at her window looking out on the soft green June grass. The summer was going by so quickly. She wondered what she would do when autumn came. She had hoped to go to London, but her father practically told her that it was out of the question this year. She watched her brothers playing marbles in the yard below. David usually won, but this time it seemed that Robert was easily beating his twin. It was interesting to watch them grow and develop. Neither was shaving yet, but David was starting to grow some fuzz on his chin. She had teased him about it until he cut it off with her sewing scissors.

Downstairs in the parlor, she had finished her fourth pillow case and told her mother that four was plenty. She had tried reading, but nothing caught her interest. Her father had numerous English novels, but today she was simply not interested in them. She wandered around her room glancing at herself in a mirror on her dresser. At once she pulled in her tummy so she stood straighter, and so her chest protruded a little more.

Again Harriet wondered what it would have been like if her father hadn't rushed into the house exactly when he did. If Cunliffe had . . . she turned away from the mirror, fluffed up her bed and pillow and cleaned up her room.

Tonight when Jennifer came over they would have a grand time, but what to do until then? Jennifer Bull, her dearest cousin and best friend, was almost her same age, and they always told each other everything. It would be the first time they spent any time together since the Cunliffe tragedy, as she was calling it. Jenny would want to hear all about it—if Jenny knew it happened. What could she tell Jennifer?

A knock came on her door and Harriet opened it.

"Hey, sister dear, remember how we used to blow soap bubbles?" Robert asked. "We've forgotten how. Will you come down and show us?"

She smiled at her brother, waved him out of the room and followed him down the steps to the parlor.

"First, you go next door and see if you can borrow two onion tops from Mrs. Branton's garden. Get the long ones off the big bulb onions. *Two of them!*" She called the last after him as Robert ran out the front door.

She went into the kitchen, found a small tinware bowl and shaved a few slivers of home-made lye soap into it, then put in some water and stirred with a spoon until it was a bubbly, soapy froth.

Harriet carried it into the back yard, where David sat in the grass, leaning against a tree and staring into the distance.

"Are you writing a poem in your mind?" she asked.

He hadn't seen her coming, but he didn't look around. "No. Just thinking."

"About what?"

"About girls. You're so different from boys in so many ways."

Harriet smiled. "Well, I'm a girl. Maybe I can answer some of the questions you have, when you want the answers. I can tell you've been noticing girls. Do you have a little lady friend?"

"No."

"Do you want one?"

"Not yet." He watched her, then openly stared at her breasts where they pressed outward against her plain white shirtwaist.

Robert ran up with three onion tops. All were bright green, hollow and over a foot long. She used Robert's knife and cut the ends of each so they were even.

"Now I remember," David said. He took one of the onion stalks, dipped the large end in the soapy water and blew in the other end. A small bubble came out, then burst. Harriet sloshed the soapy water around to concentrate it more.

David tried again and got a two-inch sized

bubble.

Soon they all were making bubbles, trying to break them off the onion stalks so they would float in the breeze. David tried blowing slowly and made one bubble five inches across before the drip at the bottom broke it.

Harriet left the boys and went into the house. She wandered into the parlor, looked at her father's newspaper, dropped it and went to the kitchen, where her mother and the cook were preparing supper. They had taken down a small cured ham from where it hung near the kitchen fireplace and cut large slices from it for frying. There would be cooked dry beans and vegetables, including potatoes, carrots and cabbage.

Sandra looked up at her daughter, love and concern showing in her eyes.

"Restless, Harriet? Why don't you take a walk?"

"I really don't think that would help, Mother. I'll go clean up my room again. When is Jennifer coming?"

"Just after supper, dear. Your uncle wants to talk to your father for some reason."

"Oh, good. I may have another nap, then." She went up the wooden steps to her room and dropped on the featherbed. Idly she wondered what really being with a man would feel like. She turned over and buried her head in the soft feather pillow. She simply would not let herself think about it. When it happened, it would happen, and there was nothing she could do to bring it any faster. With that decided, she closed her eyes and drifted into a light sleep.

Three hours later, just after supper, Jennifer arrived, and the girls hugged each other and ran up to Harriet's room. As soon as they got inside the room and closed the door Jennifer turned to Harriet.

"Now, young lady, tell me exactly what happened when that Mr. Cunliffe attacked you."

Harriet was surprised. "How in the world did you know about that? It's supposed to be a closely kept secret. Not even my mother knows."

Jennifer Bull was a small, slightly built girl, as yet with few womanly curves; a petite, attractive person with small breasts and a face that was a delight. Her green eyes sparkled over natural shadows, her nose tipped upward and her full mouth laughed and smiled often. Her hair was light brown and curled in half a dozen ringlets down her neck.

Harriet dropped on the bed and stalled. "It's a secret, Jenny, so if I tell you, it won't be a secret."

"Oh, posh, it isn't a secret now, only from your mother. Tell me, did he get his hands on you?"

"Yes, of course. It's hard to rip a shirtwaist in half without touching the woman."

"He did that? Ripped your waist in half?"

Harriet went on then, explained how he tricked her about her mother needing help, got into the house, then grabbed her and assaulted her on the couch.

"Oh, it must have been awful!" Jenny said, looking closely at Harriet. "It was awful, wasn't it?"

"Yes, of course. Terrible. I was screaming and fighting. I clawed his face, and then he had my waist and camisole off and I was all exposed."

"Then he touched you?"

"Yes."

"Then you know how it feels, don't you?"

"No, I don't think so, Jenny. I was so angry, so furious, I hardly realized his hands were holding me. Just then, Father came in, and I must have gone numb. I can't remember what it felt like when his hands touched me . . . *there*. Father beat Mr. Cunliffe and then covered me."

Harriet noticed that Jenny seemed to be breathing harder than usual.

"Didn't you wonder . . . I mean, have you ever thought what it might have been like . . . you know . . . if your father hadn't come into the house just then?"

"Yes, I've wondered. But it's sinful, and I forgot about it at once." She sighed. "Well, I almost forgot about it." Harriet went to the dresser and brought back two brushes. She gave her newest one to Jennifer, and both began brushing their long hair.

Harriet watched her cousin, her face seemed flushed. "Jenny, you haven't said anything about Andy Otis tonight. Is he still your beau?"

"He's nothing of the kind!" Her words came quickly. "I guess he's still around. I haven't seen him lately."

"What did he do to make you angry, Jenny?"

"Do? He didn't *do* anything. What made you think that?"

"Because you're acting like you still love him, and want him back. You still do like him, don't you?"

Jenny sighed, turned toward Harriet and let a tear seep out of one eye. Suddenly she was in Harriet's arms, crying softly. It took her five minutes to calm down so she could talk.

They lay back crossways on the bed, their feet still on the floor.

"He said he couldn't see me any more for a while. He had just kissed me outside my front door in the shadows and touched me and then he said he couldn't see me because he was afraid. Andy said he couldn't trust himself around me. He wanted to touch me and hold me and do just everything and he knew that was wrong and wicked and he didn't want anything to happen.

"Oh, it was just awful, Harriet. I cried and cried and he told me not to, said it was best for me. Then he kissed me again. He said he was going to work in his father's store, and he'd be busy, and he wasn't old enough to get married or even promised. I told him lots of girls married when they were seventeen, but he said that

317

he was the one not old enough. He kissed me once more and ran down the walk. That's been three weeks and I haven't seen him since."

She was dry-eyed now, her eyes red, tears still on her cheeks.

Harriet took her hand. "Jennifer, dear, I'm sure you don't have a thing to worry about. He practically asked you to marry him. He just wants to get used to the idea. The next time you see him, he'll probably go to see your father and ask his permission."

Jennifer sat up, surprise on her face. "You really think so? Honestly and truly, think so?"

"Of course. He's afraid of getting married. Mother tells me that most men are worried about taking on all the responsibility of a wife and a family and house. It's a big job for a young man to take on, once he gets promised, even."

"I see. I'd never thought about it that way. I decided I must have done something wrong, or that he didn't like me any more, or . . . or . . ." She gave a sigh and let one more shudder shake through her, then she wiped her eyes and tried to smile. "I'm so lucky to have a cousin like you, Harriet. Nobody else could have explained it to me. Now I understand, and I'll know how to act when I see Andy."

Jenny popped up from the bed. "Let's go down and tell your parents that we're going to get ready for bed and have a long talk. We'll tell them we're exchanging secrets."

Harriet agreed, and they went down. It took almost half an hour, because both her uncle and aunt had to talk with Jennifer and ask her the same questions and get the same answers. When the girls went up the steps again, they each had a glass of milk and a roundcake. They ate the snack, then undressed with their backs to each other, slid into their nightgowns and giggled as they jumped under the covers. Soon they rolled back the comforter and blew out one candle, leaving one burning.

"You really love Andy Otis, don't you?" Harriet asked.

"I . . . I guess so."

"Tell me again how it felt when he had his hands on you, on your . . . you know."

"Oh, it was marvelous, I felt so fine, it made me feel just warm all over and relaxed. I *wanted* him to have his hands on my breasts." Jennifer sat up. "Harriet, have you ever pretended you were with a man? You know, making believe he was in bed with you and you both had your clothes off?"

Harriet looked at her cousin in surprise.

"Oh, it's all right if you have. I've pretended a lot of times that way, and it makes me feel warm and wonderful. Did you ever do that?"

Harriet nodded.

"Good. I thought I might be the only one. I guess it's a natural thing." She watched her cousin, who lay very still under the sheet. "One day I was feeling that way, and pretending, and

my hand slid down there, and I was just . . .
you know, wondering. And then I touched this
one place and I thought I was going to explode.
It was the most wonderful feeling I've ever
known!"

Harriet still didn't move. She didn't know
what to say.

"Are you shocked and shamed by what I
said?"

"No . . . Jenny. No, of course not. I . . . I
make believe, too. Only . . ."

"Harriet, just don't talk to me for a few minutes. Please?"

Harriet nodded and her cousin turned away
from her.

Deliberately Harriet moved her hand down
toward her legs. It was time she found out what
her cousin was talking about.

A few minutes later, Harriet let out a soft
groan of pleasure. She didn't care if Jenny did
hear her. She had never felt anything like that
in her total seventeen and a half years.

Another ten minutes went by, then they were
talking again, both still glowing, still excited.

"Jennifer Bull, that was the most glorious
and wonderful thing I've ever known. Thank
you for telling me about . . ."

"Harriet, I should be thanking you for helping me understand about Andy. I might have
frightened him away for good. He's so sensitive.
I'm the one who owes you, Harriet Mae—and
you remember it."

They lay there a while longer, not talking, simply reliving the joy and thrill of their separate experiences.

Harriet spoke first. "Dearest Jennifer, let's always be the best of friends. No matter what we do, or whom we marry, let's never forget each other, and let's be close forever and the best friends there ever were, simply forever and forever."

After that they drifted off to sleep, each to dream her own private dreams.

The next day Jenny went back home early in the morning and Harriet cleaned her room and helped with the house things. But during that time she made up her mind. She was not the kind of person to sit back and wait for something. She'd always found it much more direct to help matters along a little, to make things happen that she wanted to take place. She had thought about it all morning, and now she was sure.

Lately she had convinced her mother that she was grown-up enough to take occasional shopping trips the few blocks to the downtown stores. Usually her mother argued, then gave in and agreed only if one of the boys went with her. This time she took another approach. She dressed to go out in her long cream and yellow street dress, with three frilly petticoats under it, and a little jacket. She wore a small straw hat with a long pin to hold it on. She felt very dressed up. She looked in her mirror and opened the jacket top to show a generous amount of bare neck and upper chest.

It was a little after noon when Harriet appeared in the sitting room where her mother sat sewing.

"Mother, I need some more thread and other things, so I'm going to walk down to the Mercantile and see if I can find them." Sandra Rutledge looked up in surprise. "Oh, well, I don't know where the boys are. I'll have Harry drive you down."

"No, Mother, don't bother. It's broad daylight. This is Boston, and I'll be perfectly safe going only a few blocks. You'll have to realize that I'm just practically grown up. I'm almost eighteen. Lots of women have two babies by the time they're as old as I am."

"You are not lots of girls. Now let me think. The boys were here somewhere. You stay right there until I look." She called once, looked in the back yard, then came back.

"Mother, I'll be fine. I won't be gone more than an hour, maybe just a little more. I don't like to be rushed when I'm picking out new thread."

Her mother gave in at last. "Well, just this time. Now, you hurry right home."

"Yes, Mother. I certainly will." She waved and went down the front walk to the street. Harriet shivered. It had been so easy. She had taken a strong position and stayed with it. She had completely fooled her mother. She walked carefully along the dusty street toward the Mercantile, for that was really where she intended to go. The Mercantile was operated by Mr. Luther Otis, and Andy worked there. That was what Jenny had confided to her last night. So far, her project was going according to plan. She wondered if the rest of it would work as well.

Near the store she paused. Did she really want to go through with it? If Jenny ever found out, the two of them would have a terrible fight, and Harriet would lose her best friend. But she had to. She set her lips and entered the front door of the store. She saw Andy at once. He was near the counter, helping two ladies select some wooden spoons. Harriet wandered around the store, looking at some wooden trenchers, at the tinware, then at the sewing supplies. She was selecting thread when Andy Otis came up to her.

"Yes, Miss, may I help you?"

When she looked up, he smiled. "Oh, I know you. Jennifer's cousin, Harriet Rutledge!"

"That's right. And you are Andy Otis, right?"

He said he was. She looked at him. He was as big as Jennifer had said, and very attractive.

"And what might I help you find, Miss Rutledge?"

She wanted to giggle, but didn't. "Oh, I'm just looking around right now. Are you running the store all by yourself today?"

"Yes. Father's ill with a bad cold and a sore throat. I finally persuaded him into going home. It was difficult, but I convinced him at last that I was old enough to run the store for one day."

No one else was in the store. She looked up at Andy, knowing he was curious about why she was there.

"Andy, I do need some thread, but I really came here to talk to you as well. Do you realize you almost broke that poor little girl's heart?"

"Jennifer?"

"Do you kiss so many girls that you can't remember which one was the last?"

"No. No, of course not." Anger flared in him and he started to turn away. She touched him and stopped him.

"Andy, I told her it was simply a little misunderstanding, that I'm sure you can talk to her and explain it all."

"I knew this was going to happen." He scowled, thinking about it. "Harriet, can I talk with you about Jenny?"

"Of course. That's why I came. But do we have to speak here, in the front of the store? Is there somewhere near the back where we can stand, so everyone who goes by won't see us?"

"Sure." He grinned and led her to the back of the store, where there was a high display of many bolts of cloth. They stepped behind the cloth so no one could see them, but so they could still look out at the store.

Andy wiped a bead of sweat off his forehead

as he leaned against the wall and set his jaw. "I suppose you must be very good friends with Jenny, if she told you about me. Did she tell you everything?"

"Jenny and I always tell each other everything."

"Oh," he said, his face taking on a grim set. "Then you must understand my problem. I like your cousin. We've been seeing each other now for almost a year, you know—and we do some kissing. Lately when I'm with her and kissing her I get so excited. I don't know if I can contain myself or not. The last time I kissed her I wanted to—" he turned. "I know I shouldn't be talking this way to you, Harriet. It's my problem, not yours."

"Andy, she likes you very much, you must know that. Maybe Jenny is having feelings like that too."

"Oh, no, not Jenny. She's good. She's so sweet and innocent, and so good. She'd never think about that."

"Andy, don't you think girls feel things, too? Hasn't it occurred to you that girls must get those same longings? Those same ideas you're talking about. They do."

His head snapped back and he looked at her. "They do? So strong? I mean, terribly powerful? I had no idea. I thought that girls . . ."

"Why don't you tell Jenny about your feelings? She'll understand. You be careful where you're alone with her, and ask her to marry

325

you, very soon."

"You aren't making sport of me, are you, Harriet? About how girls think, and feel . . ."

"Andy, girls wonder just as much how it would feel . . . I mean, we are people with feelings, and desires, and we have just as much curiosity as boys do. For at least three years I've been trying to imagine . . . *you* know."

Andy looked at her in a new way, concern gone from his face now, and a new expression there that she couldn't read. She had to make the big jump now if she were ever going to. She took a deep breath, letting her breasts swell out against her dress.

"Andy, do you want to make a little experiment, right now?"

"What . . . what experiment?"

"To see if it's just Jenny who makes you feel that way, or if it's just a girl who does it, even me. If another girl would make you feel that same way . . . you know."

"I've kissed other girls."

"The same way you kissed Jenny?"

"Well, no, I guess not. How should we do the test?"

"Well, you . . . you must try kissing me." She had said it. Now it was up to him. She waited, looking up at him. He was a handsome man, and she liked his red-tinted brown hair.

"You mean here? Right now?"

"Yes. Nobody else is here, no customers. If one does come in, that would rescue me from your clutches." She laughed softly after saying it, so he would know she was joking. His ex-

326

pression changed, he glanced into the store one more time, then stepped toward her. He looked down at her, stared openly at her breasts.

"You know, you're the prettiest girl I've ever seen. Really. I mean that." He leaned down and pecked a kiss on her cheek, his eyes glittering.

"See, nothing at all," he said.

They laughed softly. He checked the store again, then his arms went around her and he pulled her tightly against his chest and his lips covered hers. At first their lips were barely touching, then he pressed harder and held her tighter until she thought she would burst. He eased away and leaned back, but still held her close so her breasts were against him.

"Now, that was better," he said.

Breathless, she nodded and he bent and kissed her again. This time his tongue slid between his lips and touched hers in a move that surprised her. The touch of his tongue sent lightning darting through her body, and she was so moved that she groaned. This time when the kiss ended he was more serious, his expression puzzled and uncertain.

"Well, do you feel anything now? Was it that way when you kissed Jenny? Any of those feelings that you were so concerned about?"

"You know they are."

"Maybe you should make it a real test, and do what you did to Jenny with your hands, touching her."

Andy looked up suddenly, anger flaring, then evaporating. "I guess she did tell you everything, didn't she?"

"Yes, and if the test is going to work the same way, all of the parts should be the same, don't you think?" She didn't breathe as she waited for his reaction.

"I'm not sure why you're doing this, but I like it. When the prettiest girl in town asks me to kiss her, I'm not going to run away. Then when she invites me to touch her . . ."

He kissed her again, this time holding her loosely and making room for one of his hands to come between them and rub gently at the large V of exposed flesh at her neckline. She moved back slightly, giving him more room, and his fingers edged under the bodice of her dress.

Harriet gasped and broke off the kiss, but his hand kept moving downward. A million flashes of lightning sparkled through her body. His hand caressed the soft flesh at the edge of one breast, then gradually stroked lower and lower until his hand pushed out her bodice and wrapper and lay quietly cupping one of her big breasts. She sighed and reached upward for his lips again.

She sighed again and felt herself leaning against him. Never had she been so thrilled; never had her flesh been so responsive to a touch. She hoped that he would never stop.

Andy's hand moved now, caressing her breast, massaging it tenderly, then stole over to the other peak and fondled it. At last the long kiss ended.

Harriet couldn't speak. She lay against his chest, his hand still on her breast. She felt even better than she had the night before. Harriet was thrilled. She had never known that she could be so responsive, so tender. It was delicious!

Someone stepped up to the front door on the wooden entranceway, paused, then turned and left without coming inside. Harriet was not worried about them. She was too thrilled to say anything. She guessed that her voice wouldn't work. Roughly, Andy pulled her head back and kissed her again. His hand rubbed harder on her breasts.

Suddenly he pulled away from her. She looked up, startled.

"I heard someone at the door. I must look." He pulled his hands away and ran lightly to the front of the store. She saw him there at the door for a moment, then he came back and kissed her quickly.

He held her tenderly in his arms. "You were wrong," he said softly. "You don't get me excited the way Jenny does—with you it's ten times more. I want you ten times more than her." He put his hand under her bodice again and she didn't think anything about it. Then he picked her up and set her down on the floor.

"What in he world . . ."

"I was getting dizzy standing up. I thought we might fall over," he said. Then he pushed her shoulders down until she was lying on the wooden planks of the floor and he fell on top of her.

"You started this, and I found out one thing. When I get that excited, there's no way I'm going to stop. You didn't think about that, did you, pretty girl?"

She realized what was happening now, and she tried to fight him. She hit his chest until he caught her hands, then he pushed her legs apart with his legs and pulled at her skirt and petticoats. Furiously he ripped apart her underclothing and opened the front of his breeches.

"No, Andy, no!" she sobbed. "Andy, you can't do this!"

He laughed. "Can't? Who's going to stop me? You know you want me to. That's the only reason you came here today, wasn't it, to try to get me to do this. It didn't matter at all to you that I'm courting your cousin and best friend."

As she was pleading with him to stop, he plunged into her. Harriet stifled a scream as a sudden flaring pain thundered through her. She was sure she was going to die. But quickly it was shadowed by a number of other sensations, and she realized that his big shaft must be deep inside her. The pain eased to a steady throbbing.

It wasn't like she had dreamed. There was nothing wildly ecstatic or thrilling. Where was the surging warmth, the spontaneous, unstoppable wonder of powerful feeling that she had expected? Andy lay heavily on her, pounding his hips against hers. She was still confused but her curiosity was slacked. So this was what it was all about!

"Oh, but you are good!" Andy whispered through clenched teeth. He moved faster and then hit her hard with his hips five times, groaning and gasping for air as he collapsed on top of her, breathing furiously. He was finished, satisfied.

For a moment she thought he was dead, or at least had fainted.

Then he stirred and rolled away from her, sitting with his back against the bolts of imported cloth.

"My God, I actually—with the prettiest girl in town!"

She lay there watching him. So that was it. He had found his satisfaction so quickly. Why hadn't she? There was none of the power or pure joy of last night. Why? Slowly she sat up. She looked at her rumpled, soiled dress. There was a large spot of blood on her inner petticoats. Harriet stared at Andy for several seconds.

"Andy, I don't know what to say. I admit I did come here hoping maybe you might kiss me and touch me a little, but I never dreamed . . .

I mean, not right here in the store, when someone might have walked in at any minute. I thought you might touch me a little bit, but I truly never thought . . ."

Andy grinned. "That was your first time, wasn't it?" He chuckled. "Now you really know why I couldn't go on seeing Jenny so much. I want to marry that girl, but I knew if I kept on seeing her, we'd do something. I don't want it that way, not with Jenny, because I plan to marry her."

"But with me, it didn't matter?"

"Not when you almost asked me to. You wanted me to do this so much that you got all dressed up and came down here. But you still won't admit even to yourself that you wanted to. I don't plan to take you to the altar, so with you it doesn't matter. Oh, I'm glad for the good time. It was the best I've ever had, in fact. Just don't you even hint at this to Jenny." He sat there with a scowl. "Damn it, I guess I better go there tonight and explain why I hadn't been seeing her, that it was for her own protection, and then I'll ask her to marry me and I'll go in to see her father and make it all formal. I guess I don't have to warn you not ever to tell Jenny about our meeting here this afternoon."

"You don't have to worry about that. Jenny and I are best friends, but I'm afraid this would be too much for even us. No, I won't ever tell her, *if* you go there tonight and ask her to be your wife." Harriet looked up at him, admiring his rugged body, his attractive face. "Jenny is really a very fortunate girl."

He grinned, stood and helped her up. They adjusted their clothes, and Harriet found the three spools of thread and paid for them. He brushed off her long skirts as best he could, kissed her hand and took her to the front door. There he turned over a hand-lettered sign on a string that said "Out for Lunch, Back in Thirty Minutes." Andy unlocked the front door and Harriet scowled.

"So you knew nobody would interrupt us, Andy Otis. That is scandalous. You had locked the door!"

"True."

Harriet walked by him stiffly, went out the door and down the steps without a glance or a goodbye. Her sudden anger with Andy soon wore off. Actually it was clever of him to think so fast.

Soon she began to think about herself. She was shocked that she didn't feel somehow different. She had done what she had dreamed about for so long. But it had been quick and rough and really far from satisfying for her. Was it always like that?

Then, too, she had sinned terribly. She was a tainted woman, she had been ruined for marriage if anyone found out about it, and she had been with her cousin's sweetheart. She would be shut out of the best homes in Boston. Yet, she didn't feel very different. Maybe she was a little more knowledgeable now, more grown up, perhaps a little harder in her mind. She could probably handle an amorous man more easily now. No magical metamorphosis into a complete woman. No physical thrill. The thing she would remember most vividly about her seduction would be the pain of that first thrust.

Harriet walked home slowly. She had no idea how long she had been gone, but she was sure it couldn't have been an hour. A smile slid onto her face as she remembered the ingenious way Andy had gone to the front and locked the door and put out the sign. He had known very well what he was going to do when he came back to her.

As Harriet opened the gate and went up the widewalk to her home, she realized she had just passed a milestone in her life. Now she *felt* more like a woman. She was keenly disappointed with her first experience, but not crushed. There would be other times—more experienced men. She knew she could handle almost anything life could deal her from now on.

When she opened the front door, she felt so composed that in some ways she knew she had missed something, that she had been cheated. She went past the front hall and found her mother still sewing in the parlor.

Harriet showed her mother the new thread she had bought, then said she was going up for a nap and probably a cool bath. Her mother smiled, paying more attention to the complicated pattern she was working than to her daughter.

That afternoon Harriet made up her mind. It was past time that she moved into some new field, a different area of experience. She did not like music, and her sewing was only adequate, not outstanding. Why couldn't she go into her father's business?

She knew all the objections. "Nice" girls just didn't work in commerce or trade. Girls with fathers who could afford to send them to school to learn to read and write and do ciphers, were lucky enough. After that they should stay home and learn to sew and cook and keep house, and perhaps learn to play the organ or try their hand at painting pictures before it was time to marry and raise a family of their own.

It was a trap she certainly didn't want to be caught in. Once a girl married, her life was patterned and set forever. There was no way out. Before a girl married, there was at least a chance. She knew she was much better educated that most women in the colonies. She had attended several private schools, since public schools were only for boys in almost all the colonies. When she was twelve her father put her in Mrs. Adelle's School in Boston, where they taught the proper studies for young ladies of wealth and breeding. This included sewing, knitting and tatting, but there was a firm grounding in better penmanship until all the girls could write in a flowing, easy script that looked almost like fine printing. It was beautiful writing and every one of the fifteen girls had to master the art in the first year. They were also taught to cipher and do some of the more advanced arithmetic of the day, which, while not highly complex, was fascinating to Harriet. She was interested in dealing in the abstract qualities of figures and how they could relate to unknown elements.

In the school they also studied Greek and Latin, as much as many classes took at Harvard, and they made an extensive study of the history of the colonies and of England, France and Germany. Geography was one of the best courses.

Male educators looked upon the school as a ridiculous waste of time and money. One of the masters of Harvard was heard to say on many occasions that women should be either cooking, sewing, keeping house or with child. He said they should be educated to absolute harmony with those duties.

Many girls in the colonies could read and write and do simple sums, but that was usually as much schooling as they had. Soon they were needed to help in the fields and the shops, where big families were an economic asset.

Harriet knew she was extremely fortunate to have the extensive education she had. In many ways, it was as good as that offered at Harvard.

Now her mind was made up. This evening, when her father came home, she would have on one of her prettiest dresses, she would have washed, combed and arranged her hair in the twin buns he liked, and she would wear the delicate perfume he had brought home for her a year ago from France. She would bring him his pipe with a hot coal from the fireplace so he could light it. Then she would tell him she wanted to go to work in his firm. She would try every argument she knew so she could join Rutledge & Rutledge. She had as her first target the bookkeeping work. To prepare, she had practiced doing addition and subtraction for two hours. Tonight she would challenge her father to a contest in ciphers, to prove to him how adept she was at such work.

The time arrived just after dinner, as her father stretched out in front of the bay window in his favorite chair and looked out over the front yard.

"Father, may I talk with you a moment?"

Ben looked up from the *Speaker* and smiled. Harriet had blossomed into a beautiful young woman. He knew he could deny her little she truly desired. "Yes, of course, Harriet Mae, sit down."

"Father, I appreciate that you have let me have a better education than almost any other girl in Boston. But now I think I should graduate to something more useful. I'm almost eighteen, Father, and I don't want to get married right away. I've sewn pillow cases and doilies and quilts until my fingers are sore. I want to take a vacation from this and get into the practical world."

Ben frowned. He knew the Cunliffe ordeal had made a change in his eldest child, but he had no idea it had turned to this. "The practical world. Well now, daughter, what do you mean by that?"

"I want to come to work in your business, Father."

Ben had to reach for his pipe quickly before it dropped from his slack lips. A curious expression on his face showed surprise and consternation.

"In the business? A shipping company is a rough operation, certainly no place for a woman. There isn't a single female in my whole organization. No, out of the question, absolutely impossible. Maybe I could see about a millinery shop or one of those stores that handles cloth and premade women's clothes. Something like that might be more fitting, if I ever do agree to let you go into any form of business, which I certainly have not, and most likely will not." He paused, seeing the disappointment on her face. "Haven't you found some nice young man that you like yet? There must be dozens around town."

"No, Father, I do not wish to marry yet. It's a trap that fits a woman into a small life she can never get out of. I can always marry."

"But business is a man's world. There is no place for you in the business world. Marriage is what you should be thinking about."

"No, Father. I've thought it through many times. I'm a grown woman. I've been in school far too long. I'd be bored to death, stitching and sewing all day in a shop. I'm too smart for that."

Ben let the continuing surprise of it wash away, and blinked, looking at his daughter with a stranger's eyes. She was pretty, with long brown hair, wide-set eyes, and must stand about five feet and four inches, taller than the average woman. When did she grow so tall? What could she possibly *do* in a business? What in his own office? He could think of nothing.

"Father, there are many things down at your firm that I could do. For one, I could work in the bookkeeping department. I'm sure you have people who keep books, and tally up rows of figures. I'm really quite good with numbers. May I show you?"

Ben said she could, thinking the bookkeeping end of the business was a complicated one, and also the hardest for which to find good, reliable workers he could trust. They often became discouraged, couldn't do the work, or wanted more exciting jobs. As he watched, Harriet took out a sheet of paper and turned it over. On the back she had written a dozen three-digit figures.

"Watch how quickly I can add up the sum," she said.

Harriet bent to the task, running her small quill pen down the row of numbers until she came to the bottom where she wrote down a figure, then worked up from the bottom on the second row of numbers, put down that total and began adding from the top on the last column and marked down her answer.

"There, was that fast enough? You add them up and see if I did it correctly."

Ben worked on the first column and came out with a different number from what Harriet had put down. He noted his number, and totalled up the line again and found he had made a mistake. When he had the column of three digit numbers added, he saw that Harriet had been correct. She had done it at least twice as fast as he.

Ben sat back and frowned slightly at his daughter. He had no idea how his other employees would react. She would need an office by herself, with an open door. Sometimes the language around Rutledge & Rutledge became quite salty with colorful seamen's words.

"Harriet Mae, you do your sums very well, and quicker than I can, but we have no women in our offices. It would be a complicated change." He knew some firms in town now did have women working in them, but he disapproved. He shook his head. "Daughter, I'm not sure it would be the right thing to do."

"But more and more businesses now have women in them. At Edes & Gill, the printers, they have a woman there who helps out with the proof reading on the galleys of type. And your friend Dr. Warren also has a woman who helps him in the office, taking down the names of those who come in, preparing prescriptions, making out bills. Women are going to be doing more and more, clerks in stores, even managers. Some day we'll have women doctors and lawyers, and maybe even a woman in the legislature."

Ben watched her. She was so young and vital, so full of energy and enthusiasm. Why not? At least he could take a look the next day and see if there might be somewhere he could use her.

"Come here," he told her. She moved up and stood beside him. Ben held her hands and kissed them. "My very precious first born child. I'm trying to think what would be best for you. I understand that you have nothing to do here at home, that time is hanging heavily on your hands, and that you need a change. Since you say you're not ready to consider a serious suitor yet, I imagine the best thing for you would be to see if I can find somewhere in the firm that you might perform some meaningful work. You do have a beautiful hand. We might use you for some written work of some kind, or perhaps in bookkeeping. No promises, now. If there is some work you could do, and want to do, you would have to be there every day from eight to six, like everyone else, with half an hour for a quick lunch, six days a week. It will be long hours and hard work and leave almost no time for amusement. You'll have to do your share."

"Oh, yes. It sounds exciting already. I'll work hard, I promise I will." She put her arms around his neck and kissed his cheek. "I'll be the best bookkeeper you ever had. You'll see. You'll be proud of me, and I'll work just ever so hard. Oh! Let me tell Mother. She will be surprised!"

Before Ben could say anything she bounded out of the room. Sandra would be more than surprised. She would be upset. Just how disturbed he didn't know, but he would settle the matter firmly, if he had to. They could usually talk over any problems that came up. He had been watching Harriet, and ever since her brush with Cunliffe he had noticed a change, more of a womanly bearing, of knowing looks, a more woman-of-the-world feeling about how she talked and moved. For a moment Ben considered the chance that she had experienced an affair with someone, but he discounted the idea at once. She wasn't close to anyone that he knew of, and she was still only seventeen. No, it must have some relation to the Cunliffe matter. It had brought about a more significant change in Harriet than he had anticipated.

A few minutes later Sandra came in, stared at her husband for a minute, then walked to his big chair.

"You really think you're doing the right thing, to let your daughter think she might be working at the company?"

"I've thought it over. She's very determined

to do something. She has absolutely no creative or constructive activity now. Nothing that interests her. She has decided that she is not interested in marriage at the moment, and I told her that tomorrow we would go down to the office and look around and see if there might be a place where she could fit in. No final decision has been made. That will wait until tomorrow, until I get what feeling she has for the work, and also the attitude of the men working there."

"Your mind is made up on this matter?"

"No, of course not. We can discuss anything at any time, in the way we always have. But you must have noticed how restless Harriet is. We both agree she should be married by now. She should have a husband to serve and to enjoy, but that's not the case. She needs some outlet for her youthful energies, and this might be the answer."

"You know every decent family in Boston will gossip about this. They will wonder why your own daughter must go to work in a place where there are thirty men. It could be ruinous for her."

"I hardly think so, Sandra. Whether we like it or not, times are changing. Dr. Warren now has a woman in his office helping him with his paper work. Did you know that? And there is a woman working in Edes and Gill. I really don't think the 'nice' people of Boston are going to gossip if my own daughter wants to work in my business. We'll discuss it again tomorrow."

Sandra's eyes were still angry. "Very well. But I insist on coming along and approving her working conditions, if you still think that she might find a place. Would she be *alone* with all those men all day long?"

"Of course not. I'll be there most of the time. If I do hire her I'll have one man continually responsible for her welfare and safety. Besides that, she's the owner's daughter. Do you think anyone there would try to take advantage of her, knowing who she is, and what punishment he would suffer?"

Sandra rubbed her forehead, then her cheeks, with her right hand. It was a gesture she had picked up that came whenever she was nervous and not sure of herself. Now all she could do was lift her brows and walk out of the room.

Harriet had hurried up to her room to pick out the clothes she would wear. At last she selected a street dress with only one petticoat so it wouldn't be too bulky. It had a top that buttoned high on her throat, ruffles down the front, and a little jacket. For going outside she would wear a simple long black cloak. That, combined with a small felt hat with a feather in it would be stylish enough, yet practical, and would show that she was serious about working.

That settled, she began to study her ciphering again so she would be as good tomorrow as possible. With a little practice on the job, she should be as quick as any of the men in the office.

The following morning, Ben, his wife and Harriet rode in two chaises from their home to the waterfront and Rutledge & Rutledge. Harry, the groom and driver for the Rutledge household, handled one rig, and Ben the other. Harry was told to wait and the three others trooped inside.

Rutledge & Rutledge had about thirty workers in the main office building, most of them in two large rooms. One of the offices was on each floor which fronted one of the large warehouses the company owned on Ann Street, just north of Wentworth's Wharf. Ben's office was upstairs, just off the large room where the bookkeeper worked and where the other paperwork, bills of lading, accounts due and ship movements were all plotted and kept up to date.

Ben led the two women into his office, where they removed their capes. Then they stepped to the door and looked out at the row of desks with men working over books, charts, and papers.

"This is where most of the bookkeeping work is done," Ben said. "We keep track of all loads hauled, charges, payments, outstanding bills, as well as dozens of other things. But, as you see, Harriet, there's simply no private place where you could work."

"Any of those desks would suit me," she said.

Ben watched her. There was a look in her eyes he had never seen before, a determination that told him she would tackle this job, and that she would be outstanding at it because she wanted to show everyone she could do it, that she could handle the work just as well as anyone else in the firm.

Ben noted it and continued the tour, from the counting room to the downstairs offices, to the long Rutledge docks where ships were being loaded and unloaded. Back in his office, Ben seated his wife and daughter, then leaned back in his chair and looked at Harriet. He wished he had a pipe.

"Well, what do you think of the family business?"

"It's tremendously interesting. I never knew there were so many parts of it—the sailors, the ships, the docks, the warehouses and all the business end of things with bills of lading, manifests, shipping orders, storage, billing, collecting . . . it's all so exciting!"

"Do you still want to try working in all of this jumble?"

"Oh, yes. I'm more determined than ever. I want to learn all about every department."

"Any particular place you'd like to start?"

"I think bookkeeping, because then I can learn about the other departments at the same time and see how they all function together, how each supports the other and where the money goes to keep the whole business working. Does that seem a reasonable place to start?"

Ben chuckled to cover up his surprise. Never

before had he heard her talking this way. The girl had a good head on her shoulders, and what seemed to be a solid business sense as well. When Ben looked at his wife she seemed confused by the sudden talk of money and departments and bills of lading and related areas.

"Sandra, do you think it might work out all right to have Harriet employed in the bookkeeping department?"

"Well, I don't know. It does seem like the most protected area, and it's closest to you."

"Fine, it's settled then. We do have a vacancy, a training position. I'll speak with Hamilton Reeves and you can start tomorrow."

"Why not today, Father? I'm ready."

Ben laughed. This girl was going to be all right. "Yes, indeed, why not today? You're here, and set to go to work. I'll see your mother to her chaise and be right back to talk with you."

Hamilton Reeves was a small man with a big ego. He was only an inch taller than Harriet, at five feet, five inches, but he made up for his small size with a thunderous voice, a quick temper, and an astounding ability to remember dates, places, charges and costs. He had risen slowly to the very top of the bookkeeping department and records chief of all of the Rutledge business operations. Reeves was also a bachelor, not entirely by choice. He was thirty-nine years old and had been jilted at the church door when he and his intended were both twenty. He vowed never to marry, never to touch a woman again and to concentrate all of his energies on his chosen field of bookkeeping. He had done so with outstanding success for nineteen years. Ben called him in and talked to him privately for a half hour, explaining that Harriet would be moving into the vacant bookkeeper trainee slot that same day. Reeves was so outraged he could barely talk, but he agreed to let her have a chance, to see what she could do.

Ben asked that she be shown no special treatment. If she could do the work, fine. If not, she would be taken from the position.

That same day, Harriet sat at the high desk working on a set of simple books which Reeves said a child could tally and balance in an hour. Harriet did them in half an hour and asked for something else.

Sure that he would trip her up on her very first work, Reeves checked the figures and the work carefully, but could not find a single error.

In the days and weeks that slipped past, Harriet became so proficient in her work as bookkeeper that, in a weak moment, Hamilton wondered if his own position might be threatened. He chided himself and went back to work. Even though she was doing an outstanding job, Reeves found small ways to make life unpleasant for Harriet. One day it might be a set of books that some other bookkeeper had mixed up—she had to find the mistakes, correct them and redo the entries. Again it might be a set of figures that had to be done before the end of the day and would keep her late.

When Ben was not within hearing, Hamilton took delight in reprimanding some clerk close by Harriet and attaching a string of colorful oaths which he hoped would shock Harriet. If it did, she never let on. She had been moved out of the trainee category after the first month and took over regular accounts to keep in order and up to date, as well as working some of the more complex Rutledge & Rutledge profit and loss accounts.

Hamilton Reeves was still her superior and used every chance he found to talk down her work and to snipe at her. After a week in which he had taken cracks at her every day, Harriet arranged it so she would not be able to turn in an account that had to be checked by Reeves until after quitting time. She said she was almost done, and it would be about ten minutes.

Harriet saw the office clear of the other workers, waved goodbye to them and her father, then took the report in its folder and went towards Reeves' desk.

"Mr. Reeves, I have the report, but I'd like to talk to you about it privately. Let's use the office at the end of the room."

Harriet never referred to Ben as her father in the office.

"Why the hell go down there? We can talk here."

"I think you'll be interested in this report, Mr. Reeves."

"Damn women," he muttered, but stood up and followed her to Ben's office. Harriet let him go in first, then saw no one else on the floor. She went into her father's office and closed the door.

She put the report down on the desk and crossed her arms over her chest.

"Mr. Reeves, I've been very patient with you, but it seems your sickness is growing, not being cured. You simply refuse to admit that I can do the work here—most of it better than you can. And all because I'm a woman, that's your only objection to me, correct?" She didn't give him a chance to answer.

"Mr. Reeves, I'm a fair-minded person. If I do my job, I expect to be treated the same as the other bookkeepers, no better, but certainly no worse. For over two months you have been giving me the back of your hand whenever possible. Why?"

"Women belong at home, sewing, cooking and caring for babies. Does that answer your question, Miss Rutledge?"

"Typical, and what I expected." She picked up the file. "Mr. Reeves, I believe you knew a woman by the name of Abigail Dunwoody."

Reeve's face blanched, his hand came halfway to his mouth, then he exploded. "Don't you ever mention that name to me again. Do you hear, *never!*" He had raised his fist to her, but now he lowered it with great effort. His face turned cherry red, his eyes still bulged, and both his hands were clenched.

"Mr. Reeves, shortly after your campaign of slander, false accusations, and whisperings against me that you started, I began to do a little investigation of your background. This is the report I've gathered." She opened it and glanced at the first page. "It seems that the lady in question was expecting a child on the wedding date. People who knew her said that you were undoubtedly the father of her unborn child."

Reeves started toward her. Harriet jumped behind her father's desk, pulled out the flintlock pistol which she knew he kept there, loaded, primed, cocked and ready. She picked it up as if she had handled the big weapon before, holding it with both hands and pointing it at Reeves.

"Please stay right there, Mr. Reeves. It will make this so much more pleasant."

The man stopped, his eyes glaring, murderous, his hands still clenched.

"It seems that after the bride spurned you at the door of the church, you took to drink. Some two months later, you were found in a common house in New York by your family and returned to Boston under protest, where you were lectured by your stern and most demanding father, one Lucas Reeves. Am I going too fast for you to follow?"

Reeves scowled at her, his breathing ragged.

He was furious, but now surprise and respect were beginning to show.

"Thereafter you were apprenticed to your uncle Ambrose Reeves, a bookkeeper, who taught you patiently until you were a qualified sum-maker. Shortly thereafter you came into the employment of Rutledge & Rutledge, where you have been a good and faithful employee these nineteen years. It must have been tremendously lonesome, for you foreswore the touch of any woman. I should amend that to say, any decent woman."

Reeves slumped into a chair across the desk now, staring at her with round, listless eyes. The sun dropped behind the buildings across the street. It would be dark in an hour.

She put the pistol back in the desk.

"Mr. Reeves, I am determined to learn the shipping business from crow's nest to hull, on land and on the sea. You and your sniveling, backbiting little campaign will not stop me, or even slow me down. But I have learned a lot from you. I now understand and can perform any bookkeeping or record-keeping operation in this company."

His face was slack, his anger drained.

"Mr. Reeves, what I'm trying to say is that the battle is over. You have lost. I don't need your help any more. I'll be moving out of bookkeeping before long, but I don't like to leave enemies anywhere.

"I'm sure you understand me, Mr. Reeves. I intend you no harm. I may someday take over the management of this firm, so I will need loyal employees who are as talented and efficient at their jobs as you are.

"Do you have anything to say, Mr. Reeves, about my work, about the quality of my bookkeeping, about the efficient and businesslike manner in which I always conduct myself?"

"What . . . what am I supposed to say? I was insulted at first that a mere woman could do the work so well. Then I became jealous. You are a fine bookkeeper, you have a fine mind, and you are a tremendously beautiful young woman. I struck back in the only way I felt I could."

"Is that all you have to say?" She walked toward him, leaning back against the front of the desk, four feet from him. She bent slightly to look at him, letting her full, lovely figure show to best advantage. She hoped he noticed.

"Miss Rutledge, you are the most—the most beautiful woman I have ever seen. You make Abigail look like a slatternly fishwife."

"That's very kind of you, Mr. Reeves." She moved forward, bent and kissed his cheek. She saw him looking at her bodice. Quickly she moved back a step.

"Now, Mr. Reeves, I hope we won't have any more trouble. Do you think we will?"

He stood, looking as if he were ready to pounce on her and tear off her clothes, but he held. His hand came up and wiped the sweat from his forehead. "No, Miss Rutledge. No, ma'am, I don't think we'll have any more trouble at all."

Chapter Four
THE IMPOTENT TESTING

August 22, 1770

Edmund Cunliffe lay on his big four-poster bed, sipping from a glass of red wine. Today was the test, the first he had allowed himself since his . . . trouble . . . earlier in the summer; the first since his own doctor had pronounced him healed. There had been a small caution that he might not have the same ability or stamina as he had before, but there was little doubt that the organ should function almost normally.

The original injury had not kept him in bed more than a few days, but with the bandages it seemed much simpler to wear robes than the impossibly tight breeches, so he had spent most of his time in the house.

The first week he had ordered all of the females out of his sight. His current ladies had been sent back to their places of regular employment on the waterfront and the slaves were ordered to stay in the basement until he had retired, when they could do their chores. Lot brought him his food on a tray. Only gradually had he allowed the two black girls to come back and do their regular duties—but he made them wear loose fitting dresses so their figures wouldn't show. He wanted nothing to excite him. For weeks after the duel, even the thought of a pretty girl in bed with him gave Edmund immediate physical pain.

Visits by his doctor did little to lift Edmund's spirits. Dr. Pauley was a short, fat man, bald as an eagle, with half spectacles and a bawdy sense of humor. On his first visit he brought an "assistant," one of the shady ladies of the bawdy houses, whose huge breasts she promptly let fall out of her dress.

Cunliffe had screeched out a string of appropriate curses, hit her with his fists, and sent her storming out of the house. Dr. Pauley doubled over with laughter and would have been attacked himself, if he had ventured close enough to Cunliffe, who continued a steady stream of foul language until the medical men stopped laughing and wiped his tears away.

"Just thought I'd show you what you're missing, Edmund, old boy," said Pauley. When Edmund calmed down enough, the doctor looked at the bandages, removed them and made what further repairs he could. He pursed his lips as he studied Edmund.

"You realize the bottom artery has been severed," he said, then frowned and stopped.

"What the hell does that mean?" Edmund shouted.

Dr. Pauley scowled. "Are you sure you want to know?"

"Damn right."

Pauley shrugged. "I don't know for sure, just thought of it, matter of fact. If the blood supply to your organ is reduced, it could mean you'll have trouble getting a full erection."

Edmund threw a dish of sweetmeats at the doctor.

"What the hell are you talking about?"

"Just another joke, Ed. You need to work more on your sense of humor." Dr. Pauley wasn't laughing now. He used some healing ointments, changed the dressing and closed up his large black bag.

"That should hold you for three or four days. Just take it easy, and stay away from the pretty girls." Dr. Pauley walked to the door of Edmund's bedroom. He opened it and turned. "Oh, Cunliffe, just stay out of the skirts of that cute little darkie girl I saw downstairs. Humping her right now would kill you quick."

Edmund threw a pewter cup at Dr. Pauley as he ducked through the door, laughing heartily.

Edmund had long since ended visits from the ribald doctor, letting nature do its own healing work. He waited now for Roxanne, one of his favorites, a stylish little French girl who always had turned him into a flaming torch. It had been three months since his injury. He had to be ready by now.

The scene was set. Four kinds of tarts, some

hard candy, and a tray of fresh fruits. He wished he could have hired a violinist to play soft music, but there wasn't one in the city. The shades were half drawn, cutting the light to a soft, intimate level. He had bathed and freshly powdered his hair.

A few minutes later a knock came on the door. Roxanne came in, posed for him a moment to show off her new dress with the low cut neckline and sweeping skirt. Her hair was piled high on top of her head, making her slender neck seem even longer. She smiled and she came toward him with properly prim steps.

"Oh, Edmund, you are looking so handsome today. It is well to be back in your beautiful house. Oh, if only I owned this place I could bring over half of Paris and have the best brothel in all of the colonies!"

She unpinned her small hat and dropped it on a chair, then sat down on the bed and kissed Edmund. He broke off the kiss and pushed both his hands into the bodice of her dress, and laughed.

"Oh, yes, Roxanne, this is starting off very fine!"

An hour later, Edmund sat on the edge of his bed, so furious he couldn't talk. Roxanne sat beside him, shaking her head.

"I am sorry, *cheri*. I know everything about my business, every way in the world, but I am not what you say . . . the magician." She slipped into her clothes, covering large red welts where his leather belt had marked her back and stomach. "Edmund, my many times lover, maybe if I came back with two pretty friends . . ."

He shook his head and pushed her off the bed, motioning for her to leave. She dressed, took her hat and purse, now considerably heavier, and left the room without looking back. There would be no more easy money from Edmund Cunliffe. He was no longer a man. She would have to spread the word.

Edmund lay on the bed on his back, still naked. He rolled over and beat his fists into the pillow as he had done often when he was a small boy. Somehow it had always led to his getting exactly what he wanted. This time it didn't work that way. At last he began to cry.

Later, a knock sounded on his bedroom door, but he ignored it. It was more than an hour after the girl left that he got up and dressed, then went to his library where he took out his best brandy, two bottles of champagne, and a pad of paper.

As he drank, the plans began to come, one after another. This time there would be no duel. That was without question. This time he would simply pay a professional to do the job, and it would be finished quickly, cleanly and with no possible tie to Edmund Cunliffe, respected Boston industrialist.

But should it be a slow death, or a fast one? And how could he enjoy it if it went too fast?

Edmund began writing down variations, and at last settled on what would have to suffice.

He would hire someone off a ship to shoot Ben Rutledge at close range through the heart, rob him, be sure he was dead, fade back to his ship and be out of port by morning. There was no chance for theatricals or for an appealing torture death. Quick and sure. Undeniably *sure*. It would be no problem to find a man who could do the job. The more Edmund drank, the more heavily the total injustice of his position weighed upon him. It was monstrous! No man had a right to do that to another man. It would be a commendable public service to eliminate such a man as Ben Rutledge from the glorious community of Boston.

Three hours later Edmund was dangerously drunk. He screamed for Lot, who quickly came with more champagne. Lot was his manservant, driver, handyman, gardener, repair expert. He was one of Cunliffe's four black slaves. Edmund threw the empty bottles at Lot, who caught them and took them away.

Halfway through the afternoon Edmund began pitching full wine bottles around the library. He broke out two windows, smashed a mirror and spread champagne all over a shelf of rare and valuable books. Lot stood by, a faintly approving expression on his flat, black face. He wished Cunliffe would ruin everything in the library, even knock over a candle and burn down this mansion of lust.

The more Lot saw of Cunliffe's wild, drunken behavior, the more sure he was that this might be the right time. He went over carefully in his mind the preparations he had made, which had been formulated for some months now. Yes, everything was ready. Now if Mr. Cunliffe drank himself into the kind of stupor he was heading for . . .

Lot ducked a wine bottle that sailed over his head and smashed against the mantle, the wine splashing halfway to the ceiling, gushing along the mantle until it ran off the far end, making a puddle on the fine rug. Lot chuckled softly. Somebody was going to have one hell of a clutter to clean up here tomorrow.

"Lot, you black bastard, get your ass over here!" Cunliffe screamed.

Lot moved toward the man where he sat in an overstuffed chair, wine glass in one hand, bottle of champagne in the other.

"More wine, bring me more wine. The good stuff!" He belched loudly, laughed and tried to stand but couldn't and fell back in his chair. He laughed, dropped the wine glass, and found that ridiculously funny as well. At last he got the bottle to his mouth and drank.

Lot left the library, ran to the wine cellar and brought back four bottles of the best wine and placed them on the small desk near the bookshelves.

"The wine, sir. Is there anything else?"

Lot saw the surly stare, the shake of the

head, and left, closed the library doors softly and went to the kitchen where June, the cook, had just made sandwiches for everyone from coarse brown bread and cheese she had bought at the market the day before. June was a huge black woman who had lived in the north all her life. She had learned to cook at her mother's side in this very house forty years ago, and had served the Cunliffe family ever since. She often didn't believe the slaves in the south were as mistreated as people told her. Lot thanked her for the food, his eyes locking with hers for a moment. Even though he was thirty-five years old, he thought of this big, friendly woman as his mother.

He took the sandwich to the basement, and on a sudden impulse went to the wine cellar and took a small bottle of wine and uncorked it. He'd never taken any wine before, but tonight he might need it. The master would never know. He would have drunk himself senseless in another hour or two, and that would be somewhere near sunset.

Lot lifted his brows and sighed. He had worked and planned so long, yet now he was half afraid to admit that this was the time. He glanced at the loose wall board in the far corner of his basement room. He was sure that nothing had been disturbed. No one knew or even suspected he had anything hidden there. The cache behind the board held a cloth sack with his hoard of silver coins and English pound notes.

Lot gave a sigh and began gathering up his clothing. Most of it was hand-downs from the master. He laid out a pair of heavy black pants and a dark blue jacket with three buttons missing. Under them he would wear heavy long underwear, another shirt and a pair of good, home knit socks June had made for him last winter.

The remainder of his clothes he folded into a small bundle and tied them inside an old sweater Mr. Cunliffe had discarded. At least he had more to his name than the last time he was moved. He selected two heavy woolen blankets from the storeroom and rolled them as tightly as he could in a package three feet long, then tied it in several places with a stout cord. He finished those tasks, put both bundles under his bed and out of sight, then went to the kitchen.

"June, the master told me to have you prepare a quantity of food for several days. He'll be taking a trip."

"He is, is he, nigger?"

"Yes. That cheese, two loaves of bread, a sack of dried fruit and some coffee."

"How's come the master going to camp out all of a sudden, when he never did before? He always stays in the best inns he kin find 'long the way." June watched his confusion. She held up her hand and smiled. "Boy, don't you worry none. I know when somebody's gonna go traveling. We done had two travelers before, both of 'em younger'n you. They made it, I reckon. You want some of them dried beans we got, too?"

Lot nodded, smiling so broadly that he could barely keep from crying. "Yes'm, I think that would be fine. Now I got to go see the master!"

June smiled again. "Master's done fell down in the hallway, the girls tell me. Passed out of his mind, he is, drunk as he can be."

"Good!" Lot said softly, and winked at the cook.

She laughed and watched him run for the hall, wishing she were young enough to go with him.

Just outside the library doors he found Mr. Cunliffe sprawled on the rug, face up, snoring, but with one hand still curled around a half-full bottle of wine which had made another stain on the rug.

Inside the library Lot saw a broken, littered wasteland. The desk was ruined, the rug splotched with wine, each wall splattered with more wine. Lot grinned as he picked up Cunliffe and took him up to his bedroom. He had to perform as usual now so Cunliffe wouldn't miss him until mid-morning, if he were lucky. That way he would have more of a head start. Lot dropped the unconscious man on his rumpled bed, took off his shoes and began to pull up a comforter. He stopped, dug out the master's purse and took out two ten-pound notes, found a great deal more there, but put it away. He could not be charged with robbery this way if he were caught. He tucked the two notes in his pocket, then covered up Edmund Cunliffe, looked at him for what he hoped would be the last time, and closed the bedroom door.

Back downstairs he told them the master was asleep, and had the maids close up and lock the house for the night. He took the bundle of food June had prepared for him. He could live on it for at least a week if he were careful. He had a flint and steel and had much practice getting a fire going when it had died. He had a sheath knife Mr. Cunliffe had discarded. In one final act that would break his bond with slavery once and for all, Lot took one of the flintlock pistols from the set of dueling weapons, and put enough powder and ball and wadding in a leather box for twenty shots. He would hide it all in the bottom of his saddle bags for now.

Lot went back to the loose wallboard and pulled it open, took out the small cloth sack and counted his hoard. With the twenty he had taken tonight, he had over a hundred and thirty pounds sterling. A fortune. It was far more money than he had thought existed ten years ago. He could live for several years on that much, if he had to. He hid the money in several places in his clothes, and would put more in the saddle bags.

As June watched, Lot took the bundles and blankets out to the stables and quietly threw a saddle blanket over the best of the three horses, a four-year-old mare. He put on the older of the two saddles and cinched it up snugly. Then he stowed his goods in the saddle bags he attached. Inside went part of his food and most of his clothes. The rest of the food and the blanket he tied on the back of the saddle into a good traveling lashup.

June sat watching him in the early evening darkness. One huge tear rolled down her cheek. She reached out and hugged him so tightly he thought she would break his ribs.

"In the morning, woman, you know nothing. You didn't see me. You hear? Then you won't get whipped." He bent and kissed her plump cheek, then swung up on the horse and walked the mount around the big house and to the street. The mare had good strong legs, a broad and sturdy chest, and looked like the best horse for a hard ride. He had changed into his traveling clothes and now pulled an old brown bill cap from his back pocket and put it on his head. It was one the master had discarded two years ago.

At Middle Street he met the heavy fog blanket but kept going to his left and south toward the Boston neck. Once away from the house he lifted the bay to a canter and moved faster through the heavy fog. It came in wet, thick waves, rolling in from the Atlantic. But Lot made his way through it all, kept going down Middle Street to Hanover, then along Queen Street to Tremont and on past the long mall to the burying grounds. There he turned abruptly down Frog Lane and thence to Orange Street which would lead him all the way to the small neck of land that connected the peninsula with the Roxbury area.

Once off the neck, he would strike westward. Lot had long ago given up his previous thoughts of trying to go to Kentucky. He had no idea how far it was, but someone had told him it was far to the south. He had no intention of going anywhere near the south.

He slowed to a walk again as he moved the horse across the narrow neck of land, then followed the road through the marshes and bogs to Roxbury and turned right to the west and up along the Charles River. He would move west, always west, and there he would find freedom.

Once away from the Charles he moved faster, galloping for ten minutes, then slowing to a walk to give his mount a breather. He knew a horse couldn't be pushed too hard or it would quit, give up and even die. Right now it was one of his most valuable possessions, his means of getting out of this colony.

Lot, as every slave, knew well the tales about runaway slaves. He knew it was easier in the north to elude slave hunting than it was in the south, but he trembled when he thought of stories he had heard about such men. He was determined to go so far into the wilderness that he would be by himself, and no man could call him slave.

He had decided his best method would be to travel by night and sleep and hide by day. He doubted that Cunliffe himself would ride after him, but he could hire men to track him down. They would move west, asking who had seen a tall, strong negro man on a bay horse, but with luck no one would see him at all. He guessed he would have to travel by night until he got out of the colony of Massachusetts, but in truth he had no idea how big the colony was, or just how far he would have to go to that unending wilderness he had heard about that extended to the west. If he could ride far enough, then he would be free.

Now Lot found himself on an uneven road that was little more than a wagon trail between two cultivated fields. The Boston fog had long ago been left behind, and now he munched on a piece of the cheese June had provided him. As he rode, he watched the stars. Lot had practiced looking at the stars while he was in Boston, and had memorized their positions. Sometimes he thought he could see pictures of animals in the stars, but he knew that was only his imagination. He found one cluster of stars that looked like a small dipper or cup, and knew he could use them to guide him westward. Ahead he heard a dog bark. Lot rode at once into the field across from a small farmhouse to cut a wide circle around the dog and his master. He didn't want to see or be seen by another human being for at least two hundred miles. That would take him ten nights of riding at twenty miles a night. June had taught him to do his sums one winter. He couldn't read, but at least he could count and do small sums. It would be a handy skill for a freeman.

Lot cut back to the road, checked to see that it was still wandering westward, and picked up the pace. To his left he saw an apple tree hanging heavy with ripe fruit. Lot picked a dozen apples, stuffed two in his saddle bags, and the rest inside his shirt. Then he rode, eating two as he went. He would live off the land whenever he could.

A name. He would need a last name. He'd never had one before. As he thought about it he wondered what his name should be. Certainly not Cunliffe. He had seen a name in Boston on a printing plant. It was Edes. That was a short name—Lot Edes. June had taught him to write his name, Lot, but could he remember how to make the letters for Edes? At last he pictured them in his mind. Now he could do it. Now he had a name. He was Lot Edes!

Two weeks passed. Lot had ridden by night as he planned and slept by day, deep in the thickest woods he could find. As he moved further west this became easier and easier to do. The villages vanished, an occasional farm showed, and at last he began to ride by day, finding he could make much better time. He kept moving west, helped by a small compass he had found in Mr. Cunliffe's den. He had crossed the Connecticut River and forged on west. His food ran out and he shot a turkey, which he cooked and promptly ate half of.

This lasted for almost two days before it turned rancid.

The next day he stopped at a rustic cabin. He watched it for an hour and saw only two white women there. When he went up and hailed the place a voice told him to come on up. He saw the musket poked through a firing slot.

The women fed him, but made him stand up outside as he ate from a trencher piled high with beans, cabbage and a slab of venison. One woman said her husband was in a field a couple hundred yards away and would come if she screamed.

"Ma'am, I shore do hope you don't scream. I intend you no harm."

"Mama, he a real nigger? I ain't never seen no nigger before."

Her mother hushed the young girl and sent her back into the house. After he finished the meal, Lot asked if he could buy some traveling food. The woman put together what she had, a smoked ham, two loaves of bread, some dried beans and dried fruit. Lot gave her one of the silver pieces he had in his pocket. He didn't know how much it was worth, but she exclaimed over it and gave him a cloth sack filled with apples as well. He thanked her and rode on west.

Lot had not shaved since he left Boston. It was foolish to waste the time shaving in the wilderness, he decided. He rode during the day now, and once in a while, saw a rider coming toward him. Usually he detoured in the woods until the other party passed.

Lot had learned it is much harder to start a flint and steel fire in the woods than on a proper hearth with dry tinder and pieces of cloth to catch the spark. He made a fire only when the chilly nights demanded it, or when he needed one to cook meat.

It was the first week in September, but Lot didn't know or care. He was still moving west, to the land of the large lakes, if he could find it. The trees were turning beautiful colors and the evening wind whipped in colder and colder. He bought a third blanket from a cabin dweller on the banks of the Hudson River and followed the stream north, circled around the village of Albany and when he found the Mohawk river, turned west again along the stream. He heard from a settler that this river had its beginnings at the very edge of the land of the big lakes, one that was called the Ontario. He decided to continue west. Lot had no idea what he would do when he got there. How would he feed himself? He shrugged the question aside. He would worry about that when the time came. Lot was more willing now to talk to other travelers on the road. However, the road was little more than a trail for horses and pack mules. One man told him that the only way for a man to make a living in the wilderness was to hunt and trap. He told Lot that he was well out of Massachusetts now, but was still in the colony of

New York. Another day down the trail, Lot came around a bend in the river and met a tall, bearded man in the center of the trail. He walked and led two pack animals.

The bearded man looked at Lot for several seconds. The stranger was as tall as Lot and just as muscular. He wore a skin on his head for a cap, a heavy fur-lined coat and boots with Indian moccasins tied to the outside.

"I'll be dogged!" the man said, staring at Lot. "You must be one of them runaway slaves I keep hearing about. Reckon I'd run away, too, if somebody tried to brand me." He held up both hands, palms toward Lot. "No worry, friend. I ain't about to tangle with ye. Bigun', you're good sized for any kind of man. Out here a man's counted on for what he can do, shoot, stalk a deer, build a fire—the important things, not what kind of hair or skin he's got."

Lot's hand moved slightly away from his belt and the ever ready flintlock, although he knew the primer powder must be moist by now and it probably would not fire.

"Is the land of the big lakes to the west?" Lot asked.

The grizzled trapper nodded. Now Lot saw that the pack animals were heavily loaded and looked as ragged and worn as the trapper. Each animal was weighed down with furs, Lot guessed.

"True, friend. I'm running my last set of traps down here, and then heading back for

Fort Oswego. It's right on the water out there on the Ontario—big lake, looks like an ocean. It's 'bout a hundred and fifty miles, more or less, on west. You aiming in that direction?"

Lot nodded. "What you got on the horses?"

The trapper laughed. "Them is mules, friend. Don't let them hear you call them horses or I'll never get no work out of 'em. On their scrawny backs is furs. All kinds of furs. I'm a trapper."

"You catch little animals for their hides?"

"True, friend, that I do. Late getting in to the meeting this year. Most of the others moved on more into the big lakes, some down toward the Allegheny."

Lot was trying hard to understand. "Trapping, is it hard?"

"Hell, no. Not if'n you know what you're a-doing."

"Could you teach me?"

The old trapper chuckled. "We'd be a pair, wouldn't we, you and me, riding into Ft. Oswego and them traders scratching their skulls. They never seen no nigras up there." He thought a minute. "Teach you how to trap if you pay for it with that horse."

"No. Too much. She's my legs, she moves me. I got ten English sterling pound notes. For them will you teach me?"

The trapper squatted, and drew lines in the dust. It was time he had his furs turned in and went back to setting up his new lines. He was still eight days' ride from Ft. Oswego.

He stood and held out his hand. "My name's Jacobs. Hal Jacobs, and I came out into these wilds from the big city of New York to get away from people. But I'll teach you to trap for ten pounds. Fair is fair." They shook hands.

The next two weeks were the hardest of Lot's life. He had to memorize the habits and actions of the beaver, mink, marten and otter. He had to remember where they nested, how they entered and left the water, where the best chance was to find them, and how to set the traps and conceal them so the animal wouldn't smell or see them.

They set a line of traps along the Mohawk and went over them day after day. There weren't many animals left here, but the training was detailed and complete.

Lot learned how to skin out each type of animal, how to preserve the pelt and stretch it to keep it at high quality for a top price. By the end of the two weeks they had worked to within a day's ride of Fort Oswego where the British fur company would buy the catch.

That night they built a campfire and cooked fresh meat over the coals as Jacobs nipped at a bottle of whiskey.

"Never touch it, eh? You'll learn damn soon living by yourself out here in Injun country. Wonder what the first red man will think when he spots your black hide? That would be a sight to see." Before the fire burned down after their dinner, Jacobs had passed out. Lot pushed him under his blankets, then rolled into his own and went to sleep.

Lot woke up with the first rays of the sun, sat up and sensed something behind him. Before he could turn, an object pounded down on his black skull and he pitched forward, unconscious again.

The sun was halfway in the sky when Lot woke up again. He remembered surfacing once or twice, but drifting back into the mist, coming out of it for a moment only to slip away. Now he was fully awake. He tried to sit up. A pounding gong clattered in his head and some invisible hand pushed him back to the ground.

His head was on fire. It clamored and buzzed and throbbed. He lay there with his eyes open, staring at the treetops, trying to remember.

It came back slowly. He had awakened, then almost at once something hit his head. But that had been ages ago. No. He rolled over on his stomach and pushed himself up gradually. It took him several minutes to gain a sitting position. His head still throbbed painfully. Lot blinked to clear the last of the film from his eyes.

The first thing he saw was a man lying half across the burned-out breakfast fire. The figure was Hal Jacobs, his friend. Lot moved slowly, beating back the terrible pain in his head, and crawled over to Hal. He rolled him over and gasped. Jacobs' head had been split open from a heavy blow, cracking it apart like a ripe melon.

Lot looked away quickly.

There wasn't anything left of the camp. Everything but the blankets Lot had been sleeping in were gone. His horse, the two mules, the furs, all the traps, the rest of the food. Also missing were Lot's sheath knife, his pistol and all of his ball and powder. He examined his pockets. The two silver coins in his pants were missing, but all the seams of his shirt were intact. He still had his pounds sterling.

Lot stood, walked a dozen steps slowly, beat down the nausea and pain, and paced the route again. He found a sturdy stick he could use as a cane and a club, if necessary. It was two inches thick and four feet long, a straight, dry oak limb and tough as iron.

He studied the ground. There was no mistaking which direction the murderers had taken. Lot looked up the trail toward the fort, then at Jacobs' body. He knew he should give the man a decent burial, but the killers had too much of a head start already. He turned and walked up the trail, following the plain tracks the three animals had left.

Lot moved steadily for two hours, then took a rest. He had a drink of water from the stream, then went on. The riders did not seem to be in any hurry. An hour later, Lot found where they had stopped to cook a noontime meal. There were plainly two of them now. He found burned tobacco and evidences of two sizes of boot-prints. Lot walked faster, with nothing to eat but a few late berries he found along the trail. Just before dark, he came to a high ridge on the trail. He could look down and see lights far ahead, fires of some kind and what looked like a flat sheen of big water beyond that. It must be the lake and the fort. Closer by, near the foot of the ridge where the river came out of a narrow gorge, he saw what he thought were wisps of smoke coming up through the green cover of trees. Lot watched the spot for five minutes and was sure it was a campfire.

He walked faster now, jogging down the hill, alert to what was on all sides of him. When he guessed he was within half a mile of the smoke, he slowed to make sure the hoofprints were the same as those he had seen at the camp. Then dusk closed in on him. He moved slowly, advancing on the camp, making no sound.

Lot moved from one tree to the next, cautiously, with all the care and skill of an Indian. In the past two weeks, Hal Jacobs had taught him a lot more than simply how to trap. He had poured out a lifetime of understanding and knowledge of the Indians, how they thought, how they lived, how they moved. Hal said a mountain man had to be as smart as an Indian if he wanted to live among them and keep his scalp.

Lot could smell the smoke of the campfire now. He edged closer, from tree to tree. When he was certain the fire was just ahead, he faded silently into the denser brush at the side of the trail to come up on the camp from a different direction.

A half-hour later, as full darkness closed in, he slid into position behind a rotting log less than thirty feet from the campfire.

Two men sat beside the fire, roasting half a turkey. One was small, with a full white beard, a pinched face, and a mashed-in hat. He carried a flintlock pistol in his belt. The other man was huge, almost bald, and also had a full set of face hair. The larger man carried a foot-long knife in his belt.

Lot had promised himself that he would not kill them in their sleep. He would challenge them if he could, find out for sure that they had killed Jacobs and tried to murder him, then stolen their goods.

As he worked closer, Lot laid out his plan carefully. He had no desire to be shot by his own flintlock or carved up by the long knife. He would disarm the smaller man with a quick blow from his walking stick, then attempt to knock out the big man with a crack of oak on skull. Lot crawled on his belly behind the rotting log to a two-foot-thick tree just out of range of the firelight, and stood up, his club in his hand. Lot felt a rage building. He saw his own horse, recognized the flintlock as the one he had brought from Boston. They were the killers, no doubt now. He was in back of the big man who sat beside the fire, tearing the turkey apart.

Lot gripped the oak club tighter. He would slam the bald-headed man in the neck with his club, then batter the smaller one across the fire and seize the pistol.

Lot moved quietly, then lifted the club and screamed a guttural roar of vengeance as he ran the last two steps and swung the heavy stick, crashing it into the side of the big man's neck, stomping over the fire and running down the smaller man as he scurried on hands and knees to get away. Lot kicked him in the stomach, bent and ripped the flintlock out of his waistband, then spun and checked the bald man.

The big one lay where he had fallen, his head at a grotesque, unnatural angle, his neck neatly broken. Lot knew he was dead. He swept up the other one, holding him by his grimy rawhide shirtfront that smelled of a thousand campfires and just as many weeks of constant wearing.

"Now, easy, there. Easy!" the man stammered. "Okay, okay, it was him who killed your friend and tried to bash out your brains. I never done it. He did—baldy over there. I wouldn't *let* him kill you. He wanted to use his knife, but I said enough, and I made him leave you be. I saved your life."

Lot pulled a knife from the man's trousers, saw it was his own hunting blade and sheath. He checked the rest of the pockets of the trembling man, but found no more weapons. He pushed the man to the ground near his dead partner.

"I hear tell about an eye for an eye," Lot said, staring hard at the smaller man.

"You done that. Old Jonas here is dead. Your friend's dead. That's one killing for one killing. You and me still alive, so we all squared and even."

Lot worried about that as he checked the pack mules and his own horse. Everything was there, including the leather bag with all the steel traps in it.

"No sir," the small man said. "You and me, we got no more quarrel. I had to do what Jonas said, 'cause he was *bigger* than me. He made me hit you back there."

Lot plainly was not happy with that kind of talk. He looked at the man, who gave him a sickly grin. Lot wondered how many other men this killer had sent to their graves. He would give him a chance—a fair contest. Deliberately Lot turned his back on the man again and checked the packs. When he turned, the man lunged for his dead partner's blade, slid it from the scabbard and jumped to his feet.

Lot spun, his club raised. He danced on his toes for a moment, then settled back to face the attack. The stranger came in low, with his arm protecting the weapon. Lot swung the club so he couldn't miss. The thick oak hit the man's forearm, snapped bones like dry pine branches. The outlaw shrilled in pain and anger. But he still held the blade in his right hand. He lunged. Lot recovered the club but did not take time to draw it back for a long swing again. Instead he brought it end first toward his body and then lunged straight ahead with the four-foot stick like a lance, putting his two hundred pounds behind the thrust. The two-inch diameter broken end of the stick jolted into the advancing man's chest, snapped off four ribs and smashed through his lung and into his heart.

The robber shrieked as the blow struck. His eyes rolled in surprise and defeat. He dropped his knife and tried to grab the shaft to stop its four-inch journey of death. The man fell sideways, jerking the lance from Lot's hands, rolling until the oak stick stopped him. His glazed eyes stared directly up at Lot but did not see a thing.

An hour later Lot had carried the two bodies deep into the woods and thrown brush over them. He returned to the camp and cleaned up all the evidence of the fight. Lot put out the fire, checked the animals and sat up the rest of the night to be sure no other thief or murderer sneaked up to steal the pelts.

Lot stared at his hands in the darkness. His hands had killed. He had taken human life—two white men. But they were bad man who had killed his partner. They deserved to die. Yes, fair was fair. He was not at fault for what he had done. Justice had been served.

Before morning, Lot had figured out what he would do. He would go on into Fort Oswego and sell the pelts, bargaining for each group, the way Jacobs had taught him. With some of the money he would buy more traps and food. Then he would strike off to the west to find a new stream never before trapped. Jacobs had said there were many to the south and west, down toward the Allegheny river, maybe to the Ohio, or even further west toward Fort Detroit. He was a trapper now, a full-fledged fur trader. He'd need more supplies, a musket, ball and powder, salt, maybe some coffee and some whiskey.

For food he would get everything that would keep: flour, beans, and a big pack of dried apples. Jacobs had shown him how to dress out small game and said in the winter it would keep frozen for two months, maybe more. Just cut off slabs of the frozen meat and put it right into an iron skillet.

It would be a good life. He was not a slave. Only fleetingly did he think about the free black woman and her children he had once seen in Boston. He was not ready to think about that yet. He needed a cabin and eventually a farm where he could settle down. Then he could think about a wife. He wondered if there would be women at Ft. Oswego. He had been with girls before. One winter his master had forced over twenty black girls to sleep with him in one week. Many of them had borne beautiful children. But a wife would be different.

To lie with a female because he wanted to—that would prove to him that Lot Edes was indeed a freeman.

The next day Lot went to the trading post at Fort Oswego. There he sold his pelts to the traders, and with hard bargaining received nearly what they were worth, twice as much as he had dreamed he might get. He was a curiosity around the fort, and stayed only long enough to do his business. Part of that was buying a large stock of food, a new flintlock musket, new powder, shot and wadding. He practiced with the new gun for twenty rounds, till he could hit what he aimed at. It was the first time he had ever fired a musket.

Lot appraised a new tributary of the river he was following. He decided it did not show enough beaver sign to be a good producing stream, and moved on. He was wandering along a network of rivers and lakes below Lake Ontario, working gradually westward and south so he could go around the next big lake. Below it somewhere he would find the mighty Allegheny river, as wild as any in the whole of the continent, some trappers had told him. They said it was virtually untrapped.

Lot had seen Indians for the past month. He had made it a regular practice to avoid both large and small bands whenever possible. Most of the Indians had a casual attitude toward the trappers. They provided no real threat; they were there harvesting the fur-bearing animals the Indians had little use for, and the white trappers did not settle down on the land, begin clearing it or put up permanent quarters. All Indians feared log houses. They knew it was the first step as the white man moved in with women and children and stayed forever.

Lot had wandered through at least three tribes that he knew of: the Oneidas, the Cayugas and the Senecas. Other trappers had talked about them at the fort. None were exceptionally warlike, at least not at the time. With no recent prodding from the whites to take sides in wars, they had reverted to their traditional mode of life, hunting and maintaining their tribal existence.

One day's ride out of the fort, Lot came around a bend in the trail and directly ahead of him stood two braves in hunting gear. They stared at him for a moment, then walked toward him guardedly. Lot held up his hand in the peace and greeting sign, and waited. The Indians talked to each other in whispers, and one shook his head in disbelief. Lot knew they were surprised by his black skin. It was a warm day and his shirt was open, showing his hairy black chest. Still chattering to each other, they faded into the trees. Lot never saw them again.

By the end of September, Lot had found the stream he wanted on one of the tributaries that reached into the Allegheny. It was a small, virgin valley, with a meadow, forested hillsides and what he hoped was an untrapped wilderness.

First he searched the entire area for a cave, but found none. Other mountain men told him that a cave was the best kind of protection from the icy winds and the snows of winter. Not finding one, he did the next best thing: located a windfall, a giant tree over four feet thick. On the leeward side of it he shoveled out two feet of dirt and made a hard-packed floor. Then he built a lean-to of sturdy pine branches over the top, tall enough so that he could stand erect. With his axe, Lot fashioned uprights from forked sticks, then cut poles to cover the roof. He put on a double row of poles side by side, then used the shovel and dug up sod and dirt and threw it on top of the poles until he had a foot-thick covering. Inside, the logs held and his lean-to with the dirt roof was well started.

The second day there, he set out a dozen traps where he found a colony of beaver. Each morning he walked his trap line. He caught his first beaver, a big male which he promptly skinned out, and took the hide back to his lean-to, where he stretched it and hung it up to dry. Lot worked for a full week to make the lean-to as windproof and sturdy as possible. The walls were made like a stockade's, by sharpening four-inch poles and driving them into the soft dirt side by side. If he had time he would use wet clay and mortar up the chinks and holes between the logs.

The first snow came in the second week of October. It was a white coating that turned the land into a winter wilderness, but which began to melt almost at once. The lean-to was finished now. He built a firepit in the corner near the door, and cut a hole in the roof for the smoke to go through. It did not work as well as he had hoped and the inside of the hut was filled with smoke, making his eyes water. But it was better than freezing. For the door, he used a heavy bearskin Hal Jacobs had provided. Lot had heard and seen bears, so he put most of his food in his bear-proof cache, an old canvas seaman's bag tied tightly and suspended ten feet in the air from a tree branch. Inside the hut he built up a mound of dirt for a bed, and put a log frame around it. Inside the logs he piled soft evergreen bough tips, as much moss as he could find, and a blanket full of dead grass and weeds. Over it all he spread one of his four blankets. It would be softer than sleeping on the ground.

The first day it rained he sat inside all day, wondering how much the roof would leak. There were half a dozen drips, but they seemed to stop as the rain continued. The water must be packing down the dirt. Before the rain was over, the dripping stopped. He had a dry, warm cave of his own for the winter.

With the axe he had carved two shelves in the side of the old log. It had been dead and down for years, but was still solid once past the first half-inch of soft wood.

Outside he had made a pole corral for the animals, which would give them some freedom yet keep them near at hand. The corral was under a heavy stand of trees, so the animals would have some protection from the winter elements.

The next morning, Lot rose early and saw that a new sheen of snow had covered the first melting whiteness. He had set aside today to kill a deer so he could have some venison. It was cold enough now so the meat would last for several weeks.

With his musket in both hands, Lot trudged halfway up the small meadow, then angled along the side of the hill to the top of the ridge. He knew he was near a deer trail where the animals went from one valley to the next. He would simply wait until a big buck came along, and shoot it.

Lot had waited for almost an hour, and his feet were starting to get cold. He realized now that he would need more socks, and warmer ones, for his winter travels. Now he was especially glad there had been a pair of snowshoes in the goods he inherited from Hal Jacobs. He concentrated on both sides of the ridge, but saw no animals. Maybe they had moved lower to escape the snow, moving to winter pastures.

He planned on waiting another hour. Then he would start to move, try to find their tracks in the snow. He was just about ready to go when far below on the ridge he saw movement. As he watched, it turned out to be three Indians on ponies. From this distance he was not sure, but he guessed it was not a hunting party.

The trio worked toward him, up the ridge,

then turned and went toward the stream at the middle of the valley. Near the water a boulder had been upturned centuries ago, and now formed a flat face to the sun. It was about four feet wide and twice as long. When they stopped near the rock, he could see that the Indian in the center was smaller, and had waist-length hair . . . a squaw or a girl. The older of the two men got off his mount, pulled the girl down and held her. He took out a long knife from his waist band and let it flash in the sunshine so the light reflected into the girl's eyes. Then he swung the blade twice, narrowly missing the girl, before he caught her long hair, wrapped it around his hand, then used the knife to cut it off closer to her head.

When he let her go, he picked her up and pushed her onto the platform rock. The older man watched for a moment, then put his knife away and mounted his pony. He caught the third horse and the two braves rode away in the direction from which they had come without a backward glance.

Lot watched the girl. She did not look at the retreating men. She lay on the snow-covered rock where the brave had left her for an hour. Then she stood on the rock for several minutes, looking around the valley. At last she sat down cross-legged on the cold stone and folded her arms. She stared straight ahead and was still there six hours later.

Long before the sun set, Lot moved up cautiously through the brush, and using the cover he could find, worked to within fifty yards of the Indian girl. He could see her features now, and he had been correct: she was only a girl of fifteen or sixteen. Now her head was bowed and she looked at the rock. The snow had melted in a circle around her, but she did not move.

Lot sniffed the air. It was nearly freezing, and would drop even lower before the night was over. The girl would die of exposure long before the sun came up. He had no idea why the braves had abandoned her, but felt she had been banished from the tribe, kicked out for some serious violation of the tribal laws. Hal Jacobs had talked about Indian customs one night, but Lot could remember little of it. He only remembered that they were tremendously important to the tribes, and a chief would cast out his own son, daughter, or wife who violated a rule.

As dusk deepened, he knew he had to save her. He eased up from where he had been hidden and walked openly toward her. She must have seen and heard him coming, but made no move or indication that she had.

When he stood over her she looked up, and when she saw him she frowned, then looked away, saying some Indian words he did not understand. Lot took a cooked turkey leg from his small pack and held it out to her. She reached for it quickly, then pulled her hand back.

"Go ahead, eat it," he said.

Her black eyes came up and watched him. He

made the friend sign, not knowing if a squaw would understand it. She turned away from him. He laid the drumstick on her knee and walked behind her. The girl hesitated, then grabbed the leg and began to chew the meat off the bone. She threw the bone away and returned to the same pose as before, legs crossed, arms folded, head bent.

Evidently this girl had broken a serious law, and had not only been banished, but had been made to believe that she was already as good as dead. All she had to do was sit and wait for the Great Spirit to come and take her away. In summer she would have starved to death or been eaten by wolves. In winter she simply would freeze. To take food only made the ordeal last longer.

Lot shook his head at such primitive ideas and went back to the girl. He took her shoulders and lifted her to her feet, but she could not stand. She had been in the cramped position for too long, or else she did not want to try. He carried her, guessing that she weighed little more than seventy or eighty pounds. There was not time to get the horse and come back for her. She was lighter colored than he had thought Indians would be. She couldn't be more than four and a half feet tall, with a round face, flat nose and liquid black eyes that were downcast even as he carried her.

The trip back to his hut took Lot almost an hour, carrying the girl. He fell down once, and she hit the ground hard, rolling down a small hill. At the bottom she didn't move. He ran to her, and saw her breathing. At least now her legs were straightened out, which made it easier to carry her.

At the hut he swung back the bear rug and slipped inside, laying the girl on his bunk, then blowing coals into life in the fire ring. When the flame came, he lit one of his tallow tapers and set it in the hole in the big log. The candle lit the inside of the hut remarkably well, and the Indian girl stared at the candle in surprise and wonder.

Lot built up the fire with dry wood stored at the back of the hut, and when it was blazing brightly, he turned back to the girl. Again she sat cross-legged and with her arms folded, but her eyes seemed fascinated by the flickering of the candle.

"I will help you," said Lot.

She ignored him.

"You can live here. I will feed you."

There was no recognition, no sign of understanding.

Lot put the big pot of beans back over the cooking fire, and stirred it with a long-handled wooden spoon. He took out a jug of fresh river water and poured some in a tin cup. The girl watched him. He drank some of it, then gave it to the girl. She looked in the cup, then back at him, and drank all the remaining water.

Lot knew of no way to make her feel safe except through his actions. They had no words in common. He could remember none of the Indian words Jacobs had taught him. The firelight danced off her black eyes. She sat still, but now her eyes watched the fire instead of her own knees. Her soft buckskin dress fell from her shoulders to her waist, with only small bumps where her breasts were.

He took her hand and pulled her closer to the big fire in the corner. He had lined the sides of the hut around the fire with heavy slabs of rock to prevent the heating flames from burning the logs. She moved closer, reached out and felt the heat and shivered. It was the first tentative sign that she did not want to die.

When the beans were ready he spooned them out on a wooden trencher, put a cold turkey wing on it and gave her another cup of water. He set the trencher beside her. At first she ignored it, then one hand crept out, picked up a single cooked bean and put it in her mouth. A little girl's delighted grin spread over her face. She scooped up a handful of the beans and ate them. The girl ignored the metal spoon beside the trencher and ate with her fingers. When the beans were gone she gnawed on the cooked turkey wing, cleaning the bones to the last bit of meat. Then she drank the water from the cup and looked at the pot of beans.

Lot spooned more beans onto her trencher and watched her eat the steaming hot food.

He put the wooden plate and spoon away,

then tried to make her understand that she did not have to die. She looked at the bear skin that covered the door. Lot shook his head and pointed to the bed.

Lot blew out the candle, then built up the heating fire, and let the cooking fire burn down. He stood and picked up the girl and lay her on the bed, pushing her down until she stayed there. Gently he covered her with two of his blankets. Her eyes were curious, alert. When he moved away from her she seemed to relax. Almost at once she was asleep.

The big black man sat by the fire, feeding thick limbs into it, building up a good bed of coals before he put on a round chunk of oak that was green enough so it would smolder and hold a fire all night. He stared into the coals. He had saved the girl from freezing to death as a natural reaction. But had he invited trouble from her tribe? He thought about it for a few minutes and decided that even if it meant problems with Indians in the future, he could not sit there and let the girl freeze. He had seen too much of man's cruelty to other men. He had saved her, and if she wanted to, she could stay with him. He worried well into the night, and at last fell asleep near the fire, his fur coat around him.

Lot awoke twice that night to put more wood on the fire, and by morning it was still warm in the hut. The girl was sleeping when he stirred up his coffee and put the tin over the coals of the heating fire.

As he sipped the hot brew, Lot watched the girl wake up. She was smiling as she roused herself, then when she saw the hut, the fire, and him, her face took on a look of terror. Gradually it wore off and her unsmiling, stern expression came back. He did not know if she would stay there. He usually ate little in the morning. Now he offered her another cup of water. She drank it and waited. He stood, opened the bear skin door and let her go outside.

It had turned warmer, a false autumn. The snow was gone, and one bluejay scolded from an alder tree. The small Indian girl ran through the door and stopped, looking around. She seemed to approve of the hut, stared in wonder at the horses, and then walked into the edge of the brush, only half hidden, squatted and relieved herself. When she came back, she looked in the bean pot and quickly ate the remaining cold beans. When the pot was empty she took it, two wooden trenchers and two spoons and walked to the stream twenty yards away. She knelt there and washed the utensils with sand and cold river water.

Lot watched her, knowing that he had taken on either a daughter or a wife—he didn't know which. It was plain now that she would stay with him. She had no place to go and she had decided that living was better than dying.

What would he call her? She had to have a name, but he didn't know how to ask her.

Lot wondered if he would be a squawman. Would he be the first black squawman? He watched her coming back from the stream, remembering how long her straight black hair had been. Her body would fill out more, would grow. He studied her and knew that all thoughts of death had left her mind. She was young, alive, wise in the ways of the wilderness, but not yet a woman.

Lot picked up his pack, sharpened his knife and showed her one of the steel traps. He tried to indicate with motions that he would be walking the trap line. At last she nodded. When he left to walk the line, she was a step behind him. Lot smiled, not realizing how totally alone he had been before. He picked up his equipment and walked to the first trap.

Chapter Five
TWICE BURNED, ONCE DEAD

August 25, 1770

It was a full three days after Lot ran away from Edmund Cunliffe, before the master of the house came to his senses. He was in his bed, fully clothed, as he had been when he began drinking. Two empty wine bottles lay on the bed with him. One had emptied into the feathers and ticking. He got up gingerly, his head a mass of aches and booming bells and chains rattling around in empty metal drums.

Slowly, the fuzzy series of events came back to him. He had failed miserably and embarrassingly at making love to Roxanne, which had brought on his long bout with the bottle. He remembered waking from time to time, screeching for more wine, more brandy and champagne. That must have been days ago. It took him another hour to clear his head enough to scream for bath water, and then wash himself and put on clean clothes. He called for a tray of food but found he could not eat. Outside it was dark. Evening. One of the serving girls told him the day was August 25. He rang for Lot twice, and swore he would flog the laggard if he didn't show up soon.

When the maid came to take away his food tray, he asked her why Lot hadn't appeared. The girl looked frightened, backed away and said she didn't know—which meant she did know why Lot wasn't there. Damn these black bastards! He stalked downstairs to the kitchen and found the cook finishing her duties.

"Where the hell is Lot?" Edmund snapped.

June put down the pot she was scrubbing and turned toward her master. Over the years she had taken certain liberties with her position, because she had helped at his birth, had bathed him and rocked him to sleep hundreds of times. For this he permitted her some degree of familiarity.

"Mista Cunliffe, you not gonna like it, but that Lot, he done took off for parts we don't even know where is. He lit out soon as you got drunk and passed out three days ago. Took that sleek little bay mare and a saddle and some food and he's gone."

"And you helped him?"

"I gave him some cheese and some bread, yessir. I'd help a starvin' cat, why not a starvin' nigger?"

Cunliffe ordinarily would have thrashed any black who stood up to him that way. But now he sighed and leaned against the kitchen table. He knew Lot would try to run away some day. That was why he tried to keep the man as ignorant as possible, not letting him get out into the community. There were even free negroes right there in Boston. Ridiculous. Now Lot was gone. A valuable piece of property was lost. His slave had run away!

As the full impact of it pounded down on him, Cunliffe had to control his anger. He stalked out of the kitchen into the library. At the door he surveyed the damage. Nothing had been cleaned since the night he left it. He screamed for the housekeepers to come in and straighten up the room and restore it. Then he went back to his bedroom, dropped into a chair and let his anger spill out.

This whole series of disasters could be blamed on one person and only one—Benjamin Rutledge. He had been the cause, the rigger. He had fired the shot that rendered Edmund impotent. He had caused the whole affair which had now resulted in the escape of a valuable property.

There had to be retribution.

Vengeance had to be extracted.

Curiously now, Edmund sat apart from his problems, and tried to evaluate them critically, objectively. Yes, the fault was obvious, but the punishment, what should the cost be to Benjamin Rutledge?

Castration? Edmund could hire a pair of men to hunt down Rutledge and using a sharp knife tear into the roots of his manhood so he could never again satisfy a woman. It would be simple

397

to arrange. No one could trace it back to Edmund and he would be absolutely free of any blame or recrimination, either legally or by innuendo.

Perhaps he should have both of the large tendons in the back of Rutledge's ankles cut. Then he would never take another step as long as he lived. He would have to lie with his misery, his agony, just as Edmund suffered from his lack of female companionship.

No, no, that was too easy. Rutledge had to suffer, and suffer mightily, but then he had to die. Just how, just where—that planning was part of the joy of vengeance.

Edmund peaked his fingers as he thought of all the many ways the Indians used to torture their victims. Hanging a man by his thumbs over a slowly burning fire and then roasting various sections of the body, was a favorite Indian torture. First, toast a man's feet, then his buttocks, then his genitals, and at last tip him upside down and burn off his hair before lowering the head to the fire so close the blood in his brain boiled and split apart the skull, exploding it like a melon!

Cunliffe smiled just thinking about it. Yes, that might be good. Kidnaping Rutledge would be the first step, then moving him by night into the country somewhere around Lexington where they would build a fire in some thick woods. The idea grew and became more appealing. Then in a final minute of consciousness, a saber slash across his throat so he could watch his own blood flowing out of him!

So it was set. It would be done.

Edmund Cunliffe spent a week finding just the right men to do the job. They were two seamen he had used before for some of his more violent jobs. Both were in town, both had run out of money and had a full week before they sailed again. Edmund met them in the dark and made the arrangements. He would set up the kidnaping opportunity, and they would do the rest.

Two days later, Ben Rutledge looked at the message on his desk. It had been brought to the outer door of his establishment an hour before, and no one could remember who delivered it. The message itself was clear.

"I can show you how to get six twenty-four-pounder British cannon without firing a shot. If interested, meet me at Byle's wharf tonight, just after dark." There was no signature. The note disturbed Ben for two reasons. Evidently someone who shouldn't, knew about the Freedom Fighters. Someone had talked, perhaps after too much ale or wine. The second worry was, how had the person who sent the note associated Ben with the group, and even pinpointed him as one of the leaders?

There was no doubt that Ben would be at that meeting. He had to go to find out about the cannon. The Freedom Fighters could use all such pieces they could assemble for the time the real fighting began. The second reason he had to go was to discover who had sent the message, who knew so much about the Freedom Fighters.

Ben pushed the note aside and went back to work. He had a particularly tough problem of how to combine certain shipments from London so he could get it all across without one cargo damaging the others in the rough Atlantic crossing. That afternoon he talked with Lewis Lynch about the meeting at the wharf, reaffirming his decision that he should go.

It was nearly sundown when Ben left in his chaise. It was not yet dark, but by the time he drove to the south end of Boston, nearly to the Boston neck where the wharf was situated, dusk had fallen. Then the evening fog bank swept in and blotted out everything.

Ben made his way slowly the last hundred yards and tied his horse near Byle's wharf just off Orange Street. There was no indication in the note where to meet on the wharf. Ben had no intention of walking along to the end of the finger pier that extended into the bay, which was now at full tide. Ben leaned against the warehouse that sided the wharf, edged back into a doorway and waited. It was eerie, damp and quiet. Hardly any sounds penetrated the thick, rolling wetness. A dozen men could be hidden out there.

As he waited he wondered if he were doing

the right thing. By coming here he was practically admitting that he was working with some kind of an armed opposition or rebel group. Ben wished he had brought his flintlock pistol. He felt naked and vulnerable.

He hardly heard them at first, then the footsteps came surely, hard leather heels against the thick planks of the dock. They sounded steadily from the far end of the pier. The form slowly materialized in the fog. The man did not see Ben standing in the doorway.

"Looking for someone?" Ben asked.

The figure spun around, surprised, wary. "Yes. You here for a meeting?"

"I am."

"You Ben?"

"We don't need names. Come closer."

The man didn't move. His whistle was sharp and high. At once new footsteps came from both sides of them. Two more men, Ben decided. There was no way to escape. Now he wished he had brought his flintlock.

"We're ready to talk. Those twenty-four pounders. How many can you buy?"

"Where will the guns come from?"

"Not your worry."

The footsteps on each side were closer now. The man in the fog stepped closer toward Ben. When the two other shapes showed in the thick fog, Ben gave a signal of his own.

"Now, lads, now!" Ben barked.

Running feet sounded from the bay side of

the pier as three men swept toward Ben, bowling over the first man in their way. More steps came from the street side. Ben lunged forward and grabbed the spokesman. He shook free and started to pull his knife when Lewis Lynch tackled him and pinned him to the planks.

It was all over before it had well started. One of the two attackers on the pier jumped into the black waters of the bay and vanished.

"Let him go, we've got what we need," Ben shouted. The two captured men were hustled into a nearby warehouse where a lamp was lighted. Ben knew neither of them, but both appeared to be seamen. He knew by their snarling expressions that it would take a lot of persuasion to make them talk. It had plainly been a plot to trap Ben on the pier, to capture or kill him. But why?

An hour later the three-masted *Justice* crept out of the harbor in darkness with the receding tide. She picked up a gentle offshore breeze and was well into the Atlantic before the moon came up. Ben left the first mate's quarters and went up on the rolling deck.

Lynch met him. "Not a word, sir. Neither one has said a thing. They're seamen, though, for sure. I can tell by the way they walk."

Ben accepted the information. "Let's send them both for a swim, Mr. Lynch. Fifty feet of stout line over the stern with them as bait on the end might turn up a shark or two."

Neither of the seamen could swim, and both

pleaded not to be dragged behind the sailing vessel, which now was making better time with a stiffer wind.

"Tell us who hired you and you stay dry," said Ben.

Both turned mute again. They were tied securely with half-inch line, then pitched over the stern. Both bobbed to the surface, flailing arms and legs frantically in the dark waters. When the fifty feet of line played out, they were dragged behind the ship like two six-foot logs, sinking, splashing, coming to the surface—only these logs were screaming. Ben left them there for five minutes, then towed them in. The two came over the rail sputtering and cursing. They promised to tell who had hired them, but once on deck with the water coughed out of them, they went back on their promise.

"You'll die for this, Rutledge. I'll never rest until I've come back and killed you!"

"So you know my name. Why were you trying to capture me? Speak up, man, or it's back into the sea with you. This time you might not come out before you've taken on a cargo of water."

The other seaman looked up. "I'd tell you, guv'nor, if I could. But I don't know. Only Squeaky there knows. He got the job and hired me for two pounds. Two pounds for a night's work, not bad, what? But I didn't know we was gonna kill nobody."

"Then the object was my death, correct?"

asked Ben.

The second man looked away.

The next time they hit the sea they splashed for ten minutes. Their screaming came in surges, out of the blackness of the night and the sea. When they were pulled to the rail, both said they would talk but recanted before they were hoisted on board. Lynch pushed them back into the water and left them for twenty minutes. This time, when the men dragged them on board, they were barely conscious. Crewmen rolled them over barrels, pumping seawater out of them. When the one called Squeaky revived enough to talk, he stared at Ben.

"You going to kill us the next time. You ready to do that?"

"You were ready to kill me. I've killed men before."

The seaman thought about it, at last he nodded. "All right, mate, you win. No more swimming. We was paid half to capture you and take you into the deep woods by Lexington and build a fire. We get you there all tied up, and we get the other half of our money. That's all I know. The man said he would meet us there."

"Who was the man?" Ben asked.

The seaman sighed. "What will you do with us if I tell you?"

"If you speak the truth you'll go into chains until this ship is ready to sail for England a week hence. Then you'll be pressed into the crew. If you serve her a year, you'll have earned your freedom."

The sailor bobbed his head. "You swear, with these men as witnesses?"

"My word is good," Ben said.

"The man who hired us was Edmund Cunliffe."

That same night, only an hour after the seaman had confessed the name, Ben and Lewis Lynch watched Cunliffe's house. He was at home. Lynch twice saw him pacing in the big parlor. Once he went to the front door and looked down the street. Another man watched the back.

About two a.m. the last light went out in the house and Ben told Lynch and his other watchman to go home. They did.

Ben slipped up to the back door, sure that it would be unlocked as most house doors were in Boston. He moved quietly through the rooms until he found Cunliffe's bedroom on the second floor. One small candle still burned. Cunliffe lay on his bed fully clothed, with a flintlock pistol across his chest.

Ben walked silently to the bed and lifted the weapon off the man, checked to see that it was primed, then slapped Cunliffe's face. He sprang to a sitting position, his eyes wild.

"What!"

"Get up, Cunliffe. You have a confession to write and sign."

"Who? Rutledge? What the hell are you doing in my house?"

"I'm here to kill you, Cunliffe, unless you do exactly as I say." Ben held flintlock pistols in both hands now, one of them pointing at Edmund's heart.

"Why? For God's sake, why? I wake up out of a sound sleep and find a madman has set upon me in my own house."

"You know why, Cunliffe. Your plot failed. We captured two of your conspirators. They are put away for safe keeping. And you will write out a complete confession I can turn over to the judicial court tomorrow."

"Never! I have nothing to confess."

"Cunliffe, you lie worse than you shoot. Now get up, move over to your desk and take out quill and paper and write as I dictate."

"Why should I?"

"If you don't, I'll put a pistol ball through your head. Is that sufficient reason?"

"You wouldn't. My servants would hear it."

"But they wouldn't raise a hand in your defense. Think about it. Isn't it true? Which of them would give up her life to defend you?"

Slowly Cunliffe got off the bed and moved to his small writing desk. He took out paper.

"My quill is in the drawer. May I bring it out?"

"Slowly."

Cunliffe reached in the drawer. He moved faster than Ben thought he would and the flintlock pistol came up and fired, all in half a second. The quickness destroyed the aim, but Ben felt the ball whizz past his chest. Ben's own flintlock centered on Cunliffe's heart. He held fire.

"No, Rutledge, I know you won't shoot. You're a law-abiding man. You want to defeat me legally and proper, right? You wouldn't shoot me unless you had to, to save your own skin." As the man talked Ben moved closer, but too late he realized that Cunliffe had planned well. He had not one but two primed and loaded flintlock pistols in the drawer. Ben saw him drawing out the second one. Ben had a fraction of a second to make up his mind what to do. Survival took over. He hardly remembered the next few seconds. His pistol held on Cunliffe's chest. Edmund picked up the gun and raised it. A split second before it swung to point, Ben squeezed the trigger and saw his ball slam into the carriage maker. Ben watched Cunliffe blasted backward, tipping over a chair, sliding along the floor.

Cunliffe's weapon went off as well, but by then it was pointing at the ceiling.

Ben didn't need to look at Cunliffe. He knew the man was dead. He ran to the bedroom door, down the hallway and out to the steps, then out the back door and across the open lot into the next street. Ben walked quickly then, taking huge gasps of breath, trying to steady himself. He had never killed a man up close before. At musket range it was so different, so impersonal. You didn't see the expression, notice the hatred in the victim's eyes, see the ball strike and penetrate and do its deadly damage.

Ben walked for another half-hour before he returned to where he had parked his chaise, two blocks from Cunliffe's house. Ben looked down the street but saw no lights on in the mansion, no activity around it. Cunliffe's servants were used to wild noises in that house. It would be morning before they found the body.

Ben tried not to think about the killing any more. He should have done the job the first time. When you have a snake in your sights, kill it when you have the chance.

He hardly considered Cunliffe a man. He hadn't planned on killing him. He'd rather have had the confession and brought the two seamen to testify to the foul plot of murder. But this was faster and cleaner.

His hands trembled as he untied the reins and drove slowly through the early morning darkness toward home.

This was another of the small battles they were waging. Cunliffe had been a Tory. Now he could not spread what he knew about the Freedom Fighters. It was another victory, but no one but Lynch would know about it. Murder most foul, the newspaper would call it. So be it.

Edmund Cunliffe was one more victim of the yet undeclared war of the colonies for their independence.

At home, Ben slid into bed beside Sandra gently, without waking her. He thought he might have trouble sleeping, but when he relaxed he was asleep at once.

Chapter Six
TEA FOR TWO—OR THREE

October 22, 1770

Ben sat with his pipe and newspaper, completely relaxed, catching up on what Sam Adams had been shouting about in the colonial assembly. He was making much noise but didn't seem to be winning on many issues. Ben put down the paper and stared at the log burning in the big fireplace. The boys had filled the woodbox and now Ben was ready for a quiet, thoughtful evening.

Sandra looked up from her needlepoint and smiled. "It's good to have you home, Ben. You've been working so many hours at the office that sometimes I only see you coming and going." Her smile warmed. "Ever since word came about the breakup of the non-importation agreements, it seems you've been working twice as hard."

"Yes, true, Sandra. Things are on a very even keel right now—and very busy. The business is surging, with more shipments than we can handle, so we must pick and choose. Those two new ships being built will help, but we could use them right now."

Ben shook his head in wonder. "What truly amazes me is that daughter of yours. How in the world did you do such a good job with her? She could take over the bookkeeping department at any time, if she had to. And now she's handling all of the land and property operations for us. She knows more about the buildings and docks and value of city land than any of us. She is simply a marvel of organization and efficiency. Already she's pointed out several warehouses we have where utilization could be much higher and she's working on plans for a new building on some leased land."

"You're very proud of her, aren't you, Ben?"

"Yes, of course. She's the smartest businessman in town, I'd say—man or *woman*."

Sandra stitched on her needlepoint. "The boys enrolled today in Beekman's Preparatory. From what they said, they're going to enjoy it." Sandra had seen that both the boys went to bed early, after a hard day.

Ben wanted the boys to have two years at Beekman's. Then, when they were well ready, they would enter Harvard. If there was time. When would it happen, when would the British become so overbearing, so outrageous, that they would bring about that spark to ignite the powder keg and thrust the colonies into a revolutionary war?

Ben watched the blaze work on an oak log, then looked back at the newspaper. There was little talk in the partisan Whig press about the British. Only a minor scrape by two junior officers. Nothing like it used to be, with long columns of charges against the hated redcoats. It was amazing how a full belly and the relaxation of certain restrictions could change the temper of a land. Now there was a period of calm. How he wished it would change soon. Of course his business was on the firmest foundation it had ever been. He had money in the bank, more ships and more property than ever before. But money in the bank? Would cash in a colonial bank be any good in case of a war? Would all of the assets be frozen, so no withdrawals could be made? That could ruin him. He'd have to find out about that from Dr. Warren or Sam Adams himself. Perhaps they should think of opening a bank that would remain loyal. Or perhaps there were such institutions. He would ask John Hancock at their next meeting.

"This was the boys' day to go hunting with Mr. Lynch," said Sandra. "My, he is such an interesting man. Royal Marine, you said? Well, he took them across the Charles and they came back with two turkeys. We had one for dinner and the other went to those new people who moved in down the block. Mr. Lynch said I should tell you that both boys are good enough shots now to make private in the Royal Marines."

Ben nodded and mumbled a reply to his wife, then puffed on his pipe and turned the page.

The Freedom Fighters were growing restless. Each captain had cautioned the troops about absolute secrecy. They were told to hold fast, to stay in training, and to keep their powder dry. A force might be needed at almost any time, even on a minute's notice. Since they couldn't fight now they could still think back and remember how well their outing had gone against the *Richard* when they burned her to the water.

Weekly musters of the companies were changed to monthly, with firing set for each three months. The weekly meetings of the council continued, but there was little for them to do. They kept ready, watched and waited.

After the regular Monday night council meeting Ben made his usual trip down the alley and into Sadie Wythe's upstairs apartment. She had seemed restless and preoccupied at the meeting, as they talked about possible ways the council could work toward independence. Now she stood by the small stove and let the tea water boil furiously without noticing.

Ben closed the back door, took the water off the fire and made the tea, then as it steeped, he put his arms around the small woman and kissed her cheek.

"Now, little lady. Do you want to talk about it?"

"Talk about what, Ben?"

"Talk about whatever is bothering you.

412

You're not your usual self tonight. All during the council meeting you were as vague as an old Irishman giving directions in a London fog. Is it something I've done?"

She smiled. "Oh, yes, it certainly is! I might say that it definitely is at least half your fault." Her face was stern yet he saw a twinkle in her green eyes.

"My fault. Let's see. If loving you is it, then I'm guilty."

"Yes, that's it, that's most of it." She reached up and kissed him. Then she put her arms around him. "Darling Ben, at last we're going to have a baby!"

He lifted her up, stared at her, then kissed her mouth and she held him tightly.

"Are you sure?"

"Yes, love, absolutely sure. This is the second month I've missed my flow." She watched him, her eyes taking in his every reaction, every movement. She wanted him to be as happy as she was.

The smile that flashed across his face was the most beautiful sight she had ever seen. It was full, warm, honest, and she knew he meant it.

"Sadie, darling, that's wonderful! It's exactly what you wanted, so I want it too, and I'm delighted. You'll make the most wonderful mother any son ever had."

"Daughter. She told me she's a girl."

Ben wagged a finger at her in gentle reproof, then turned around and set her on the small chair. He poured tea, put in a lump of sugar and sat down across from her.

"No wonder you weren't worried about politics tonight. Do you have a name chosen?"

"I've tried to make a girl's name out of Ben and Benjamin, but I get absolutely nothing. So I've decided on Aretha, or Arthur."

"Why?"

"After King Arthur. I read a book about him. Jonathan sent it to me. I like the name. If it's a girl, she will be Aretha. It's a Greek name."

Ben thought ahead. "Two months. So you have to leave here in another few weeks, at the latest, right?"

She nodded. "I've written to my sister, Ardelle, in New York over a month ago. I should hear from her in a week at most."

"And you're sure you can stay there?"

"Oh, yes. She's my older sister and most understanding. They never have had any children, and she'll be delighted."

"But she knows when your husband died."

"Yes. I'll just have to talk about that with her. It will be all right."

They spent an hour planning and talking, and before Ben knew it, he was late getting home. He kissed her gently and said he would come again the next night. Ben gave her twenty pounds in five-pound notes and told her to put them away. He would bring her more each time he came so there would be no money worries when she was in New York. Ben left with a slight swagger in his walk. He hadn't been so excited about anything in months.

Sadie watched Ben go down the steps, and her heart nearly burst. She had never known the meaning of happiness before. Now she did. New life was growing in her body, a new person would soon be delivered and grown into a man or woman, a living continuance of a part of her and Ben.

Sadie sat near the stove and sipped the fresh cup of hot tea. She had no idea what a transformation a month or two could make. What an amazing difference! Her whole outlook had shifted, and now she thought of so many different things.

At last she stoked the small kitchen stove full of wood, and went into her bedroom, leaving the door open so some of the heat would get into her room.

She had two to keep warm for now.

Sadie hummed as she glanced over at the wall clock which Ben had bought for her. It was large and had all sorts of complicated weights that had to be lifted every seven days. It was far too complex for her to understand. Now the time showed as 11:30. Goodness! She had to get to bed. Sadie blew out the candle and lay there under the two comforters thinking about all the happy, healthy babies she had ever seen.

The next day she worked as usual in the millinery shop. She had made so many beaded handbags now that she thought she could do it in her sleep. Another of her jobs was to put decorations on straw hats made in the West Indies and brought in on ships. She worked steadily now, with a song on her lips.

She wondered if Ben would come past that night as he had promised.

Right after work she hurried home and baked an apple pie from the last of the winter apples she had saved. She wished there was some cream to whip but he would just have to like it that way. It was slightly after six p.m. on her big wooden clock when she heard a knock on her front door. Seldom did anyone come calling at the front. Could it be Ben?

She ran to the door, but when she opened it she found Lieutenant Arnold Compton standing there. He was so well dressed and his hair so slicked back that she hardly recognized him. He wore a waistcoat and ruffled white shirt under a greatcoat of very heavy cloth.

Compton nodded, stepped inside, closed the door and picked up Sadie and kissed her lips. When he set her down she was still so surprised she could hardly talk.

"Mr. Compton . . . I don't understand."

He peeled off his great coat and stood with his hands on her hips and grinned at her. "Of course you don't, muffin. I've just started. I've come to announce that I'm courting and that we will be married come the first of January. I won't take no arguments."

She wanted to laugh. He looked so out of place in his fancy waistcoat, the white ruffles at his neck under his farmer's sunburned face, and the breeches were so tight they were nearly indecent. But she stifled it, took his coat and hung it on a hook by the front door.

"Sit down, Mr. Compton. Just when did you come to the conclusion that you had permission to come courting?"

"Well, like I figure it's kind of like deciding whether to plant wheat or corn. I just don't go out and ask the field, and I sure as hell, begging your pardon, I sure don't ask the seed corn. So I figured you with no kin here, you was needing somebody to take care of you, and I sure as hell do need somebody to help warm up my bed these cold winter nights. So I just decided. Figured I'd get permission after I got started in the courtin'. I'm a little out of practice."

It was quite a speech for Arnold. He hunkered down in a small chair and watched her, his broad face open, honest, ready for her complete acceptance of his idea, of him and of his soon to come proposal. She was sure Arnold would not believe in long engagements.

"Well, Mr. Compton. I'm overwhelmed. It's not every day that a handsome man comes charging up and tells a girl he's courting and won't take no for an answer. But I'm surprised too, my mourning . . ."

"Your husband died more than a year ago now, Sadie."

"Oh, why yes, that is right. Well . . . would you like some tea?"

"Sure, yeah . . . great."

She brought tea and poured for him and herself, then put the pot back on the edge of the hot kitchen stove and sat down, looking at him.

"Mr. Compton, I don't think I'm ready to be courted yet, not again."

"But it's been over a year . . ." He put down his cup and stood, picking her out of her chair as if she were a toy. His lips crushed against hers and she wanted to scream at him, but she didn't. He broke off the kiss and still held her tightly against him.

"Look, girls got to be shown they are appreciated. Damn, you got the best looking body of any woman I ever seen. I like it. I want it. But I ain't about to tear your clothes off 'fore you say it's all right. You're the prettiest little thing I ever did see, Sadie, and I'd be pleased as can be if you'd marry me."

As he talked he continued to hold her, but now his hand came down and rubbed at her breast through her dress.

"Oh, I know I ain't as good-looking as them town gents. But I got a good farm, a big one, and I'm making hard money every year and putting it away. Got a big garden spot for raising vegetables and a good root cellar that's full, and I got me about a dozen fruit trees, and more 'taters than you know what to do with, besides pumpkins and squash, and meats all dried and hung, lots put down in salt too . . ."

His hand kept rubbing her breast and in spite of herself Sadie felt herself responding. She didn't know how to reject him without hurting him terribly. And how could she tell him not to touch her there? He was a big, rough farmer who could shoot straight, but she wished desperately that he wouldn't rub her breast that way!

"Look, I can take care of you. I know a woman needs to be loved and kept. Easy. I know you've been married and all that and I ain't, but I've had lots of romps in the hay with girls." His hand moved to her other breast and she gasped but he either didn't notice it or ignored her. How could she stop him? Her body was slowly responding to his maleness, his size, his heavy masculine scent.

He kissed her again and she felt herself soften, felt the tension go out of her arms, her knees buckled. Compton caught her. His hands pushed between the buttons on her blouse. She never knew when he had opened them. What did he think he was trying to do?

The kitchen door squeaked, the one leading to the back stairway. Sadie stiffened in alarm. Oh, no! It wasn't time for Ben to come yet! But it must be him. No one else ever came up the back steps. She broke off the kiss and pushed away from him. She was confident and sure now. If it were Ben he would sense that she had a visitor and he would not come in.

She stared in anger at the big man facing her. Sadie pointed to a chair and told him to sit down.

"Now, Mr. Arnold Compton, there are a few facts that you should know. The first is that you are my second in command, and a good soldier, a fine shot and a strong man. The second is that I have no romantic interest in you whatsoever. I am not a destitute widow ready to throw myself into a brothel to earn my daily bread. I was left with a fairly good inheritance from my late husband, and as you know I work daily in the millinery shop. I thought I made it perfectly clear to you after the burning of the *Richard* that I didn't want you courting. I *do* want to keep you as a friend. You are a very handsome man, wealthy, and a fine catch for any young girl. But not for me. Wouldn't it be a shame if all of the men in the world liked the same woman? What a mob around the same house. What fights there would be! But we're all different. I just don't happen to think of you as a beau, but I'm sure lots of girls would."

She stopped and watched him. His frown was heavy as he tried to think it through. She went on quickly.

"Besides, Mr. Compton, I'll be going to Philadelphia within a month. My only sister lives there, and she is very ill. Her husband has asked me to come and stay with them. There's a strong probability that she will not recover and if so, my brother-in-law and the baby will then need my help. So you see, there's a double reason why I cannot allow you to come courting. It would be pointless, and I'm going to be moving shortly."

She watched Arnold slowly wilt. His shoulders sagged, his head lowered, he didn't know where to put his big, work-roughened hands. When he looked up there was a trace of wetness in both of his eyes.

"I've wanted you so long," he said. "That whole shooting contest was just so you'd notice me, and I could talk to you. I guess I've always loved you, Sadie Wythe."

She wanted to go to him and hold him, and kiss his forehead, but she knew he would misinterpret it. Instead she tried to think of some good news she could tell him. A second later she had it.

. "Arnold, there is a bright spot. Since I'll be going away, I'll be resigning as captain of my company. I'm going to recommend to the council that you be promoted to captain and take over the group. Would you like that?"

It was dark to daylight. His face exploded into a grin, his eyes sparkled and danced, and his mouth formed a shout she was sure the neighbors must have heard.

"Yaaaaaaaaaahoooooooooooo!"

Sadie laughed at his sudden change. He was like a little boy now with a new plaything. "Of course there is one drawback, Arnold. You'll have to be the best shot in the company, then you'll have to pick a second in command, and you'll have to take your place at the weekly council meeting as one of the five full members!"

"Yaaaaaaaaaahoooooooooooo!"

She stood. "Now, Captain Compton, I do have to start my packing. I'll be gone for some time. Do you mind if I shoo you out?"

He stood, shaking his head. "No, no. 'Scuse me, I didn't mean to . . . oh, hell. I'm going. Just want to apologize for busting in this way like some damned yearling bull . . ."

"Arnold, it was most flattering, and I'll always remember what you said."

He shook her hand at the door, then saluted and did a smart turnabout and yahooed as he ran down the steps to the street where his broad-beamed stallion waited.

When she was sure he was gone, Sadie closed the front door and looked at the kitchen.

"You can come out now, wherever you're hiding."

Ben laughed softly from the kitchen. She ran to him and threw her arms around him.

"I've never been so glad to see anyone in my life. You know that Arnold Compton was trying to seduce me?"

Ben put his face in her hair, which was loose now and flowing in a blonde cascade over her shoulders. It always smelled so fresh and clean.

"Maybe I should give Arnold some lessons. I could tell him exactly what you like." He ducked her soft slap and carried her to the sofa.

"Arnold came barging in about twenty minutes ago and insisted that he was going to court me. He just picked me up and kissed me before I had a chance to say yes or no. He was very forceful. I didn't know he had such a big farm."

"I heard a lot of it, remember?" Ben said. "I thought you handled him very well and expertly. That promotion you gave him was a beautiful move."

"He deserves it."

"Now, young lady who seems to attract suitors like a queen bee out of her hive, we have to do some planning." He patted her flat little belly. "We have to plan right now, because some things, such as that son of mine—just won't wait a mite longer than he cares to."

She kissed him softly. "Ben Rutledge, no woman has ever known a better husband, whether in name or not. I love you so much, I hate to leave. But . . ." She left it hanging there, both of them knowing she had to, both knowing that he would be making many more trips to New York than usual in the next few months.

On November 6, 1770, Sadie Wythe boarded one of Ben's boats for a trip to Philadelphia where she would stay with her sister. Dr. Warren, Jonathan Clark, Lewis Lynch and Ben were all at the dock to see her off. Each of the men had a small going-away gift for her. She took four trunks with her and said she did not expect to be back for a year, maybe two. It depended on the state of health of her sick sister. This was the only family she had left and Sadie was going to help take care of her.

Ben and Sadie had made their good byes the night before, making love one last time so tenderly that they both cried and pledged that they would see each other as often as they could. Ben would be with her for the happy day, if possible.

The facts had been planted early in the council meetings that Sadie might need to go to Philadelphia. In reality she was heading for New York, where her sister lived, but they decided such a minor subterfuge would be needed to help shield Ben's visits as business when he went to New York to see Sadie.

The four men paced the docks as the ship pulled away, then Lynch suggested a quick stop at a tavern.

Later, back at his office, Ben found plenty of work to keep him busy. He had sent his personal check in the amount of five hundred pounds to a New York bank to be deposited in the name of Mrs. Sadie Wythe. He would send additional money as needed. He only wished that he could be with her for the whole term, to watch his child grow and see him come into the world at last. But such was not to be. It was part of the price of loving two women. It would be a month before he could schedule a trip to

424

New York, but then they would be together again for a few days. Ben shook his head and looked down at his work.

On his desk were plans for one of his new ships, the *Avenger*. Curiously she was fitted so she could take on sixteen cannon if need be. He told the designer it was a dual-purpose ship. He could use her as a freighter, but in case a need arose she could be sold to England as a fighting ship. This was the excuse he used with anyone in Boston whom he knew had Tory leanings.

Ben laughed softly. Right under the British noses, he and John Hancock were starting to build an American navy, and there wasn't a thing the redcoats could do about it.

Chapter Seven
THE DAY OF ARTHUR WYTHE

May 1, 1771

Ben tried to remember where the past seven months had vanished. He couldn't. The boys were just finishing their first year at Beekman's. Harriet had settled down to her work at Rutledge & Rutledge, where she was now in charge of all purchasing, land development, buildings and equipment and handled all employee relations. She was doing an outstanding job.

Ben had traveled to New York three times on business, and each time he marveled at the way Sadie relished her role of coming motherhood. She showed an entirely new side of her complex personality, and Ben loved it as much as the rest.

Now in New York, Ben stared down at his son, born on April 29, 1771. He had missed the joyous event by only two days. The baby had absolutely no hair, his eyes still squeezed shut so tightly they didn't want to open, and now he sucked greedily at his mother's full breast.

"He's such a good baby," Sadie said. "In another month I wager Arthur will be sleeping through the night."

"That's because you're such a good mother and feeding him so well. He's probably stuffed most of the time."

"He looks like you, Ben. Do you see that?"

"You'll never be able to prove it in court." He laughed, bent and kissed mother and child. "That was a bad joke. I'm sorry. I told you that you're a remarkable mother." He let his smile fade. "I just wish you could come home right now."

"I do, too."

"When can you come back?"

"It depends on Arthur. Perhaps when he's six months old I can leave him, but only for a month or two before we arrange to bring him, too." Her voice took on a desperate tone. "It is all right if we bring him back, isn't it? We can say he's my sister Ardelle's child the way we planned . . ."

"Of course, yes, that's what we planned."

She looked away. "I know, darling, but sometimes . . . I mean, it does happen that people change their minds."

"I'll be waiting for you both to come just as soon as we can work it out. But I suggest it should be after he's weaned. That might give away the truth if you nursed him!"

They both laughed.

"Oh, I know people are going to talk. They will remember when I left town and how long I was gone, guess how old Arthur is and figure back. I can just see them doing it now!" She moved Arthur's hungry mouth to her other breast. The child snuggled down, his hands pushing at her soft, white skin. "But I don't care, let them gossip. I *do* have a married name, and I am not afraid of whatever they say."

"That's my girl. Now, no more of this down-in-the-mouth talk. As soon as this hungry lad finishes his dinner, I'm going to take you out to the finest restaurant in the whole city of New York, and we'll order everything on the menu and eat until we can't hold another morsel!"

A week later, back in Boston, Ben tried to judge the feeling of the people. In the past year there had been drastic changes. No one pelted the redcoats with rocks now. There was little jeering of the soldiers on the streets. They had few duties, but surprisingly they stayed out of major trouble. It seemed that everywhere new buildings were going up. Men were working, houses were spreading out toward the Boston neck. More homes showed across the bay in Charlestown. Imports were at an all-time high, and Ben's business was stretched to its absolute capacity until he built or bought more boats.

One new shipping concern had begun in Boston since the end of the non-importation agreements, and it was doing very well.

There had also come an upsurge of light manufacturing: nails, tools, some lumber, everyday furniture. But still the majority of their ready-made goods was imported from England, according to the laws laid down in the navigation acts. Ben sensed the colonies were gathering strength, and at the same time building up a pressure that would eventually burst. Shipbuilding was the only major manufacturing industry in the colonies. There should be so much more done here. The artisans were here, men who could make many things. England couldn't hold the colonies down forever in this kind of economic slavery.

Ben struggled with his task of holding the Freedom Fighters together. There had been many who had quit. The average company now had only twelve men instead of twenty, but those left were rock solid and hard, knowing it was a waiting proposition and guaranteeing that they would be ready when needed.

The Rutledge twin boys were doing well at Beekman's school, in their second year and growing taller by the day. Both could look their father straight in the eye, and both, when fully grown, would be a hand taller than Ben.

Harriet had concentrated so on the business that she had no beaux at all. Her mother worried. At last she had Harriet's agreement to give a twentieth birthday ball on December ninth. It was held at their home, the rugs rolled up for dancing, and they had musicians and wine punch and champagne. Sandra seemed to enjoy the event as much as Harriet did.

By the middle of December, 1771, Sadie

Wythe came back to town. There was no fanfare. She arrived on a Rutledge ship and moved into a small house in a new district a dozen blocks from Ben. She did not reapply for membership in the council, but did make calls on Dr. Warren and Jonathan to let them know she was back. She told them that her sister was simply hanging on. They had brought in a woman to help care for her, but Sadie had missed her friends and wanted to return home. She had put on weight having the baby, but she lost it in the last two months so her weight was the same now as when she left. It had made her a little pale in the process. Dr. Warren promptly prescribed a tonic and told her what she must eat to get the pinkness back in her cheeks.

The second night she was in town Ben went down an alley, found the right gate and went up to her back door. It was the first time they had seen each other since New York. She flew to him. Ben held her so tightly he was afraid he might hurt her, but she smiled and kissed him and wished that she might stay in his arms forever. When they moved apart, she took his hand and he promptly led her toward the small bedroom.

"Darling Sadie, it's been so very long since I've felt the delight of loving you. I can't wait another second!"

They didn't leave the bed until almost one a.m. Then Ben kissed her goodnight and crept out of the room, walked through the alley and drove away in his chaise.

A week later Sadie had her old job back in the millinery shop. She didn't lack funds, but she needed something to do with her time. The work was interesting and somewhat different. She made some new types of beaded handbags, and even created a few small needlework goods that sold well, though she knew designing was not her main talent. She was better at politics. But so far, she had not been able to rejuvenate her concern for the state of the colonies. All she was interested in now was waiting a few months until her sister in Philadelphia would "die" and Sadie would be "saddled" with the youngster, who was almost two but small for his age. Arthur had grown rapidly, and was big for his age. Saying he was almost two instead of almost one might help to allay suspicion.

A dozen blocks away, Ben sat at his desk at home and watched the fire. In the year—no, nearly a year and a half since they had burned the *Richard*, there had been few bad British mistakes or intrusions in colonial affairs. The politicians still argued, the men in the colonial assembly still passed regulations and chaffed at the British troops because they were stationed in Boston. There was little unrest and almost no talk now of independence.

Even Sam Adams seemed slightly less adamant than before. "Wait, lads," he said. "Just wait. They will make a mistake, or we will help them create a crisis. Just you wait!"

Ben and the council kept the small fire alive, recording what they could of the outrages which daily dwindled and became more petty.

Sadie was not at the meetings. She seldom talked with Ben about politics. She was totally concerned with the calendar. The new year came and then slowly the blush of the first spring blossoms.

In May, 1772, Sadie was on one of Ben's boats sailing for New York. There she packed up all of Arthur's belongings, kissed her favorite sister and brother-in-law goodbye and thanked them for boarding Arthur, then she left for her home in Boston. She had prepared the town well, letting it be known to all who would listen, about the tragedy of her sister's illness. Dr. Warren knew the specific problem and he was surprised she had lived as long as this. Jonathan as well was relieved when Sadie's sister was at last taken from her misery.

The four men met Sadie at the dock for a homecoming and took her to her new home. Little Arthur now had stiff black hair and looked nothing at all like Sadie, but more like Ben. For that, Sadie was doubly glad. The small house was not at all ready for a baby. She had planned that. Jonathan and Lewis Lynch helped her remodel one room into a nursery. Ben watched and left early.

At the shop, Sadie said she had to quit to take care of her sister's child. An inheritance from her sister would keep her and the child for five or six years. When Arthur was old enough to be by himself more, she would go back to some kind of employment. "Who knows," she told them. "I might even find myself a husband."

So Sadie settled down in the little house and loved her baby, who was now just over a year old. Every day he was growing and developing and Sadie thanked God she had been able to have a child and to know the joys of motherhood. She had Dr. Warren examine Arthur and he pronounced him in fine health. Dr. Warren paused as he watched her dressing the child.

"Sadie, are you sure you're happy with this new responsibility?"

"Oh, yes. The child has given me a real purpose. Maybe because my husband and I couldn't have a child, the good Lord has provided me one this way. I'm only sorry it had to take Ardelle's death to make it come about."

"But," he paused. "I hope you are thinking of remarrying."

"Oh, yes. That would be nice. If I could find the right man. But then he would have to want a ready-made family, wouldn't he? There aren't many of that kind around."

"I'm still here." Dr. Warren said it softly. His face was open, honest, willing to be hurt in order that she would understand.

"Dr. Warren, I'm truly touched, and flattered. I had no real idea . . . But right now I have a lot of adjusting to do with one new man

433

in the house. I simply couldn't cope with two."

"Can I talk about it again in six months?"

Sadie turned and smiled. "Dr. Warren, I'd like that. Any woman needs to know that she is appreciated and wanted. Yes, in six months or a year, Arthur and I should have our contest of wills all worked out." She laughed. "By then I'm sure this little rascal will have convinced me that he is the boss around our house."

In June, 1772 an event took place which was to be one of the opening gambits in the huge chess game of moves and counter moves by the colonists and British which would lead to the outbreak of the revolutionary war. Ben beamed as he told the council meeting in the room over the bookshop.

"And so, on Monday next, the royal commission will begin its investigation of the burning of the *Richard*. The navy tried to hush it up because of the captain's suicide. So nearly two years late, they will come—late, but here. The commissioners will have total power to summon witnesses, conduct a complete hearing with the whole purpose to put in chains and return to England for trial anyone implicated in the destruction of British Crown property and the death of the captain of the *Richard*."

"What can they hope to accomplish?" Dr. Warren asked, then he nodded. "Yes . . . to them it's wrapping up a loose end. They can't

434

let us colonists get away with anything."

Lewis Lynch grinned, his one eye flashing. "Burning of what ship, Mr. Commissioner? I don't recall any British merchantman by that name in the Back Bay."

They all chuckled. Twenty-one persons were at the site, took part in the affair, and Ben guessed that not one of them would be ferreted out and asked to appear before the commissioners.

The Boston *Gazette* headlined the story the next day: ROYAL COMMISSION TO INVESTIGATE *RICHARD* SINKING. JUDGE TO QUESTION ALL WHO SAW OR KNEW ABOUT SINKING. FEW LOCAL PEOPLE HEARD ABOUT DISASTER UNTIL NEXT DAY.

After the headlines the *Gazette* moved into a serious condemnation of the whole idea. "We can see only one logical reason for the commission to be sent here at this time for such a belated investigation: the cowing of the Massachusetts people and their represented assembly, the grinding down under the British Lion's paw of what few liberties we still have left; the further restriction on our God-given rights to freedom and happiness. There can be no success in such a farce. Either the commission will hound some Massachusetts citizen into confessing to something that he did not do, or the commissioners will come up empty-handed. Surely, those who were responsible in running aground the craft (and we have not heard any-one boasting about this feat) will not volunteer to come forward and testify so that he will by such an act incriminate himself.

"Not only is the Massachusetts colony on trial here, the entire seaboard, every one of the thirteen self-governing colonies is involved, be-cause if the Crown can come in and blunder about seeking retribution, TWO YEARS AFTER AN ALLEGED CRIME, how safe is any of the other colonies from the same or worse treatment? It is the time for us thirteen colonies to unite as we did for the Stamp Act Congress in 1765 and show that together we have great strength which will permit us total safety from the English Redcoat menace! The clarion call must go out now and throughout this spurious Royal Commission hearing—now is the time to unite and demand an end to such arbitrary and unwarranted breaches of the com-mon law. We must stand on our feet and pro-test like free men, or we will be herded into con-venient colonial pens like the sheep we surely will be, and quietly channeled through the chute into the shearing hall and from there directly to the slaughtering rooms. United we are strong!"

Ben put down the paper and smiled. He saw the delicate hand of Sam Adams behind the front page story. It showed in the phrasing, the choice of words. He felt sure that Sam would have more to say about the commission every day the paper came out. Later, Ben followed the hearings as they progressed. Several of the seamen involved were brought to testify. When the sessions began, Ben sent Lewis Lynch to New York on a ship. He would work out of the Rutledge New York office until the commission was finished with the hearings, and would return only on Ben's orders.

The young lieutenant who had been left with the captain's body was brought to testify. His descriptions were hazy. He did remember a man with a black patch over one eye, but now he couldn't decide which eye it was. The man had either been a seaman or a military man, he said. The lieutenant did testify that the captain had taken his own life with a pistol shot, which settled one of the hottest questions in the hearings. Now no one associated with the attack could be charged with murder.

Once that determination was made, the proceedings turned into a running joke for Bostonians. Numerous men were called to testify, but each was either out of town, in the country, or if he had been on the waters that afternoon, had suddenly developed one of the worst memories in the colonies.

The commission sensed the tone of the people, the feeling, and began calling as witnesses men from the gallery watching the hearings in Boston Town Hall on Kings Street.

Two sailors did admit that they had seen a white ship of some thirty feet come into the harbor that evening some time after dusk, but they forgot where she anchored. They were so unsure they decided it could have gone right by the north part of the port and on past Mimot's "T" Wharf into the south harbour.

Travelers across the Boston neck that night were sought out and questioned under oath, but none would admit to seeing a "band of some twenty" mounted horsemen coming back into Boston an hour after darkness.

There was little the commissioners could do. In the end they concluded that the men who had lured the *Richard* into shallow waters where she heeled over and was burned, were undoubtedly "men of estate and property who were rebellious-minded and acted in a criminal manner after the ways of pirates. Since these men were generally known by the community, and had position and wealth, no common citizen dared risk his life by giving the true evidence the Crown was looking for."

Ben watched the newspapers from around the various colonies rip into the commission. They were called a court of inquisition which combined the blatant wrongs of that holy tribunal and the unfairness of a Star Chamber.

One newspaper editorial shouted: "This makes the position of Americans infinitely worse than that of a subject of France, Spain, Portugal or any other of the most despotic powers on earth."

Other journals called the commissioners: "A pack of English tyrants and their deeds are the most insulting violation of the rights of Americans that can be devised."

After seventeen days, the commission had to give up and the members confessed their failure. Instead of finding and punishing the guilty arsonists and pirates, the commission could only slink back to England. This spectacle of the American rioters again slipping through the hands of the British government deeply pained the Crown's officers.

The collector of customs in Rhode Island wrote that this "marked the end to security of government servants . . . an end to collecting a revenue and enforcing the acts of trade."

Ben was overjoyed by the results of the commission's failure. The council began keeping detailed newspaper clippings about the hearings and soon a pattern began to emerge: the British indecision, their rapid veering from appeasement to severity, and the inability of the British to punish the colonists effectively encouraged Americans to regard the Atlantic ocean as a barrier beyond which the long arm of Great Britain's power could not reach.

Dr. Warren puffed on a pipe and smiled. "It seems we need have little fear of punishment from the doddering old lady called England. Certainly, the failure of the British government to punish anyone for what we did to Capspree and the *Richard* must be direct encouragement to a revitalization of our stand. It should make us watch and be on the alert for more acts of independence we can undertake."

Ben read a quotation from one Britisher: "Admiral Montague says the Bostonians are ripe for independence, and nothing but the king's ships in Boston harbor prevent their going to greater length, as they see no notice taken from home of their behavior."

Jonathan Clark lifted his cup of tea in a salute. "Now that sounds more like it. I like that admiral, indeed I do. From what I've been reading, it looks like this whole affair has given us another big push forward. The Commission of Inquiry has been shown around the colonies as not just an attack on Boston, but an attack upon liberty in all America. More and more newspapers and journals are urging every colony that we must unite and stand our ground with a truly 'Roman spirit of liberty.' Now, I like that turn of phrase. It seems, people, that we're starting to move again. Perhaps it's time that we bolster our ranks, get each company up to its stipulated strength of twenty men."

They talked about it. Everyone was glad that the pendulum had at last started to swing the opposite way. But there seemed no immediate need for a larger force. They could muster fifty men if they had to, and that should suffice for a while.

Even Captain Arnold Compton had felt the change in attitude. No longer was the feeling personal against individual redcoats, now it was deeper, more intense, a feeling coupled with an

American pride.

Near the middle of the inquiry by the commissioners over the *Richard*, another event took place that went unnoticed for a few days by all but a few vitally interested men.

On June 13, 1772, Governor Thomas Hutchinson, the agent of the king of England, told the Massachusetts Assembly that he neither needed nor would he accept any further salary from the assembly, since the king had made provision to pay him from the customs revenues.

Sam Adams, sitting in the assembly, was thunderstruck. He more than any other man in the group saw the long-reaching connotation of this act. In one stroke the Crown had freed the royal governor from any dependence on the assembly. No longer could the assembly attempt to gain favor or bring pressure upon the governor by withholding or delaying his salary grants.

A short time later, the governor announced that judges of the Superior Court would likewise receive their pay from the Crown. Now the highest judges in the colony would not be subjected to any control or influence by the assembly. This left Hutchinson and the judges to do precisely as they wanted, or as they felt the king wanted them to do, without fearing any financial embarrassment. Sam Adams had jumped to his feet and quickly informed the governor that this was an untimely withdrawal of one of the basic checks and balances of the democratic form of government, and he feared that there could easily arise a despotic administration without the assembly's restraint.

Governor Hutchinson was startled by such an open attack, but he could only smile, knowing he had at last struck a mighty blow that could help him defeat Sam Adams.

Most of the population did not like Governor Thomas Hutchinson. The people thought of him as having a long nose in a long face on a long, skinny frame. They liked him less because he was always courting royal favor. On the whole he was an honorable man, but he swore his duty to the king, and wore his honor with the haughty air of a nobleman. This alone was enough to turn most of the common men in Massachusetts against him.

Sam Adams was physically the opposite of Tom Hutchinson. Sam was round-faced and with a tendency to carry too much weight. But under that soft-looking body functioned a man much harder and more dedicated than Governor Hutchinson dreamed.

As Sam Adams sat in the back room at the Black Horse tavern, he eyed those around him: John Hancock, Dr. Joseph Warren, Lewis Lynch, Ben Rutledge and a dozen other men known for their commitment to unification and liberty for the thirteen colonies. He stood up and the room quieted.

"All of you gentlemen are aware of the latest

form of ingenious slavery to which the pompous lords of London have subjected us—and that dictated by the king himself. It must not be allowed to stand! They have made a move, and now it is our turn to try for a checkmate as quickly as possible.

"I suggest we make some dramatic counterplay with an eye to uniting our own colony, then attempt to extend such a movement into the rest of the colonies. Here's my plan, which, if you agree, will be proposed at the Tuesday night Town Hall meeting, and for which I hope you will generate vocal and deliberate support. My plan is simple. I suggest we form a committee to send out letters and other correspondence to as many surrounding hamlets, cities, towns and villages as we can, listing a statement of colonial rights, and follow that by showing a long recitation of the violations of those rights by redcoats, the Parliament and the king. We will make these lists of violations as detailed as possible, including the attacks by the revenue ships, the robbery and cheating of the Board of Customs Commissioners, the troops in our city, and the villainous Boston Massacre.

"This will not be a riotous extra-legal Sons of Liberty kind of operation. We propose that it have the total and complete blessing of the Selectmen and the Town Meetings, emphasizing the democratic manner in which we are proceeding.

"It is our hope that we can urge each group

to which we send our list, to circulate a list of its own, of local outrages by the British during the past several years. It has been suggested that we call this the Committee of Correspondence. As we get the Commonwealth of Massachusetts behind the program, we will strike into other colonies and urge them to circulate to all cities their own recitations of illegal and immoral British acts. This way, our friendly newspapers will have fresh fuel for the fires of dissent and, we hope, eventually, of liberty!"

Sam sniffed to clear his nose, wiped his eyes with a linen handkerchief and looked around the large table.

A cheer sounded in the room, then another, and soon it was a chorus of shouting agreement about the plan.

For the next half-hour they discussed the idea, refining it, trying to come up with quicker methods for achieving their goal.

"Gentlemen, if this works, we should have our campaign in high gear once again, our plans for working toward independence from England will be strongly launched, and we will be jabbing the English lion in the rump so hard she will never forget it!"

A dozen mugs of ale were lifted into the air, and the group voted unanimously to promote the plan at the coming meeting.

The Boston Town Meeting selectmen heard and approved the plans, and on November 10, 1772, Samuel Adams, working through the Boston Committee of Correspondence, wrote the first report, which was sent by post and messenger to every town in Massachusetts.

"The colonists have been branded with the odious names of traitors and rebels only for complaining of their grievances; how long such treatment will be, or ought to be borne, is submitted." That was the opening line of the report.

Ben sat with Sam Adams looking over a basket of letters the committee had received in the two weeks after the letters were circulated. Most of the returns were similar in content, blasting the British and the redcoats for a variety of evils, and it seemed that each city tried to outdo the next in the extent of its outrage and the call for redress of their complaints.

Newspapers all over Massachusetts began publishing the letters, selecting the best and most anti-British. At once the sentiment was brought to the public's mind about the cause for more freedom from England. Anti-British feeling rose at an astonishingly fast rate.

The committee expanded its scope and wrote to other colonies urging them to circulate letters of complaint and to organize similar committees within their own jurisdictions.

Ben had gone directly from his meeting with Adams to the small house off Timberly Lane and tied his horse in the alley. Now he lay in bed beside Sadie. They had just put Arthur back to sleep after his fitful waking. Ben could think of little else besides the Committee of Correspondence and the fine way it had lighted the fires of the freedom movement again. He told the whole story to Sadie, and she listened, asked some questions and agreed with him that now they were back on track again. This might be the time it would keep building all the way until the first shots were fired.

Ben had urged Sam Adams to be sure that the Massachusetts militia, controlled by the assembly, was kept at a considerable strength, and that the citizen-soldiers were well trained and ready to fight. Sam had taken the cue and did what he could toward readiness by the Massachusetts militia groups all over the colony.

"Ben, darling, you've been so quiet just now. Are you worried?"

He kissed her cheek and shook his head. "Excited is more the word. It's an invigorating time to be alive, do you realize that? We are in the process of winning our liberty from a great world power. We are in the very first stages of establishing what I hope will one day be a fine nation, and a world power itself. Think of the tremendous responsibility we have! What if we do something wrong, or we don't act correctly when we should? Generations of Americans who then will still be under British domination will curse us for centuries. But, if we take it a step at a time, wait for the surging swell of public support, for the demand by the farmers, the shippers, the artisans, the ordinary people *for their independence*—then we will be thanked by those same untold future American generations."

She kissed his lips. "And you think the Committee of Correspondence has launched the final push that will make all this happen?"

"Oh, yes. It's been the spark we've needed. At least it looks that way so far. I thought the Boston Massacre might do it, but our people weren't ready. Now, two and a half years later, we might be set for it. The next few months will tell."

"Darling, I'm so glad you're involved, and that you're one of the leaders in the movement . . ." She pushed against him, snuggling as close as she could. Slowly his hands came down and covered her breasts and his lips reached for hers. He was totally committed to the cause of liberty, but there was something much closer at hand that he should think of for a little while.

Chapter Eight
THE BOSTON HARBOUR TEACUP

March 1773

Through the last half of 1772 and the first three months of 1773, the Committee of Correspondence had spread rapidly all over the colonies. It seemed the right time had come for more vigorous action against the British. In March of 1773 a proposal went out from the Virginia House of Burgesses to coordinate the movements on an intercolonial basis. This was set up quickly and by the summer of 1773 the thirteen colonies had fast and efficient routes of communications set up, so whatever happened in one section of the colonies would be circulated to every other American.

The committees continued to point up deficiencies in the British colonial system, berating the faults of Parliament and standing ready and eager to flash the news of any outrage by a governing body, British officials or troops.

Parliament was the whipping boy, since it caused the colonists most of their anguish, including the continuing tax on tea. In the fall of

1773 the people were waiting to see what the lords across the sea would try to foist on them next as irrefutable law.

Even after the repeal of the Townshend duties, there was still a tax on tea. The colonists had openly defied the tax by smuggling in any kind of tea they could find. It was socially popular and thought of as non-criminal to smuggle tea to beat the British tax. Once inside the colonies, such tea was openly offered for sale. The British lost the tax on all of the smuggled goods, and it was a constant source of irritation to them. Officials estimated that at least half the tea used in the colonies during those years was smuggled in.

Local importers who brought in legal, taxed tea were held in low esteem by most of the people. Tea was an important part of daily life, being a common drink with meals, and also taken in the morning and afternoon. It was the national drink.

Ben Rutledge had watched the tea controversy closely. He had refused to carry the taxable, legal tea on board his vessels. But now there were rumors about the troubles of the East India company, the gigantic corporation representing England's investments in India. Ben heard from London that the feeling was in Parliament that they might be able to save the firm if they allowed it to sell tea directly to the colonies.

Until that time they had to ship the tea from

the Far East to London, where it was sold at auction to wholesale merchants. The London buyers then sold the tea to American wholesalers, who in turn sold to retailers and thence to the public. Each hand the tea passed through increased the price.

Parliament decided that by going around the middlemen, they could allow East India to sell directly to tea agencies in America, who would sell directly to retailers, thus cutting out both British and American wholesalers, and bringing down the price. East India Company agents could then sell their tea even under the price of the smuggled variety, capture most of the huge colonial market and recoup its fortunes. In May of 1773 Parliament passed such legislation and word arrived about a month later in the colonies. The issue was far from clear and there was confusion and anger.

In August the true picture came out and merchants banded together and rushed forward, shouting "Monopoly!" They reasoned that the cheap tea would put legitimate tea wholesalers and merchants out of business. Then, with the whole market, East India could raise the price of tea to whatever high level it wished.

The Committee of Correspondence flashed the anger of the people around the colonies. Soon every hamlet, village, and country store knew about the scheme to make the colonies pay to keep the East India Company from bankruptcy.

Governor Hutchinson of Massachusetts was interested in the idea, and his request that his two sons be appointed consignees or wholesalers of East India tea in Boston was granted.

By mid-October tempers were rising. Ben called a meeting of the Freedom Fighters to order and immediately brought up the matter of tea.

Jonathan Clark was the first to rise. "Gentlemen, I'm glad to say that the tea merchant in our city, one Jonathan Clarke, and that's the one with an 'E' on the end, is of no relation, kith nor kin of mine, thank ye. I'm the bookseller and binder, this is my store. That other Jonathan Clarke, is the one who has been appointed one of the major consignees of the East India tea here in Boston town. I'm embarrassed that my name is so similar, but I'll take notices in the newspaper tomorrow telling everyone that it's he and not me who is involved in this unholy monopoly effort."

Dr. Warren took his turn. "The people are highly concerned about the monopoly aspect of the East Indian tea. The feeling seems to be that first it will be tea that gets special treatment, then all the Townshend duties will be back and other firms will be added and move in with total monopolistic rights until the American merchant is nothing more than a petty supplier of non-essentials. As you know, we have fought the importation of duty tea. But there has been little else we could do. Now, gentlemen, now we have a cause, and the newspapers are helping us and the committees are working hard at it. Almost daily some pseudonym cries out in the papers. Today, 'Reclusis' objected to the vast amount of currency the monopoly would take out of the lifeblood of Boston. And he is right.

"Yesterday Edes and Gill in their *Boston Gazette* suggested that we ship the tea *and the consignees* themselves back to England. They pointed out it was another way to provide enough revenue to pay the salaries of the governors and judges, rendering them totally independent from the local government till.

"On October 21, a week hence, the Committee of Correspondence here will send out letters to all surrounding towns calling attention to the dangers of the tea plan and seek cooperation from other groups and ideas for methods that might be used to prevent its taking place."

Dr. Warren sat down.

Arnold Compton never stood when he spoke, but his voice was strong and usually loud. He was getting used to the talk at the council meetings, although he couldn't attend all of them. He smoked a black cigar and frowned. "We got along without tea before, during the non-importation thing. Why don't we declare tea illegal for any patriot to buy or use? Then, even if East India did bring in the tea, it don't matter 'cause nobody's gonna buy it and they won't stay in business long."

Heads around the table nodded in agreement.

Ben looked at Lewis Lynch, but he waved his hand. "You guys get too damned complicated for me. Makes my head hurt just thinking about it."

Ben stood and walked slowly around the table.

"Gentlemen, I've been following this problem carefully. I would suggest that it is going to become more and more critical as the days progress. I know some of the captains involved and I'm afraid that a few will accept the shipments of tea even under these conditions. I don't see how we can avoid a direct confrontation. It's my suggestion that we start planning right now and devise some contingency operational plans, so we'll have them ready if we need them. We might think along the lines that we are going to need to have some type of a reception ready if and when that tea comes into port and someone starts to unload it."

Ben made his suggestion in the form of a motion and the vote went around the table. It passed. Ben said he'd have some ideas for their consideration at the next meeting.

The days passed. Ben worked out plans, and the Freedom Fighters listened to them, approved one and then watched the developing crisis.

Early on the morning of November second, Richard Clarke awoke to loud noises at his front door. He opened the second-story window and saw two men in his courtyard below.

"Quiet, you ruffians! I'm trying to sleep up here!" Clarke shouted.

"You won't sleep another night, Clarke, unless you come to the Liberty Tree Wednesday at noon and make a public resignation of your commission as consignee of the East India company's tea shipment."

"You've no right to ask, no authority . . ." Clarke began.

"Legal and binding summons," one of the two men in the yard said. He threw the summons, tied to a rock, at Clarke. The missile sailed through both the raised and fixed windows, smashing the glass in both.

"You be there, you damned Tory, or we'll have you fried and quartered for our dinner tomorrow night!"

The other agents for the India tea received similar threatening summonses that same night. By daylight on November second, handbills had been posted all over town urging the citizens to assemble at the Liberty Tree and witness the public resignation of the consignees of the hated East India Company.

That evening the Committee of Correspondence met with the North End Caucus in the Green Dragon tavern to map out some plans for what the next day's action might take.

Wednesday at noon, the Liberty Tree was spangled with flags and banners. Church bells rang, the town crier ran his specified route, and soon five hundred people collected at the tree. Sam Adams, Joseph Warren, John Hancock and Ben Rutledge were all there. None of the consignees who had been summoned made an appearance.

Word soon spread that the wanted men were gathered at Clarke's store at the foot of King Street. A delegation was sent to protest the affront to the public gathering and demand the verbal resignations of the tea agents. Mr. Clarke scorned them, saying they were not a legally constituted public meeting or forum, and had no standing. He refused to heed the order.

The crowd started to disperse. Then someone turned and stormed the open door. The door's hinges were ripped off and men piled into the store. The consignees fled upstairs to the counting room, where a strong locked door protected them. It took the angry crowd an hour and a half to disperse, but no one was hurt.

Ben sat in his chaise nearby, remembering another angry crowd throwing rocks in the Boston street. He wondered if this would have the same kind of ending. As he moved away he resolved it would not. Action was the key here, not waiting and then reacting to what the British did. A new plan began to formulate in his mind.

Ben watched the maneuverings, the hearings, the meetings, and the counter-moves by the authorities. All through November the two sides sparred in an effort to force the importers of the East India tea to resign. Someone even sent threatening letters suggesting tar and feathers, and some murder.

Then a meeting of the Committee of Correspondence from all the surrounding cities was called to be held in Faneuil Hall. The idea was solidarity of all the neighboring communities. Mr. Clarke requested an appointment with the group and pleaded his case now, saying he did not really want the commission to sell the tea but the tea was already on its way, and there was no way the ships could be turned back. By law tea could not be re-imported into England, so he would lose the tea and be fined and this could ruin him. The committee suggested that as soon as the ship came into port it be turned around and sent back with a letter explaining that due to local conditions beyond his control he could not accept the tea or the commission. Clarke would not budge, and the compromise was not consummated.

Governor Hutchinson became daily more concerned about the danger of the situation he saw building. After the November 22 meetings he openly wondered if he should retire to the Castle William in the bay where the king's troops were stationed and where he would be safe under British guns.

A bluff-bowed ship worked its way through the outer islands off Boston on Sunday, November 28, 1773. It anchored in the sheltered waters of the harbour and soon everyone in town knew that the first ship with East India Company tea had arrived. She was the *Dartmouth*, nine weeks out of London, with one hundred and fourteen chests of first-quality tea and assorted other freight on board.

The crisis was met.

This was the first of the tea ships to arrive in America. None of the other ships had yet ported at New York, Philadelphia or Charleston. In New York the consignees had been forced to resign by furious public opinion. Reports from Philadelphia indicated the same situation was about to happen there. As word spread through Boston that Sabbath day that the tea ship was in port, the men of Boston realized that what they did in the next few days might well influence what happened at the other port towns as well.

Ben and his band had twenty days to act. Under long-time port law and practice, the customs officers could seize goods on which duty was owed if payment were not made within twenty days after the ship entered port. This tea on board was legally taxable under the Townshend Acts duty. The end date was December 17.

The day was full of activity, which was unusual on the Sabbath. The Boston Board of Selectmen, the town's ruling body, met at noon, hoping for some new proposals from the consignees through Clarke, which would settle the problem. None came from Clarke, but he promised to have something for the selectmen on Monday.

Sam Adams and Joseph Warren were also busy. They had summoned the surrounding Committees of Correspondence to hold a joint meeting in Faneuil Hall the next morning.

Monday before noon they came, soon overflowing Faneuil Hall, so the convention was moved to Old South Meeting House where more than five thousand men converged. The unanimous resolve was that the tea be sent back to England and that no Townshend duty payment would be made. They also had the *Dartmouth* moved to Griffin's Wharf and placed a twenty-five man armed guard on her to prevent any mob violence and also to block any attempt by Captain James Hall to unload his tea cargo.

More meetings were held, but each side remained adamant in its stand, and time slipped by. The governor could do nothing. His troops were on Castle William, allowing patriots and extremists to control the town and the wharfs.

By December seventh, the *Eleanor* and the brig *Beaver*, both with tea in their holds from the East India Company, had arrived and were ordered by the Committee of Correspondence to dock at Griffin's Wharf as well so all could be controlled more easily, with a smaller guard force. The fourth and last tea ship headed for Boston, the brig *William*, had been blown ashore and foundered on the back side of Cape Cod, and the vessel declared a total loss.

Ben and Lewis Lynch held long conferences. The Freedom Fighters studied the problem for a week, then decided on a course of action. All fifty of the Freedom Fighters were given explicit instructions. Lynch worked out the battle plan, giving detailed targets, weapons, even the uniforms they would wear.

The crisis worked down to the last day, as Ben had feared. On Thursday, December 16, more than five thousand men of Boston and vicinity jammed into Old South Meeting House at ten a.m. Outside, a cold rain fell.

Ben and the rest knew that the next day the customs officials would be free to seize the cargo. The owners would then gladly pay the duties and the goods would be landed. If anything were to be done, it must happen now.

The ships' captains were summoned and ordered by the Committee of Correspondence to take their vessels out of Boston harbour. They said they could not do that. The big 32-pound cannon at Castle William would blow them out of the water unless they had the proper papers. To get the papers they had to pay the duty and unload the tea. One of the boat owners said he would try again.

The meeting reconvened at three p.m., but Francis Rotch was still seeking the papers and permits to move his vessel, the *Dartmouth*. By five p.m. he had not returned from the governor's country place. The crowd waited restlessly.

At 5:45 p.m. Rotch arrived. It was almost dark. Two dozen candles feebly lit the great hall. Rotch told the meeting that the governor had refused to grant him a safe pass so he could sail past the British guns on the Castle.

"A mob, a mob!" someone shouted.

"Let's burn the bloody tea!" another cried.

The chairman got the unruly crowd to quiet and restored order. Thomas Young stood and made a brief defense of Rotch, saying the man had tried hard, he was in a difficult situation and he had done everything that could be done to settle the matter. Young urged that no harm be done to Rotch or his property.

Sam Adams followed that plea and when the large assembly had quieted so a whisper could be heard, he spoke. "Gentlemen, I see nothing else that the inhabitants can do to save our country."

Immediately a curdling war-whoop came from the gallery. Near each of the doors, voices repeated the cry. The men quickly pulled on blankets, dabbed paint and soot on their faces, and soon looked like poor imitations of Indians.

"The Mohawks are here. It's an Indian raid!" someone shouted.

Arnold Compton jumped out of his seat and ran for the back of the hall. "Hurrah for Griffin's Wharf!" he yelled as he ran, whipping a tattered blanket around him.

Now there was a confused milling as men made their way for the exits. Someone else in the crowd by the door gave the last understandable shout of the meeting: "Boston Harbour will be a teapot tonight!"

It was only then that the majority of the men in the big hall realized what was taking place. Some thought that Sam Adams' statement may have been a signal: others said they were sure that it was the pre-arranged phrase to start the action. Soon there were fifty men with blankets wrapped around themselves and with dabs of soot and paint splotched on their faces. They pushed through the crowds to the doors, then ran in three efficiently assembled groups toward Griffin's Wharf.

Ben caught up with them before they got to the *Dartmouth*. He hurried up the short gangplank onto the ship, shouted two words to the armed patriots on board. Fifteen men swarmed onto the ship behind him. They knew exactly where to go, and pushed the heavy chests of tea out of the holds and up to the deck. Other "Indians" opened the chests and threw them over the side into the bay. The tea bobbed and floated about for a while like leaves in a china cup, then slowly sank out of sight.

Ben paused a moment to admire their work. On the other two ships at the wharf, the *Eleanor* and the brig *Beaver*, he could hear the shouts and a few scuffles, then there was quiet until the splashes came, and he knew more chests of tea were spicing the harbour water.

"Lively now," Ben called to those on the

Dartmouth. "The quicker the better. We want all one hundred and fourteen chests of tea, lads, keep it moving!"

Ben had his flintlock pistol in his waistband, and tonight he had brought along a two-foot saber, not really sure why, but hoping he would have no need for either weapon. Surely he wouldn't need them against the crews of the ships or the patriot guards.

It took them thirty minutes to dump the tea from the first ship into the harbour. The men danced around the deck for a moment, then hurried away to help on the others. A crowd had gathered at the dock and they cheered the "Indians" when they knew for sure what was happening. Ben ordered the rest of his men off the *Dartmouth* to disperse and remove their disguises. He ran to the *Eleanor*, saw the men had almost finished there and hurried on to the *Beaver*, which had been the last boarded and still had the most tea in the hold.

Lewis Lynch urged the men on, but Ben knew it was taking too much time. He had learned half an hour before the start of their Boston Tea Party that there was a fifteen-man contingent of Royal Marines stationed at the governor's house to prevent looting and vandalism, while the governor hid out of the danger in his country place in Milton. At the first report of an attack on the tea, Ben was certain that the detail would march toward the ships in a show of strength. He wanted to be well gone by that time.

Ben ordered Lynch and his men off the ship. They came reluctantly, before the job was done. Just as the last man jumped from the gangplank, Ben heard shrill orders and saw the crowd around the wharf parting. The dozen Royal Marines with bayonets fixed on Brown Bess muskets came through the crowd in a narrow wedge, sharp steel poking anyone not moving aside.

Ben squatted beside the big ship, saw three more of the men huddled nearby. He glanced again at the smallest of the three and sucked in a quick breath. It was Sadie. He'd know the tilt of her head and that profile anywhere. He rushed toward her, caught her hand, and led eight men the opposite way as the marines were coming.

Sadie looked up as they ran down the street.

"Sorry, I just couldn't miss out on the fun," she said.

Ben nodded. He knew the feeling. "Break up, men, scatter up the streets. Don't pick dead-end lanes. And get rid of your blankets and paint. They can't follow us all!"

The men darted into different streets facing the wharf, pounding away at a fast run. Ben pulled Sadie along another street. He stopped as he heard a musket shot behind him. Looking back, he saw a man stumble and fall. The victim wore an Indian blanket. So the marines had orders to shoot. It was war! He pulled his flintlock out of his waistband and ran on.

Sadie was tired. "You're not in good condition, soldier," he said, slowing down, then walking. She was panting too hard to answer. Instead she took a flintlock pistol from under her jacket and held it in both hands.

"Two more blocks," Ben said, "then we can slip into the alley, go through a store and lose them." She took time now to unpin the Indian blanket that had been her disguise. Sadie still had the smudges of soot on her cheeks and forehead. Ben heard boots pounding the cobblestones behind them. The British too had scattered to chase down the patriots.

"Run! Up this way!" Ben said, pulling her into an alley. They ran hard, and when they came to the other end, Ben saw his mistake. Two marines were just turning into the alley. Ben shot one in the chest, knocking him down, then pulled out the short saber. At once the other marine was on top of him trying for a shot with the Brown Bess. Ben dodged the bayonet, tripped the man and swung the saber at his falling body. Ben slashed the marine on the arm, making him drop the musket, giving Ben a chance to advance on the marine. He scrambled up and turned to run, but saw the other two marines coming up the alley. Ben lunged forward, slashing at the enemy, making contact and slicing a deep wound across the marine's face. The man screamed, turned and ran down the street. Ben grabbed the heavy Brown Bess and brought it up to fire at the two men charging down on him. It misfired.

Sadie had shrunk to the brick wall, her pistol lowered as she watched Ben. She was too surprised, too shocked to fight back. But as the new threat came closer, she gathered her senses, and as the marines ran within twenty feet, she lifted the heavy flintlock and fired. The ball struck one marine in the shoulder. He stumbled toward her. The marine swore, and holding his musket in both hands, drove at her. She guessed he had fired once and hadn't stopped to reload the musket. Sadie dodged one way, then the other, but the marine was a veteran of many combat fights. He moved with her, then lunged with a slashing thrust of the sharp bayonet.

Sadie screamed. The steel cut through her thin coat like a green sapling, the tip slicing deeply across her belly, slanting upward, breaking a rib and swinging free.

Ben swore at the misfiring Brown Bess, and lowered it to try the bayonet. He'd never used one before. None of the Freedom Fighters had them on their weapons. Instinctively he fought, pushing the other man's thrust of the bayonet aside as he would a saber. There was a similarity. He slashed at the marine, made him take a step backward. Then the marine charged. Ben smashed away the oncoming shining steel and pulled his own blade back just as the marine plunged into it. The heavy steel pierced the marine's chest, entered the left lung, and then severed one of the major arteries from his heart, killing him instantly.

Ben had lost his grip on the musket as the marine fell, the blade still in his chest. Ben found the last marine still on his feet, holding an ugly shoulder wound. He had just swung his bayonet at Sadie. Ben ran toward him, slamming into the marine's side with his shoulder and drove the marine against the brick wall, dazing him. Ben had no weapon. He had lost the saber somewhere.

He fell on top of the redcoat, pinning him down. As he did he saw Sadie lying near the brick wall, her eyes glazed, hands holding her stomach. Blood seeped between her fingers. Ben roared in·outrage, his hands fastening around the half-conscious marine's throat, squeezing until the man coughed and wheezed and bucked like a wild animal, trying to throw Ben off his back. But Ben's anger was stronger than the marine's fear of death. The redcoat's movements came slower and with less strength until at last he wheezed one final time and died.

Ben crawled six feet to Sadie, picked her up and carried her down the street. They weren't far from Dr. Warren's office. Ben broke a rear window, unlocked the door, then carried Sadie into the treatment room. She was barely conscious and hadn't made a sound since he picked her up.

"Sadie, I'm sorry. I failed you!"

She smiled through sudden tears. The pain

was so bad she didn't know how to react. It was so far beyond any pain she had ever known that it numbed her. Tears spilled down her cheeks, but her mind remained clear. "Ben, it wasn't your fault. You did all you could. I'm a bad shot. I should have killed that one who cut me."

She winced then, gasped and shuddered. Ben held her. She screamed, her eyes projecting her terror and pain, then she went limp. Ben knew what to do. Find Dr. Warren!

With a fury he had never known before he slammed through the office to the front door, unlocked it and ran into the empty street.

"Dr. Warren! Dr. Warren!" Ben screamed it twice into the night. He saw a new light flicker on across the street. Ben ran to the end of the block, saw a group of people.

"Have you seen Dr. Joseph Warren?" he demanded.

They shook their heads. Ben saw his hands were covered with blood, as was the front of his jacket. He ran the other way. No one there.

Ben was crying now. He couldn't stop. Tears poured out of his eyes and down his cheeks. He ran a block toward the docks and found another group of men. One person lay dead to one side, his Indian blanket still wrapped around him. Ben didn't want to see the face. A British marine lay wounded at the other side under a sputtering pine torch. A man bent over him.

"Dr. Warren!" Ben screamed. Joseph Warren looked up, saw Ben's anguished appeal in the dim light of the pitch torch. He stood at once and ran with Ben back to his office.

Dr. Warren worked with all the skill and understanding of the human body he possessed. The blade had gone deeper than he first believed. Several vital organs had been damaged. There was nothing he could do. He stopped the bleeding with a massive compress, which he still held over the wound. Tears now came from his eyes as he looked at the lovely young woman.

She had not regained consciousness while he probed and searched the bloody wound eight inches long on her lower torso. Now her eyes flickered and she groaned.

"Oh, dear God!" she whispered.

Ben was at her side, his hand holding hers, his lips brushing her sweat-beaded forehead. She saw him and tried, but couldn't smile.

"Ben, it hurts!"

"Don't worry, you're going to be fine, just a little cut."

"Ben, I've been over on the other side. It won't be so bad. I knew when he . . . when he hurt me that it was the end of me. It's so . . ."

She stopped, grimacing as her face twisted in unbearable pain, but she held on. "I don't want to faint again, just give me a little time, Ben, just a little more time."

Dr. Warren looked at Ben, then left the room.

Sadie smiled, and Ben was startled by the remarkable beauty of her face.

"Darling Ben, we have so little time, kiss me."

He did. Her lips clung to his for a long moment, then he kissed her nose and eyes.

"Ben, promise me you'll take care of Arthur for us. He's such a good baby."

"You're going to be all right," he said, fighting a feeling that was ready to explode in his body. "You'll be fine." As he said it he couldn't keep the tears from coming again.

She didn't argue.

"Ben, it's been the happiest three years of my life, knowing you, loving you. And I'm proud I was with you tonight at the tea party. History will remember this night for as long as men can read. I'm so proud of you. Stay strong, darling."

He bent and kissed her again.

"Sadie, I'll always love you. Always."

"Ben, I love you."

He reached down to kiss her again, but a small cry stopped him. Ben had never heard such a sound before, a gentle wail, a call, not in pain or anger, perhaps it was the sound of the release of a pain-tortured soul. He straightened. She was no longer breathing. Her eyes were open.

"Dr. Warren!" Ben called.

The doctor was there at once, listening with his ear to her chest. He pinched her nostrils together, then closed her eyelids.

"Ben, I'm sorry."

Ben started to turn, but before Dr. Warren let him leave, he wetted a towel and washed the soot and paint off Ben's face, wiped his bloody hands clean and made him change out of the bloodstained coat.

"There's half a regiment out there now. They sent the longboats over and are on the lookout for anyone with Indian marks on him. You go straight home, Ben, or stay here the night. It's best not to be out on the street tonight."

Ben waved at him and walked out into the blackness of the chill December night. It might snow before morning. Sadie, dear, sweet, beautiful Sadie. He had lost her.

Ben walked away from the docks, out to the mall and the common. He saw no one. Once a pair of British marines looked sternly at him, but he barely noticed them, walking with his head down.

Why?

So young. So beautiful. A mother with a child to raise. Why would she be chosen for death?

No! No, she couldn't be dead. It must have been a nightmare, some elaborate dream, some fantasy from which he would awaken.

God, how had it happened? His fault, he had not been fast enough, good enough, quick enough. He should have clubbed both men, run in front of her, kept them away from her. But he had expected her to defend herself. That fact he would always have to live with.

Ben sighed. Only now did the crushing reality of it come smashing down on him. He shoved his hands into the pockets of his coat. His ears should be cold, but he didn't feel them. Ben walked on.

Quicker, he should have been quicker. He had seen another dead "Indian." Ben wondered how many were dead. How many casualties had his little tea party cost the Freedom Fighters? In a war there are losses on both sides. They had absorbed some more tonight. How many? He wondered about so many things, but forgot them at once. There were a million things to be done, to cover up any part in the affair, but his numbed brain wasn't focusing on them.

Sadie was gone, his own sweet Sadie was dead! How could he go on? He walked south, past the burying grounds, out to the very edge of the bay and turned north. Ben was not sure where he was going. He didn't care. He walked ankle-deep in the marsh before he turned inland, skirted the wet and then followed the shoreline. Ben kept on walking.

After two hours of wandering the shore and then the streets, Ben's grief turned slowly into anger. He began running. He ran for a mile toward the spot near Old South where he had tied his horse.

Ben walked the last few blocks, untied the mare and drove home at a gallop. Part of his life was finished. This was a new phase, one in which he would strike out with every ounce of strength he had left. Sadie Wythe must not have died in vain. He would strive to make her dream of a free America come true. For this he would pledge every cent he had, every muscle and power that was his, every bit of wisdom and skill he possessed—even his life itself, if it must be.

The Freedom Fighters would work harder. The time must be close at hand; the day had to be near when musket would answer musket and the birth of a great new nation would begin. That would be the day he would go to Sadie Wythe's grave and assure her that her life had been given for a great cause.

Ben closed his eyes and pictured Sadie, with her beautiful smile.

"All of this to you, Sadie Wythe, I do solemnly pledge!"

BOOK THREE

Chapter One
SURPRISED INTO DUTY

Boston, January 11, 1774

As soon as Harriet Rutledge saw the chaise halt half a block ahead of her, she urged her mount into the shadows and stopped, watching the rig at the edge of the soft gray nighttime fog that slithered through the streets with animal-like stealth, advancing in long tentacles, a whitish, wet mass that ebbed and flowed from one street to another, leaving some of its salt-laden moisture clinging to the frozen boards on the buildings and coating them with hoar frost.

Harriet pulled the jacket tighter around her, and wiggled her fingers together in her mittens as she held Black Princess's reins a hundred yards behind the chaise. She had dressed warmly, since she did not know how long this trip might last. Someone came out of the blackness and boarded the chaise. It moved down the street, its wheels crunching through the late afternoon's snow that had now developed a rough frozen crust.

The girl urged her mount forward with her knees and realized that she was something of a sneak, a point she conceded to no one else, not even her favorite stable boy who readied her horse at odd hours without a question or surprised glance.

The chaise turned right, moved eight blocks through the quiet, dark streets, and stopped two blocks from the wharves where both passengers stepped down, adjusted their overcoats, and looked around. Harriet had stopped just around the corner and they could not see her. Her father tied the reins and then the pair walked quietly toward the bay.

Harriet slid off the black, tied her to a hitching post in front of a tannery and hurried after the two dark figures.

For over a month now she had been curious about where her father went on certain evenings, and as a lark she decided to try to find out. Initially her attempts were awkward, and the first four trips were failures. On three occasions she lost him entirely. On the next he turned back and she fled so he wouldn't recognize her, since then she would have to invent the most outlandish story to avoid suspicion.

Now, with practice, she was more efficient. She knew when to move closer, and when to hang back. Four times she had followed her father to The Old Boston Bookshop, which seemed closed, and indeed the door was locked when she tried it.

Twice more he ended at taverns well known for their rebel activity and as rebel gathering places; she of course could not go in and see if her father were there, since her disguise was suitable only for the darkness of an occasional lamplit window. Now, as before, Harriet was dressed in bulky men's clothes, with a cap to hide her long brown hair. She looked like a slight youth of sixteen in her boy's clothes, but she was really twenty-two years old and curious about everything in the world, including her father's strange behavior during the recent Boston Tea Party. She was sure he had taken part in it, but he never mentioned it, and she could not ask. She hoped to learn of his involvement with the rebels so she could join them. It was a driving passion with her now to be a part of the rebel movement!

Harriet pressed close against a shop wall now as she saw her father meet four other men, all dressed in dark clothes. They vanished into a hardgoods store. Harriet settled down in an alley fifty yards away to watch. She had learned patience, and in this case she could see there was only one entrance to the store, so she could not lose them that way. No alley served the rear of this business, and other stores crowded both sides and the back.

Soon two more men came, then a group of four. As she watched she counted twenty-two men going into the building. She wished there was a window she might look through, but the front glass remained dark, which meant they had to be meeting in a back room.

Harriet kicked at a pile of snow that had been pushed off the sidewalk and leaned against the wooden side of the building. She had her mittened hands deep inside her coat pockets now, but even so her teeth began to chatter. She tried to relax to ease the tension, and as she did the hardgoods store door opened and four men came out. All wore heavy, bulky coats and she wondered what they might have under them.

Now Harriet had a new problem. She could not tell which of the men was her father. She knew he must be there somewhere in the group. She watched six sets of men leave in fours, and decided that must be all of them. She trailed along behind the last ones, staying just far enough back so they wouldn't see her, but close enough to keep contact. She slid from one doorway to the next, trying to walk silently in the crusty snow. They passed across one street and she walked normally, then moved in closer as they came toward the docks.

The cold Boston wind whipped through the dark streets, keeping Harriet cold despite her activity, and the shivering didn't help her nerves. At last she had stumbled onto something her father was involved in, but what in the world was it? She suspected all sorts of things they might do to harass the British, because she had decided this must be a group of the famous

Freedom Fighters that she had once heard whispered about. If only she could become a member of such a glorious movement!

The last four men in front of her slid into an alley and Harriet realized that it would lead them directly to the area beside Griffin's wharf. Ahead it was darker, and now there was no way to disguise her footsteps in the crunching, frozen snow. She moved cautiously, and sensed that men were waiting ahead of her.

Behind her came the sound of running feet and at once two men dressed in black ran toward her. She turned just as they came up to her.

"What the hell you doing way back here?" a rough voice asked her. A hand hit her shoulder and rushed her along as they ran. "You were told to stay with your group, now get up there with them."

She ran ahead of the two men, keeping her face toward the ground the best she could and pulling the flaps of the hat around her face. Half way down the alley she saw other men kneeling on each side, some now with flintlock pistols out of their belts, loading them or checking the loads and primers. She knelt behind the last man and watched him working with the pistol. It was almost completely dark in the alley, but the man poured powder down the barrel of the pistol, put in a paper and rammed it home, then put in the round ball and a bit more wadding and rammed it again. He worked quickly, wasted no time or motion. When he was done, he flashed a smile at

Harriet.

"There, that damn well will take care of any son-of-a-bitch of a royal marine who gets in my way."

Harriet nodded and moved back a little and pulled the cap flaps up so only her eyes showed. Someone came past her, touched her shoulder and motioned a group of them closer. He was Lewis Lynch, a man she knew. He was her twin brothers' hunting instructor, a former royal British marine who had lost an eye in combat and been mustered out because of it. He had worked for her father for several years. She ducked her head and held the flaps over her face as she listened to him.

"All right, lads. You all know what you're supposed to do. We send the first two people on board as returning sailors. Their job is to take care of the sentry and the watch crew, which shouldn't be hard. It's Saturday night and only a dozen men are left on the ship. The rest are off on shore leave. This old tub is being laid up for repairs. It should go smoothly. No using your pistols unless absolutely necessary. We want to be quiet as two dozen mice. Remember, lads, we have no more than ten minutes on board to do our work. Let's go up to the front of the alley now and wait the signal."

Harriet moved forward when the man in front of her did. Sailors, a ship, which meant a British ship! They were going to board an English ship of the line? And why was a man-of-war at Griffin's wharf? It was usually reserved for merchantmen with cargo.

She wondered if she should hold back and fade away in the darkness as the others moved, but then felt someone behind her, someone close. There was no place to sneak away! She was trapped. She pulled the cap flaps closer to her face and waited, shivering.

The group of men stopped at the very end of the alley and she could see the three tall masts against the sky. There was a half moon shedding some light, and she noticed the five lighted lanterns at the bow of the British naval ship. That should mean lots of men, and weapons . . . suddenly Harriet was frightened. People could be hurt doing this. She had never seen a man die. She certainly had never caused anyone to die.

As they waited, Lewis Lynch came down the line double checking every man's assignment. She heard the replies clearly: "Arms locker for the pistols and Brown Bess muskets." Another man said he was to lock the forecastle and trap any men inside and make sure they stayed there. "Port side security," another said. "Bow security." "Arms locker." The man just ahead of her also said he was on duty at the arms locker, and Harriet decided that's what she would say, too, but just then Lynch heard the signal, the plaintive, familiar call of a bobwhite. Lynch turned and ran back to the head of the alley.

"They've done it, lads, all clear. Step lively now. Let's move. Remember, by two's and no running. Move on board casually, then go directly to your post and get to work.''

Harriet was so nervous she wanted to scream, but she stood there biting her lip until she knew it turned white. She saw the first pair of men walk across the street to the wharf and then go up the short gangplank to the British ship of the line as if they belonged there. It was a huge three-masted warship.

Suddenly it was her turn. Harriet found herself shoved forward by a man behind her and she was walking across the street beside someone she didn't know. She decided to follow him, to go where he went and do what he did.

The street had never been so wide, so long. Finally they reached the gangplank. She could be hanged for this, she knew, but she plunged ahead, walked up the gangplank with long strides matching the man beside her. On deck he ran forward and she stayed behind him. He must know where he was going. He dropped down two ladders off the gun deck to the main deck, lit now only by a pair of flickering coal oil lanterns. On the main deck he went forward where he saw a British seaman just coming out of a cabin. The sailor held up his hands at once, and Harriet saw that the freedom fighter had his pistol trained on the seaman.

''Turn around, mate,'' the man with her said. When the Britisher turned, her companion brought a short iron bar down across his head. The seaman groaned and slumped to the floor, unconscious.

They rushed past him to a more forward area where her fellow conspirator tried a door, then kicked at it until the latch broke. He rushed in with his pistol ready and cocked. Harriet followed him and found the cabin empty. He told her to run back and bring the last lamp they passed, which she did quickly. She wanted to stop and check on the man hit on the head, but she didn't. Now she stepped into the cabin and saw that it was an officer's stateroom.

The man with her took the lamp and looked around, found a cabinet and gave her the lantern to hold. He pulled a hammer from under his coat and pounded the lock and hasp until it broke from the cabinet. Behind the doors were rows of Brown Bess muskets, some of the finest shooting long guns in the world. He handed them out to Harriet. She sagged under the load. The weapons were five feet long and weighed over ten pounds each. Harriet held three in her arms and staggered away, trying to remember which way they had come. Soon another man and then a second rushed past her, heading for the arms locker. She got to the first ladder where a man from above called quietly to her to hand up the weapons one at a time. She did, then ran back to the locker to bring more. She passed other men carrying five of the guns and she felt like a shirker. Harriet made two more trips, this time with four, and dropped one on the way. Someone else picked it up.

"Too heavy for you, lad?" came the remark, but she only nodded and hurried to the ladder where she handed the guns upward. Now, all the men were returning from the locker. It was empty, their job here was done. She followed the men up the ladders to the lower main deck. There the Freedom Fighters picked up the weapons again and took them to shore. She carried three Brown Bess muskets and followed the men to the gangplank and down it to a wagon which had materialized from the shadows as soon as the muskets arrived. They all ran back for another load. Three trips and they were done, with more than fifty of the standard British issue muskets in the wagon. The guns were quickly covered with shocks of hay and the rig wheeled away.

Harriet and the others faded into an alley and rested in the shadows.

"We did our part," one of the men whispered to her. "We sure nailed the bastards good tonight. And we ain't done yet!"

Harriet blushed in the darkness, glad that the big furry flaps of the hat covered most of her face. She was not used to hearing foul language, but she nodded at him and leaned against the building, resting. She was sure her arms would fall off, and her feet ached from the weight of the oversize men's shoes she was wearing.

Three minutes later she saw flames showing through the ship's gun ports, and quickly after that ten more men streamed off the British man-of-war. They waited only a moment in the alley, then all moved at a quick trot through the crusty snow to Belcher's lane, and on to Cow lane.

Just as they entered the second street they heard a massive explosion, and Harriet guessed the powder storage on the ship must have been blown. It was muffled, but a powerful sound, and a short cheer went up from the men. Harriet had seen her father only once, but now she heard his commanding voice.

"Silence! Enough time for cheering later." Ben sent one man back to the docks to report on the extent of the damage to the ship, then led the rest of them to the same hardgoods store they had used before. Harriet knew she had to slip away, but when she tried to hang back, she was good naturedly hustled forward. She attempted to go right past the doorway, but someone grabbed her coat sleeve and turned her into the opening and there was nothing to do but follow the rest to the rear where a keg of beer had been opened and all hands were lifting mugs.

Ben stood at the far end, counting heads as they came through the door. Harriet hung back in a corner where the light from the three lamps was weakest. Ben Rutledge frowned, and counted again. "We have a small problem, troops. I sent one man back to check on the ship, and now I find that we still have twenty-six here. That's one too many. We picked up a stowaway along the route somewhere. A spy, perhaps?''

Everyone looked around, and Harriet knew some were looking at her, so she turned and looked at someone else.

''All right, let's have a formation. Everyone fall in right now up here in two lines.''

As they formed up, Harriet remained in the corner, her knees shaking, her teeth chattering and not from the cold. One of the men from the formation saw her, grabbed her wrist and pulled her roughly to the front of the room. She struggled and as she did she knocked off her cap, and her long brown hair spilled out.

A chorus of surprised shouts went up, and she lowered her head to hide her face.

The man holding her at once released her wrist, and she stood where she was, staring at the floor. A moment later she saw two new boots stop in front of her.

''All right, young lady, we're not going to hurt you. But we do want to know how long you've been with us, what you know about our group, and, of course, who you are.''

Harriet set her jaw firmly and lifted her head, looking steadily into his eyes.

''Hello, Father,'' she said.

Ben Rutledge stared down at the girl for a second before he recognized her, then he didn't know whether to be angry or amused. But he burst out laughing and threw his arms around Harriet, hugging her tightly.

Benjamin Rutledge was in trim condition for

his forty-two years, and at five-feet eight weighed a hundred and fifty pounds. His dark brown hair was full under his black cap and his brown eyes sparkled now as he held Harriet away so he could see her.

"I doubt if the boys would approve your wearing their clothes," Ben said, his face one big smile.

Lewis Lynch stepped forward and grinned at Harriet. "I don't believe it, sir, but this really is Harriet."

"I'm afraid so, Lewis. She pulled a neat trick on us, and we were the ones being so careful." Ben let go of Harriet and turned her around to the group. "Gentlemen, I'd like you to meet my eldest offspring, my daughter, Harriet Rutledge. This young lady has some tall explaining to do. At least our immediate problem is solved; I don't think our security has been irreparably breached. Continue with the celebration while I interrogate the prisoner."

The other Freedom Fighters, all civilians who ran shops and businesses or worked as clerks or artisans during the day in Boston and surrounding areas, began talking about this surprise helper and then reliving their raid on the British ship. The bung in the keg of beer kept popping.

Ben took Harriet aside to a pair of chairs and seated her. He watched her for a moment as her soft blue eyes stared back at him. Her eyes were wide set over a small nose and a chin that was slightly pointed. Right now the lamplight picked

487

up the red glints in her brown hair.

"Harriet, I think you have to explain how it is you're here."

"Yes, Father. I know I shouldn't be here. I shouldn't even have left the house tonight. But I got curious. About a month ago you were out of the house so much and I saw you come and go and you never told me where you were going on what you were doing. I decided you were one of the leaders of the rebel movement, and one day I followed you. I lost you in the crowd and tried again, and finally I found that you were going to the Old Boston Book Shop, but always after it was closed.

"Tonight I followed you again to that hardgoods store and then again when all of the men came out. Father I want to join your group. I want to be a Freedom Fighter too!"

"And I thought we had good security. We're going to have to tighten up a lot of procedures. He sighed and looked down at his daughter. "I can understand your following us out of curiosity, but how in the world did you ever get *included* in our group?"

She explained how she was moving down the alley after the men when someone rushed up behind and scolded her for lagging, forcing her up to the end of the line of men.

"I figured that I could get away later and I didn't want to make a scene. I was afraid you would be angry with me."

"I would have been, at that point, and I am

now." This was an escapade that Sadie Wythe might get into, but he hadn't suspected that Harriet was interested in the same kind of things.

"Then when did you leave the group? You surely didn't go along and participate in the raid. You weren't on the *East Indian*, were you?"

"Yes, of course. There was no way I could get out of it unless I took off my cap and started screaming. So I helped break into the arms locker and carried out the Brown Besses. Why are they so long and so heavy?"

Ben lifted his brows and shook his head. "I may have to lock you in your room with a ball and chain." His scowl was fearful. Very few times had she ever seen him looking so grim, so serious. At last he spoke. "And then when you got off the boat again you waited with the group of men and then came directly here with the others?"

"Yes, Father."

"Stay right there," Ben said, stood and went to one side and talked to Lewis Lynch.

Harriet watched the two closely, wondering what they were talking about. When her father came back and sat down, he wore the serious face.

"Harriet, we are not playing games here. In the past four years we have lost four of our members. Four have been killed. We are deadly serious, prepared to die if that is what it takes to help win freedom and independence for this new land. For what we did tonight, we all could be hanged, tracked down by British officials, tried and put to death. This is a life and death struggle for us. We are not officially an army, an attack force—we have no legal standing with the colony, with Boston, with anyone. But soon we will be needed. It is my firm estimate that we will be at war with England within a year, fighting for our independence, a revolution. Knowing this, I must ask you to forget everything that took place here tonight, and at the ship, and not to mention a word of this to your mother, your brothers, or to anyone else."

"I promise, Daddy."

"Be sure you keep that promise, because the life of every man in this room rests on your word." He stood and lifted her by the hand. "Now, it is time to get you home before your mother misses you and calls the constable."

"Father, the explosion. Was that the ship blowing up?"

"Yes, we think so. I sent a man back to be sure, we should know about it soon."

"Father, could I join your group? It seems like I've been sitting in the audience and watching the whole thing grow around me. I want to be in the struggle, I want to be doing something. You know I'm not any good with guns, but there must be something else I could do. Please let me join you. Haven't you ever had a woman member?"

Ben felt a lurching beat of his heart as he

nodded. "Yes, we had one, she was killed by a Lobsterback the night of the Tea Party. We all miss her very much."

"I'm sorry, Father. I didn't know." She brightened and touched his arm. "Then if you've had one woman member, why can't I join? I'll take a pledge to secrecy or anything else I need to do. Father, I really want *to do* something."

Ben watched her, trying not to remember what happened to Sadie, that terrible night when she too had dressed like a man for the foray against the British, only to be discovered and then trapped in an alley and Ben's sword had been one stroke too late to save her life. "I'll take up your application with the council, Harriet. We'll see if it will approve. Now, let's get on home."

A man came bursting through the inner door waving his hat.

"She sunk! The damned old tub went to the bottom! The *East Indian* suffered a hole in her side, took on water, rolled over and went down dockside. Half of her barnacled bottom is showing beside Griffin's Wharf right now!"

A cheer went up from the men, then the messenger worked through them to report to Ben.

"Sir, the explosion done the job all neat, it sure did. Blasted a big hole out through her side just below the waterline and by the time I got there she was heeling over. Somebody got the fo'c's'le door open and some men were splashing around in the bay. She's down for good. I sure wouldn't want to try to raise her."

"Did they lose any men, Barlow?"

"I don't know, sir. We'll hear about that tomorrow."

"Aye, Barlow, that we will." Ben dismissed the messenger, caught Harriet's hand and worked toward the door. There he stopped and got the men's attention.

"Excellent work tonight, men. It's a night the royal marines and his majesty's navy won't forget in a hurry. And we added considerably to our store of arms as well. Celebrate, but be sure that everyone is home before one a.m. The raid is important, and a good victory, but also important are our security and our secrecy. I'll take care of our security slip tonight, myself."

He waved and took Harriet to the front of the store, then into the bitter cold. They walked to the chaise, found her horse and tied it on behind. On the way home they talked and she asked him how the Freedom Fighters started. He said that he might tell her later. He did say that theirs was a highly secret organization, not like the Sons of Liberty, which had not been effective and was more bluster and talk now than action. She must not breathe a word about the Freedom Fighters, not even the name to anyone, no matter what the council did about her membership application. Harriet agreed eagerly.

When they were safely home and the horses put away, Ben stirred up the coals in the main fireplace, added some wood, then motioned for Harriet to sit down.

"I think I owe it to you, Harriet, to tell you how our group first got started, and explain something more about what it is and does. I also want to explain to you that Sadie Wythe was one of the founders, and a member. In fact she was a captain with a company of men in her command."

He went on talking about the group, the various raids they had made and how they spearheaded and organized the Boston Tea Party and the burning of the revenue ship. By the time the fire had burned down, Harriet understood how her father felt about the group.

"Harriet, if you still want to join, I would insist that it be on a non-action basis, that you could work on our books and our organization, perhaps keep our minutes, but you would have no voice in command or in operations."

He held up his hand when she started to reply. "Now, don't make any decisions now. First, we'll see what the council says, then you'll make up your mind. Now, off to bed. Remember we both have to go to church tomorrow on time, that's one of the requirements after any action by the Freedom Fighters, life as usual."

Chapter Two
COUNTERPUNCH

Captain Horatio Bleeker had been roused at midnight by a pounding on the door, and now listened as Annabelle spoke briefly with someone in the other room. Despite the cold in the bedroom he was bare to the waist and sitting up in the bed, fully awake now and waiting for Annabelle to get rid of the distraction. She was a friend of a friend in London who had insisted that he must look up Annabelle the moment he came to Boston. For the past six months he had been looking at her every night and he still liked what he saw.

A moment later she opened the bedroom door and Captain Bleeker swore when he saw his third mate Miller in a bedraggled uniform that looked wet and had a sleeve half torn off. The mate was about thirty years old and not the captain's favorite. He stuttered as he began to report and Captain Bleeker yelled at him.

"Say it, Miller, or I'll have your tongue cut off!"

"T . . . Th . . . The ship, sir," Miller said. "She sunk, turned over and pulled the davits off and sunk, went down right beside the dock, sir, she's on her side in three fathoms."

"What in hell do you mean, sunk? How could she go down?"

"A raid, sir. Rebels caught us off guard. Fifty rebels swarmed on board, broke into the arms locker, bashed four men in the head and then set a fuse in the powder magazine. She blew before the rest of us knew we'd been boarded."

"Sleeping, Miller?"

"Uh, yes, sir."

"Scum! Lousy incompetents! Where was the marine officer? Where were the bastard royal marines, the guards . . . Goddamn bastards to blow up my ship. Get out of here, Miller, while I get dressed. Wait for me outside, move, damn it!"

Captain Bleeker rolled out of bed and began dressing. He stood six feet tall, with a thick body of more than sixteen stone, dark hair and a full beard. His eyes were small and black and he was the son of a full admiral now retired. His hands pulled on his uniform hastily but with caution. A competent officer is never seen without the proper uniform.

Annabelle stood near the door, watching him, letting her robe fall open so that one breast slipped out invitingly.

"Horatio . . . "

He looked at her and shook his head. "Not

now, woman, not now! I've just lost my ship, my command! I'll be charged with it and my days in the navy may be over. I'll never be trusted with anything as big as a longboat again. I've no time for you right now. Out of my way!''

He pulled on his boots and stomped through the small house to the front door where Third Mate Miller waited.

"Well, well? Where's the chaise, the horse?''

"I walked, sir. There's no horses, no cabs, this time of night.''

Captain Bleeker swung his big fist at Miller, grazed his head with the hard knuckles and knocked him to the frozen snow on the sidewalk. The captain stalked off toward the docks a half mile away. He hadn't walked that far in years. Miller caught up with him.

"Any casualties, Mr. Miller?''

"Yes, sir. Two missing, two dead, five injured.'' Miller said it but was sure he was far enough away so the captain couldn't hit him again. He understood the fury of his commanding officer. Miller was well aware what this could do to the captain's reputation and his future service. It wouldn't look good on Miller's record either but he was only the third mate— the end responsibility for losing the ship was the captain's.

Captain Bleeker grew more angry with each step. The insufferable stupidity of these colonial swine! Didn't they know when they were well off? Now they even wanted to be treated as

Englishmen when everyone knew they were a dozen ranks below the lowest Englishmen. They were colonials, only a notch above debtors, prison trash, the French and the Indian savages. Now they were demanding "rights?" Christ! They should be smarter than that. They spoke the King's English poorly but still they should have the basic good sense to understand the words. They were less than men, more like negligent children. Unfortunately a child behind the trigger of a Brown Bess can kill a lieutenant, or a mate or a captain just as easily as a trained royal marine.

Goddamn! He wouldn't have it! Sink his ship, would they? If the navy did not find out who did it, he would launch his own campaign of retribution. He would personally rout out this band of criminals and with his bare hands he would strangle each one of them until all fifty were dead. By God, he would do it if he had to leave the navy! He scowled at the thought, knowing that after such a fiasco as this there was little that he could do but offer to resign his commission. Only Admiral Leeds, the commander in chief of naval forces in America, could save him, and he and Admiral Leeds were not on the best of terms. Admiral Leeds knew his father, but that might not mean much now. At least his meetings with the second in navy command, Admiral Edwards, had been pleasant.

Captain Bleeker looked to one side but saw that Miller was too far away. He wanted to hit someone and Miller was his best chance, but the third mate stayed out of reach.

At the wharf it was as silent as a newly dug grave.

Captain Bleeker ordered a dozen torches lighted. He commandeered a small boat and was rowed around his foundered vessel. As he watched the terrible truth unfold, Captain Bleeker spouted a steady stream of profanity aimed at the rebel criminals. The side of the *East Indian* with the hole was under water. The captain's cabin was in the dry side. Bleeker studied the possibilities of righting the vessel and knew it would work. She drew only sixteen feet and the harbor was little deeper than that at this point. It would involve two dozen strong teams with ropes and an open pulling area to right her, then a crew to patch the hole in her side, and last, a pump to clear her holds of water. She could be floated again, if only the admiral would let him try.

Bleeker sent the third mate Miller and a crew of three into the captain's cabin to remove all of his gear and records, everything that would move and could be salvaged. The men worked with torches and had his cabin cleared before daylight.

Captain Bleeker sent a messenger boat to Castle William, a fortified island three miles into the outer harbor where the British military's high command was situated. He reported the incident to Admiral Edwards.

It was well past sunup when Captian Bleeker saw a longboat pulling briskly through the choppy, cold waters, heading directly for the sunken ship. It was an official party of three officers who made a cursory inspection of the *East Indian*, then invited Captain Bleeker into the boat for the return trip to Castle William.

Bleeker would not talk to the other officers. He could well imagine their report, and he realized that before he knew it his fourteen years of service in His Majesty's Navy could come to a sudden and tragic end. He was trained for nothing but the navy. He would not be trusted with a civilian ship. His whole future hung in a delicate balance, all because of some colonial rebels!

As Bleeker was piped aboard the *New Victory,* Admiral Edwards' flagship, he was more impressed than ever with the strict pomp and formality of the craft. Every hand wore his dress uniform, every bit of brass was shined to a gleaming mirror and the decks were spit-and-polish clean.

"Admiral Edwards requests your presence in the saloon, sir," a fuzzy faced midshipman said, as Bleeker stepped on the deck. They proceeded forward, Bleeker with dread building in his heart. He could smell a naval inquiry, and now he knew that he would not fare well, not well at all.

The saloon was adjacent to the captain's quarters, where three bulkheads had been torn out and replaced with beams, creating an open space twenty feet long and ten wide, a vast open area on a British fighting ship where space was at a premium.

A large table had been bolted to the deck and chairs placed around it. At the other end of the room overstuffed chairs were arranged in a semi circle, and Captain Bleeker snapped to attention as soon as he entered the end of the saloon.

"Captain Bleeker, of the *East Indian*, reporting as ordered, sir!"

Admiral Edwards turned and nodded. "Yes, Bleeker, come in, come in. Relax, man, this is not a board of inquiry, just an informal gathering of some details about your misfortune. I understand you were not on board at the time of the attack?"

"No, sir." As he said it Captain Bleeker felt his knees begin to weaken. Sitting in the chairs were all of the top naval officers in America, including two admirals he knew or had at least seen, and one more he did not know. But the man who struck his soul with liquid terror was at the center in the biggest chair and wearing the admiral pips and a frown. He was Admiral Leeds, the commander of all British naval forces in America. What was going on?

"Captain Bleeker, we thank you for coming," Admiral Leeds said. "I'm not a man to rush into engagements, especially without definite instructions from the home office. My friends here disagree heartily with me and say that we should take some sharp action in direct retaliation for the deaths of our men and the scuttling of the *East Indian*. What is your position, Captain?''

''Sir, the riffraff, the blackguards, the scum who have blown up my ship and killed my men must be routed out and hanged before sundown. It would be my suggestion that ten rebels be hanged for every British seaman or marine killed.''

''Ten to one, eh, Bleeker?'' Admiral Leeds asked.

''Yes, sir. I've seen that ratio highly effective in other colonies for controlling rebels, sir. It makes them think long and seriously before they kill any more British military men.''

Admiral Leeds lit a cigar and rolled it between his fingers, taking his time, knowing they would wait for him.

''Captain, do you have any idea where to start looking? How do you find a handful of rebels out of, what, thirty thousand souls in Boston?''

''We have certain intelligence, sir, and our spies are useful. I believe Admiral Edwards has specific names on a list that could prove effective if they were questioned.''

''The Sons of Liberty?'' Admiral Leeds asked.

Admiral Edwards, a medium sized man with a long beak of a nose and a powdered wig, stood and looked at Leeds. ''Oh, now, sir. I wouldn't think so, sir. These Sons of Liberty have been a vociferous bunch of rabble, but it seems they actually *do* very little. As far as we can tell, they are loud but ineffective. Our spies say that they have no practical organizational structure, function on emotional impulses and are more banter and bravado than they are given to action. So it is our guess that they were not involved in dumping the tea a month ago, and it is our guess that they were not involved in the scuttling, either.''

"Still someone must have planned it, it seems to have been done in a highly organized and efficient way, almost a military operation, from what we have heard so far.''

"Yes, sir,'' Bleeker said. "It was. I've heard from certain civilians that there is a small band of about a hundred men who train regularly, who are set up on military lines, and that the organization is lean and hungry and thrives on action. The members are said to be dedicated to harassing us into an actual armed conflict.''

"What is your source for this information, Bleeker?'' Admiral Leeds asked sharply.

"Why, civilians, sir. A tailor for one, and a reliable woman recently moved here from England who has a good ear and uses it well. I assure you their information seems to be reasonable and up to date. However I cannot claim a solid informant within the rebel camp. They seem to be dedicated, and close mouthed. Too many mugs of ale seems to be the best way to loosen a tongue or two.''

Admiral Leeds took a long puff on the cigar. "Edwards, I'm a reasonable man, but I would expect any intelligence of this sort to be in my hands at once. I trust the reason I didn't know about it was because you didn't know about it." He frowned slightly, puffed on his cigar and tried to blow a smoke ring, which failed. He frowned again. "Foul habit, smoking. I don't know why I indulge myself." The admiral looked back at Bleeker. "Captain, your ship, can she be salvaged?"

"Oh, yes, sir. I believe so. The explosion blew a hole in the port side just below the water line. The water put out the worst of the fire and some of the men put out the rest with buckets. I'd say two dozen good teams of horses and some block and tackle . . ."

"I don't want the details, Captain. Just raise her, repair your craft and get her back into the line as soon as you can. I had two ship return to England last week and I don't want to be short-gunned any longer than necessary." He looked at Admiral Edwards who had sat down and now was leaning forward, his face working. "Edwards, what is the trouble?"

"It's unusual to try to salvage a ship without a board of inquiry on the spot, sir. This vessel seems to be badly damaged and half under water . . ."

"Hang the procedures this time, Edwards, we'll have a hearing later. Bleeker said he could do it, let him try. What have we lost if he fails?

As to the rebels, I will not permit any serious armed confrontation against them at this time. I will allow no wild, frantic search for the perpetrators. It is my duty here to avoid rushing into hostilities. I do not believe that these rebels are all that dangerous, or that adept in their desires to prod us into war. They will calm down if I can reduce the pressures of the friction between England and the colonies. They do not have the intent, and if some have the notion, the majority do not have the will, nor the abilities to wage an open conflict with us. Therefore we will move with all due caution against them in every way. Caution and prudence. There shall be a naval inquiry into the sinking, but not a public one. A diligent attempt should be made to locate the culprits, but no larger scale provocative actions such as massive house searches and interrogation of the men on your suspect list. There will be no actions taken by our troops or ships that might incite or inflame the population. We certainly will not permit another Boston Massacre!''

Admiral Leeds stood and adjusted his saber. ''I hope everyone here will understand my policy and follow it to the letter. It is also my desire than Captain Bleeker receives nothing more than the mildest of official rebukes for the sinking of his vessel. Obviously it could not be prevented and he was in no way at fault. Certainly no incompetency or dereliction of duty could be found.'' The admiral sat down and nodded at the captain. "Bleeker, you may be excused. Work through regular naval command for materials and funds you'll need to raise your ship."

Captain Bleeker saluted smartly, did an about face and left the saloon with his spirits higher than they had been since he had tumbled Annabelle in bed earlier that night. Now, he had a mission, and he would complete it and save his ship.

The *East Indian* went down Saturday night. Monday noon, Harriet Rutledge left the firm of Rutledge & Rutledge, Importers, where she worked for her father, and took a noon-time walk past Griffin's Wharf for a look at their handiwork. There was a curious crowd of people watching the first futile efforts to raise the ship. Teams of horses were attached to a long rope which was tied to the top of the main mast. They were attempting to roll the ship upright from where it lay half submerged.

Harriet smiled as she watched the attempts and saw the large rope break in the effort, allowing the ship to settle lower in the water.

She walked back to her office slowly. Last night she had had second thoughts about wanting to be a part of the Freedom Fighters, but now she knew that she must join. There were so many things she wanted to do, So much she wanted to accomplish! She must help nudge the thirteen separate colonies toward a united confrontation with England.

Harriet settled down behind her desk and

looked at the list of jobs she had to do for the company. There were not many women working at Rutledge and Rutledge. Only three on the whole second floor. But Harriet had wanted to work, and had finally persuaded her father that he should let her try her hand in the accounting department. She had been good at it and after a year she had moved on, and now was in charge of the real estate, building and land purchasing department. She had worked hard and learned as much about the business as she could. Now she was ready to make another survey of the company warehouses, to see which ones were being used properly, and if they should keep them all, sell some, or if they needed more or simply should utilize them better.

Even though her father owned the importing firm, as had his father before him, Harriet had earned her place in the company. She knew little about the shipping side of the business, which was the largest and which made the most money, but she knew she could learn that, too, if she needed to. Rutledge and Rutledge was the second largest shipper and importer in Boston, second in size only to John Hancock and his fleet of ships. Mr. Hancock and Harriet's father were good friends, although rivals for some of the business. Both were boosters for independence too, she had learned.

Harriet thought about the Freedom Fighters. Now, more than ever she wanted to be a part of the force, the movement, to help in any way that she could. For a moment she hesitated. What if Malcolm didn't like it? Or would she tell him? Her father said she could tell no one. But what if she married Malcolm? Still the ban would apply, she was sure.

Harriet was not at all positive that she wanted to marry Malcolm Trotter. He was a jeweler and diamond merchant on Middle Street. She had met him at church one Sunday, and then the next Sunday as well, and for four weeks in a row! After that he asked if he might come courting and appeared three times the following week. Malcolm was attractive, and pleasant, and he seemed interested in her, but was that enough? She felt very little toward him. Her cousin, Jennifer Bull, was married now, Jennifer Otis. Harriet felt confused and uneasy every time she thought of Andy Otis. She had teased Andy one day in his father's store, and the tease had ended with Harriet flat on her back on the floor with her knees parted. Andy had taken her roughly, quickly, before she really knew what would happen. It had been her first time, and she had been surprised, shocked, a little thrilled and then disappointed.

But what about Malcolm? She had never permitted him any intimacies, not even a kiss. And she knew that he was getting restless, unhappy. She was afraid he would propose to her before she knew what she would answer. That would be terrible.

Malcolm was coming to the house that

Monday evening. They would play a game of chase with the boys, and then go into the library, leaving the door open, of course, and listen to a new music box Malcolm had given her. But did she love him? Harriet closed her eyes and then looked down at the papers on her desk. She knew the answer already. If she had to ask if she loved a man, then it was plain and obvious that she didn't. She sighed, put the papers away and looked at a note a messenger brought to her desk. Her father wanted to see her in his office as soon as she was free. She went at once.

Down the end of the long hall in her father's big office, she sat down and smiled.

"Harriet, you aren't going to like this."

She widened her eyes in mock surprise and sat up straighter. "Is it about my membership?"

"No, not that. We're not that fast. It's about something else just as important. Let's talk about Malcolm Trotter."

"Oh, is he going to join, too?"

"No, Harriet. Definitely not."

"Then you've been investigating him as a prospective son-in-law?"

"Frankly, yes I have, Harriet. The fact is every young man in the past three years you have shown more than a passing interest in, we have had routine background checks made, to find out about family, what troubles he's been in, the usual character reference type of questions."

"Then since this is the first time I've heard about it, this is the first time you've found a bad one, right?"

"Yes, Harriet, I'm afraid so. Oh, not that Malcolm is dangerous or anything like that."

"Then what's his trouble? I really don't know him very well, yet."

"Harriet, he has what we consider to be extremely strong and active Tory sympathies."

Harriet let that penetrate for a moment and tried to evaluate it. He was sympathetic with the British. But she had not noticed a single thing to indicate that, nor had he said anything of the sort, even hinted at it. Of course she said, she couldn't remember discussing any kind of politics with him and surely not the rebel cause.

"Which in itself is a bit suspicious. Most men these days feel very strongly about the political situation." Ben Rutledge put his fingers together forming a peak and looked over the top. "Harriet, the idea has occurred to us that there may be more to his courting you than simply romance."

"Now, Daddy, that is not very flattering." But it sent her mind racing, exploring possibilities she had never thought of. She looked up at her father then, her eyes bright with excitement.

"You mean that you think Malcolm is courting me so he might discover something about you that would tie you into some anti-British operation or rebel group?"

"Exactly. That was the center of our idea. And by us, I mean by the five member Freedom Fighters council. Trotter had concerned us for some weeks now, and with your baptism in action the other night, I feel that now it is more important than ever that you should know about our fears."

"Tell me everything that you've found out about him so I'll know. Then I can probe gently and see if he gives me the true facts about himself."

Ben handed Harriet two sheets of paper, which had been carefully printed on by a good hand in close but easy to read lines. She went through it:

"MALCOLM TROTTER. AGE 28. ADDRESS: 15 MILLWAY ROAD. OCCUPATION: MERCHANT, JEWELRY, DIAMONDS, FINE WATCHES. BORN: LONDON, 1746. FATHER WEALTHY MERCHANT, DIAMONDS. BOTH PARENTS LIVING, LONDON. SCHOOLING: BRITISH ROYAL ACADEMY, AND OXFORD. MILITARY: TWO YEARS ROYAL MARINES, FIRST OFFICER. DIPLOMATIC SERVICE, TWO YEARS.

APPEARS TO MAINTAIN UNUSUALLY STRONG TIES TO LONDON WITH FATHER AND FRIENDS. KNOWN TO ASSOCIATE WITH OTHER TORIES IN THIS AREA. SEEN ENTERING CUSTOMS HOUSE ON SEVERAL OCCASIONS WITHOUT KNOWN CAUSE.

UNMARRIED. COMFORTABLY WEALTHY. MER-

CHANT POSE MAY BE A FRONT FOR OTHER ACTIVITY. HOBBIES: RIDING, ARCHERY, BROWN BESS TARGET PRACTICE. CONSIDERED DANGEROUS TO FUTURE ACTIVITY WITH HIS DIPLOMATIC AND MILITARY BACKGROUND."

Harriet lifted her brows when she finished reading.

"When did you get this?"

"It was completed two weeks ago. His presence in our home has been of some concern to our intelligence people."

"Well, I can assure you, Father . . . "

Ben held up his hand to stop her angry reply.

"Harriet, I know he has not gained any information from our home or from you or me. So put your anger away. We may be dealing with a highly sophisticated spy network. We need to be more careful of him and any apparatus they may have set in place. But we must also be extremely cautious not to let anyone know that we suspect Malcolm of anything except his apparent interest in you. Anything else would alert him and he would be replaced with someone we don't know. Do you object to continuing to see him?"

She took a deep breath and without realizing it blinked her eyes several times. It was a nervous habit she thought she had eliminated.

"No, Daddy, no, of course not. I want to help in any way I can. I wonder how long it will take me to catch him in a lie? If I do, and if he is no longer any use to us in place, then I want to humiliate him publicly.''

"The humiliation we can talk about later. I just wanted you to understand what was going on. Now, I hope that you can work very closely with us against Mr. Trotter. It may be that some of the British are a little smarter in this matter than we gave them credit for being. We thought they had given up their campaign to find us, but evidently they have not.''

"They'll never find out, if I can help it,'' Harriet said. I'll work hard to throw them off the track any way that I can.''

"One thing does worry us, though,'' Ben said. "How did they suspect that I might be connected in some way with the anti-British movement?''

Harriet laughed. "Daddy, you must be joking. Everyone in town knows that you are a staunch supporter of colonial power and rights. You're as publicly anti-Tory as anyone. Probably half the important men in town who are anti-Tory have spies working on them right now.''

Ben Rutledge filled his pipe and slowly lit it, then looked at Harriet. "It is entirely possible. However, I can't imagine Admiral Leeds coming up with any plan quite so practical and at the same time so carefully laid out. It simply doesn't feel like it came from the admiral's hand.''

Harriet agreed, then said goodbye and went back to her own desk, keyed up now, and busy making a copy of her own of the report on Malcolm. She would read it and re-read it until she had it memorized. Tonight she would start to ask him some questions about his family, and if he asked her why, she would say coyly that a girl liked to know as much as possible about each of her courters. That would sound natural enough. But she already wished she knew some of the answers that he would give to certain vital questions!

Chapter Three
MALCOLM TROTTER, ESQ.

As Harriet left his office, Ben Rutledge watched her with a strange uneasiness growing in him. The only woman who had ever been in the Freedom Fighters had been tremendously important to him. Sadie Wythe had been there when they got the idea and began it. Neither she nor Ben had even thought about falling in love, but they had, and suddenly they were lovers and Ben realized that he had a mistress—without planning to, without even considering the consequences.

He and Sadie had been tremendously happy for nearly three years: three years of hidden meetings, of snatched moments after the council meetings, of formal, polite conversations when others were around. Then Sadie had wanted a child. More than anything else in the world she wanted a baby. They talked about it and tried and soon she conceived. She went to New York for a year at her sister's house where her son was born and then brought him back as her sister's orphan. Ben had been ecstatic about his new son, and Sadie faded from the Freedom Fighter's movement. Then on the terrible night of the Boston Tea Party she had thrust herself back into the action and became involved. Ben tried to protect her, hustled her away from the ships before the redcoats came with their muskets, pistols and sabers.

They had been trapped in an alley and, while Ben fought with two of the enemy, a third got through and slashed Sadie before Ben killed him. Sadie was hurt seriously. Ben picked her up and ran with her to Dr. Warren's office. He wiped her hot face with a cloth as the physician did all he could for her. Ben held her hand as she died. Then, cursing himself and God, he walked the black streets of Boston until the small hours of the morning, and at last vowed that Sadie Wythe had not died in vain. Her contribution would spur him on to ultimate victory and freedom.

Since then Ben had spent many painful hours thinking about Sadie, her bright smile, her quick answer, her dedication to the cause of independence and liberty.

Their son, Arthur Wythe, had been placed in a home where there were two other small children. The man in the family was in the Freedom Fighters and he understood. Arthur would always have everything he needed, including the family's tender and loving care. Ben and the others contributed to a special fund in Sadie's name to help the family, and Ben's gift had been substantial.

Ben sat down and put his face in his hands.

First Sadie, now Harriet. Did he dare let her become involved with the Freedom Fighters? He knew there were hundreds of arguments against it. He should tell her just enough to satisfy her, then tell her to stay home and remain safe.

But he wouldn't. Harriet had made up her mind to participate, and there would be little he could do to stop her. That girl had a mind and a will of her own.

Ben rose and went to the window, watching the bay and the big ships moving around with the tide. He had heard that Captain Bleeker was having troubles trying to raise his ship, the *East Indian*. The horses seemed unmanageable, the ropes kept breaking, supplies he needed didn't get delivered on time. Ben figured it would take Captain Bleeker at least a week to realize that he must have his own men in charge of the horses and the ropes before he could make any progress. It was a highly unpopular cause, the raising of the ship, and Lewis Lynch would manage to have at least one Freedom Fighter or sympathetic hand in the crew every day to help slow down the works.

Ben thought back to his major problem. Yes, he was sure now that Harriet should be permitted to join the group, but only as a non-combatant. She could keep records, perhaps even continue the Journal of Outrage, that Sadie had started, but she absolutely would not be permitted on any action operations.

Then he thought about Malcolm, perhaps working for the navy, or one of the Tory magistrates. He would be neutralized and left in place. It was far better to know who he was and where he was. The other leaders would be warned about the possibility of such spies around them as well.

Ben's next problem was to maintain a lookout for any reaction by the British forces to the sinking of the *East Indian*. There would be something, but Ben had no idea just what. An investigation by the naval authorities was certain. He hoped it was not a full blown public affair as they had with the sunken revenue ship, *Richard*, a few years back.

Would there be a show of force, any belligerent action in retaliation for the loss of the ship? Ben expected something, but so far nothing had been reported. There was no roundup of agitators, known rebels or "trouble makers," no restrictions of movement around the docks, no doubling of the guards on the ships. That was good. Admiral Leeds was in command of the navy and was taking a moderate course.

Ben sat down in his big chair and stared at the work on his desk and knew he should be doing it. The stack would keep him busy well after it was time to go home. But the wheels of commerce must grind on. He loved his business, his work. Ben picked up the first letter and began working.

That evening in the Rutledge two-story house on Hanover street, Harriet prepared carefully for her caller. She had a delicious bath with scented soap from France, and now she combed her long brown hair and brushed it until it glistened. Harriet decided to leave her hair down, hanging loose. The right dress to wear had been a puzzle, but at last she chose a dress with a tight fitting blue velvet top and a skirt of matching deep blue that flared into a bright swirl. She would wear at least six petticoats under the skirt to make it stand out. The velvet bodice was cut enticingly low. She might even need to tease Malcolm a little tonight if she were to discover anything important about him. She laughed in nervous anticipation. This was so much different than trying to find out what her father had been doing. Now she *knew* that Malcolm was suspect and she had to try to trap him. It would be an exciting evening, a fine spy adventure, and the best part was that he did not know that she knew what he was there to find out.

Harriet looked in her mirror. At least her eyes were wide set and blue, and her smile pleasing. That would help. She put a touch of scent behind her ears and at her throat and knew that Malcolm would have to be a very good spy to discover anything tonight.

When he arrived just after seven, they sat in

the parlor talking. Malcolm Trotter was five-nine, slender, with lots of dark hair which he wore without a wig. He also had a full moustache that never crossed his upper lip and was always carefully trimmed. His dark brown eyes were alert and inquisitive, and he had the breeding and manners of a proper English gentleman. Malcolm sat on the settee, his brocaded waistcoat in sharp contrast to his black breeches and high white stockings. The silver buckles on his shoes gleamed in the lamplight. His ruffled shirt contained a large diamond stick pin. He wore one diamond ring on each hand, the stones in heavy masculine settings.

Harriet had worked the conversation rather skillfully, she thought, from the weather and the hoped-for early spring, to the warmth of the fireplace, and now to the scuttled ship.

"Mr. Trotter, I don't know anything about politics and all that, but it does seem a shame that grown men have to go around destroying things, like that boat someone blew up in the harbor."

"Ship. That's a ship. A boat is a small craft that is carried aboard a large ship."

"Oh, see what I mean, I don't even know the difference. But it does seem odd to me that grown men would do something like that." She moved a little closer to him. "I wonder who did it? Evidently someone who isn't happy with the British?"

Malcolm Trotter smiled at her and flashed his

even, white teeth. He wondered if she was always so flighty, but when she talked about the ship it seemed almost as if she brought it up deliberately. Mentally he shrugged it aside. No, she was a pretty bit of fluff, an empty-headed female like all the rest, more worried about the depth of her cleavage than the extent of her mind. He moved a little toward her and put on his best serious expression.

"Well, Miss Rutledge, I know your father has ships, so you're concerned about all ships. Evidently someone wasn't quite that thoughtful about the *East Indian*. You may not realize it but to some men politics is extremely important. Not to me, of course, I'm interested in beautiful jewels." He looked at her and his smile was full, his eyes straying to her cleavage. "And I must say, Miss Rutledge, that when it comes to jewels, you are a perfect example of a one-of-a-kind rare gem."

Harriet blushed and looked away. She didn't need to pretend now, and even though she knew he was turning on his charm, it had affected her. She would have to be careful, watchful. Her mother and father had left earlier to go to a church deacon's meeting or some such, and the twins were upstairs in their rooms.

"Now, Mr. Trotter, that's just a bunch of flattery and you're not supposed to do that. Instead why don't you tell me all about yourself. You said you were born in London. Are your parents still there?"

"Yes, Father's a merchant. He tried to stand for parliament once but didn't get elected. He's a wine importer."

Lie number one, Harriet thought. "Have you ever been in the military service?"

"Most Englishmen have, at one time or another, but I, fortunately, missed the press crews and worked in my father's stores. Then I wanted some adventure so with my father's backing I came here and set up business."

Lie number two. "So you went from wine to diamonds. At least you can't drink up the profits that way."

He smiled at her, curious about her sudden interrogation, but he let it pass. "No, as a wine merchant neither can you wear diamonds on your fingers or give gems to beautiful women."

"There you go again, Mr. Trotter. You're trying to turn a girl's head. Now don't you do that. I'm just making a few unobtrusive inquiries about your background and you are supposed to be gentleman enough not to notice."

"Then you do have a certain interest in me, Miss Rutledge?"

"Mr. Trotter! I do swear. You know better than to ask a question like that. A girl would put herself at a terrible disadvantage—why that's downright naughty of you, Mr. Trotter."

He laughed and when she saw the way crinkle lines came around his eyes she liked the effect. He truly was a handsome man, and despite what she knew about him, he was kind and she liked him. Something remembered stirred deep inside her, but she shut it out and looked back at him. He was now sitting close beside her, his leg pushing against her skirts.

"Mr. Trotter!"

"Now, stop it, Harriet. You know that you like me to come calling, and you love to be complimented and told how pretty you are. Why not admit it? What is it going to hurt? Besides, you do like me sitting close to you this way, don't you?"

She looked up at his strong face, his glittering eyes, and that something remembered pounded at her again, but she shoved it to one side and leaned away from him.

"I'm sure, Mr. Trotter, that I don't have the slightest idea what you're talking about."

Before she could move he caught her shoulders with his hands, leaned in and kissed her lips. Harriet wanted to shriek and pull away quickly, but she did neither. She sat there and let him hold her and kiss her, and he murmured deep in his throat as he did. When he leaned back she slapped him gently. His eyes glistened and he kissed her again, this time pulling her toward him, his arms tightly around her. She drifted through the kiss in a soft haze, not quite realizing it was happening on one hand, but knowing quite clearly that he was kissing her passionately, even brushing her lips with his tongue. She let him end it and then he still held her close.

She pulled back with a start, leaning away from him.

"My parents!"

Malcolm shook his head, laughter in his eyes, now. "No, they went out half an hour ago, remember?"

"My two brothers."

"I bribed them to stay upstairs."

"You did not."

"Can you be sure that I didn't? I talked to both of them while I waited for you to come down."

Harriet stared at him frankly. She kept telling herself over and over that he was a spy, that he was devious, that he felt nothing for her, he was only trying to get information about her father. He would even pretend that he loved her if he needed to get vital information. She pushed him away. He followed, caught her shoulders and turned her so she had to look at him.

"Harriet, you don't know how long I've dreamed of kissing you that way."

"Really, flattery again, Mr. Trotter. . . . " She was saying the words, desperately trying to think of something to get away from this dangerous romantic situation. She could think of nothing. Should she accuse him of being dishonest, of being a British spy? No, that was what they did not want. She must be wary, must ward him off, but must be careful.

She stood. He stood beside her at once, now his arms came around her and pulled her close to him until her whole body touched him from knees to shoulders.

"Sweet, precious Harriet. I didn't mean to frighten you. I assumed that you had been kissed before."

She looked at him sharply and he retreated a little.

"Oh, no disrespect, but a girl as beautiful as you are with such a glorious figure, and lips so perfect . . . I simply expected that some man must have swooped down on you and kissed you, before you could protest, of course."

Harriet was confused. Malcolm was nice. He didn't sound like a spy. And it felt good with his arms around her. Little by little she eased her resistance to him, and she knew he could tell. Slowly his mouth came toward hers, and almost without willing it, her mouth moved toward his until they met and now the remembered urging she had felt before spoke plainly to her, and her body began to react to his kiss as she grew warmer and more thrilled, more excited by the second.

His arms pressed her tighter against him, pushing her breasts to his chest. She felt them respond, warming, and for one wild moment she relived the minutes with Andy Otis and that surprise seduction on the floor of his father's store.

Harriet turned her head away and pushed back from him.

"No!" she said sharply. "You simply will not

do that, Mr. Trotter. I think it's past time that you should leave."

He looked at her, surprised, and stepped toward her again, his eyes troubled. She put her hand on his chest and held him away.

"No, Mr. Trotter. Do I have to raise my voice and call the boys? Either one of them could throw you right down the front steps with no trouble."

"Harriet. Miss Rutledge. Surely I had no intention of frightening you, or harming you, or doing anything you did not want me to do. Believe me, I have only the highest respect for you."

"Then you won't mind leaving at once?"

He shrugged. "If you want me to. I had thought perhaps we could play some chess. You're really quite good. Or we might listen to your music boxes."

Harriet hesitated. Perhaps she could find out more about him tonight. She looked at Malcolm slowly and took her hand away.

"Well, if you promise to behave yourself. And not even touch me, then perhaps we could have just one game."

"I promise not to touch even the hem of your skirt unless you give me your permission." It was his turn to frown. "I did sense a willingness to be kissed, and with the questions you were asking about my background . . . well, it seemed to me that you were more than a little interested in me. Are you, Miss Rutledge?"

"Interested? Of course, Mr. Trotter, or else you would never have been back here for your second visit. But even if I am somewhat interested in you, that still does not give you a license to become forward—to drink from every wine bottle in the winery, now, does it, Mr. Trotter?"

"No, of course not, and I do apologize. I was simply carried away by your beauty, and that fascinating perfume, and your delightful, youthful vigor. I must admit I am quite taken with you, Miss Rutledge. Now I have to convince you that you simply can't live without me by your side."

She laughed and they walked into the den, found the chess board and the box of pieces and arranged them on a table near the fire.

Before the evening was over, Harriet had caught Malcolm Trotter in another lie about his background, but the curious part was that he made absolutely no probes about her father, his politics, or his activities. Malcolm never once mentioned her father after that first time. When she showed him to the door a little after nine, she let him peck her on the cheek, and sent him dancing down the steps.

Harriet stared after him, totally confused. If he was a spy for the British, why didn't he try to get some information? If he wasn't a spy, why did he give her deliberate lies and misleading statements about his background? In her room, Harriet took out a quill and ink pot and wrote down everything she could remember about Malcolm, and his answers to her probing background questions. She said nothing about their kisses.

Upstairs in their rooms, the Rutledge twins heard little that went on in the parlor or den. They were both working hard at their studies. They were in their first year at Harvard, well into the second half of it now, and both enjoyed it.

David was amazed at the extent of the books and new ideas he encountered daily. He took to literature and philosophy naturally, and made good marks.

Robert was interested in the physical sciences, and the practice of business. He earned the better grades of the two because he applied himself more to the points that interested the professors. David would work for months on his own, perhaps at an angle to the professor's wishes. But in the end they found a common ground, and David was in his own heaven.

Robert had been interested in this suitor who had called on Harriet. He wished she would get married. Robert talked to Trotter for a while, then went upstairs when Harriet came down. He tried to hear what they were talking about but couldn't, so he went back to his books.

Robert was studying a fascinating book about the inventions of Leonardo da Vinci. It was amazing how far ahead of his time he was. He had ideas and theories and physical concepts that only now the best minds of the day were starting to figure out and build upon. Da Vinci was a brilliant man in such diverse fields as painting, sculpture, engineering and astronomy. There was no man like him before or since who could do so many things so well. His talents dazzled Robert.

His thoughts strayed to Harriet again. She certainly should be married. Maybe this was the courter who would marry her. She should stop working in the family business and realize that since she was a woman, she should be wed, with three or four children running around. She was almost an old maid.

For a brief moment Robert remembered that day he had been passing Harriet's room and the door had been open a crack. He glanced in and saw his sister standing in front of her mirror without a thing on. Her back had been to him, then she turned and for just a moment he had seen her breasts and the dark ''V'' of hair at her crotch. He had never seen a woman's breasts before and he didn't realize that they could be so large. Robert had slipped quietly away and run to his room. He'd been seventeen at the time, and he knew almost nothing about girls. By now he knew a lot more, and had even stolen a few kisses in the dark. Once, on a hayride, he played with a girl's breasts. There had been twenty people on the old wagon in the dark. That was all she would let him touch.

He shook his head and tried to get back to his book. Girls didn't worry him that much. He knew sex was there and it would come, but he had no big anxiety to rush into it. He was afraid that he might make some girl pregnant and would have to marry her. Marriage was the last thing he wanted to get involved in right now. He turned to his required literature book and began reading the first chapter of Plato's Republic. Robert had never before had to wade through such uninteresting writing in his life. But he dug into it.

Suddenly Robert slammed the Plato book closed and then scowled and opened it again and began painfully to read. He understood very little of it. What in hell was this old Greek talking about, anyway? Robert read on.

At nineteen Robert had most of his height, but he would fill out more in the shoulders and torso. Even so, he was five-feet-eleven inches tall, and weighed a hundred and seventy pounds. He had good shoulders, a thick set neck and a head that looked more square than rounded. He wore his hair long around his ears and had it cut only when his mother insisted. Robert was one of the young rebels who would not wear a powdered wig, calling them foppish, frivolous and ridiculous. In general appearance he and his identical twin were hard to tell apart, but there were ways. Robert had chipped a tooth five years ago, one of his front ones, a small notch that was easy to notice, for those who knew what to look for. Robert's eyes were a little deeper shade of brown than his brother's. As with any identical twins they had gone through the stage of answering to each other's names, and playing tricks on teachers and classmates, but now that was past. They never dressed alike, Robert being the more correct, more formal. David was casual and on the sloppy side. His mother often had to suggest that he wear a certain item or change his clothes entirely. It simply didn't matter to David what he wore.

They were splitting further and further apart in other ways as well. David's main loves were literature, poetry, the humanities, philosophy and history. David was quickly and quietly efficient at nearly everything he tried. When their father took the boys out shooting when they were thirteen, David had absorbed the instructions and proceeded to out-shoot even his father on a large "V" target. David's one difficulty was in trying to get interested in the subjects and projects the teachers assigned.

Lately he had been concentrating on poets, reading them silently, reading them aloud, and trying his hand at writing poetry as well. He worked on everything from doggerel to sonnets.

David combined his love of poetry and literature with an active interest in the ladies. His first weeks at Harvard he had gone to a brothel with a new friend on a bet, and ever since his introduction to the joys of sex, he had been more alert to the possibilities around him. Once a month since then he had discovered willing partners in the most surprising places.

David smiled, remembering, and put the last episode out of his mind, turning back to the poems he was studying.

But David could not concentrate for long. He kept wandering to the window of his room and looking across the lawn and shrubs at the house next door and the window where he knew that Millie Livingston should be. It was her bedroom and once in a while they looked at each other and waved. Millie was a little over seventeen and getting anxious. One day he had teased her when they both had been in the yard, and he knew she was interested in him.

He moved to the window and pushed the curtain aside and stood framed in the light, looking at her window. She was not there. One of these days she would be, he knew. He had seen the frank way she looked at him in church one day, and he knew that she was interested in him.

Chapter Four
MILITIA TIME

Ben Rutledge had arrived at the Old Boston Book Shop a half hour before closing time, and browsed along the racks for a while. Then when there were no customers, he waved to Jonathan Clark, owner of the store, and went through a curtain into the back where the living quarters were and up steep steps to the third floor. At the landing there was one door which opened into a windowless room twelve feet square. It held only a sturdy table, six chairs, a slate and some chalk.

Ben had lit a candle in the back room to show his way up the steps, and now he fired the wick of a bull's eye lamp. This well made pewter lamp was over a foot high, held a tank of whale oil and a wick at the top with a three-inch diameter lens of unusually pure glass on each side to give off a truly brilliant light. It was better than any other artificial light Ben had ever seen.

He settled down with the papers he had brought with him, intent on getting some study and planning done before the rest of the Freedom Fighter's council arrived.

A half hour later when Dr. Joseph Warren came, Ben had his thoughts well in hand. Dr. Warren was a physician, thirty two years old, tall, fair, with blue eyes that jolted out bolts of lightning when he talked about the Freedom Fighters and independence. He shook hands with Ben warmly, grateful that Ben had snapped back from the depression he had suffered after Sadie Wythe's death. The night she died, Dr. Warren had been there and had sensed a special relationship between Sadie and Ben and when Ben had carried Sadie's child to his new home, the medic had known for sure that Ben was the child's father, but he would never say a word about it. The affair was none of his business.

"I see you've been doing your homework, Ben."

"Yes, Joseph, it's time we shared our experts with the standing militia. It seems to me that part of the reason the British don't take us seriously is the way our militia has performed in the past. None of this colony's citizen-military units have fought well when they were called up to battle against the French or the Indians. The record is clear on that. And most of their training sessions have been little but boisterous holidays with light talk, heavy drinking, and damn little military training. Some of the men in my old militia company didn't even know how to load their muskets."

Dr. Warren sat down at his chair. "Precisely why we put together a crack military outfit, the Freedom Fighters. We can fight, we can function."

"Joseph, I've been looking at it this way. We have the experts, the Massachusetts military, the manpower. If we could get two of our men into each militia unit as trainers, we could put them on a firm military basis within a year. At least we could give them some basic fundamentals in loading and firing their weapons and in tactics. Of course, we can never make real soldiers out of them with only one day a month, but we can get in some fundamentals, and then when they need the skills, they'll be ready to perfect them."

Lewis Lynch came in then. He had changed his black eye patch to one more flesh toned to make it less noticeable. He had been on an extended assignment in New York for Ben working out of the Rutledge office there. It was standard procedure for Ben to get Lewis out of town immediately following a Freedom Fighter action, since he was the man most easily identifiable. Lewis shook hands with both men and took his usual place at the table. Ben had discussed the idea with Lewis and worked out the numbers of men they could spare and how they would utilize each. Lynch was all for the idea.

Captain Arnold Compton arrived at the

stroke of seven with Jonathan Clark. Compton was a huge man, and a farmer out toward Lexington. Three years ago he had challenged Sadie Wythe to a shooting match and Sadie had beaten him in a shoot off. When she moved to New York to have her child, she had selected Compton to take over her company.

Greetings were exchanged all around and they looked to Ben to start the meeting.

The five of them sat around the table. Each with one hand extended on top of the rough wood, fist closed. One by one they opened their hands, palm up, and lying in each was a small gold coin.

"Freedom or death!" they said in unison. Then the coins with special Freedom Fighter words and emblems engraved on them vanished back into pockets and the meeting began.

Ben laid out his plan carefully, talking mostly to Arnold and Jonathan who had not heard of it before. When he was done, the council voted unanimously to start the program.

"I'll talk to Sam Adams tomorrow and see how we can integrate the sharpshooters into the various militia units, have them move from one training session to the next. Sam can take any action necessary in the Massachusetts Colonial Assembly to approve such special training."

They talked about some routine matters, and then Ben brought up another sensitive point.

"You all know about our success with the *East Indian*. The operation went smoothly, with no firearms discharged, and none of our men lost or injured, however there was one slight problem. My daughter, Harriet, stumbled into the operation and participated in it without anyone noticing. It was dark, and cold, and everyone was so bundled up that she became involved really without trying to. Looking back, it isn't too surprising that it happened."

"I'm still surprised," Lewis said. "And I was one of the ones right next to her, talking to her."

"Needless to say, Harriet now is aware of our movement, and my involvement, and she has asked that she be allowed to join us a a non-combat member. She says she wants to help in any way she can, writing letters, or keeping books, working with records. What's the feeling of the group?"

Five minutes later they voted to approve her membership as a non-combatant, in charge of correspondence and bookkeeping.

Two weeks later Harriet attended her first council meeting, where she had no vote but did have duties of recording what was talked about and what actions determined. All records were kept at the bookstore, some in a secret compartment in the upper room, others in secret wall safes downstairs. All work on the books and records had to be done inside the bookstore, and then only after the outer doors were locked. Harriet was so thrilled that she could hardly talk. When they started home she found her tongue and bubbled over.

"Daddy, this is the most exciting thing that's ever happened to me! I don't know how to tell you. To think that what we do might have some real effect on launching a whole new nation!"

They rode in silence for a few blocks. Then she touched her father's arm. "Daddy, I think we're all wrong about Malcolm Trotter. I've seen him once a week now for three weeks and he simply has made no moves to try to find out anything about what you believe or what you do. Nothing. The only time your name even comes up is if I mention it. Have we found out anything more about him? Any real evidence against him?"

Ben Rutledge drove awhile in silence, then shook his head. "No, we haven't, Harriet. I know of nothing more we have discovered except the circumstantial. There's nothing more than what I told you before and what you heard tonight at the meeting. If Mr. Trotter is a spy, he's certainly not working very hard at it right now. Perhaps that's only to throw us off the track?"

"Daddy, I don't see how he could be quite that sneaky, so underhanded. It just isn't like him to be deceitful."

Ben turned and looked at her through the chill February night. "You really like this young man quite a lot, don't you, Harriet?"

"Yes, Daddy, I'm afraid that I like him very much!"

The days eased by. Sam Adams came through

with the permissive orders and two by two the Freedom Fighters attended various militia training days around the immediate Boston area. Then they began working out farther. They took six militia men each, and drilled them and trained them carefully in the quick loading procedure for the flintlock, then trained the twelve men in fighting tactics they had picked up from the Indians: how to use the terrain as concealment and protection, how to fight and attack and never be seen. It was training that could come to good use later on.

Ben watched everything, managed his business and kept an eye on Harriet, who seemed to be spending more and more time with Malcolm Trotter. Their special file on Trotter did not grow much. He seemed to be inactive as a spy. But he had deliberately lied to Harriet about certain aspects of his background, including his goverment service, and that would be hard to explain away. Harriet reported that he carefully skirted politics whenever it came up. And he certainly was not observed in any more meetings with the military commanders or the other Tory hardliners.

Captain Bleeker had at last ordered out troops to man his work party and a week later had the *East Indian* upright so the carpenters could repair the hull. The job was now underway and pumping would be the next process. Within two or three months the *East Indian* would be back to active duty.

Each evening at dusk, the captain himself posted the watch, ten armed men on deck from dark to dawn, and the gangplank was pulled on board and secured. No one could board or leave the *East Indian* except by working along the tie down ropes. As far as Ben knew, no one tried.

But the *East Indian* and even the Freedom Fighters were two of the last things Harriet was thinking about tonight. Her only thoughts were on a man named Malcolm Trotter. She had questioned herself every way she could and now she was certain that Malcolm was not trying to spy on her father. Twice in the past week they had been out, once to a lovely dinner at the Judson House hotel dining room, and again to a concert by a small chamber orchestra. Tonight they were going to Boston Hall to a string quartet recital. Harriet had never been to one but Malcolm said they were very popular in England. He said he hadn't heard such glorious music since he left London. He would come pick her up in his chaise about seven o'clock. Harriet had been ready for fifteen minutes. She sat in the parlor watching the blaze in the fireplace. By now she had known Malcolm Trotter for almost two months. Today was March 4, 1774, a Friday, and she hoped that tonight Malcolm might indicate just how serious he was about her. He had gently hinted that he wanted to be more than a friend, and once his kisses had become most insistent, but she had fended him off. He would never come out and say in so many words that he loved her.

Each time now that she thought of Malcolm she marveled at how soft and gentle his voice was, at his polite manners and his obvious good breeding and charm. She had never met a man like him before, and in Boston she guessed that she might not meet another one. Oh, yes! But she did love him, and she wanted to marry him.

They had kissed many times. It had become a little ritual to walk in the dark near the front of the house each time before he left. She let him kiss her twice, and once three times. She could feel his excitement grow each time they kissed, and she knew very well that her color always rose measurably, so she was glad they were in the dark and she didn't give herself away.

Malcolm was so unlike Andy Otis that she had to laugh just thinking about a comparison. Malcolm had everything Andy lacked: charm, good looks, intelligence, fine manners.

She heard someone coming up the front walk and she hurried to the front door. Harriet opened the door just before he knocked and it was Malcolm. He frowned.

"What if I had been a robber, Harriet? You really must be more careful."

"Yes, Malcolm," she said, inviting him inside. "But, if it had been a robber, I would have charmed him half to death and then stomped on his toes and frightened him away."

Malcolm rubbed his clean shaven jaw. "Yes, I really think that you might." He smiled then and it lit up his face. "But seriously, Harriet, you should be more careful."

They left shortly, he helping her down the steps, then handing her into the one horse chaise, with its high step and the long shafts the horse stood between.

It was a brisk night for the first of March, but most of the snow had vanished from the streets. They knew there would be more snow, and more cold as well. Both of them were bundled in heavy coats. He touched her hand as they sat in the rig and on an impulse she reached over and kissed his cheek. He turned, surprised and pleased.

"Why, thank you, Miss Rutledge. That was a sweet and charming thing to do. May I return the compliment?"

She smiled, nodded, and let him kiss her cheek. Then he took the reins and drove down the street. They were halfway to Boston Hall when Malcolm pulled the rig to the side of the street and stopped.

"Damn!" he said softly.

She looked at him, surprised, because she had never heard him swear before. He glanced at her, his frown deeper now.

"I'm afraid that I forgot our tickets to the concert. I left them in my other waistcoat. Now I'm wondering if we have time to return to my apartment and get the tickets?"

"What else can we do?"

"We could buy more at the door."

"No, that would be wasteful and extravagant."

"It's only a mile or so back to my place." He looked at his pocket watch. "I think we'll have time. Should we try?"

"Oh, yes."

"Then we'll make a race of it." He flicked the reins against the back of the chestnut and hurried it down the street. They raced along for a block, then he turned twice so they were heading back the way they had come. A few minutes later they had turned three more times, and Harriet became lost in the unfamiliar streets. But before long Malcolm stopped at the side of the street in front of a medium sized house. It had lights burning in one side. "This is it," he said and stepped down, but turned back.

"I really shouldn't let you stay alone here in the street."

"Oh, I'll be all right. Just hurry."

"There have been reports of some street toughs around here at night. Why don't you come to the front door with me, then we can talk and I'll know you're safe."

She nodded and reached for his hand as she stepped down to the street. Harriet felt a little tingle of excitement as they walked up to the side door. She felt wicked—here she was going to a man's apartment alone with him! He explained that he sublet the rooms from an older couple who owned the house.

Malcolm put a key in the lock and turned it,

then let himself in and left her at the door. There was a flickering oil lamp burning very low so there would be a flame to turn up when he came back. He went to the lamp and turned it bright, then carried it back to her. "Why don't you step just inside the door while I find the tickets. Then you'll be out of the wind."

She did and he vanished through a door, leaving the lamp on a small table, He was back in a moment.

"Odd, I don't find them. I know I left them right on my dresser or in the pocket."

"Why don't we take the lamp, and I'll help you look," Harriet said.

He nodded and picked up the lamp and led the way into the other room which was his bedroom. Harriet shivered as they stepped through the door, then held his arm tightly as he went past the bed to a dresser where he set the lamp and looked around. He checked in back of it on the floor and on both sides. Malcolm slammed his hand down on the dresser.

"I know I had them right here."

"Could we still get more at the door?"

"No, I don't think so. It's a small auditorium and I remember I got some of the last seats. I feel like such an idiot. A grown man doesn't lose concert tickets!"

He turned and sat on the bed, his face in his hands. She walked to him and put her hand on his shoulder.

"Well, now, Malcolm, it isn't all that bad. We

simply won't go to the old recital. We can go back to my house and play some chess, or read poetry.''

"But I promised to take you to the concert. I feel stupid.''

"No, please, don't feel that way, Malcolm. I'm sure it will turn out not to be your fault after all. And we know each other well enough that it doesn't matter. You'll probably find them in a shirt pocket or under the rug or somewhere next week and we'll have a good laugh about it.''

"I'm not laughing now.''

She bent and kissed his forehead. "Come on how, cheer up, it isn't that bad. We can always talk to each other. You haven't told me about your home in England, where you grew up.''

"You're patronizing me. You do think I'm stupid.''

"Of course not, Malcolm. Don't you think I've lost things, too? Things like that just happen.'' Now for the first time the impact of where she was came through. In the bedroom! "Maybe we should go into the other room, you may have left the tickets there.''

"You're disappointed, I know you are.''

"Yes, a little, but I'll live though it. We really should go. After all, Malcolm, this is your bedroom.''

"Oh, yes, so it is and you're . . . He stood and smiled. "Sorry, I just wasn't thinking too clearly. Kiss me and make me well.''

She laughed. "That's our farewell game.''

"But we're about to leave the house."

"Yes, that's true."

He moved close to her, his arms went around her and his lips found hers. The kiss was a long one, and at once Harriet felt its impact on her. A throbbing rush of blood poured through her veins and her breath came faster. Then her knees trembled and she was afraid she might fall. Gently, and still holding her in the embrace he bent his knees and they sat on the bed. She broke the kiss and looked at him.

"I was afraid that you were going to fall."

"I wasn't, and Malcolm, you shouldn't kiss me so seriously."

He was still holding her as they sat on his bed. He didn't reply. His arms pulled her tighter and he kissed her again, watched until her eyes closed and then his tongue brushed against her lips and Harriet groaned in a sudden surging desire.

She clung to him with both arms even after the kiss ended and pressed against him, not ever wanting him to leave her. It all felt so good, so right. He moved and kissed her nose, then her cheeks, her eyes and at last her lips again.

"Darling, Harriet, you're so beautiful, so marvelous. We don't have to go back to your house. We can stay right here and kiss each other for as long as we want to, all we ever wanted to!"

"No, Malcolm, sweetheart, I can't do that. You know that we shouldn't do that."

"I know," he said softly. "I know." Then his lips touched hers again and he kissed her hard as they clung together almost desperately. At first she didn't understand what was happening, then she knew that she was moving backwards, that he was gently pushing her down on the bed, and then he was lying half on top of her, his tongue brushing against her lips until she groaned in delight and opened them and let his tongue probe gently into her mouth.

Harriet lay there in delicious agony. She knew that she had to push him away, knew that she had to get up and walk to the door, and knew that he would come with her and would not think any worse of her. The agony was knowing that she did not want to move. Her breasts were burning now where they pressed against him and she wanted his hands on them, wanted him to touch her, touch her bare skin . . . .

His lips still kept her fire burning, his lips on her nose, her cheeks, then her mouth and down to her neck until she wanted to scream at him because it felt so delightful, so wonderful! Never had she felt this way before, never had she experienced this kind of sensual feeling, as if she were going to melt, as if he could do any-thing that he wanted to with her and she would only accept it and encourage him.

A half hour later Harriet still lay on the bed, the bulky, heavy coat was on the floor. The top of her dress unbuttoned and pulled off her shoulders revealing her breasts, her skirts and petticoats rumpled and bunched around her waist. Malcolm lay beside her, naked and on his stomach. She thought he was asleep so she didn't move, not a muscle. She didn't want to think, she kept her eyes closed and tried to breathe very shallowly. There was no tomorrow, no right or wrong, no problem, there was only the delight and the rapture of the here and now, and it was enough.

Slowly the soft, warm glow filtered out of her system, and the fogs cleared, and blankness of her mind faded and she realized that life would go on and that she would be a part of it.

She thought again about the whole experience with Malcolm and smiled. Oh, yes, it had been glorious, amazing. That was more what she had expected, what she had heard that it was like to make love with a man you cared for. It was a million times better than the rough mindless coupling with Andy Otis.

Rape? No, she had not been raped, rather she had been seduced by a man who knew exactly what he was doing. Now she was sure that there had been no tickets for a concert. The whole scheme had been put together carefully, planned and refined and probably used before, with the precise results that had come about this time. It had been an elaborate seduction plot that had worked to perfection. Malcolm Trotter probably had been through the script dozens of times. So was he sincere in his feelings for her, or was he really a spy? She looked quickly at him and found him in the same position, his breathing deep and regular, he was still sleeping. Now was a chance to see what she could find in his room, time to do some spying of her own!

She sat up with care, pulled her chemise and the bodice of her dress back in place, buttoned her dress, then worked her way carefully off the bed so she wouldn't awaken him. She pushed her skirts down and stepped gingerly to the floor. When she found her shoes she would be socially presentable.

For a moment she looked down at Malcolm, and saw that he was still sleeping soundly, one arm over his head, the other at his side. An odd thought swept into her mind. Despite her two months of courting by him, she realized she really didn't know Malcolm Trotter very well. She *would* look through his things.

Softly she moved toward the bedroom door and swung it open, then she took the lamp from the dresser and in her bare feet slipped out of the room and closed the door but did not latch it.

Where would he hide things he didn't want found? Would he hide them at all? Either way she would make a report to the council—she frowned. But then they would know she had been here with him and they would think the worst. She put it out of her mind, first she would search.

Kitchen, living room and bedroom. She went to a small desk in the living room and began going through it first. Nothing on top looked of any value, books and papers. No headings, no names or addresses. Below some papers she found some envelopes addressed to him here and evidently brought by some ship and hand delivered. No letters were in the envelopes.

In a drawer she found more pads of paper and envelopes all unused. Below the paper nothing was hidden. In the last drawer she found an envelope at the very bottom. She opened it and found it contained a list of all British ships and their commanders in the area. She was putting it back when her hand touched the bottom of the drawer just above the one she had opened. She felt it with her hand and then knelt down and looked under the drawer. Glued to the bottom she found a folded piece of paper.

Carefully she pulled it away from the glue, and opened it with trembling hands. She look at it in terrified fascination.

"Major Malcolm J. Trotter, Royal Marines. Assigned to temporary duty in the American Colonies. March 1, 1772.

"Major Trotter: This will acquaint you with your new duties, to wit:

1. The observation of the civil population of Boston with an eye to discovering and relaying all vital intelligence you might find of military value.

2. Placing yourself totally within the framework of the colonial situation and following their style of life to gain the confidences of the

colonies.

3. To report on a monthly basis, directly to the British commander in chief or ranking naval officer at Fort William, all intelligence you gather.

4. To maintain an active interest in all rebel leaders, and to get as close to them as possible with an eye to gaining information about proposed plans and future actions they might plan or launch against His Majesty's forces.''

She had read enough. She put everything back the way it had been, except the letter which she folded twice more and placed inside her chemise next to her breast where it could not slip out. Quickly she checked to see that she had arranged all the papers the way they had been, then she took the lamp and slipped back into the bedroom returning the lamp to the dresser.

Malcolm lay where he had been. She sat down on the bed, jolting it. Malcolm groaned and rolled toward her. He eyes came open and he heaved a big sigh and sat up beside her, his hand on the inside of her leg.

He stared at the anger on her face and winced. ''Now don't start crying, for God's sake. My darling Harriet, I know, I know I should have been strong and waited. I should not have touched you until after we are married, but I'm not that strong. And you are so beautiful, and delicious and enticing that no normal man could have resisted. I simply couldn't control myself. Do you understand?''

She stared at him with fury, not for seducing her, but for his outrageous masquerade as a spy and how he was using her.

"Look, I admit I started it, but you could have stopped me, the way you did the other times. You *wanted* to just as much as I did. You helped, so it's just as much your fault as it is mine."

"Malcolm, will you stop sniveling like a school boy and take me home. I really have a lot of thinking to do, and you had better plan on seeing my father within the next day or two and ask for my hand in marriage. If you don't, I'll tell my father, and he'll come and kill you."

Chapter Five
THE FIVE KEYS

Slightly before his usual closing time of six o'clock, when the nearby church's big bell always rang out, Malcolm Trotter was surprised to see Harriet Rutledge come into his diamond and jewelry shop. She was smiling, which was a great relief to him, since she had hardly said two words to him after they started back to her house the previous night, and he was worried about how she might feel about him now. He smiled back and went forward to greet her.

"Miss Rutledge, it's a pleasure and an honor to have you in my small shop."

"You're absolutely right about that, Mr. Trotter," she said, then motioned at his clerk who was closing some of the display cases. "Can you send him home right now?" she asked quietly.

Trotter went to the clerk, spoke to him a moment and at once the clerk put away his key to the cash box, found his coat and went out the front door. Trotter followed him, pulled down the blind and locked the door, then extinguished one of the lamps and smiled at Harriet.

"Now, shall we go into the back room to talk about this, whatever it is that's on your mind."

She followed him to the rear of the store where a door led into a combination storage and packing room. The former owner had used part of the back for living quarters. Harriet saw an outside door as she had been informed there would be, and she turned toward Malcolm.

"Now, Mr. Trotter, about last night. You owe me a great deal more than just an apology."

His face worked into a frown, then surprise and at last he could not hide his irritation.

"But, I thought we agreed last night that. . . ."

A pounding at the rear of the room broke into his words and he walked to the panel which had a sturdy looking bolt.

"What do you want?" he shouted through the partition.

"Delivery off the *Liberty* out of London. Special parcel we must deliver into your hands only."

"Just a moment." He pulled the bolt back and unlatched the door. Before he could open it, the panel slammed inward and four men, all with loaded and cocked flintlock pistols boiled into the room. One of the men knocked Trotter down, and another tied his hands behind his back. The other two closed the door and bolted it.

All four men wore head hoods completely masking their faces. They stood Trotter up and ranged in front of him, with Harriet in the center.

"Now, Mr. Trotter, we have a few questions for you. Is it true that your father is really a diamond merchant in London and not a wine dealer as you told me?"

"What is going on here? Who are these men? I demand that you untie me this instant. This is an outrage!"

A fist lashed out, caught the side of his jaw and spun him around into the wall. A man caught him and put him back on his feet.

"Answer the question, Mr. Trotter," Harriet ordered.

"Yes, all right. So he's dealing in diamonds, not wine. What's the difference, he's still a merchant."

"It shows me that you lied, Mr. Trotter. Isn't it also true that you spent at least two years in the Royal Marines as an officer, and that you were two years with the British Foreign Service?"

"No."

"Mr. Trotter, we know that you're lying again. How much punishment can your face take?

One of the hooded figures moved toward Trotter, who backed away.

"All right. Yes, both statements are true, I did serve in both groups."

"And isn't it true that this very instant you are a major in the Royal British Marines?"

"No, no, of course not."

"Do you wish to reconsider your answer, Mr. Trotter?" Harriet asked.

Trotter looked at the big men on both sides of him, their fists balled and ready. He licked his lips, his mind racing. "Look, I don't know what this is all about. What if I were still in the marines, what difference would it make? I'm a fulltime businessman, a merchant, I sell diamonds and precious stones."

"And you are a spy, Mr. Trotter, you spy for the British."

"No!"

"Yes, Mr. Trotter. Do you know what we do with spies caught during wartime?"

"No one is at war. This is not a war. You are a colony of England. No one is at war."

"But you are a spy."

"Certainly not, I'm a merchant."

Harriet took out the letter from the navy and showed it to him. "Mr. Trotter, a team of experts examined your quarters today. You were good, you hid it well, but we knew that you must have some identification, some orders, and we at last found them pasted to the bottom of a drawer in your desk. Clever, ingenious, but not quite good enough. Now, do you still deny that you're a British spy?"

"I demand to see the head port commissioner at once!"

"Denied. You know what we do with spies, Mr. Trotter? We shoot them. In your case, we'll make it appear that your store was robbed. It won't be hard. We'll take most of the valuable gems from your displays and safe, and it will be a robbery, true enough, but unfortunately you were killed in the struggle with the gunman. Too bad, in a way."

"No, no, no! I'm not a spy. That paper has no validity at all!"

As he spoke three of the men formed in front of him and drew their flintlocks. They checked the primers, then cocked them and held the weapons pointing at the ceiling in a precise military ready position.

Harriet, the only one of the rebels who had talked, stood to one side.

"Take aim," she said.

The three pistols came down, centering on Trotter's heart from ten feet away.

"Ready. . . . " Harriet barked.

"No, no!" Trotter screamed. He fell to the floor and began crying, babbling, begging them not to shoot him.

"No! I'll do anything you say. They made me spy on you. I didn't want to. I never turned in anything against you. My father made me do it."

It was hard for Harriet to watch him turn into such a spineless creature. But for all he knew he had come within a few seconds of execution. On her signal one of the men cut the bindings on Trotter's hands and marched him to a small desk. Harriet found a pot of ink and a newly sharpened quill and gave him a piece of paper that had writing on it.

"This document affirms that you have sold your entire stock, fixtures and your business in this shop to the bearer, and that you have received just compensation for such goods, and that you hereunder release all rights to such goods, property and goodwill so included. Do you agree to this statement?"

He looked up at her. "And I thought you were soft, I thought that you were apolitical. How I laughed at the way I was fooling you. Ha! You're twice the spy I am, or ever will be. Yes, I'll sign, and then you shoot me anyway, right!"

"Sign it, Mr. Trotter."

He took the quill and signed his name carefully, so there could be no doubt of its authenticity. He then looked up at the muzzles of the weapons, but all were well out of his reach.

"So who kills me?"

"No one, Mr. Trotter, but you may wish you were dead soon. You are hereby sentenced to two years under sail as a deckhand. You will suffer the dangers, lack of food and water, and be at the mercy of the wind and waves as any other common seaman on a two year's journey to China, around Cape Horn and up through the Pacific. By the time you return we will be in open warfare with the British, and your information about us and our people will not matter in the slightest.''

Trotter's hands were retied behind him and a hood placed over his head. Then he was led out the back door for a quick ride to one of John Hancock's ships that was ready to sail the next morning with the high tide.

Once Trotter was gone, the two remaining men took off their masks. One was Ben Rutledge, the other Dr. Warren. Ben smiled at Harriet. "Excellent job, Harriet. I couldn't have done it better myself. Now let's see just what we have won in our chess game tonight. I would estimate gems valued at something around five thousand pounds. A fine night's work.''

Across town, Captain Bleeker sat on the bed with Annabelle close beside him. She was worried because he was worried.

Almost two months had passed and he still had no real idea who the one-eyed man had been who seemed to lead the attack on his ship. There were two men with eye patches in Boston he had checked on, but both were clearly not involved. One had a wooden leg, and the other one had been bedfast for a year. Only within the past week had he heard about a third one-eyed man, but locating him had proved to be the problem. He would do more searching, and sooner or later he would find the man. Perhaps he had kept out of sight after the raid to confuse any searchers.

Annabelle snuggled up to him and let her hand wander to his leg where she rubbed higher and higher. The movement disturbed Captain Bleeker's concentration and at last he roared in delight and pushed the woman flat on the bed. She rolled over on her stomach and shrilled in pleasure as he spanked her naked bottom. With every slap his need rose higher and higher.

He would find this one-eyed man! He would. Bleeker was determined that rebel blood must be spilled to balance out the deaths among his crew.

Annabelle squealed and jumped astride of him and pushed him on the bed, then began undressing him.

March soon turned into April, and Harriet felt the days dragging. Malcolm Trotter was now somewhere on his way to China, and her social life had come to a total stop, but she had expected that. It would take a while for the eligible young men of Boston to realize that she was back in the available category. A notice appeared in the *Speaker* that one Mr. Malcolm Trotter had sold his diamond and gem business and was returning to England. The new owners would retain the shop in the same building. One of the young Freedom Fighters who had been working for John Hancock took over the store and kept it open, selling a few items, but not restocking anything. All profits went to the organization's treasury. In a year or so they would phase out the store and sell all the gems.

By the middle of April the weather broke and the sun shone gloriously for a week. The false spring couldn't last but it was fine while it was there. The political front still stormed and boiled.

Ben put in more time working with the Committee on Correspondence, which exchanged and circulated outrages by the British anywhere in the Thirteen, and generally hit hard on the point that all the colonies must stand together, and that an attack on one would be an attack on all. If they did not bind themselves together, England could easily beat them one at a time.

Now Ben was pacing his big office. It was late at night, and Dr. Warren sat across the desk from him. Both had been writing and rewriting and at last Dr. Warren held up a document and gave a small cheer.

"Ben, I think we have it. This time it has exactly the right flavor; it is firm, yet polite, it calls the devil by his full name, and lays out exactly what we expect for those who will go along with the sense of the proposal. I think we have something here that will work, that will be passed and that may someday be an historic document."

Ben stopped walking and looked over the final draft that Dr. Warren gave him. He held it near a bull's eye lamp and read it through.

"Yes, Joseph, yes. And I like the title: 'The

Solemn League and Covenant.' Now if we can just get approval by all thirteen colonies.''

"I hope we can, Ben. If we don't, you and I did a damn lot of work for nothing. But it is a real weapon we can use against England. It is a pledge that they will listen to. Hit somebody in his pocketbook and it gets an immediate reaction.''

"Of course, Joseph, this is going to hit John Hancock and me right in the purse as well.''

"Yes, but only for a short time. Three months at the most should do it.''

"If everything goes right.''

"How can it fail? All the covenant does is get a pledge from each of the Thirteen Colonies that if we need to, and call for it, all Thirteen will cut off all imports from England, and all exports to England. It is an economic club that we can shake at the British, and they will quake in their boots. Think what the big shippers in London will do as soon as we start turning their loaded ships around. They'll come down on Parliament like a herd of half-starved wolves!''

"True, Joseph, true. I only hope we can make our own people here see the wisdom of this reasoning.''

At the next meeting of the Freedom Fighter's Council on Monday, April 18, Ben and Dr. Warren laid out the Solemn League and Covenant for the other members. They had just begun to discuss it when Jonathan Clark held up his hand for quiet. He tip-toed to the door, opened it carefully and stared down the dark steps from the third floor. Lewis Lynch followed him with one of the bull's eye lamps and shone the light down the stairs.

"Don't move, either of you!" Lynch roared. "Hands against the wall, up high!"

Lynch went down the steps carefully, his flintlock pistol in his right hand.

"Mr. Lynch, it's us, don't shoot!" A voice came from below.

"What?"

"Robert Rutledge and David. Don't shoot!"

A moment later Lewis saw that it indeed was the twin Rutledge boys he had known for years. He told them to go back down the stairs and called for Ben and the others to come down.

Lewis sat watching the two young men as the others trooped into the living quarters.

"How did you get in through a locked door?" Lynch asked sharply.

David held up a key. "With this, Mr. Lynch. There are only five types of locks generally used in Boston. With those five keys, you can open ninety percent of the locks if the door isn't bolted."

Ben and Harriet came into the room and Ben tried to hold his anger inside.

"Just what are you boys doing here? Why did you break and enter into this business?"

David chuckled.

Robert felt so frightened he was almost sick. "We saw you and Harriet go to a meeting, and we got curious. You never say what your Monday night meetings are about, so we tried to find out. We followed you and when the lights went out down here, we tried David's keys and found one that worked so we came in. Then we heard voices upstairs, and we were going to come up and say hello."

"You certainly had no right to break into this establishment. That's a serious legal, a criminal, offense. Also, Robert, curiosity can get you killed, do you know that? This is not a game, it is a serious business. And I want both of you to apologize to Mr. Clark for breaking in here."

David had been looking at the people assembled. Dr. Warren, and Jonathan Clark, his father and Lewis Lynch, all of whom he knew were strong, outspoken rebels. He didn't know the fifth man. This must be what they suspected.

"Father, is this some kind of a meeting of the officers of the Freedom Fighters?" David asked.

Ben lifted his brows. "Now whatever gave you that idea?"

"It's true, isn't it? That's the only thing I can think of that could mean so much to you. It doesn't matter, I really don't want to join. I don't want to be shot at, but my brother does. He's been wanting to be a Freedom Fighter ever since he heard about them."

"Please, Father, let us join you," Robert said.

Ben turned and scowled, motioning both boys

toward the front door. "Now, listen, you two. I want your word of honor that you'll say nothing to anyone about seeing us here tonight. Also I want you to forget all about this. If I see someone from the Freedom Fighters, I'll ask them if they are looking for any volunteers, which I doubt. Now, both of you apologize to Mr. Clark, then go out the front door and directly home. We'll talk about your unpardonable behavior later."

"Yes, Father," Robert said.

David paused, faced his father, and announced, "From a rational point of view, I agree with your strong stand for independence, and I applaud it. But I really don't want to join the group. I'm more interested in the political side of the struggle than the military. Good night, Father."

The boys gave their apologies to Clark and went out the front door.

That evening the six of them decided that they must begin meeting at various times, and at different locations. If the boys could trace them here, why couldn't a British spy?

The council approved the Solemn League and Covenant. Dr. Warren was to urge Sam Adams to take it to the Boston Committee on Correspondence for adoption. Copies of the resolution would be sent to all twelve Colonial Legislatures and several cities and Committees or Correspondence with the hope that they all would adopt it as soon as possible.

Ben drove home with Harriet. He admitted to himself he was still excited over the potential of the Covenant, but uncertain whether it would pass everywhere.

And the twins. What on earth was he going to do about them?

Chapter Six
AN END AND A BEGINNING

Lot sat beside the fire in his strongly built trapper's cabin on a tributary of the mighty Allegheny. In four seasons here he had created a whole new life for himself. Four years ago he had been an unhappy slave in the home of a Mr. Edmund Cunliffe in Boston town. One night when the master had a serious bout of drinking, and Lot knew he would be drunk for two or three days, Lot had gathered up his small pouch of money, borrowed a second rate horse from his master and ridden into the West. He had seen free blacks in Boston, and vowed that he would be free, too. He had ridden by night and hidden by day, and did not rest until he was out of the colony of Massachusetts and far into the West toward the great inland seas. One day he struck up a friendship with a trapper who taught him the trade, and they began working their way to the trading post.

While they slept one night a pair of murdering bandits killed Lot's new friend, and thought they had split Lot's head as well, but Lot survived and went after them. He found them not far ahead, and challenged them, and both died. Lot recovered the horses and mules, but nothing would bring back his friend.

Lot rode into the trading post, sold the furs, bought new equipment and a supply of food and struck out to locate a virgin land where he could trap and live and be a free man.

He had found this untouched valley on the upper reaches of the powerful Allegheny and settled, building a first rough shelter against a giant fallen tree. Later he expanded the shelter into a kind of half cabin, half lean-to, with the big log as one wall. He pounded four inch logs into the ground to make a new outer wall, put on a roof of strong logs and covered it all with dirt and a solid sod roof. Inside he scooped out the floor to make the enclosed space high enough to stand in. There was a fine creek running past the door. He even had two fireplaces, one for cooking and one for heating, each with its own smoke hole in the roof.

The first year there he found an Indian girl who supposedly had done some great evil in her tribe and had been brought by the chief and placed on a large rock in the snow and left to die. Lot found her and carried her, half frozen, to his cabin, warmed her, nursed her and saved her life. Gradually she decided that she did not want to die. Lot guessed she was no more than fifteen, and he did not know whether he now had a daughter or a wife. She taught him where edible berries grew, where they could find good roots, and which bark made the best tea. Soon he had a wife.

Each spring he took his furs to the Ft. Oswego trading post where they spoke French and flew British flags, but Lot did not care what flag they used as long as they bought his furs. It was a time to talk to other trappers, buy new supplies and food, and bring home something for his squaw and son.

Lot watched his squaw chewing a deerskin to make it soft. He knew he was a lucky man to have her. Many times she had saved him from bad mistakes in the wilderness, and she made his life much more pleasant, and complete. His son was called Jumper, and was now over a year old. He was even walking some. At the trading post last year he heard that the settlers were pushing westward, but he knew that it would be twenty years before they found his sheltered valley.

Now spring was coming fast. The heavy snow cover was fading, and soon the pelts would be worthless as the animals began to shed. He could trap only a few more weeks.

Lot rose from his bed of leaves and dry moss and put on his great coat made of the skin of a brown bear. He would not need the snow shoes this time, since he was on the close line today.

His winter's work would soon be done.

Lot came out of his cabin, closed the door and walked away fifty feet, then looked back. The dwelling blended well into the surrounding landscape. The only clue that there was a cabin there was the smoke coming from the roof. Grass and weeds had grown up around the sides, and from fifty yards away even an Indian could walk right past it.

He was not thinking about savages as he worked along his trap line, only wondering who would be at the jamboree this spring when he took in his packs of pelts. It was always a week-long celebration. Lot rounded a bend in the creek and ahead of him stood three Indians, a long range hunting party, he judged by the equipment they carried. They must be on the third day from their lodges looking for venison. He could not turn back. They had seen him. Lot made the usual greetings and peace signs, then walked up to them.

They stared at him. Lot was accustomed to stares. Most Indians had never seen a black man before. He made more signs, then tried out a few words of the Seneca tongue he had learned from his squaw.

The Indians understood the words, looked at each other quickly, and he wondered if he had made a mistake. They asked in sign language where he was from and he made the signs for far, far away.

They shook their heads, indicating he had

traps and no long-range provisions.

· He tried to tell them he was a trapper who was moving on. They seemed to understand and he made the peace sign again and continued up his trap line. He turned into the deeper woods and watched the three red men from behind a big tree. They talked, then seemed to argue. One came forward, following Lot's trail. The others went on each side, in what would be a three pronged attack. They wanted to surprise him so he couldn't use his pistol. Lot had no idea why they wanted to kill him, but now he knew they did.

Lot avoided Indians when he could. Some of the red men would spot a trapper and follow him back to his cabin, kill him, and make off with his pack animals and everything in his shack they could haul off. They never took the pelts; rather, they looked for fire sticks, horses and mules.

Now, Lot ran toward a natural fort where he could shelter between a ten foot high cliff at his back and a big log in front for protection. He plowed through snow to the spot, jumped behind the log and quickly dug out the damp primer in his flintlock and filled it with fresh, dry powder. Then he waited for the savages. Lot crouched behind the log and lifted his head to look over it just as the first Seneca came into view. The Indian darted back out of sight and sent an arrow into the log two inches below the top. Now Lot wished that he had brought his musket instead of his flintlock pistol, which was a short range weapon.

Lot lay motionless in the snow for an hour without hearing a sound from the Indians. At last he lifted his head and peered over the top of the log. Directly ahead, not twenty yards, he saw the brush move, then it moved again. One redskin was there, but Lot couldn't make out a target. His eyes swept the land in front of him. There were dozens of hiding places.

Suddenly one Indian stood up in front of him in plain sight. Lot brought up his flintlock and started to sight in on him when he realized something was wrong. No Indian would do that unless . . . . Lot rolled to one side, pulling his long hunting knife as an Indian landed where Lot had lain. The Indian held a six-inch knife and slashed toward Lot. The black man lifted his longer weapon and lunged at the red man, but pulled back, slashed him on the arm, jerked his weapon back and kicked forward with his boot, catching the Indian's forearm and snapping it with a crack. The Seneca screamed and looked down at his arm just as Lot drove the big knife into the Indian's chest.

Lot turned and brought up his pistol, firing it two feet from a charging red man, blasting a hole in his chest and killing him instantly. Lot felt blood on his arm, and saw where a knife had slashed through the heavy bearskin coat. He dropped to the ground behind the log, pushing one dead Indian out of the way and watched the area in front of him. Lot saw nothing else move. Quickly he reloaded his flintlock, rammed the ball home and waited.

Four hours later, when dusk fell and quickly turned into night, Lot left the place of death and broke a new trail back to his cabin. He would look at his wounded arm as soon as he got home. Lot moved in quick spurts, then stopped and listened. He changed directions and back tracked, then surged ahead again. Lot knew there could be another Indian out there watching him, trying to follow him in the darkness. Or the third red man might have left to return to his tribe and report the loss of two braves and to bring twenty with him to settle the matter.

For the first time Lot felt concern for his squaw and his son. He shouldn't have left them alone for so long. No, that was his fear talking. They had stayed alone for two weeks each time he went to the jamboree. Even so, Lot hurried. A mile downwind from his cabin he sniffed the wind, but could smell no smoke.

Lot began running. No smoke meant no fire, and no fire . . . .

He came to the rough door made of hewn branches and saw it standing ajar.

In a rush Lot drove into the cabin with flint-lock pistol. A savage, roaring scream of protest and anguish gushed from his mouth as Lot fell on his knees in front of a slashed and mutilated body. There was no question that she was dead. His scream of torment blasted out again as he saw his son lying in the heating fire, his small body broken, half charred and his head split open.

Lot lay in the cabin for two hours, sobbing out his heartbreak, cleansing his soul of his loss. Then he got up and went outside. The stars were brilliant in the cloudless sky. He found his shovel and slowly dug a grave. Gently he laid his two loved ones in the half-frozen ground, and covered them with a warm blanket of soil. He camouflaged the surface so no one would be able to find the bodies.

Before the moon set near midnight, Lot had gathered his belongings. Now he knew that the savages had come upon his smoke and found the cabin sometime shortly after he had left. They must have discovered the "X" burned on his squaw's wrists and knew that she was an outcast, so they had been required by tribal law to kill her and any issue. Then they came after him, tracking him, then circling in front. With him dead they would return to the cabin and take everything away on his animals.

Lot put his traps, his pelts, everything in the world that he owned on the mules, mounted his horses and began moving away from the Allegheny. He would leave the other traps rusting in the stream rather than risk running into the last Indian, or a whole scalping party that soon would be tracking him from the lodges of the Senecas.

Lot rode west down the trail. He would move

as far as he could by sunup, then stop for a quick meal and press on, ever forward into the wilderness. He must leave the Seneca lands far behind for now he was a marked man, he was one who had saved and harbored a forbidden woman.

Lot would go far, far to the West. Beyond the inland seas beyond the flat lands he had heard spoken of to the great mountains where the valleys were always green. Lot would stop at the jamboree and sell his winter's catch, buy salt and a few new traps and strike out traveling light across the great unmarked wilderness to a virgin land where Lot Edes Freeman could build another life for himself, and perhaps start a new family and where he would forever be free.

Chapter Seven
A SPY IN YOUR EYE

During March and April of 1774, while Ben and the Freedom Fighters watched and waited for some retaliation to the Boston Tea Party, Parliament was reacting with shock and anger to the tea tax rebuff.

Parliament enacted the first of what was to be a series of laws called the Coercive Acts, which were designed to strangle the port of Boston and bring the rebel bastion to its knees in quick surrender.

It wasn't until a month after the acts' passage that ships coming to Boston brought the news and the colonists found out what the Tea Party was to cost them. Ben looked at a report in the *Speaker* newspaper of Wednesday, May 11, and shivered in anger. The article outlined the Boston Port Act, which closed the port of Boston to all commerce, setting up a British blockade to begin June 1.

To carry out the closure, General Thomas Gage was commissioned as military governor of the colony of Massachusetts. General Gage was also the commander-in-chief of all British forces in North America.

Ben threw down the paper in anger. It was divide and conquer, exactly what he had warned the other colonies about. It was an effective and powerful tactic. Boston would be starved out. His own business would be shut down here, possibly ruined. His ships would have to operate out of New York and other ports. There would be a lot of work for the Freedom Fighters to do. But where should they start? And what about the Covenant that he and Dr. Warren had worked so hard for and in which they had so much faith?

They received word quickly from New York on the Covenant. The New York Legislature and town meetings had admired Massachusetts' spunk and anger, but in all conscience they said they wanted to have some kind of a joint meeting with the other colonies before taking such a drastic step.

Soon messages came back by couriers from other colonies. Within two weeks it was obvious that the long sought total embargo against the British would not take place. However the reports did contain cause for optimism. Almost every one of the couriers from the legislatures, assemblies and cities, said they would like to see a congress, a Continental Congress of all the colonies, to discuss this and other problems. It was suggested that they all meet in Philadelphia in September of 1774.

Ben had fought for the Covenant, but now it was defeated. He and Dr. Warren took some satisfaction in the emergence of a Continental Congress which had long been hoped for by those men who saw the Thirteen Colonies as cooperating against the British. Their call for the passage of the Covenant had stirred the first great step toward unity.

That evening, May 11, Ben and Dr. Warren and about twenty other rebel and assembly leaders met in the back room of the King's Road Tavern. There was much talk of fighting the blockade.

"This is an open act of undeclared war!" Ben thundered. "Before we rouse ourselves, British ships will be firing at our cities, our women and children! I say we must arm ourselves now and fight. We should attack the British garrison here and on Castle William as quickly as possible before any more troops can be landed. We are at war with a powerful enemy, and we must strike now while we still can!"

Another voice was raised, saying that a slower course might be needed.

Then Sam Adams took the floor. "Gentlemen, no one is more anxious than I to begin our conflict with the British. However, it seems to me that we need to wait and see exactly how the British enforce the blockade. Now, I appreciate

Ben's call for fighting, but I don't think that our people are ready yet for open warfare. The people are not angry enough. Once they become furious, once England trips the wrong trigger somewhere, then the people of these Thirteen Colonies will rise as one man and drive the British into the sea.''

The talk ranged from these points of view to several others, including those of shopkeepers who would be ruined by the blockade, to shippers, to the working men.

At last Dr. Warren got the attention of the men, and while fresh pitchers of ale and warm beer went the rounds of the tables, he laid out a moderate course.

"Gentlemen, we must watch and wait. I must agree with Mr. Adams that we simply aren't ready to declare war on England. We now have the Continental Congress coming up, we need that tool of unification, that corporate body. We fight them, but we fight them another way. Right now we need to be working out alternate sources of supply to feed the people of Boston who will be out of work. Also we'll need to establish better land roads. Do you realize there is not one good wagon road from Boston to New York? Just feeding our people is going to be a monumental job. I say we do what we can right now to lay in food supplies before the blockade goes into effect on June first.''

That seemed to sum up the thinking of the group and the men began drifting away. As Ben and Dr. Warren walked out to their rigs, Ben shook Dr. Warren's hand.

"You capped it just right, Joseph. I was a little fast on the trigger, I guess. I can see now that we will have a shooting war, and perhaps sooner than we expect, but we can't push it, we can't make it happen. I'm going to ask both boys if they want to join our forces. I'd rather they have good Freedom Fighter training and learn correctly before they are thrown into some untrained militia unit and get pushed into a battle somewhere."

The next day Ben invited both boys to join, but only Robert did so. David agreed to fight, but only when the need became urgent.

Ben was working fourteen hours a day in his office trying to plan his business move to New York. He loaded one of his ships with the vital business records and sent it to New York where a trusted man set up shop. Ben had a little over two weeks to complete the move and he knew it would be only a partial success, but he had to get as much of the business situated in New York as he could before the British frigates moved in.

Later that day Lewis came in with some papers for him to sign, and Ben looked up at him and wrinkled his brow in amazement. Lewis had on a new suit of clothes, quite proper breeches, knee high white stockings, black shoes and a waistcoat over a vest and a white shirt. Ben hadn't seen Lewis so dressed up since Sadie Wythe's funeral.

Ben took the dispatch from Lewis and motioned to the chair beside his desk.

"You'll be wanting to come to New York with me," Ben said, sure that the former British royal marine would go.

Lewis sat stiffly, unused to the waistcoat. He put one hand to his patch and moved it slightly, then gazed at Ben from his one good eye.

"Aye, that's me trouble, sir. I'm not knowing right now just which way the wind is blowing for me. You see, I've met this snip of a girl, I have, and it seems that she takes a fancy to me. I never thought that I'd be so . . . . Sir, it's a bit of a struggle for me to decide right now."

"Two weeks is all we have, Lewis, before the port closes. After that it'll be a long ride on some sway-backed horse to New York. General Gage moves his men-of-war into position on June 1." Ben laughed softly. "So it's a woman, is it? Well, if she's a proper sort, I'm more than happy for you. Take your time, Lewis, nobody deserves a good woman more than you do."

Lewis nodded and went out the door and through the next big office area that was now almost deserted, many of the desks and cabinets gone as well. Lewis knew that a number of Ben's people were already in New York setting up the office. Now it was almost his turn to decide.

At the front door of Rutledge & Rutledge he went outside and walked quickly along the street that was warmed now by a friendly May sun. Splashes of colored flowers showed in window boxes and in pots along the sidewalks. It would be summer before long.

Lewis was well aware that he had only met the girl two days ago, and he had taken to her at once. The strange part was she seemed to like him as well. He had no idea how he really felt about her. How could he after only two days? Could he know after two weeks? He had to try. The girl's name was Annie, and she was pretty, youngish, and was well shaped. At first he wondered why she took such a shine to him, but after she told him her story he understood. She was frightened and lonely.

Annie had lately come on a ship from London where her mother had passed on, leaving only the most meager of an inheritance, little more than passage money and enough to secure a room here for a few weeks. She had hoped to gain employment as a maid or perhaps a governess in one of the wealthy Boston homes, she said. In her dear mother's last effects she had found a small letter written a few days before she died. It included the name, Lewis Lynch of Boston town, and only said that he was a former royal marine, and he might still be working at Rutledge and Rutledge. As soon as she came to port she had looked up Mr. Lynch with the hope that he might be an old friend of her mother's who could help her find employment.

But Lewis told Annie Conners that he had never known a Connors in London, and certainly no lady old enough to be this girl's mother. Besides, he said he came from the north country.

At first he looked upon her as an unfortunate. He loaned her ten dollars and said he would ask around to see whether he could obtain a position for her. They arranged to meet at a fresh foods market two days later, and that was where Lewis was headed now. He saw her standing by a counter heaped with foodstuffs. She wore a pretty print frock and smiled when she saw him.

"Well, Mr. Lewis Lynch, you can call me proud! I got meself a position, I did. As companion to an old lady who needs some help around the kitchen. I've got a nice room and all, and I'm eating and she even bought me this dress."

"Annie Connors, you're an enterprising girl, you are." Lynch said. "All this and only four days in the country. Let's celebrate with a dinner."

They went to a small tavern, the Oxen Pair, which had one room reserved for ladies and dinner guests, and ate heartily on a meal of country stew, and slabs of fresh brown bread and unsalted butter washed down with mugs of beer. After the meal they went outside.

"Could I see you to your new home, Annie?"

"That would be most thoughtful of you, Mr. Lynch," she said, beaming a smile at him the likes of which Lewis had not seen from a pretty girl for more years than he cared to remember. He felt almost boyish striding along beside this attractive girl. She must be just over twenty, and he was only thirty-four, not too much of a difference. Lewis chided himself. What in the world was he thinking of?

They walked for fifteen minutes through the streets and lanes of Boston, then entered the less prosperous section where she turned in at a small white clapboard house. At the door she looked up.

"Thank you so much, Mr. Lewis, for seeing me home safely. I'm really very lucky to have a strong man like you to protect me in a strange land. I appreciate having an arm I can lean on sometimes. Really, this country is all so frightening." She paused. "Oh, my manners! Please come in and meet Mrs. Mayberry. I'm sure she'll want to see you."

Before Lewis could protest she opened the doors and drew him inside. They walked through the four rooms but Mrs. Mayberry was not there.

"Oh, she said something about having a meeting to go to this evening at the church."

Annie stepped in close to Lewis and leaned against him.

"Mr. Lynch, I thank you for being so gallant and taking me out to dinner and seeing me home. I really do appreciate it."

She reached up and kissed his cheek.

For just a moment Lewis wanted to put his arms around her and pull her close and kiss her, but he resisted the temptation. She was a lady, he couldn't do that.

Then the moment was over, lost forever as they moved apart and walked to the door. She tugged at his waistcoat.

"Mr. Lynch. I had me a boy friend in London, and he was kind and gentle, but he got pressed into naval service. He used to give me a little kiss good night. Would it be all right if you did it now, to make me feel all safe and secure here?"

Lewis glanced down at her standing close to him. There was a touch of homesickness and fear in her eyes. He reached for her gently, saw her close her eyes and he kissed her lips tenderly, then with a little more pressure, and pulled away, not wanting to at all.

"Oh, my, Mr. Lynch. That was lovely, and I thank you. Would you come to dinner here tomorrow night? I could cook a chicken and some nice fish. Would you like that?"

Lewis could hardly talk. He hadn't kissed a pretty girl that way for so long he couldn't remember. He bobbed his head and furiously tried to gather his scattered thoughts.

"Yes, Miss Annie, I'd be pleased to come." Lewis turned and bolted for the door before she could change her mind. He hurried half way down the long block, then turned and stared at the little white house. He'd never forget what it looked like!

The next day, Lewis told no one about his small miracle. He treasured the very thought of it. He kept her in his mind no matter what else he was doing. Toward the middle of the afternoon, Mr. Rutledge called him to his office.

"Well, Mr. Lynch, I must admit that yesterday as I was coming from the docks, I saw you squiring a most pretty young girl down the street. She had looks of a lady about her. Was that your lady friend?"

Lewis grinned and laughed and Ben couldn't remember seeing him quite so pleased and happy. He told Ben about the small affair, and Ben slapped him on the back and told him what a lucky man he was. He warned Lynch not to forget that he still wanted him to go to New York, but if this made the difference, to be sure to let Ben know quickly. They parted and Ben frowned.

When Ben saw the pretty girl on Lynch's arm he knew at once that she was not from one of the brothels. Those women were not in the habit of flaunting themselves with their customers in broad daylight. Then who? Lewis Lynch was not an ugly man, but his eye patch frightened most women, and over the years he had not taken care of his person as well as he might. As far as Ben knew, Lewis had not been involved with a single woman during the past seven years he had been in Boston.

Ben had cautiously observed the pair and followed them to the white frame house, had carefully written down the number on the door. That same evening before dusk he had a man watching the place, making notes of anyone coming or leaving and trying to get the girl's name and background from neighbors.

By midday next, Ben knew that her name was Annie Connors, as she had told Lewis. But he had disturbing reports of a sailor arriving at her door, presenting her with a letter and waiting outside for her reply. He left a short time later with a letter tucked in his jacket. A sailor was a sailor, but the lookout did not know whether he was American or British. Ben held his tongue, talked to Lynch, and did not tip his hand that he had been watching the house.

That evening Lewis ate fried chicken and worked on a huge slab of whitefish that was indeed baked to perfection together with four vegetables, a very good porter and delicious fools and trifles that left him licking up every bit of custard and whipped cream.

"Miss Connors, this is delicious," Lewis said. He leaned back in the chair and watched her blushing daintily, the color spreading up from her neck. His eye again caught her low cut dress which showed the very tops of her creamy breasts and an urging rose up in Lewis that he had thought could never recur.

"Let's just leave the things and sit by the fire, would you like that, Mr. Lynch?"

"Indeed I would."

There was a big rug on the floor in front of the hearth and Annie sat there, reaching out to the fire to warm her hands.

"I love sitting on the floor, watching a fire," she said. "It reminds me of my childhood back in London."

He sat beside her, awkward now in such close quarters. His eyes were drawn to the dark shadows between her breasts and his need kept building.

"Mr. Lynch, my father was a military man, and I know how you must miss the excitement, the travel,the camaraderie of the military life." She moved, exposing even more of her bosom for him to see. Lewis cleared his throat.

"Miss it? Oh, no, I have another group I'm working with." For a moment he almost told her about the Freedom Fighters! He'd never done anything like that before. But he caught himself in time and hurried on. "I work at Rutledge & Rutledge, and there's always lots of excitement there. The ships, the ports, going to far-off places."

He wondered if she realized how close he had come to telling what he should not. Of course she wouldn't even care. He took a deep breath and looked at her face, not her breast.

She was smiling. "Mr. Lynch, I do admire you for striking out in the new world. A new beginning. That's what I need. I . . . . I must admit that I didn't leave London with any fanfare. I had been accused of stealing, so I got on a boat as fast as I could. I simply did not steal anything. Now I need to find a man who is big and strong, and honest, like you, Lewis Lynch, who will promise to take care of me, to look after me."

She leaned against him and his arm came around her. She looked up, and a moment later he was kissing her, a passionate, hungry kiss. When their lips parted she sighed.

"Oh, Mr. Lynch, but that was nice. Once more?"

They kissed again and she moved her breasts against his chest and it was more than Lewis could stand. He groaned deep in his throat, caught one of her breasts and began to rub it.

Now Annie moaned through the kiss, and slowly they toppled over backward on the big bearskin rug, still locked in their embrace.

She caught his hand and pushed it under the bodice of her dress. "Oh, yes, darling Lewis, yes, make me feel just so fine. Make me feel good all over!"

Three times that night they made love, and Lewis Lynch greeted the just risen sun as he came out of her house early the next morning.

Lewis shook his head in amazement. Annie was quite a girl. During the hours of bed play he discovered that Annie was not quite the pristine lady that he had at first thought. Some of the tricks she knew could come only from a highly traveled man, or from some woman with considerable experience. Either way he was not worried about it. He was happy. He would take her to dinner that evening at the fanciest hotel in town.

That day Lewis didn't get to work until after noon and found a notice waiting for him to go see Mr. Rutledge at once.

Ben was approving a final list of ships that would home port in New York, and which ones would move to other ports. It was a staggering job. He looked up when Lewis came in and asked him to wait a few minutes. When the distribution was done, Ben sent the two men who had been helping him out of the office and turned toward Lewis.

"We've been friends for a long time now, Lewis. You know I wouldn't do anything or say anything unless I was extremely concerned and I thought the organization was in danger."

"Yes, I understand that, Mr. Rutledge. Have I done something wrong?"

"I don't think so, Lewis, but the chance is so potent that we do have to talk about it."

"Yes, sir."

"Last evening you were with a Miss Annie Connors. You left her rooms about five-thirty a.m. This does not concern me, or didn't, until I realized who her visitor was at seven this morning."

Lewis was choking back his protests. Ben had no right to spy on him, no right at all. But he heard the part about the next visitor, and he held his tongue and waited.

"Lewis, just after seven this morning, a captain in the uniform of His Majesty's Navy went into the house, let himself in with his own key.

His name is Horatio Bleeker, the captain of the *East Indian*."

Lewis slumped in his chair, his hands over his face.

"Oh, God . . . . Oh, no, it can't be!"

"It is, Lewis. Bleeker has been living in that apartment for the past six months, the neighbors tell us, and he is there almost every night. He makes no secret of the fact he lives there."

"And the girl?"

"Better known as Annabelle to her neighbors, she is from London, came about eight months ago. She had no means of support and evidently is living off the bounty of her friendly Captain Bleeker."

"They trapped me, they ambushed me. She's a damned spy!"

"I'm afraid so, Lewis. Did she find out anything?"

"No, I'm certain. I almost slipped once, but didn't. And she did ask me some prying questions. Would it be about the ship attack?"

"Yes, we're sure. Bleeker is probably the one behind it all. I've contacted the other two one-eyed men in town, and both said there were Britishers prying about, asking questions about them. You must have looked like the best prospects." Lewis stood and paced to the window, then back to the desk and to the window again. Ben sat, letting him think it through.

"At least this answers some questions," Lewis said. "I know I'm not a handsome man, but she seemed to take to me, right away. And she said my eye patch didn't bother her, not a bit. I should have known, then. It means she's a whore who took me to bed, and not the other way around."

"I'm sorry, Lewis. But she was careful enough and worried enough about going slowly, to take five days before she seduced you. That's a long time in her league. How do you feel?"

"Like I lost something, a little puffed up pride, I'd say, by the way my gut aches. But I'll get over it. Sometimes I can see these things better with only one eye. Well, now, Mr. Rutledge. What shall we do next? What about our Annabelle?"

"Why, next, Lewis, we trap the trapper!"

That afternoon, on Ben's suggestion, Lewis paid a small boy to take a bouquet of flowers around to Annabelle's house. Lewis called for her promptly at six-thirty with one of Ben's chaises behind a high-stepping black.

"I borrowed it from a friend," Lewis said. "This is going to be a grand occasion and deserves the best transportation."

Annie had taken some of the flowers from the bouquet and pinned them to her shoulder. She looked charming. A painful barb tore through Lewis's heart as he handed her into the rig, then stepped up beside her. She was beautiful, by far the prettiest woman he had ever known, or touched, or made love to.

"Where are we going to have dinner?" she

asked.

"In the very finest dining room in all of Boston," Lewis said, and slapped the reins on the black, moving him down the street at a canter.

He drove for ten minutes, and pulled up at the outskirts of Boston, near the thin neck of land connecting the peninsula with Roxbury. She had not noticed where they were going, now she looked up in question.

"Where is the hotel? This ain't no hotel." A trace of anger and fear touched her voice.

"True, small girl, very true," Lewis said. "But we have to change vehicles to get to it."

"I ain't for sure moving out of this damn rig!"

"Lass, you've lost some of your polish. A bit of the cockney street urchin is showing through."

"Take me back to town, you blithering, one-eyed idiot!"

"Soon. Now step down and we'll continue our trip."

She wouldn't, so Lewis reached in, picked her up and carried her to the edge of the bay on the harbor side where he called out sharply. A longboat nosed in from the mists over the water and touched land. Lynch waded into the water, dumped the girl into the arms of two seamen who sat her on the seat between them, as Lewis pushed off and jumped on board the craft.

They rowed into the harbor toward the south end of the deep water, and soon Lynch saw her, a merchantman with two lighted lanterns forward swinging on an anchor chain. She was showing few lights, and from her movements, Lynch knew it was nearly high tide. She could sail at a moment's notice.

"I won't get on any damned ship," Annie said.

Lewis ignored her. They came alongside and Lewis stood, slung the girl over his shoulder like a sack of barley.

"Unless you want me to drop you into the bay, lass, you best hang on tight. We'll be on board in a jiffy." Then Lewis went up the rope ladder to the deck and swung on board.

He dropped the girl on the weathered boards and a lantern appeared casting a shadowy light over her and the others on deck.

Ben Rutledge stared down at her and shook his head.

Lewis Lynch scowled. "Wench, you should know that when you get into the game of spying, the rewards may be sweet, but the penalty for being caught is a damn lot worse than a simple tongue lashing."

Dr. Warren watched her and his face was sad. "It does seem like a tragic waste, doesn't it? Such a pretty little girl who thought she could fool us."

Only Harriet Rutledge was angry. "Let's not waste any more time on her. Let's get the trial over with so we can hang her."

Chapter Eight
SUBSTITUTE HUSBAND

Annabelle Connors' bravado left her. She stared at them through tear-stained eyes.

"So help me, guv'nor, that's the slice of it. Sure, I been living with Captain Bleeker, a girl's got to keep some food in her belly. So maybe I did ask the one-eyed man a few questions, 'e didn't have to answer 'em."

They were in the captain's cabin where the light was better and Harriet held up both hands.

"That's enough, there you have it, gentlemen. She just admitted being a spy, so I see no need to continue."

The others nodded, Lewis, last of all. "Aye, it seems so, How could you do this, Annabelle?"

"I done nothing! Get away from me, you ugly one-eyed monster! Captain Bleeker was just trying to find out who blew up his ship. Treated that damn hulk better'n 'e did me."

"So it was all Bleeker's doing?" Ben asked.

"That's right. Bloody navy doesn't want anything to do with the damn Freedom Fighters, whoever they are. Bleeker wanted blood, an eye for an eye, 'e said.''

Harriet pounced on it again. "There you have it. She's admitted she's a spy again, and this is war. So let's hang her and drop her body out at sea.''

Dr. Warren shook his head. "Wait a bit, she might have something else to tell us. Did Bleeker have any orders? Are there more British ships coming? When will General Gage come to Boston?''

"I don't know, I was just concerned with a one-eyed man, I wanted to see if this one was the one on the raid. That was all.''

"Was I the right one, Annabelle?'' Lewis asked.

"You sure as hell was, mate, only I didn't know it till just tonight. With this bunch, you damn near got to be. I'll have a batch of names and faces to tell the captain about, sure as hell I will.''

"From the grave you mean?'' Ben asked.

The girl looked up quickly. "No, 'cause you ain't gonna kill me or hang me or nothing. You're not the bloody killing types, I can tell.''

Ben looked at Lewis. "Is that Dutch captain still of a mind to make a bargain?''

"Aye, sir, he is.''

"Then you might as well take her over. He'll be ready to sail in an hour.'' Ben looked at Annabelle. "Have you ever been a ship's whore, Annie? Well, you're about to. The captain will keep you as long as he's able, then he'll probably auction you off to the highest bidder. By the end of the year's voyage to South America, you'll have earned your freedom. The captain is a fair man, he'll stick to his word. By then who knows what might be happening in Boston town?''

The girl shrugged. ''It's better than dead, and I don't tend to get seasick.''

''And you won't spy for the British any more,'' Harriet said.

The following morning a runaway horse pulling a heavy chaise slammed into Captain Bleeker as he left his rig in front of a white clapboard house. The captain was seriously injured and was removed to Castle William in the bay where the British command had its hospital facility. The driver of the rig could not be found as his runaway kept right on going after the crash. The Freedom Fighter's Council members drew a sigh of relief and considered the matter closed.

Ben continued putting in long days at his offices making sure that everything was in order for the move. Half of his operation was already in New York and functioning. A picket ship was placed just beyond Castle William to warn any incoming Rutledge ships about the blockade. All edibles were brought ashore to stockpile for the coming blockade, and the empty ships were sent on to New York. Ben had a dozen ships return from his new headquarters loaded with barley, oats, potatoes, any foodstuffs that he could buy which would last for a good period of time. He had one warehouse partially filled in Boston, but he knew it would not be nearly enough.

The Committees of Correspondence around the Colonies shouted out the facts of the Coercive Acts as they became known in the Colonies. The Port Act was the worst for Boston, and the other committees wrote that when it went into effect with the blockade of Boston on June 1, the other cities and colonies would shower gifts and food on Boston.

The last week in May came and Harvard was closed for the summer. Robert went to the office and helped his father with the move. David preferred to stay at home and catch up on some reading. He also was well aware that Millie, the girl next door, was at home. They had talked once or twice recently and she had hinted that she would welcome him if he would come courting. David had only smiled and squeezed her hand and said perhaps that could be arranged.

All morning David had been at his books. Now he stood, stretched and went to the window which looked toward the Livingston house. Millie sat in her second floor window, reading. He raised the shade and watched her. A few moments later she saw him, waved, and then pointed toward the far back corner of their yards where they had met once before, in a patch of trees and brush.

Often as children they had played there. David smiled and went down the stairs and into the yard, working his way to the trees and then into them. He hurried to what had once been a crude rail fence between their properties, but which now had rotted and fallen down.

Millie Livingston sat on a rock that had been too large to move when they cleared the land. She looked up at him and smiled. Millie's skin was so fair that she couldn't be in the sun more than a half hour at a time without protection. Her eyes were a soft green, some said blue-green and her hair the color of freshly threshed wheat straw. Her nose was a little too large, and her eye brows so faint David could hardly see them. She was an attractive girl, not beautiful, but interesting and vital and just a little eager. She was well proportioned, David thought, now looking at her, but he wished her breasts were larger. He put his foot on the rock and grinned.

"What in the world are you doing here, playing hide-and-seek?"

"Yes, and you?"

She said it with a slightly defiant air which intrigued David more than ever. She had always bragged when they were little that she was going to marry David when she grew up. She never looked at Robert. It was always David and she could tell at once when they tried to use each other's names. Today she wore a going-to-meeting pink dress.

"I'm looking for a pretty girl. Does your

mother know you're out here?"

"Of course," she said. "But she doesn't know that *you* are off your leash."

"I've been untied for months now."

"Ever since you kissed me behind the church?"

"About then." He sat beside her.

At once she leaned against him. "David, don't you like me even a little bit?"

"Of course, I do, Millie. What a silly thing to say."

"But you haven't come courting, not once. And I told Mama I was so excited about your coming."

"If I come courting, then I can't kiss you." He bent and kissed her cheek, and she turned toward him. He kissed her lips and she clung to him. When it was over she leaned back.

"David, David, David. You are not supposed to sneak up on a girl and surprise her like that."

"But you liked it, didn't you?"

"Mother tells me that kissing is for married people. She says it leads to other things."

"But you liked it?"

"Yes, of course, but . . ."

"But a nice girl never says she likes it? Horsefeathers, all girls like to be kissed."

"Oh, and have you kissed all of the girls in Boston?"

Instead of answering her, he put his arms around her and pulled her tightly against his chest, then kissed her lips and watched as her eyes closed and she sighed.

She turned away from him after the long embrace and looked up. "You know I can't let you do that. Now let go of me!"

"Let go of you? You're the one holding onto me. I can't do what, kiss you? We've done more than that, remember?"

"No, David, I won't remember. That never happened and you are not a gentleman to mention it. That was just a weak moment and I got excited, besides, I was ill. Yes, that's it. I was ill and almost fainted and you didn't know it . . . and . . . and all."

He still held her close, now he reached down and kissed her nose.

"Stop that."

"I could go back to my room."

"No, David, you stay right here."

"Give me one of your best kisses, then I can stay."

She smiled and turned toward him, her lips touched his then parted so his tongue could push into her mouth, and she groaned in delicious response. As he held the kiss his hand worked between them and rested on her breast. She tried to shake her head in protest but he held her tightly as his fingers closed, cupping her breast.

David wondered if this were the time. Robert was down at the office, his mother went shopping. It was safe on his side of the fence. He held the kiss a long, long time, and rubbed her breasts more, then he came away from her.

"David, you shouldn't . . ."

He put his hand over her lips and helped her to stand.

"Come over here, that rock is too hard to sit on. The grass is much softer."

She looked at him, and when he nodded and kissed her lips lightly again, she turned and sat on the grass. He put his hands at once on both of her breasts and kissed her, and that's when he knew that this was the time.

They made love slowly, taking their time, because each knew no one would come looking for them. Afterwards they pulled their clothes back in place and sat with their arms around each other.

"I'll love you forever, David."

He kissed her in reply.

"I'll never love anyone else, David Rutledge. We are going to get married, aren't we?"

David watched her closely now. "Married? I'm not even out of Harvard. I can't get married yet."

She cried. He held her and petted her until she stopped.

"But what if I . . . I mean girls sometimes do get pregnant when they make love. I might. I have been seriously exposed, you know."

"You don't have a thing to worry about, I'm sterile."

"David, don't even joke about that."

A week later they met in the same place in the brush behind their houses. David caught her hand and led her to the grassy place where he had spread a blanket.

"You know what might happen here, Millie. So why did you ask me to meet you here again?"

"Because I wanted to talk to you . . . and see what would happen." She blushed. "David, don't you think a girl can like to do it, too? Well, this one can. I do."

She assured him that her mother was gone for the rest of the afternoon and no one else was home; anyway, they could see if anyone came their way from the house. So this time they undressed each other and lay down luxuriously on the blanket.

David fell on her hungrily, and he had just gained his satisfaction with a half dozen powerful hip thrusts when he looked up and saw the sturdy figure of Mrs. Livingston standing over him and Millie. David shouted in shock and anger, then rolled away from Millie, covering himself. Millie lay where she had been, a soft smile on her face.

"Now, David, darling, you are going to have to marry me. If you don't agree to it right now, my mother will go see your father tonight. Isn't that the way we planned it, Mother?"

Mrs. Livingston stared at David and the shirt that he had pulled over his crotch. She wet her lips, then at last looked up at his face and nodded.

"Yes, David. You will marry Millie within the next two weeks. I won't have a bastard grandchild on my hands!'' She shook her head in surprise and admiration. ''Millie, girl, you sure were right. Your David is a big stud who knows what to do with it all.''

That night, after everyone in the Rutledge household was sleeping, David got up, took a carefully packed carpet bag, his musket and a flintlock pistol and went down to the stable where he saddled his horse, a four-year-old mare, and walked her a block away from the house before he got on and rode toward the Boston neck and then turned west. He had no idea where he was going, or how he would get there. David wanted to find a tavern ten or twelve miles from Boston and spend the rest of the night. From there on he would let chance lead him. He certainly was not going to stay around Boston and be forced into a marriage with Millie Livingston.

Two days later when Jed Livingston heard the whole story, he approached Ben in the evening at his house. They discussed the episode, all told from Millie's point of view, but with Mrs. Livingston's testimony there could be little doubt that David was the guilty party. Jed put his ultimatum bluntly.

''Ben, your boy has ruined Millie. The only way to save her is to find the boy, bring him back and have a quick wedding. I don't know how we can do that quietly, but Ben, I hope we can. We've been friends for too long to let this come between us.''

Ben fired up his pipe, took a puff and put it down on a cherrywood secretary. He had been shocked when David left home. David had left a note explaining that he was being pressured into a marriage that he had no intention of making, and he simply had to vanish for a while.

Now Ben discussed the various possibilities, but none of the usual seemed practical.

"Jed, we don't know if the girl is pregnant or not, do we? If she isn't and we keep this all to ourselves, she still has a fine chance to marry and be happy. Why don't we wait and see?"

"And if she is with child, we'll have to arrange a hasty marriage, and then a five-month child for everyone to talk about? No, Ben, not for my girl. She's ruined and ruined proper, two times Millie told us about, and it could be more. She's pregnant, for sure, so it's up to you to make good. Your son has run off, but he'll be back, and when he shows his face I want you to grab him and get them to a preacher. It's the only thing I'll stand for!"

"Jed, I don't see how I can do that. David is almost twenty. He's a man, and he's old enough to make up his own mind about things like this. Remember when you were twenty years old, how you felt?"

"That's why he has to marry her. He'll settle down, it's going to be a good match. If you don't do it this way, Ben, you leave me no alternative. I'll go down to the city-house tomorrow and swear out a complaint of assault and rape against David. I'll let the law go after him."

"Jed, I hope you don't do that."

"Nothing else I can do, Ben. It's my family's honor at stake here."

Robert Rutledge stood at the entrance to the library where he could hear the men talking through the partly open door. He had heard it all, and he knew what had happened. He opened the door and walked in, cleared his throat so they both looked at him.

"Gentlemen, I have the perfect solution to your problem," Robert said.

Four days later Robert and Millie were married quietly. Robert was the happiest of the lot. He had loved Millie from afar ever since his first schoolboy crush, through the tongue tied stage when the lump in his throat was no match for the lump in his breeches. Millie accepted him as second best, knowing she could always pretend it was David lying beside her. Jed Livingston and his wife were satisfied.

Their daughter had married into ten times the money his small law practice produced and she was set for life. And it had been done with no scandal or gossip. Ben thought it was a terrible sacrifice Robert was making, but when Robert explained that he was glad to get Millie under any terms, Ben went along with it.

Now Ben concentrated on one crisis after another. The time was short before the blockade began. Willis Southgate would run the New York office for Ben. There was a small cove by

Strawberry Point, about a twenty mile horseback ride to the south, where Ben had arranged meetings every Saturday with a ship from New York. If there were any troubles or emergencies, he would go back on the ship and handle them, returning to the same point by ship when he could.

He had only a skeleton crew left in Boston, mostly to furnish foodstuffs to the markets and stores from his warehouse for as long as the supply would last. Ben had spearheaded a group in the Committee on Correspondence to start improvements and widening of a wagon road to Lynn, north of Boston, where it would be possible to land small boats or at least painters and longboats from merchantmen with vital foodstuffs. But there was no assurance that the British would allow even that. Plans were also made to lay out a passable road for wagons in both directions from Boston, north all the way to Salem and Marblehead, and south into Rhode Island to the port of Providence. For a hundred years the only highways Boston had needed were made of water. Now that roadway was blocked, and she had to look inland.

Boston realized the blockade was soon at hand. Ships of every size and shape streamed out of the port moving anywhere they could find a sheltered harbor: Salem, Marblehead, Gloucester, even around the Cape in New Bedford, and some all the way to New York.

General Thomas Gage arrived at Castle

William in Boston Harbor on May 1. But it was a week before the population knew he was there. He would be their "little" king after June 1, ruling the whole colony with military authority.

Ben was ready. Most of Boston was not, that June 1, 1774, a Wednesday. General Gage ordered the Customs House and commissioners moved to Salem, since they would have no work in Boston. He also changed the seat of the colony's government from Boston to Salem to make it more secure. Just after daybreak on June 1, a regiment of British grenadiers landed at Long Wharf, marched out King street and through several more blocks to the Boston Common where they encamped, setting up their long rows of tents on the green. Watchers from the tallest buildings on the waterfront reported two frigates patrolling the approaches to Boston Harbor. There would be no business done at the waterfront wharfs in Boston today.

Ben drove his chaise along the docks and stared toward Castle William. He had watched the British troops land, and for a moment wished he had been commanding a regiment of militia and Freedom Fighters to resist them.

The occupation went smoothly. The colonists watched in silence as the tent stakes were driven into the lawn. A few catcalls and slanderous shouts came, but the British troopers had heard much worse and ignored them.

During the first week, Ben watched the mood of the people slowly change from one of passive anger, to a more vocal, more demonstrative tone. Redcoats walking the streets were pushed, jostled, often crowded off walks. Some were spat upon, and sooner or later some of the Englishmen resisted. There were fights, more taunting of troops on guard duty and a few acts of theft and harassment at the troops' quarters on the common. The first week ended without any major trouble, then a big fight was reported among three civilians and four Redcoats. A complaint was filed and the Redcoats found guilty of assault and battery and sentenced to thirty days in jail. The civilians were not held.

Two days later General Gage removed the judge who heard the case and appointed a known Tory sympathizer. The new judge reversed the decision, quashed the sentence and dismissed the charges against the Redcoats. Boston fumed.

Then a problem arose that kindled hatred in the heart of every red-blooded Boston male. Rum supplies were running short. Taverns began limiting drinks to one per man. There was talk of lynching General Gage.

Some foodstuff staples usually brought in regularly by ship were running low. Shopkeepers set up a limit on certain goods, and the public understood and went along with them. Bostonians began to feel that they could stand anything the British navy could force on them and still come out cantankerous and ready to fight. It was the first real sign of an angry, united population that Ben knew the colonies needed before they could have a popular uprising—for independence.

The second week of the occupation passed and then word came from a British naval vessel that two new laws had been enacted by Parliament. They were printed and distributed and soon it hit the newspapers.

Ben looked at the reports in the *Speaker*:

"Two New Acts Harass Boston! King Spanks Boston for Tea Party" He read the story. "May 20, 1774. London. The British Parliament passed two new acts aimed at punishing the Colony of Massachusetts for her refusal to pay the illegal tax on tea. The first is called the Government Act, which provides that the King, and not the Massachusetts Assembly, has the power to appoint the Governor's council and all colonial judges. It also forbids all town meetings except to elect town officials.

"All Bostonians and Massachusetts citizens will bemoan this act, which turns the Governor's council into a sham and gives the Governor the right to name his own keepers, and his own conscience. The Act's provision for the appointment of all judges by the King concludes the point that any form of democratic representative government has been smashed by Parliament, and the Colony of Massachusetts is now a puppet of the King and must jerk arms and legs on his command.

"The second act is the Administration of Justice Act, and allows any accused to be sent to Nova Scotia or to England to stand trial if he thinks he can not get a fair trial in Massachusetts. It would let all soldiers, judges, appointees of the Crown and any Tory sympathizers to go to an 'impartial' jury where they could easily be acquitted of a just charge.''

Ben read on, seeing that the Boston Tea Party was becoming more and more expensive, but that in the long run it could fire the Americans to an anger hot enough to lead to war.

The Freedom Fighters met in their monthly training sessions to sharpen their shooting eyes. They picked up as much about fighting Indian fashion as they could, knowing how sharp would be the contrast to the standard British system of orderly rows of marching units. They watched and waited, and kept their muskets handy.

The militia became better trained as more men volunteered for duty as part time citizen-soldiers, and with the tutorial help of the Freedom Fighters, the militia began looking more like soldiers and less like weekend party goers.

Nothing was heard from David at the Rutledge household. He had simply vanished into the Massachusetts countryside. Robert and his bride moved into a house provided by Ben, and Robert took over a responsible job with the firm, handling many of the local problems, while his father was on his frequent trips to New York.

Each time Ben returned, he drove the streets in his rig and tested the temper of the population. Each week the people were more angry, more sullen, less able to put up with what they felt was continuing and expanding oppression by England, the country that was supposed to be protecting and nurturing them.

Soon, Ben thought. Soon, the people would be worked up to an explosive pitch and then there would be one spark and the whole colony would detonate into a people's war for independence.

Chapter Nine
TWO FOR ONE: YOU'RE DEAD

Robert Rutledge had put in a long day at the offices of Rutledge & Rutledge and it was nearly dark on this summer day as he started home. He had been unsuccessfully trying to trace a lost shipment of goods for a Boston merchant. It had gone either to Salem or New York, and Robert could find no manifest showing it in either place.

He rode his horse, Starfire, letting him walk home now, neither one in the mood for a fast ride or even a canter. Robert was in no rush to arrive home. Millie had turned depressed and angry, and each time he asked her if she were pregnant, she burst into tears and wouldn't talk to him for a day. He decided she must surely be with child and that this phase would be over soon.

However, as long as it lasted, it was extremely irritating.

Robert was passing an alley off Queen's street when he heard a muffled shout, then a scream that was choked off, apparently coming from the alley. He knew it was a woman, and a woman in desperate trouble. He wheeled Starfire around into the alley, trying to see through the gloom, but now the only light was a half moon sailing overhead.

Near the end of the blind alley he saw figures, and wished he had brought his flintlock. He often carried the pistol now. With all the Redcoats abroad with their muskets and bad tempers, a little equalizing firepower could keep him out of a bad situation. Robert rode up the alley and suddenly he saw a figure rise and lift something. Was it a musket? He leaned close to the neck of Starfire and charged the figure. A firearm exploded at close range, and Robert felt something hit the horse's neck and graze the back of his hand. Then he was upon the gunman before he could reload, and Robert saw Starfire's hooves strike the Redcoat and fling him to one side. The man had been a British Grenadier and Robert spotted another one ahead, rising from the alley floor. Robert tucked his left leg across the saddle as Lewis Lynch had taught him for a quick running dismount and he came to the ground six feet from the soldier who was fumbling with a musket. Robert surged forward with his momentum from the horse and in an instant he saw the girl on her back in the alley, the top of her dress ripped away, screaming her defiance at the Grenadier. The Redcoat had found his Brown Bess but couldn't bring its five feet of length into play quickly enough.

Robert dove at the soldier while he was still

on his knees, connecting with his shoulder and flattening the Grenadier. Robert rolled on over and came quickly to his feet. The Redcoat stretched toward his musket but Robert jumped toward him, kicked the Britisher in the side and then swung his booted foot hard at the Redcoat's head, connecting with his chin and snapping the Redcoat's head back sharply. The soldier crumpled to the ground and didn't move. His head set at a strange angle to his shoulders and a quick look showed Robert that the Redcoat's neck must be broken. At any rate he would not bother them any more. Robert turned toward the girl, who had come to her knees. She was still naked to the waist, her eyes wide as she watched Robert dispatch her tormentors. She reached out to him, and he caught her hand and lifted her to her feet.

"It's all over now, it's finished. Don't worry, I'll help you. Do you live close by?"

She nodded but couldn't speak yet. Robert watched her a moment, then began pulling her dress up to cover her and she turned her face away and finished the job as well as could be done. Robert did not know her.

"Where do you live?" he asked. "Can I take you home?"

She still couldn't speak, or wouldn't. She pointed down the alley, and Robert walked beside her, leading Starfire. When he came to the first soldier he paused, and checked him, but saw that the man's chest had been caved in from one of the hooves. He was plainly dead. Robert thought of taking the muskets, but decided not to. It was a serious offense these days to steal a British Brown Bess, and he knew he had little chance of doing it without being caught. He asked the girl if she wanted to ride, but she shook her head.

They hurried to the mouth of the alley, and the girl turned right. Almost at once Robert saw the man coming toward them.

"Minerva?" the man asked while still several yards away.

Robert saw the girl look up, then she was running, and the man caught her in his arms. She cried furiously and the man took a flintlock pistol from his belt and advanced on Robert.

"Sir, is this your daughter?" Robert asked.

"Indeed she is, and I should shoot you down right here!" the man growled. "What did you do to my poor Minerva?"

"Nothing, sir."

The girl grabbed her father's hand and pushed the pistol so it pointed away from Robert.

"No, not him. Two soldiers. He saved me."

"Then I thank you, sir. We'd better get away from here. I heard the musket shot, so others did too, perhaps the guards."

Before they could move, a horse galloped up, spotted them and the rider brought his horse to a halt in front of the three, his flintlock pistol out covering everyone.

"Who fired that shot? Did you fire it, sir?"

asked the young lieutenant of Grenadiers on the horse.

"No, I've not fired. Smell the bore, if you wish. What shot? We heard no shot here. I came to meet my daughter and thought this man had mistreated her, but it turns out to be only her imagination."

"Sir, there was a shot fired. We must find out who fired it, since we have a missing sentry in this area. We're searching for him."

"I've seen none of your soldiers."

"Since you display a weapon in the presence of an officer of His Majesty's Grenadiers, I'll have to ask you to come with me to speak to the captain."

"I'm afraid that's not either possible nor legal, sir," the girl's father said. "We're about to have our evening prayers."

Robert stepped into the stirrup and swung into his saddle. The officer turned to look at him closer now.

"You, young man. Who are you and where are you bound?"

"I'm going home from work. Is that illegal now, too?"

"No, sir. If we find nothing amiss here. You, too, will come to speak with the captain."

Robert watched the young officer carefully. When Robert consented with a nod, the officer lowered his weapon and put it back in its place in his belt.

"Well, then, if you three will walk ahead of

me, we'll get started." He turned, swinging his mount's head around, and momentarily blinding him to Robert. As he did, Robert dug his boots into Starfire's flanks, surging ahead. Robert's mount hit the officer's horse with its chest against the officer's leg, bringing a scream of pain from the Redcoat. As Starfire brushed alongside the other horse, Robert grabbed the Grenadier's arm and jerked him off his mount dropping him to the street.

"Run!" Robert shouted at the surprised man and his daughter. They turned and rushed off in opposite directions while the unhorsed lieutenant screamed in pain and anger as he searched on his hands and knees for his fallen pistol.

Robert spurred Starfire down the street, turned and raced up another, then kept riding hard until he came to the house he now called home and put the sweating horse away in the small barn. Robert had his handyman rub Starfire down well and cool him out. Then he went inside, ready to face another few hours of tight-lipped anger from his sullen wife. He now was sure Millie resented his "saving" her good name. It was clear that he must somehow win her love or live with her anger forever.

He thought briefly about his fight with the Lobsterbacks, but dismissed it until he realized that in the heat of the battle he had actually killed two men. Then when he thought about the confrontation with the lieutenant, he guessed that there was a three man searching patrol a block or so behind the officer. He had been lucky. If the patrol had found the dead Lobsterbacks first, right now he'd be in a British cell waiting a quick trial and a sure hanging.

Robert opened the side door and was delighted to see a smile on Millie's face. It was such a sudden and welcome change in her that he forgot all about his battle in the alley.

Later that evening, Robert rode to his father's house and explained in detail what happened in the alley and street.

"I'm afraid I reacted from instinct, Father. I did not stop and reason it out. I should have rescued the girl without damaging the Redcoats so severely."

Ben smiled proudly at his son. "You did just what I would have done if I'd been there, Robert. Now don't worry about it. Let's look at that hand." He sent for some ointments to treat the wound and had the stable boy check Starfire's neck.

Harriet came in when she heard Robert arrive and listened as he explained his confrontation.

"There's nothing we can do until they start to search for the person responsible," Harriet said. "And since they have no facts to go on, we don't have anything to worry about. There is no connection between Robert and the girl, or her father, so even if the British do find out who they are, Robert is safe."

Ben nodded. "I agree with Harriet. Robert, you have nothing to worry about except that hand. Get it looked at by Dr. Warren tomorrow. Go to your job tomorrow morning and do everything you usually do.'' He paused and smiled. ''Robert, your actions tonight were magnificent and courageous. I commend you most highly for your good sense and your selflessness, as well as your cool and calm response when you were under fire.''

That same night after Robert went home, Harriet and her father talked a long time and decided that the Freedom Fighters should put together a series of small attacks on the British forces. They would harass the troops and the command as much as possible in retaliation for the Coercive Acts. Perhaps they could mount one such action every two weeks through the summer. It would take some of the pressure off the Freedom Fighter captains by the men who were itching for action, and at the same time it would be a continual warning to the British and General Gage that the opposition was strong, organized and was not submitting meekly to the latest insults and abuses.

At the next council meeting Monday evening, Ben made the motion for the small harassing actions and the council approved it without discussion. Ben asked Lewis if he had any suggestions for such actions and he presented three that he had designed. The council chose what Ben thought was the hardest of the three to complete, but he agreed that it would be the most unsettling for the British navy.

Harriet tingled with excitement just thinking about it. She knew she could not go along on the actual mission but she helped in the preparations. She listened to Lewis:

"I've seen three of his demonstrations now, and it works. He calls it a burning fuse. It's made of nothing more than black powder sprinkled on a special sheet of fast burning paper. The paper is rolled and glued together. The powder burns faster than the paper and the flame follows along the roll of paper that's smaller than your little finger. I've seen these more than four feet long, and it burns from one end to the other every time and sets off a black powder charge."

"And it functions in any position?" Dr. Warren asked. "Could it be hanging straight down and still work?"

"Absolutely. It is different for each handmade fuse, and usually it burns about a foot a minute."

"So with a three foot fuse, you have three minutes to get away?" Harriet asked.

They nodded.

Two days later, Harriet sat in a chaise on the waterfront with Robert beside her. This time he did have his flintlock pistol primed and ready.

Some two hundred yards off Long Wharf sat a British frigate, a small fighting warship with forty guns. She was anchored about midway between Long Wharf, which extended over a quarter of a mile into Boston Harbor, and Hancock's Wharf. The two piers were about five-hundred yards apart. The frigate had as its job to be a watchdog on the most active part of the Boston harbor and to be sure that no ships got to the wharfs for loading or unloading. At night she took a position between the wharves and some two hundred yards seaward.

The craft's name was the *Crusader*. She was fully manned and on an alert status as a vital link in the blockade of the Port of Boston.

Lewis Lynch and three other swimmers wearing cut off pants and bare to the waist, entered the cool waters of Boston Harbor from Hancock's Wharf and swam straight ahead for a quarter of a mile or so.

They were seaward of the *Crusader* and still two hundred yards north. They pushed three casks of black powder with them specially fitted out with small floats, and another package, an oilskin bundle containing the specially made fuses, more dry powder and a tin with hot coals in it all carefully padded. The men pushed the kegs and packages slowly forward, swimming an easy breast stroke, making no noise.

Harriet wished she knew what time it was, and how long the men had been gone. She asked Robert, who grumbled. Few persons in Massachusetts had timepieces, but Harriet knew that he did, a handsome gold pocket watch with a gold chain. He pulled it out and tried to read it in the moonless night but he couldn't. The night for the strike had been chosen only after the clouds rolled in during late afternoon and a fog was also predicted by the seafaring men.

Treading water, Lewis Lynch helped the last man up with the group. They had asked for the strongest swimmers in the companies, and all three beside Lewis were good, young men in fine condition. Lewis passed the slower man the oilskin and he took the other fifty pound keg of powder. The group turned at a right angle to their previous swim. This put them on the seaward side of the ship, where the lookouts should be less watchful. They swam another two hundred yards and Lewis signaled for a halt.

He could just see the outline of the frigate ahead of them. There had not been a word spoken since they left the wharf. Each man in the group knew exactly what to do, and had been swimming in the back bay for a week. When they swam silently and with only their heads and the four floating bundles out of the water, it was hard to see them from twenty feet away. Fifty yards gave them absolute protection. As Lewis watched he saw the sea fog bank rolling in behind them. He moved the men out quickly now, aiming them toward the harbor and directly at the *Crusader*. If the fog arrived before they did, the ship could be missed as they swam by, fifteen yards from her unlighted hulk.

As they approached the *Crusader*, they stopped twenty yards away. The fog was still behind them and not moving. There were no lanterns burning on her bow. It was after midnight and all hands except the usual watch were below and asleep.

Lewis had spent half a day on the end of Long Wharf studying the *Crusader* through a telescope. He had at last found what he was looking for. They needed a firm anchor for a rope so the kegs of powder could be tied and suspended just above the waterline on the *Crusader*. He found what he wanted in the rat lines, those webs of rope that extend from each mast to either the deck or the sides of the ship and up which the crew hurried to get to work on the sails. In the case of the *Crusader*, there were a dozen lines that extended down the outside of the ship well below the second row of gun ports and almost to the water line. They were anchored into the side of the ship and sturdily set. These ropes were strong enough to hold the three kegs of black powder which would shortly present a surprise for the *Crusader*'s captain.

Lewis motioned the number one man toward the ship. He carried only a coil of quarter inch hemp rope around his torso, and he dived and swam underwater to the side of the *Crusader* then surfaced silently. He found the rat line he wanted as close to midships as possible, scaled out of the water and up three feet on the side of the ship to loop the end of the rope around the rat line, and noiselessly let himself back into the water. He made the end of the line fast, and tied a series of loops designed to hold the casks of black powder.

As he finished his work, the number two man touched his shoulder and floated a keg of powder to him. Together they lifted it out of the water, fitted it into the loop and pulled the rope tight and tested it. It held the keg neatly and they let it rest against the side of the *Crusader*.

Quickly the other two men brought in the other kegs of powder. They were grouped so two kegs rested against the hull of the ship at the same level, and the third one sat on top of the lower two. All were tied securely in place, then specially placed bungs were opened on the top of the two lower kegs, and the bottom bung opened on the top keg, so one fuse would set them all off at once.

They worked quickly, efficiently, not making a sound. They were so close to the ship that a lookout would have to bend far over the rail to see them, and since they made no noise there was no reason a guard would inspect the sides of a ship two hundred yards into the bay.

Lewis checked the work of the other men and pointed them toward the nearest point of exit, Hancock's Wharf, some four hundred yards away north and west. He indicated they would have five minutes to swim before he lit the fuse. They nodded, motioned that they would stay together, and moved out slowly but noiselessly on a straight line for the dock.

Lewis estimated the time, knowing he would give them ten minutes or perhaps fifteen. As he waited he opened the oilskin pouch, and being careful to keep everything dry, took out the packet of black powder and sprinkled this over the top of the two lower kegs to help insure a dry powder contact. Then he unrolled two paper fuses and pushed one of them into each of the two lower kegs.

Lewis wished he had a burning torch so he could simply touch flame to the fuse when he wished to and swim away, but it wouldn't be that easy. But he had practiced on shore and in the water. Now he took out the protected hot tin, and opened it. From another tin he scooped out tinder and put it against the hot, glowing oak log coals in the first tin and blew on them until it burst into fire. Holding the tin with a padded glove, Lewis brought the flame to both of the fuse ends at once and let them start burning well. When he removed the flame he heard the steady sputter as one of the black powder grains after another burned in a chain.

They were lighted, and burning! He let the small flame in the tin die as he put the cover back on it, then plunged it into the water, dropped it and the glove and swam to the stern of the *Crusader*. He looked back and could see faint trails of smoke near the kegs. Lewis smiled, sank under water and swam as far as he could away from the ship and toward the pier.

When he surfaced, he was thirty yards from the *Crusader*. He swam again, a faster stroke now, to get some distance between him and the ship. At last he could no longer see the craft and decided he was about two hundred yards away. He turned over on his stomach, looked toward the spot where the ship should be and kicked leisurely, paddling with his hands under water, careful to keep his head out of the water and waiting for the explosion.

He had not timed it in his mind and the first blast took him by surprise. It was followed almost immediately by the second explosion, a larger detonation that lit up the night sky and sent debris flying through the air, some landing near him. At the same instant a giant vise squeezed his chest as the compression of the explosion transferred through the water. He was thankful that his head wasn't below the surface when the explosion went off, or his brains would have been scrambled and his ears useless for life.

The explosion ended in fire, and Lewis could hear voices shouting, screaming, on board the *Crusader*. The fire lighted up the sky, and he turned and swam with a fast overhand stroke toward the pier, aware that he might get caught up in a search for survivors when rescue boats came. Two hundred yards farther he rested, turned and saw the fire burning brightly and the big ship heeling over to one side. Bucket brigades were at work, and in the calm of the night, no other sailing ship could come near her. Lynch reasoned that the *Crusader* would not sink, she had not been hit low enough, or with enough charges. The powder magazines had not blown, being midships and low down where cannon ball through her sides or decks would not reach.

At least the *Crusader* would need extensive repairs, and the good General Gage would have to pull another ship off his line to do picket duty in this spot. Gage would know soon that he was doing more than standing guard over some street rabble.

Lewis Lynch turned over and swam steadily for the Hancock wharf. He soon came up to the small floating landing alongside and found his three men lying on the rough wood, cheering quietly. They all shook hands, then went up the wooden ladder to the wharf and were met by a pair of sulkies which took them off the waterfront and to their homes.

Harriet and Robert picked up Lewis a block inland and drove him to his house. Lewis gave Harriet a complete report on the way and asked her to relay it to Ben.

As Lynch left the chaise, Harriet touched his hand.

"Again, Lewis, congratulations. That was an outstanding and brave act. I may even nominate you for a medal."

They smiled, Robert shook his hand, and Lewis went into his rooms to get warm and get a change of dry clothes.

By the time Robert drove the chaise to his father's house, Ben had already returned. A smile broke over his face when Robert reported

630

that all four men returned from the attack and none was injured.

"Fine, fine," Ben said. "Well done! That should be a great calling card for General Gage. Tomorrow is July 1. That's a fitting anniversary for him, he's been in command for a whole month now. We should have another small surprise for him about the fifteenth."

The next morning Ben's smile wasn't quite so bright. There would be a military inquiry into the attack on the *Crusader* and all known rebel leaders and dissidents would be called to testify. Ben's name was listed among those to be questioned, along with Sam Adams, Paul Revere and John Hancock. But more disturbing were the notices that Lobsterbacks tacked on walls and buildings around Boston that same morning.

Parliament had passed another Coercive Act, the fourth, and this one brought instant irritation to all of Boston. It was called the Quartering Act, had been passed by Parliament June 2, and only now had news of it arrived by ship from London. The act granted His Majesty's troops the right to be quartered in the city of Boston, lodged in community structures, in private buildings or private homes, wherever the commander determined.

The outcry was immediate and overwhelming. For two days British soldiers were kept off the Boston streets. Everywhere the British were cursed, shouted at, often Tory sympathizers were set upon and pummeled. Gradually the shock wore off, and Boston home owners realized that the number of troops quartered in homes would be few in number—but the threat of such an act was there, was now the law of the land, and it infuriated every Bostonian patriot.

More and more talk came now about a Continental Congress, and soon a definite time was set. The elected representatives would all meet in Philadelphia in the Pennsylvania colony from September 5 through October 27th. The people thought this might indeed be a historical meeting.

Harriet had little to do in her job at the company these days. More than a dozen warehouses sat empty, office spaces that once buzzed with workers were unoccupied. Most of the work was taking place in other cities.

A week after the *Crusader* incident she stopped by the nearly lifeless main office building and talked with Robert. He grinned and waved her into a chair but she didn't sit down. She frowned and looked at his left hand.

"Why haven't you had that hand taken care of?" she asked.

"Oh, it's nothing, should heal in a few days."

"I bet Dr. Warren hasn't seen it yet, has he?" Robert shook his head. "How long has it been all mottled and puffy this way?"

"Four or five days, maybe more, I don't remember."

"Get your jacket on, we're going to see Dr. Warren, right this minute."

Harriet would not be talked out of it, and about eleven o'clock that morning they sat in Dr. Warren's front room waiting for him to see them. Shortly a young apprentice who was studying to be a doctor under Dr. Warren's instructions, came out. He was twenty-five, as tall as Robert with clean, sharp features, a lot of red hair and a growing red moustache. His smile swept over them like a soft breeze.

"I'm sorry, but Dr. Warren is still with Mrs. Devine. She promised us she would have that baby at five a.m., but somehow that little fellow won't be rushed. Is there anything I can do to help you?"

Robert held out his hand, and the young man's eyes took on a note of interest.

"I was concerned about it, Doctor . . ." Harriet began.

"No, I'm not a doctor yet, an apprentice. Maybe in one more year, if I can please Dr. Warren. My name is Daniel McCallister."

"Can you work on my hand?" Robert asked.

"Yes. We need to lance it and drain away that buildup and the puffiness, then we'll put some healing ointment on it. Let's do that and then you come back tomorrow and let Dr. Warren have a look at it." He hesitated and looked up. "You're good friends of Dr. Warren?"

"Yes, why?"

"Well, I'm sure this is a gunshot wound, they're always slow to heal, and we have strict orders from the new military governor to report all gunshot wounds to the captain of the guard."

Harriet smiled. "Daniel, are you a very good friend of Dr. Warren?"

"Yes, I certainly hope so."

"So you must know that Dr. Warren does not do much of what the new governor or the captain of the guards say. I'm sure he would not want you to report this gunshot wound."

"Yes, you're right. I'll need to tell him who you are, so he does know."

"Robert Rutledge, and this is my sister, Harriet."

Daniel looked up and smiled. "I'm sure you don't have to worry about any report, Miss Rutledge. Dr. Warren and I are equally strong minded about the British and what they are doing to us. We also treated the young girl that Mr. Rutledge here saved from the soldiers a few weeks ago. Her family is most appreciative."

"How did you know about that?" Robert asked.

"Dr. Warren and I believe alike in almost everything, politics included."

Harriet looked at Daniel McCallister with a more critical eye. He was just short of being handsome, his eyes green and his smile delightful. It was a strong, good face.

"Mr. Rutledge, why don't you come into the next room and let me treat your hand. It won't take but a minute or two. If you will excuse us, Miss Rutledge?"

"Yes, of course. I'll wait right here." She sat

down and looked at a newspaper. It was the *Speaker*, the same one her father read. She smiled. Daniel was the most interesting young man she had met in a long time. She hoped that she would see him again. She could always bring her little brother back to have his hand checked. Harriet smiled more broadly this time. Yes, she thought, she certainly should take more interest in that wounded hand, and be sure that it healed exactly right.

Chapter Ten
A MAJOR PROBLEM

July fled rapidly into August. The Boston town situation grew worse daily. The whole community now had split into two definite factions: you were either loyal Tory or you were Rebel. The loyalists accounted for no more than ten percent of the population, and usually these persons were closely tied to England by job, family or position.

Ben watched the temper of the people, judging it, measuring, testing, pleased because more and more men were saying that the time for peaceful means had slipped past. There now lay no true course except total independence, even if that meant there must be a war of revolution against England. But many still shied away at this point, looking in vain for a compromise that might yet provide liberty and a measure of self government, without breaking all ties with England. Who wanted to contest the mightiest military force in the world? Attack the global British Empire and its thousands of ships, hundreds of thousands of troops? Many still felt such an action would be foolhardy and, in the end, a failure.

Robert's hand healed nicely, and Harriet did go back to the doctor's office with him again. She told him it was only to be sure that Robert went because he had been so careless about his injury. But Robert and Harriet both knew very well that she went along hoping for a glimpse of the young apprentice doctor. She did see him, and a week later he came calling on Sunday afternoon.

The following night Harriet sat in on the regular meeting of the committee which was being held in Ben's study at his home this time. They had Robert on guard duty outside the study windows, to forestall any snooping, and had worked out the third "small action" they were taking against the British to counter the psychological effects of the blockade.

The city of Boston was slowly dying. Commerce had been her lifeblood, and now she crept along on all fours, not able to stand, but not flat on her back yet, either. The wagon road to Salem was almost done, and a trickle of supplies was coming in, but it was a long and expensive route, and merchants often took a loss on goods rather than charge for the transportation as they should. The shipments were grouped in fifteen or twenty wagons, pulled by oxen, mules or horses. When a stream crossed the road it usually had to be forded, and horses, ropes and biceps helped get each wagon across the water. Each wagon train had armed guards with it.

At first they had a "stump road" in places where trees had been sawed or chopped down two feet from the ground just low enough so a wagon axle would roll over them. For the wheel paths they chopped the trees out at the ground making a narrow track through the wooded sections.

There were few bridges, and only two in the process of being built by local communities along the shore of the bay. The road and bridges were ten year programs, but Boston couldn't wait.

All shipping firms in Boston were at the starvation level. Not even a rowboat could break through the stranglehold the British men of war held on the city. John Hancock had moved all of his ships to Salem and New York, as Ben had, and they shared facilities in certain areas. In Boston their docks, warehouses and offices were shuttered with only a few watchmen patrolling the structures.

Daily more shops and stores in Boston closed because they ran out of goods and could not get any more. Building of new houses and stores ended abruptly when the supply of lumber and imported bricks ran out.

One of the early shortages was food. However, this would not be critical as long as the fruits and vegetables were available in town and in the countryside across the Back Bay. But for the first time Ben could remember, many of the poorer families in Boston were going to bed hungry. It made him angry just thinking about it. Programs were set up to help find and distribute food. One of them manned by the Freedom Fighters was called the Greater Boston Welfare Association. Ben sat down at the council session in his own study and it got under way. Lewis Lynch began talking about the next proposed action.

"The attack on the *Crusader* went well. The ship suffered serious structural damage, has been taken out of action and is due to be put into drydock soon for extensive repairs. In the middle of July we ambushed a six-man patrol, took all of their equipment and provisions, then made them undress and sent them running back to their tents on the Common in their underwear.

"Now we have a new plan. On King street is a warehouse that has been appropriated by General Gage and turned into a supply depot for his land based men. The warehouse is carefully guarded and highly important to the British. It's my suggestion that 'we raid the warehouse, eliminating the guards, and loading as much of military equipment and food as we can on wagons and carts and move it away."

Ben broke in. "That warehouse is where they keep most of the food supply for the troops on the Common?"

"Right, sir. A lot of food that Boston can eat immediately and extend our supply."

"If it could be done quietly, without alerting the rest of the regiment, we could have all night to carry off the food and equipment," Dr. Warren said.

"I have a plan that might just do it that way," Lewis said.

"A diversion?" Captain Compton asked.

Lewis shook his head. "No, I don't think so, Captain. That could alert the rest of the troops to check on other areas that might be attacked as well. This one will take a lot of patience, silence and stealth, and no gun shots at all."

Lewis was given authorization to plan the operation and to utilize the entire Freedom Fighter's manpower if needed to carry it out sometime in August.

Harriet had worked all day distributing food to the older people in one area who couldn't get out to find it for themselves. She was exhausted when she came home for a quick supper. She had arranged with Arnold Compton to let a wagon pick up the pumpkins from his fields that he didn't have the time to gather and sell. Two flat bottomed wagons should get them all. She needed to find the two wagons, one more driver (she would drive one of them) and some help to load the pumpkins.

A little after the seven o'clock hour struck on the big clock in the hall, she heard a knock on the front door, and when she answered it, found Daniel McCallister.

"Oh, Mr. McCallister, this is a surprise, come

in." She knew she blushed deeply when she saw him. It was unusual for a man to come visiting on Tuesday night.

"Hello, Miss Rutledge. Is your father home?" He was smiling broadly at her, amused by her surprise.

She bobbed her head.

"Good, I hope to say good evening to him and deliver a message. Then perhaps you and I can talk or read some poetry or I could even listen to you sing."

"Mr. McCallister, are you courting me?"

"I most certainly am trying the best way I know how, that is, if I have your permission?" He watched her closely, hoping that there would be some hint of encouragement.

Her smile grew slowly, then broke over her face like a brilliant sunrise and she closed the door.

"You certainly may, Mr. McCallister. I would have been disappointed if you hadn't come, but I don't sing, and we shall talk politics, and don't mind if I seem to be talking a lot, just running on and on, because I simply am showing that you have surprised me twice and I'm nervous and trying very hard to make a good impression on you, which I probably am not, but if I don't stop this pretty soon, I'm going to be totally out of breath and your call here will turn into a medical occasion because I'll probably faint dead away and you'll have to revive me."

Daniel McCallister laughed. "Well, I'm certainly glad that you didn't faint after all. Now where can we find your father? I have a message from Dr. Warren."

Her father was in his study, reading the *Speaker* and writing a strong protest letter to the editor. He looked up in surprise when the two of them walked in.

"Well, McCallister, good to see you. Is Dr. Warren all right?"

"Oh, yes, sir. He's fine. He has a message for you." Daniel looked at Harriet.

"It's all right, McCallister, she's one of our number. Harriet is the secretary of our council. I don't think you knew that."

"She is?" He lifted his brows. "I didn't know." Dr. McCallister rubbed his chin with one hand. "Mr. Rutledge, you have a rather remarkable girl hĕre, did you know that?"

"I've known that for years, Mr. McCallister. Now, what was the message?"

"Oh, Dr. Warren said to tell you that he has lined up all twelve of his wagons and drivers on a standby basis. They'll be ready whenever we need them."

"Thank you, Mr. McCallister. I'll tell Lewis."

"Mr. McCallister came to see me as well, Father. We'll be in the parlour."

Ben smiled as they went out. The young doctor-to-be would be a good match for Harriet. Ben admitted that he was concerned with her apparent lack of interest in marriage. But he hoped that this time it would be different. Harriet was an "old maid" by community standards, but on the other hand she had done more things in business and other activities than most women did all their lives. Perhaps she was just a little ahead of her time.

In the parlour they talked and Mr. McCallister asked her about the Freedom Fighters.

"You're actually on the council? What do you do?"

She told him and when he asked how she discovered the group, she recited her participation in the attack on the *East Indian*.

Daniel McCallister whistled. "You were along on that raid? That's tremendous! They wouldn't let me go. Dr. Warren told me I was on standby medical duty, just in case we had any casualties. He and I were set up in one of your warehouses near the docks, and that's where anyone hurt would have been brought. Luckily we didn't have to do any work that night."

"Are you a regular Freedom Fighter too, Mr. McCallister? Do you take training and fire your muskets and everything?"

"Yes, of course, but I'm only fair with a Brown Bess or a flintlock pistol."

They went on talking, about the Freedom Fighters and about his work as a doctor in training. He hoped to go into practice right there in Boston within a year. Dr. Warren had told Daniel that in a year or so he would be ready.

The big grandfather clock in the hall struck

the hour and Daniel jumped up, surprised.

"It's ten o'clock already?" He shook his head in amazement. "I don't know where the time went." Then he smiled. "It seems that I enjoy being with you, Miss Rutledge. I hope I haven't overstayed my welcome."

She stood, her smile frank and wide, her eyes dancing with delight.

"Mr. McCallister, I don't think you could ever overstay your welcome in this house. But it probably is time for you to go."

"When may I come back?"

"Thursday night?" she said.

"Yes. About seven-thirty?"

She said that would be fine and they walked to the door. He opened the oak and walnut panel and smiled at her. "Miss Rutledge, I can't remember ever spending a more delightful evening. I'm going to be looking forward to Thursday."

She touched his hand and felt a shiver dart through her.

"Mr. McCallister, I hope Thursday comes quickly. Do you think we could do away with Wednesday?"

They both laughed. He touched her chin, turning her face slightly into the light. He watched her a moment, then smiled and went out into the night.

Harriet closed the door, walked to the first chair she came to and sagged into it. She was limp with excitement. Daniel McCallister had seemed as interested in her as she was in him! She felt it with a steady glow, a sureness, a wonder, but at the same time a knowledge that they were suited for each other, that they held the same beliefs in politics, and they both had achieved something of success.

Ben came past her and lifted his brows.

"Father, I like that young man a great deal. What do you think about him?"

Ben touched her shoulder. "Harriet, that's one suitor I am not going to have to do any checking up on. He's solid gold in my book."

Harriet went up to her room humming a little song she had learned when she was a small girl. Her mother had always called it Harriet's happy tune.

The planning was done. Over a hundred Freedom Fighters were in place. Dr. Warren and Daniel McCallister had set up their emergency treatment center in an empty warehouse. Twenty-four wagons, drivers and horses were ready to roll on command.

Harriet huddled on the roof of a two-story building directly across from the Weyland warehouse on King street. That was the target. There was a bright moon tonight; it would be full moon in another three days. She looked through the false front of the building and could see the two British guards pacing in front of the warehouse. It was a big building, between two other structures that extended through the block with two guards at the rear. The guards back there patrolled just across from Faneuil Hall.

The guard would be changed at midnight and then again at four a.m. The raid was scheduled just after the change at midnight.

As the new pair of guards marched into view, Harriet knew the action was about to start. Below on King Street the two guards had just settled into their routine when a pair of Freedom Fighters appeared behind them, clubbed them over the head and dragged them back into the alley and out of sight. The Freedom Fighters, dressed in identical Lobsterback gear which had been captured a month before, then took over the guard positions.

The same action took place at the back of the warehouse, and the moment it was done a signal was sent, and the wagons rolled, four at a time up to the big back door. The loading began. Spies had earlier determined a rough layout of the warehouses and mapped approximately where the goods were inside the structure. Forty Freedom Fighters began loading the wagons. They worked quickly, running with their loads along planned routes, filling wagons rapidly, and moving them out into the shadows of the alleys. First they took the military equipment and supplies: forty Brown Bess rifles, three mortars with a quantity of twenty pound shot, and two small six pound cannon with plenty of shot.

Next were thirty barrels of black powder,

then a large quantity of bayonets which almost none of the Freedom Fighters had, blankets and other stores. When the military stores filled the first eighteen wagons they were waved off and took roundabout routes, working slowly through town with their canvas covered loads until they formed up into a long wagon train at Boston Neck, then drove across and headed around the far side of Back Bay toward Concord.

The remaining wagons were filled with the foodstuffs. When the first two were loaded, they moved through a guarded alley and two streets to a vacant warehouse where the food was unloaded and the rigs returned for more. By three o'clock the weapons wagons were all gone, and a messenger returned and reported they had cleared Boston Neck and were moving toward Concord. They now had an escort of thirty armed men with them, carrying both muskets and pistols, loaded, primed and ready to fire.

The forty loaders in the warehouse drained the last of the portable food from the stores, loaded it all in the wagons and sent them on their way. There were flour, beans, wheat, potatoes, hard biscuits, pumpkins, melons, carrots, and a dozen more piles of fresh fruit and vegetables.

By three o'clock, the last wagons were filled, the door of the big warehouse fastened and the Freedom Fighters faded away, leaving the four guards bound and gagged, missing their weapons, powder, shot and all other military hardware.

Harriet had left her perch just after two a.m. and hurried to the warehouse where the food was to be taken. When the first wagons arrived she had designated locations for each type of food and soon had a plan worked out for how it would be distributed.

By ten minutes to four, every Freedom Fighter was off the street, either back home in bed, or safe inside the food storage warehouse. Ben, Harriet, Dr. Warren and Mr. McCallister looked over the huge pile of edibles and smiled at each other. This part alone had been worth the risk.

When the sun came up another group of Freedom Fighters would fan out through the poor sections of Boston, informing the people that the head of each household could report to the warehouse for twenty pounds of food.

A sign had been painted and swung over the inside of the warehouse. It said: GREATER BOSTON WELFARE ASSOCIATION, Food Distribution.

A few tables had been set up with the food displayed on them. The people would be told to bring burlap sacks or pillow cases for carrying their supplies home.

By eight o'clock the first disbelieving men and women began to arrive at the warehouse. They laughed and shouted when they discovered the story they had heard was true, and most carefully selected items of food they could use, and some to store. By ten o'clock there was a line half way down the block toward the waterfront.

Dr. Warren and Mr. McCallister had to go to their office, but Ben stayed, keeping in the background, while Harriet and a dozen fresh Freedom Fighters kept the people in line and helped them work through the bounty.

About noon a British major in full dress rode his horse through the big door and demanded to see the person in charge. Harriet had been designated as the least vulnerable and she said she'd be glad to meet anyone who came asking questions. Now Harriet marched up to the major who still sat on his horse.

"Major," she barked at him. "This is a food distribution warehouse. I'll thank you to get that filthy beast out of here at once. If you wish to return on your own two feet and act like a gentleman, I'll be glad to talk to you."

She stared at him when he lifted his riding crop as if to protest, then swung the horse around and rode outside. Two minutes later he was back, his riding crop slashing into his gloved hand with each step. The angry, embarrassed color still had not drained from his neck and face.

The major stopped in front of Harriet and she quickly put in the first attack.

"Major, I don't know why you are here, but we are extremely busy trying to feed the very people you are trying with all of your guns and ships and soldiers to starve. I am not favorably impressed by grown men trying to starve babies. The Greater Boston Welfare Association is valiantly trying to save these youngsters, and old folks and defenseless women from your greed and your viciousness. Now, what do you wish to say?"

The major found himself without words for a moment. His color had turned to a fiery red again and he stammered, then whacked his leg with the riding crop and found his voice.

"Madam."

"That's Miss, if you please. Miss Harriet Rutledge, and who might you be, in spite of your lack of manners?"

"Begging your pardon, Miss Rutledge. Major Harrison Stanley at your service. I'm here to ask where you suddenly found so much food and vegetables and flour to distribute?"

"I'd like to say it came off ships that ran through your blockade last night, but there was no fog and the night wasn't dark enough. We have obtained this food, Major Stanley, by begging and borrowing and pleading with those communities around Boston which grow more food than they eat and always ship the surplus to us or out through our port, which you have sealed off. The Greater Boston Welfare Association will go right on trying to save our women and babies from starving to death since your foul warships are still there. And by the way, you'd better watch your horse. Good horsemeat

651

is hard to tell from beef, if it's cooked right. Have you ever eaten horsemeat, Major Stanley?"

The major's eyebrows shot upward, he turned and looked at the big door which his horse was near, and then back at the slip of a girl who was defying the whole British army and navy.

"Miss Rutledge. Last night our warehouse on King street was attacked and robbed of a large quantity of goods, material and food. Much of it was the same as you are distributing here."

"Major, are you accusing me of stealing your food? If you are, I will invite you to move yourself out of my warehouse at once." She motioned to two men in farm clothes, who came up quickly beside her, both carrying pitchforks with three steel tines held at the ready in front of them.

"Miss Rutledge, you jump to conclusions. I only wished to make a quick inspection of your foods, with the hope that I might be able to utilize some of your sources to replenish our stores. We are constantly looking for food for our men here both on and off our ships."

"You already know our sources, because you have bought up much of the normal supply. Because of you we can't find enough food for our own people. You could solve your own problem and ours, Major, by removing your illegal occupying forces and sailing your navy back to England."

"Miss Rutledge, I could close your warehouse by calling for a squad of armed men."

"Yes, of course, you could, Major Stanley. You could also bayonet half the women in line and then drown their babies, but I don't think you'll do that, either. How many Redcoats were killed in Boston last month, Major?"

"Killed, casualties? We are not at war. There were—some accidents."

"Major, you had at least six Redcoats killed in Boston by irate townspeople, according to reports I read in the newspapers. You close down this distribution, or molest one of our women, and I promise you, Major Stanley, that you will be losing six to ten men *dead every day*. Now I'm busy, I have work to do. Please leave by the back door, or my friends here will be delighted to assist you. Good day, Major Stanley."

Chapter Eleven
CONTINENTAL CONGRESS

Ben had spent two weeks in New York working on his business, one in June and another in July. Now he was looking forward to another trip, this one to Philadelphia in September for the convening of the Continental Congress on September 6 at Carpenter's Hall. All over the Atlantic seaboard the American colonists were electing delegates. Some did so by their Colonial legislatures, the Assemblies or Houses of Burgesses. Massachusetts elected its representatives at a meeting of the Massachusetts General Court called to order in June to consider the state of the colony. All but one of the members were staunch patriots and that one Loyalist was cleverly excluded when the court voted to send five men to Philadelphia to represent the colony. They were Sam Adams, John Adams, James Bowdoin, Thomas Cushing and Robert Treat Paine. Ben would go along as an aide to Sam Adams.

Thursday morning, September 1, 1774, Ben

led the five delegates and three aides on a horse-back ride to Strawberry Point, some fifteen miles from the Boston Neck and the point where Ben met his regular messenger ship from New York. The rump-weary delegates arrived and met the long boat which promptly rowed them to the merchantman, *Harriet*, for the two day cruise to Philadelphia. On the way they talked, planned and worried over what the Congress would do. No one knew what to expect, because there had never been a meeting like this. They were thirteen separate colonies of England, but bound together by many problems and desires that were common. They were meeting to try to work out what they could do about a myriad of problems created by their mother country. No-thing like this had ever happened in history. It would be a unique assembly and one that Sam Adams said they must use to start binding the Colonies together into a firm and solid union, so strong that it would rise to the eventual call for a revolutionary war against England. He flatly predicted that such a conflict would take place within a year.

Ben sat in one of the cabins where Sam Adams was holding forth on the absolutely vital nature of this Congress. Ben thought back three months ago, when news of the Boston Port act first slammed into the Thirteen Colonies. By the last days in May all of the major Colonies except South Carolina had reacted to the signi-ficance of the act. During May a new wave of resentment toward Great Britain swept through all of America. This feeling was much more widespread and intense than anything previously seen. Now it was no longer a legal point for lawyers to argue about the technicalities of Parliament's right to tax the Colonies. The Boston Port act was a cruel blockade of a city, and England had now shown her true colors with an act of naked and flagrant tyranny for everyone to see. The second of the coercive measures, the Massachusetts Government Act, stirred the fires anew, showing the other Colonies that the charter of any one of the Thirteen could be changed, reversed or cancelled at the whim of any Parliament in session.

As a direct result of this anger, the call for the immediate non-importation, non-exportation and non-consumption of any British products came, and was debated hotly. The Colonies did not want to take such a drastic step as single units and decided they should talk it over as a group. The result was the Continental Congress where all issues could be plainly considered.

And now Ben was on his way to that conference. It made his own pulse race at the prospect. It was a chance for total unity which he had been working toward for four years. It could also permit some kind of united action of a substantial nature to help Boston before she was frozen and starved into submission.

Most of the delegates from Massachusetts found quarters near Carpenter's Hall and at once charged into the rounds of luncheons, dinner parties and breakfasts that had begun as soon as men from different colonies arrived.

John Adams sized up some of the delegates in his journal: Charles Thomson was called the Sam Adams of Philadelphia and was subsequently elected secretary of the Congress at its first meeting even though he was not an official delegate. John Rutledge of South Carolina, who was not related to Ben, was complimented on his appearance, but thought not to be a promising delegate. William Livingston of New Jersey seemed to have "nothing elegant or genteel about him, but he was sensible and learned."

While John was looking over the individuals, his cousin, Sam Adams, was busy politicking, buttonholing delegates, talking them around to his point of view and checking out the opposition. Sam knew the Congress represented many points of view. One of the strongest was that of Joseph Galloway of Pennsylvania who would propose a strong Tory plan of conciliation.

The first few days of the Congress were given to organization and a kind of testing the water, getting acquainted and lining up votes.

Then on September 16, Paul Revere brought a resolution from Massachusetts that was to set the tone of the First Continental Congress. Early in May men in Suffolk County, Massachusetts, had met in session and Dr. Joseph Warren had drafted a resolution that was adopted by the group and became known as the

Suffolk Resolves. This paper denounced the Coercive Acts as patently unconstitutional and recommended that the people commence military training and that an immediate cessation of trade with the British Empire be adopted by the other counties. The Suffolk group said it would confine itself to defensive measures, "So long as such conduct may be vindicated by reason and the principles of self-preservation, but no longer."

Sam Adams at once began to pull his votes together and to lobby for the passage and acceptance of the Suffolk Resolves by the Congress. Joseph Galloway quickly found out how strong Sam was. Galloway said of Sam: "He eats little, drinks little, sleeps little, thinks much, and is most decisive and indefatigable in the pursuit of his objects."

Two days later, on September 18, 1774, Congress unanimously endorsed the Suffolk Resolves, and the ultimate direction of the Congress was established—hard toward the Rebel causes.

Ben stayed at the Congress long after he knew he should be attending to business, but the intercourse of great minds and historic acts fascinated him, and he lingered. He cheered when the Congress voted to postpone indefinitely the discussion on Joseph Galloway's resolution for a Grand Council in America in which all colonies would have delegates. The plan would supposedly solve the problem of just representation. The king, however, would appoint a president-general to govern the colonies and the actions of the Grand Council would have to be approved by Parliament. The delegates brushed aside Galloway's conservative ideas here, and later other conservatives suffered similar treatment.

Ben watched as Congress adopted on September 27, a resolution banning imports from Great Britain after December 1, 1774. Three days later they voted that unless grievances were redressed by September 10, 1775, all exports from America to Great Britain would be halted. This led to the signing of the Continental Association, committing all colonies to the policy of commercial retaliation against England, and establishing procedures for its enforcement throughout America.

Ben had to leave shortly after that, and he was in New York when the Congress adjourned on October 26, after having made provisions for another Congress to be held in May of 1775, unless all grievances by England were redressed.

By the time Ben got home to Boston, landed at Strawberry Point and rode to his house, the *Speaker* had completed a series of articles on the First Continental Congress and listed its accomplishments under bold headlines. Ben saved every copy for his late night reading. He would treasure those few weeks he spent in Philadelphia for as long as he lived.

When David Rutledge had slipped out of his father's house in May and ridden away from Boston, he wasn't sure where he was headed. He only knew that he would not stand by and be trapped into a marriage of convenience to Millie Livingston. She had sprung the trap on him neatly, he had to admit that, and he had fallen into it without a question.

He pressed forward, rounded the Back Bay and rode the dark roads toward Cambridge. David was heading generally north and west with little more plan than that. He did not want to continue into the wilderness, he had no urging for that kind of a life. Immediately he wished to vanish out of the sight of the Livingston family. He slept in the woods that night and continued the next day, stopping at a roadside inn for a solid meal, then rode on. The first full day on the road he reached a village called Lexington and turned west again. In the afternoon he saw a farm and stopped, hoping he might stay that night in the barn.

A woman answered his knock at the back door. She had a baby clutched in one arm and a flintlock pistol in the other hand. She refused to let him sleep in the barn and told him to ride on. She watched him until he was out of sight. David turned back the moment she couldn't see him and rested in some woods beside a stream where he drank his fill. When it grew dark, he returned through the woods beside the stream, tied his horse and then crept into the hay loft and slept.

The next morning he got up when he heard someone milking a cow below. Quietly he investigated and found the same woman, in the same clothes, a long skirt and blue flowered blouse under a man's work jacket. A felt hat hid her brown hair as she milked. She relieved the dun bovine of three gallons of milk and when she finished David dropped out of the loft and smiled at her.

"Good morning. Do you suppose I could bother you for some of that milk? Nothing gets a morning off to a good start like a cup of fresh, warm milk."

She had stopped in mid-step when he jumped down, and now glanced at the pistol which lay on a pile of hay fifteen feet away. She shrugged and reached for a dipper instead, that hung on a peg on a hewn beam, and handed it to him.

"I figured that you'd be back. You had a determined look on your face, and I knew you weren't a country boy who'd take to sleeping outside. I'm not really surprised."

She poured the dipper full of milk and watched as he drank it.

"I suppose it wouldn't be friendly of me if I send you on your way with only a cup of milk in your belly. Would some fresh eggs and bacon sound good to you, along with some slabs of fresh made bread?"

"Oh, yes, ma'am, it most certainly would!"

"Then clean out the barn, put some fresh

straw in the stall and let Mathilda here out to pasture through that door. Then wash up at the pump and come into the kitchen.''

She smiled and he saw, even though she was tanned and windblown, she wasn't as old as he had first thought, maybe thirty. Her eyes were dark brown, her hair the same color where it fell from under the old hat. She reached for the dipper.

"Well, are you hungry, or not?''

David let the cow into the pasture, then found a pitchfork and began cleaning the stall, throwing the manure out through a small side window made especially for that purpose. When he was done he put fresh bedding in the stall and went out the other barn door and looked for the pump. It was between the barn and the house on slightly higher ground, with a small building made around it to keep it from freezing. He primed the pump with a tin can of water and pumped out a bucket of water which he used to wash his hands and face, then took off his shirt and washed his chest as well and dried off in the early morning sun.

The place had the appearance of near abandonment. It certainly was run down, and he couldn't quite nail down the cause. Boards were missing on the house, the fence had one post knocked over, weeds and wild rose bushes grew near the front door. It had a strange, neglected appearance. He knocked on the back door.

"Come in, if your nose is clean,'' the woman

called.

David grinned. He hadn't heard that old saying since his grandmother Rutledge had died ten years ago. The door led into the kitchen and he smelled the bacon frying before he saw it.

The kitchen was clean and orderly, as neat as a military camp. Everything seemed to be in its place.

"Since you're working and eating here, I might as well tell you my name. Katherine, *Mrs*. Katherine Kellogg." She turned the bacon in the heavy skillet on the small wood burning kitchen stove. Katherine looked up at him again. "I'd say you're one of them college boys who got in trouble for punching the dean right in the nose and you lit out, afraid to go home and face the music."

David laughed and sat down, straddling a wooden chair, and leaned against his crossed arms on the chair back. "Wish it were that simple, Mrs. Kellogg. But that's close enough. My name is David and that's about all I'd rather say."

She lifted her brows, put the bacon on a clean cloth to drain and dropped four eggs into the bacon greased skillet expertly keeping them separate and flipping them over without breaking a yolk. A moment later she slid the four eggs and four thick slices of bacon onto a pottery plate and placed the food in front of him on the table. A tray held slices of light brown bread, a pad of butter and some fresh made crabapple jam.

"Come and eat, David. I had my breakfast before the sun came up."

He went to the table and ate, now realizing how hungry he had been. The eggs and bacon vanished quickly and then he ate the third slice of bread and jam. She sat across the small wooden kitchen table watching him.

"Sorry I don't have any potatoes and onions fried for you. Karl always . . ." She stopped and turned away, looking out the window.

"This is just fine, Mrs. Kellogg. I appreciate it."

She turned back, her face composed again. "Where are you headed? Not much on west of here. Concord is out there a piece, and then after that it's not much but the wilderness."

David shrugged. "I'm not really sure where I'm going."

She brushed back her thick brown hair and smiled. "Which just tells me again you're not *going to* something, you're *running away* from something. A girl?"

David looked up quickly and Katherine laughed softly. "Well, that figures. The handsome ones like you always do wind up that way, either you have to marry the girl or you take off, fast. Looks like you are the moving kind."

David finished the breakfast without saying anything more and when he pushed back the chair, he stood.

"Mrs. Kellogg, you're alone here, aren't

you? Did your husband die?''

She nodded, not looking at him. ''Near a year ago, now. I never saw him after. Neighbor man went looking, said it was that old hook-horned bull we had. We always let him run in the pasture. He never had been mean before. One day Karl went down there, working on the fence . . .'' She stopped and stared out the window again. ''They made a box and buried him out by the garden, wouldn't let me look inside. Neighbor said it must have happened real quick.'' She sighed. ''But don't make no difference, I'm still just as much a widow.''

''I noticed a few things outside that could be fixed up. The near fence, the well house . . .'' He looked up at her and saw she had snapped back and had lost the vacant stare.

''You're a city boy, David. What do you know about a farm? Probably don't know one teat from the other.''

He watched her. ''I could learn. I catch on to things very quickly. I can fix up things a little, get the place through the summer anyhow. You got any crops to put in? Bet you haven't planted a lick since . . . in the past year. Just show me what to do and how to do it. I learn fast.''

She sat down across from him and he settled back onto the chair again.

''Tell you the honest, God's truth, David, I was thinking about that. That and other things. A man in this end of the county ain't easy to come by.'' She looked at him critically again, frowning. "You ain't running from the law, are you, David?"

"Just from a girl."

"You like kids? I got me two. One three and little Josie you saw yesterday. Josie is ten months."

"I get along with kids, I used to be one myself."

She laughed and he realized that she must not have had much to laugh about for a long time. When she quieted, her eyes met his and there was a look of longing there that he had seen before and he silently acknowledged it.

"Mr. David No-name, will you promise to stay out of my bed?"

"Mrs. Kellogg, I'll not be sharing your bed until you ask me to."

She frowned at first, then smiled and broke into a laugh that he knew was a screen for her true feelings, but at the same time it stripped her naked.

She stood and held out her hand. "David, I think you'll make a good hired man. I got no money to pay you. Food and a bed . . . of your own!"

"That's fine, Mrs. Kellogg. I have no use for money. I'll go get my horse and put him in the pasture, then you make a list of things you want me to do, and I'll start getting them done!"

Katherine Kellogg watched David walk past the barn and into the woods. She smiled, wondering at this stroke of luck. Wondering as well what he would look like without his clothes on. She shivered. It had been so long. Where had he come from? She wasn't sure and now she didn't care. He was here, and she would have an adult to talk to. Sometimes she grew so tired of talking with a three year old that she could scream.

Katherine looked in the mirror over the wash basin. She hadn't glanced in the glass for at least a month. It was so spotted and dusty she could hardly see her reflection. Katherine Kellogg hummed a little tune as she cleaned off the mirror and then tucked some stray strands of hair back into the tie at the back of her neck.

Chapter Twelve
DOWN BUT NOT OUT

Ben almost wept when he drove through Boston's quiet streets that Monday morning, December 5. Only a few months before there had been many happy faces, going about their jobs in business and commerce, but now there were few faces at all and those were rushing from one warm building to the next. Hundreds of shops had been closed, and only the barest of essentials were available in the stores still open.

The Freedom Fighters had loaded their diamonds and other jewelry from the old Trotter store into boxes and taken it all to New York under guard and sold the goods there to a dealer at a wholesale price. The money went into the Freedom Fighters' treasury.

Ben's business was struggling to survive even in New York's busy port. He was not on hand for the many small day to day problems which can be so important to a firm.

Many of the unemployed people who could get away had fled from Boston. Hundreds went into the surrounding towns and villages to stay with friends and relatives. There they found a better food supply. The farmers generally put away most of the food they would need for the winter in salt or in root cellars. Quantities of potatoes, squash, pumpkins, dried beans, peas, corn and bushels of dried and fresh apples were usually on hand. There were always a few chickens that could be sacrificed for a Sunday dinner and, if times grew bad, there was a yearling bull calf ready for slaughter.

Farmers had never had so many friends to help them with their harvests that fall of 1774, but by December they were wishing their shirttail relatives would go back to Boston. No one was returning to Boston who wasn't bodily thrown out of a farm house.

Boston Town Meeting leaders, in unofficial meetings, reported that they had lists of seven thousand persons on relief. They demanded food from the British authorities to feed the hungry but did not even receive a reply. More than one honest man turned to thievery so that his family would not starve. Each day wagons arrived in Boston with gifts of food and even coal from other colonies, but it was a trickle, compared to the flood of the need. Ben's own ships, coming in at Salem now, were transporting food, but the time and sweat in getting the loaded wagons to Boston over the twenty miles of "Salem highway," as they were calling it, were incalculable. Wagons broke down, the streams couldn't be crossed. Sometimes whole wagons loaded with food would be swept down a stream when stout ropes broke and horses failed to find footing on the opposite bank.

In the homes the people heated only the most used rooms, the kitchen, and maybe a parlour. Never the bedrooms, or living rooms. Even whale oil was scarce, and nighttime reading and three-lamp lit rooms were a thing of the past. Much reading was done in front of the kitchen fireplace.

British troops in Boston were feeling the pinch as well. Supplies that ordinarily would be purchased locally for the troops had to be obtained elsewhere in the colonies, brought by ship to Boston, and then distributed. General Gage had a partial solution to his problem, but he put it off as long as he thought he could. Now he had to act.

Ben came home from a meeting with John Hancock. They discussed ways to cut their operating costs, and then came to grips with the problem that all of their shipping contacts were in Great Britain. They were prevented by the Maritime Acts from trading with any other nation. If and when war did come, they would have to make entirely new contacts, new markets and new sources of supply. The reorganization would have to be set up quickly. France was the most likely nation to approach. But what about the problems of language, the medium of exchange and financing? There would be hundreds of details to work out. John thought about sending a representative to Paris to consider the matter.

Ben was mulling all this over when he came into his home through the rear entrance. His wife, Sandra, waited for him near the door.

"There are two men here to see you, Ben," she said. "I don't like it at all. They are British officers and both have their packs, bedrolls and gear."

"How many?"

"Two, what are we to do?"

Ben looked at his belt. He had not taken his flintlock pistol with him that morning.

"You stay in the kitchen, and keep everyone else there, too. I'll take care of them." He strode to the hall and down it to his den where he picked up his flintlock and checked it, shook out the primer and put in a fresh supply, then pushed the twelve-inch weapon through the front of his belt and marched down to the parlor where the two officers sat.

Both were alert, evidently having heard him arrive. As soon as Ben entered the room both men jumped up, snapped to attention and saluted. The older of the two spoke.

"Lieutenant Smith-Edwards, sir. We have orders from General Thomas Gage. Here they are with his compliments, sir."

Both officers dropped their salutes and stood at attention.

Ben took the offered paper, three thicknesses

and folded, then sealed with wax and a royal symbol embossed in it. He broke the seal and opened the papers.

In a moment Ben knew what they were. Quartering orders! General Gage intended to quarter two Lobsterback lieutenants in his house, under his roof, eating his food. He wouldn't have it!

"Request denied, Lieutenant. You may take your gear and return to your tent and convey my regrets to your general that I am not equipped to take on boarders, neither do I wish to. Your request is denied, and you are instructed to leave my house at once!"

"Sir, this is not a request, but an order from the general. You are no doubt aware of the Quartering Act, passed by Parliament in June? This is the implementation of that act. You cannot refuse a legal and lawful order of your military governor."

Ben had the flintlock out before either of the men could make a similar move.

"Primed, loaded and cocked, gentlemen. This is my house, not the Parliament's, not Tom Gage's. You can tell Tom that if you wish and tell him he can take a flying leap off Castle William, for all I care. Or if you wish to contest me, you can both die right here, trying to get your weapons."

Neither officer moved.

"Well, what's it to be?" Ben asked.

"Sir, you may be familiar with the Quartering Act, but did you realize that refusal to accept troops when so ordered by the commander leaves the corrective action up to the discretion of the military governor? You may wish to read the second paragraph on the first page, sir. It indicates that any home owner who refuses to board men or officers so assigned, may have his home sold at public auction. Or the owners may be evicted and the entire structure used by troops, or the officer in charge has the option of burning to the ground any house where quartering is refused.''

Ben ripped the pages open, found the second paragraph and read it quickly. The Lobsterback lieutenant spoke the truth. Tom Gage had expected refusals, and like a good military man he was, he backed up his orders with punishment and reprisal. No man would risk having his home burned down by refusing to board the troops. Ben read the paragraphs again. They said nothing about the quality of the lodging or where in the home it must be done. Ben had an idea.

"Gentlemen, pick up your gear and follow me.''

"Don't you have servants who could . . .''

Ben stopped him with a withering glance. "My servants serve me and my household, not interlopers and the unwelcome. If you want that trash, you carry it. If it's there when I come back, I'll burn it.''

Ben turned and walked down the hall, giving them time to grab their packs and bags and stumble after him. He went through the back parlor and out the rear door. Ben walked deliberately to the stable where he opened a door and went up a flight of open steps to a room over the horses. It had been fixed up at one time as a play room for the children, and later the stable boys had slept there. Now they were in the big house for the cold months. There was no heat in the room and it was not built to hold out much of the bitter cold.

"Here are your quarters, gentlemen. If you will read your orders carefully, you will find that they do not say a word about the quality of the lodging or the food. This building is an integral part of my home. If you will look further the orders do not say that your quarters must be comfortable or heated in winter or shaded in summer."

Ben smiled at them as they dropped their belongings on the two old cots that had been left there in the fall.

"Neither does it say anything about providing you with beds, furniture or conveniences. Lodging, it says, food and lodging, and indeed that is all you'll get." He paused and looked at the scowls on their faces. "Do you have any complaints, gentlemen?"

"No sir," the younger one said.

"You know very well this is in violation of the spirit of the order," the older man said. "It might be permitted for some common soldier . . ."

"But you think you're better than your own soldiers? You flatter yourself. You bleed, do you not? You weep. So do they. Anyway, I am not a spiritual man, nor is that a spiritual order you gave me. It's a factual order, and factually I have obeyed it." He walked to the door. "Neither does it say anything about furnishing you with light, however—out of the goodness of my heart you can utilize the small lamp on the stand. However, you must provide your own whale oil—if you can find any at the stores. The military occupying forces have been buying it all up, for the officers' barracks, I hear."

Ben watched them. Both were fuming, but holding back their anger, waiting for their rage to explode where it would not hurt them or give Ben any more satisfaction. Ben wanted to laugh.

"Oh, do you sleep lightly, gentlemen? We sometimes come home late at night, and our stable boy is a loud and demanding person who drinks often to excess and shouts a lot at night. But you'll get used to that after a few weeks. The cold, aye, that's what will bedevil you. You'll need to apply to your quartermaster for more blankets. Now, just one more thing. I am not a Tory sympathizer. I consider both of you my enemies. I predict we will be in a shooting war with you Englishmen within six months, a war for the independence of this land, as our Sam Adams has so long perdicted. If I hear the opening shots before you do, yours will be the first British throats that I'll have the pleasure of slitting open."

Ben slammed the door and walked down the steps to the stable with a fury that was unusual for him. If tomorrow he found out that he alone was singled out for "occupation" he would go directly to General Gage himself and protest in the strongest possible terms.

Back inside his home, Ben made arrangements for minimal meals to be sent to the British officers twice a day. He left specific instructions that a hot meal should be left to cool until almost tepid, and the poorest cuts of meat were to be served in smaller portions than usual.

The next day Ben discovered that more than a thousand troops would be assigned to live in Boston homes.

It didn't make Ben feel any better, but he knew he was not alone. He urged his acquaintances to set a standard of minimal existence for the British house guests, to provide them with little better than a starvation diet. They should be fed separately and treated with contempt.

Ben talked to the Committee on Correspondence and saw that a hundred letters were sent out explaining this new outrage against the people of Boston, and how the quartering had finally taken place. Ben knew that the only thing that Boston could do was tighten its belt and watch and wait.

Harriet disliked having the two British officers in the stable house as much as her father did. She made it a point never to be within sight of them. The Freedom Fighters meetings were transferred back to the Old Boston Book Shop on Tuesday nights. Training sessions had been slowed to one each two months. The cadre training the militia reported excellent results, and now a new order came down from the council. Each Freedom Fighter must join a militia unit if he was not already involved. It was becoming obvious to the council that, when war came, the militia would stand the first line of defense or make the first strike. The units had political acceptance, funding and a chain of command. The Freedom Fighters would blend in and should soon rise to places of command and authority. Ben went back to his old company as the commander and a ranked captain.

Harriet worried and wondered where she could find more food for those near starvation. She had given up any pretense of working with Rutledge & Rutledge and now spent all of her time searching for food. She took Robert with her and another armed Freedom Fighter on a hazardous horseback ride toward Providence, Rhode Island colony, hoping to find some new sources of food, but the expedition came back empty handed. Again the problem of almost no roads complicated the matter. She would not let these people starve!

Once more she set out with Robert and another Freedom Fighter, contacting the farmers around Boston to see if they could sell or give stores to the hungry people. This time they picked up a wagon at the first farm and soon found a few hundred pounds of potatoes, squash, pumpkins, and some sacks of dried beans and wheat and corn. They hurried the goods back to Boston, taking a ferry across the bay from Charlestown. They made dozens of trips in the next two weeks and managed to save many families from starvation.

After the third such week, Harriet collapsed at home, and Dr. Warren ordered her to take a complete week's rest.

That evening Dan McCallister came to see her. He felt her forehead and then held her hand.

"I understand this treatment is said to be excellent medication by some experts," he said.

"I know what would help more," Harriet countered. He leaned in and kissed her cheek and she pretended to faint. Then she smiled, her heart so full she didn't think she could stand it. He was the most handsome man she had ever seen!

In the last four months they had seen each other twice a week without fail. Their mutual attraction had grown into a strong, sure love and, while there was nothing official, they considered that they had an agreement, that they were "promised" to each other.

Tonight Daniel's face was a little flushed, and she sat up in bed and arranged the comforters and hand stitched quilts around her.

"Young man, I'm no doctor, but I'd say that

you have a bit of a fever. Your face is flushed."

"Well, Harriet Rutledge, it's about time you noticed!"

"Noticed what?"

"That I'm as excited as a turtledove on a spring morning."

"Does that mean all worked up?"

"About as jumping around excited as a turtledove ever gets." He reached into his inside waistcoat pocket and handed her a card.

"My new card, miss, just off the press. You're the first to see it."

She read it, then looked up, but her glance shot back to the card and she screeched in delight.

"*Doctor* Daniel McCallister! *Doctor*. You made it, you finally passed your tests with Dr. Warren?" She reached out for him and kissed his lips and hugged him so tightly that Daniel had to laugh and pull away.

"Hey, hey, you're supposed to be resting up, not wrestling with your doctor."

"Oh, Daniel, that's the best news I've heard in just months and months and months! I'm so happy!"

He sat there holding both her hands. "And when you're happy it makes you even more beautiful. You're the most beautiful little girl I've ever seen. The way your eyes sparkle, and that funny little nose of yours."

"Darling Daniel! You could even open your own office now, couldn't you?"

"Well, no, not for a while. I've been talking with Dr. Warren, and he says there's no hurry for that. There are other things coming up that are more important."

"But Boston doesn't have enough doctors. You've told me that. You've said that we have seven or eight in the whole city, and that we need twenty or twenty-five more. Anyway, what could be more important than your own practice?"

"We will have our own practice, eventually. But right now I'd only just get started and have to stop."

"Stop? Why stop? I thought . . ." She closed her eyes and bobbed her head. "Oh, you mean the war, that we're going to have a revolution and it's getting closer and closer, and the soldiers will need the doctors more than the civilians, and you would be one of the first to volunteer, and . . ."

He put his arms around her and held her tightly. "Yes, my love. But I'm not going to wait until the shooting starts. I'm going to sign up now with one of the best militia units. Dr. Warren has been spearheading a drive to get one doctor for each three companies of militia. If anything happens, I report along with the other men, try to assemble a group of materials, set up a medical treatment position somewhere to the rear of any fighting, but close enough to be of some help."

She was crying. Tears seeped from Harriet's

eyes and ran down her cheeks. He kissed them away, then kissed her lips and her eyes to open them.

"And I think we should set a wedding date, our wedding date."

Harriet looked up at him. Then the tears really came and she held him tightly again, trying to talk through the tears. But the words came out only in gasps. He couldn't tell what she was trying to say, but he got the idea she was crying happy tears, and he let her cry it out, then wiped her eyes and let her blow her nose.

"Now, let's try that all again. I said I thought we should figure out the exact date of our wedding and you said . . ."

"Daniel McCallister, I love you!"

"That's what I hoped you said." He kissed her and eased her back on the bed with the pillow behind her so she sat up comfortably, then he stood and paced to the window.

"Back to the wedding. How about sometime in February? Would that give you enough time to do all the things that women seem to think are so important?"

"Yes, Daniel," she said softly.

He looked surprised. Then teased her. "Now that is a change, the submissive, dutiful woman. Well, I might as well bask in it while I can. Knowing that independent coltish nature of yours, you won't be able to put up with docile humility for very long."

"Darling, why did you mention February for

the wedding?''

"It will be warmer then, maybe we can use a church."

"No, now be serious, you had another reason, too. What was it?"

"Everyone I've talked to lately says that we will be at war when warm weather comes. Sam Adams, Dr. Warren, Captain Hancock, even John Adams and Paul Revere admit that we will be firing musket balls at the British before the Second Continental Congress convenes in May. I want us to be properly married, man and wife, and with some time together before this all happens."

"You'll go with the first shots?"

"Yes, and perhaps before, depending on what unit can use me and where I'm sent. I'll be in the army then, and I'll do what they tell me to do."

"But you won't be in the battles, you won't be . . ."

"Shot at? It all depends. Battle lines can move and shift, you never know."

"I wish we were married right now!"

"So do I, but we're not, and you're ill, and you need to get well, and I have to make a house call before it gets too late. You get to sleep early tonight and I'll come see you tomorrow, if you promise to stay in bed and rest."

"Promise, I promise, if you'll kiss me once more."

He did and then lifted away and smiled at her.

"Little girl, I like you. You watch your manners and you may get free medical advice for the rest of your life. Now, I have to go see Mrs. Jennings. You talk with your mother, and then be sleeping by nine-thirty."

"Yes, doctor," she said and smiled as he left the room. Harriet closed her eyes and let her fondest dreams float across her mind. This was a wonderful day, a beautiful day, one she would cherish and remember and glorify for ever and ever!

That evening Harriet and her mother talked until well past ten o'clock before they noticed the time. They had so much planning to do, lists to make, people to see, dresses to get ready. When her mother turned out the lamp and closed the door, Harriet smiled and thought about Daniel. "Good night, my darling Doctor Daniel McCallister," she said, a beautiful smile lighting her face.

Chapter Thirteen
THE DISCOVERING OF DAVID

Harriet soon recovered from her exhaustion and flew back into the fight to save the starving. She read the *Speaker* one night and cried over a report that a family of four had starved to death not a mile from where she sat because they had been too proud to ask for help. The father had been ill and had refused to let his wife go out of the small house to ask for fuel or food because they had no money. They were found by a neighbor, all four huddled together with their arms around each other, their emaciated bodies frozen to death.

Two weeks during January and again in February, Harriet led teams of six Freedom Fighters into the country with big wagons. They went from farm to farm asking for any extra food or grain or corn they might have to give to the Boston starving. At every farm now they found food waiting: a sack of potatoes, a wooden box filled with oats, sometimes a sack of dried beans or a few sacks of wheat or barley. Dried apples were plentiful; everyone had dried apples and they all shared.

The last week in February, Harriet and Dr. McCallister were married in her father's big house. They opened up the living room and the parlour and invited in a few close friends. After the ceremony they moved into a small house Dr. McCallister had rented two months before. There was no time for a wedding trip. Dr. McCallister took off three days, then went back to work to help Dr. Warren.

A week after her wedding, Harriet and Robert set up another trip into the countryside. March came in like a lion that year with cold winds, more snow, and lowered temperatures. They had worked the closer farms and now were just the other side of Lexington. So far on this mission they had filled three wagons and sent them back and were now working on the last one.

Robert started to kick his way through an errant snow drift to get to the front door of a small farm house, then changed his mind and went up to the rear door. Most farmers lived out of the back of their homes, he knew. His knock was brisk and the door opened promptly.

Robert hardly recognized the man who faced him. His hair was long, he wore a beard and a moustache, but there was no denying those eyes.

"What . . .? David. Well, hello!"

David lifted his brows and smiled. "Afternoon, Robert. Are you alone?"

"No, Harriet is with me. May we come in?"

"Of course."

A few moments later Harriet hugged David and sat near him by the fire. They had been introduced to Katherine Kellogg and her two squirming youngsters, and after a few moments the farm woman stood to leave. David took her hand.

"No, Kate, I'd like you to stay. You deserve to hear whatever is said." He looked at Robert. "I told Kate about Millie. She knows all about it. If you're going to scold me for shaming the whole family, I understand."

"There was no shaming, no scandal, David," Robert said.

"Robert married Millie four days after you left, David," said Harriet. "That put a stop to any rumors that could have started. Right now Millie is home almost ready to give birth."

"So then it could be . . ."

"No, David, you don't have to think about that. Millie is bearing *my* son, that's been decided for sure, *by me*."

David smiled and reached out and shook hands with Robert. "Congratulations then, Daddy, and I thank you for solving a nasty situation. But remember, I have a side to the story as well." David shook his head. "I just can't imagine my brother as an old married man."

"He's a wonderful husband, David. He went to work in the firm and didn't go back to Harvard. A lot of the boys didn't go back this year for a lot of reasons.'' She looked at David and smiled. ''I *like* you with a beard, it just seems to fit. Every poet should wear a beard.''

''I haven't been writing much lately. Too busy.''

''David, you don't know about Harriet's new husband, either, then, do you?'' He went on to tell about Dr. McCallister and how he was tied in closely with the Freedom Fighters and now with the militia. That led to questions about other people David knew, and time drifted past.

''I had heard about someone coming to the farms looking for donations for the starving Boston poor,'' David said. ''I should have known it would be you two. Is your battle almost won?''

''It will be in another month,'' Harriet said. ''What do you have to give to us? A few potatoes or some beans?''

David held up his hand. ''We've been saving up for you. We usually feed our older potatoes to the hogs, but this year we saved them. Kate and I talked it over and we want to butcher out two of our hogs for you. Just before you head back we'll get them ready. Now, tell me more about this Dr. McCallister. You sure his middle name isn't Trotter?''

Harriet poked at him with her fist and scowled at him in mock anger.

''Dr. McCallister was an apprentice with Dr. Warren, and is the nicest, sweetest man I have ever met.''

They talked for another hour and by then it was so late that David asked them to stay for the night. Robert unhitched the team and put the horses in the barn.

It was a fine evening, Harriet reflected that night as she curled up on a couch in the living room. Robert was already sleeping on some blankets in front of the fire. She had never really known David before as a person. He was bright, quick, intelligent and so closely in tune with other people and sensitive to what they thought, how they felt. He shouldn't be shut away here the rest of his life. Harriet wondered about his relationship to Mrs. Kellogg, and decided they were sleeping together, but that was none of her business. She was glad they had found David. Now they would have a chance of getting him back home, back to Boston where he could pick up his life again.

The next morning at breakfast she asked David if he were coming home soon. He shook his head.

"No, I have a farm to run and four mouths to keep fed, and Kate couldn't get along here without me now. She tried, but things were breaking down and falling apart. A farm is no place for a woman who's alone, especially in times like these."

"David, Father thinks we'll be at war soon."

"Yes, we hear the same thing. I've signed up with the militia, Captain Parker's unit in Lexington. They've worked out a series of signals to call us. Greg Smith, my closest neighbor, will get word from his neighbor and will ride over and call me. We're the farthest ones out. They say some of them can respond in a minute after they're called. So we'll be ready here, when the time comes."

"Father will be pleased about that. I just wish you'd come back home with us."

"I can't do that, Harriet. Kate wouldn't like that a bit."

Katherine came over and poured more coffee for them. "He's right, Mrs. McCallister. I wouldn't like it, but I have no real hold on him. I know that David is young and ambitious, and smart and a real dreamer. And I know that when it's time for him to pick up and go, he'll go. Nothing will be able to hold him here. So I'll just treasure those days that he's here, and be thankful for them."

David got up and smiled at both of them.

Then the dreamer and poet went outside and butchered two hogs. He put them in the bottom of the wagon, and covered them over with straw. They would be frozen within two or three hours.

An hour later Harriet and Robert were ready to leave. They shook hands and Harriet kissed David's cheek and made him promise to write to their father. They set a time when they would be in Lexington to see him, Harriet suggesting the middle of next month. She would be at Buckman's Tavern in Lexington on April 18 and hoped to see him there that evening. David promised that he would come to see her in the evening about six. Then they drove away.

They hurried now, straight back to the flat bottomed boat at Charlestown and the quick trip across the water to Boston. Harriet let Robert see to the food distribution from the wagon and went to see her father and tell him the news about finding David.

By the middle of March, 1775, there were over 4,000 British soldiers in Boston. Many lived in Boston homes, in warehouses, in barracks, anywhere General Gage could find a place for them out of the wind and the weather.

The military units controlled the town. Food was still scarce; no crops could be planted yet, let alone harvested. Salt pork and salt beef were even running in short supply, and many a farmer's chicken coop was raided by those so hungry they were reduced to stealing.

Many of the strong Tories had left Boston, some traveling to Canada, others back to England. The ones with the biggest investment in shops and stores stayed on, hoping against logic that the problems could be worked out and war prevented.

With each passing week the Rebels built up more shot and powder in the farm storehouse at Concord. Weapons were lost by the British Redcoats, or stolen from them, and they all found their way into Rebel hands. Soon a stiff penalty was set for any civilian having a British

Brown Bess musket.

Twice Robert headed a three-man party taking more powder and weapons to Concord. This trip they chose a roundabout way, became lost once, and then, using back roads, got to within two miles of their destination, an obscure farm, when a six-man British mounted patrol rode up quickly to meet them.

Robert wore farm clothes and a slouch hat and did not have a weapon. A pitchfork was jammed into the load of loose hay they had picked up, filling the wagon and covering their load of weapons. The two Freedom Fighters behind Robert did not show any weapons either, but flintlock pistols loaded and primed lay under the hay near all three men.

"Evening," Robert said easily.

"Where are you men going?" the officer in charge asked.

"Right up the road, the Glendenning place, about five miles. We got low on hay."

"How much livestock do you have there?"

"Just two old boney milk cows. Keep the family and the little ones in milk. You ain't planning on taking the only cows we got left, are ya, army officer?"

"The British army does not *take* things, young man. At times we must buy food from you colonists, but we always pay."

"Yep. We don't see you Redcoats so far from Boston very often. Lookin' for somethin' special?"

"Certainly not milch cows. Now on your way."

Robert waved at the officer and moved the horse ahead at a walk as the Lobsterbacks stepped their mounts aside and let him drive through. As they cleared the area the men in back told Robert that the squad watched them for some time, but since they continued on slowly, normally, the soldiers lost interest and jogged on down the road toward Boston.

The roving British patrol worried Robert. What if one of them by chance stumbled on to the arms storehouse? Or what if they had found the weapons hidden under the hay in the wagon? The British officer must have been a city man; he had no idea that such a small load of hay would not require three strong men to load and unload. Robert made a note next time to use only two men on such a mission, and put on more hay. It would make the whole trip less suspect.

Robert did not like to think what would happen if a British patrol did stumble on the arms storehouse, really several small buildings on a farm outside of Concord, that no one even had a name for. The trouble was, so many knew about the arms, that Robert was surprised that the secret had remained as well kept as it had.

They made their delivery, gave the farmer the hay as well, and with a jug of cider began their homeward trip. Robert was concerned about the scarcity of protection around the storehouse. If he were commanding it, he would have a series of concealed positions ready to block off the roadway, and a semicircle of firing positions dug into the landscape where musketeers could defend the arms. He would talk to his father about this as soon as he got back to Boston.

But by the time the wagon made the twenty mile trip back to Charlestown and across the bay to Boston, it was extremely late, and the men had taken turns driving and sleeping. Now, near exhaustion, Robert stumbled home and fell into bed with not a thought about the lack of security at the Concord farm.

The next morning Robert was up for breakfast and jolted to a stop in surprise as he came into the kitchen. A British Redcoat sat at the table waiting for his food. The Britisher was a member of the 10th Regiment and was always talking about the valor of his commander, a Colonel Smyth. This sergeant had been quartered in Robert's house now for a month, and still Robert found it hard to accept.

The sergeant had been in the army for ten years and had served all over the world. Millie was quite taken with the stories of his adventures, and she insisted on feeding him just as well as she did her husband, even though she was now nine months and one week pregnant, and Robert expected her to bring forth at any moment.

The sergeant put on his large red coat with the

shiny buttons and as he did Robert realized what perfect targets they would make in the sun at a hundred yards, perfect aiming points right down the center of the man's chest. He waved goodbye to the sergeant and suddenly remembered the lack of security around the Rebel arms cache. He would talk to his father about that this very day. And he promised himself he would bring his mother-in-law to live in with them until the baby came. Millie shouldn't be doing the cooking and all, nor should she be left alone, although there were times he had to be gone.

He had told Millie about joining the militia, but she knew nothing about the Freedom Fighters. Not that he mistrusted Millie, but she did talk, constantly she talked. If she didn't know about the Freedom Fighters, there was no danger of a slip of her lip.

Ben listened to Robert's report on the transfer of the weapons to Concord and made some notes about the lack of protection around them. Up to now they had thought a natural and normal appearance of the farm buildings would be the best camouflage, rather than an area bristling with obvious fortifications. But perhaps some compromise could be made. There were enough men in the militia units in the area to defend the arms unless a huge British force marched to capture it. That was unlikely. He would talk to Sam Adams that very day.

Ben said goodbye to Robert, who was on his way to the Livingstons' to pick up his mother-in-law. Ben had the highest regard for his son, who had stepped into a difficult situation and straightened it out without any recriminations or whining. He was glad that David had surfaced, and that he was doing something productive, no matter that he was living in sin with the widow. That would work itself out. What really eased Ben's heart was David's commitment to the militia.

Last week Ben had won permission for Dr. McCallister to function as his battalion medical officer. They had worked long hours putting together two portable cases filled with most of the medical items that Dr. McCallister would need to set up an emergency medical treatment center as close to the front line as possible. Dr. McCallister had found three young men to serve with him as medical aides. They would carry flintlock pistols and be assigned full time to helping the doctor, assisting him in any way, from an amputation to holding down a patient, or moving the equipment forward or to the rear.

Ben was pleased to have Dr. McCallister. He would serve the three companies in the battalion and provide Ben's men the best medical help they could expect in a wartime battle.

Ben was also happy with Harriet's marriage. She had taken to it grandly, and at the same time continued to track down food for the city's poor. He was sure she had singlehandedly kept more than a thousand persons from starving during the coldest of the winter months.

Ben had stopped sampling the people's feelings. He knew that most in Boston were at the critical breaking point. The whole population was angry, furious, ready for action. He knew it, Sam Adams knew it, and he had agreed to have the members of the Massachusetts Assembly hold an unofficial meeting the second week in April. They would call the group The Provincial Congress of Massachusetts, and meet at some nearby city outside Boston, but the place would not be known until three days before the date. That would give General Gage less time to learn about it and to try to break it up.

Ben smiled, not because he knew they were getting closer to war with each breath, but because he realized that at last these colonies were pulling together, and all they needed now was another spark, some violent stroke by the British to spill Rebel blood, and the people would explode into action, a revolution, that could end only in independence for America.

Chapter Fourteen
IT HAS BEGUN

The meeting ended Saturday, April 15, at Concord. Sam Adams had called together the newly formed Provincial Congress of Massachusetts, and most of the regular Assembly members were there, meeting in a semi-secret session to frustrate the forces of the military governor, General Gage. Word had come to the group that Samuel Adams and John Hancock should not return to Boston. Informants said that General Gage had been instructed to capture the two fiery rebel leaders and transport them to London for trial on treason charges, and probably a quick hanging. The British now had decided that the Rebels and the Whigs were going too far in their rebellious talk, and a few hangings of Rebel leaders would cool down the hot heads and bring the colony back in line.

After talking over the matter, both men said they would wait in Lexington, some six miles closer to Boston, until it was time for them to go to Philadelphia in May for the meeting of the

Second Continental Congress. They would stay at the parsonage of the Rev. Jonas Clark, one of Hancock's kinsmen. They were still there on the night of the 18th of April. They felt safe there, where they had a military guard of militiamen. If there were any British move to capture them by troops from Boston, they would be advised in time for escape.

Back in Boston, Dr. Joseph Warren had returned despite the rumors that his name, too, was on the list for capture by the Redcoats. He knew there had to be a link between the high command of Adams and Hancock and the rest of the Rebel operation. When he arrived home Saturday, he found the situation more volatile than he had expected.

Paul Revere's watch-guards, who had been patrolling the streets nightly, reported something stirring in the Redcoat camp. They at once suspected that General Gage was getting ready to move some of his troops, perhaps to raid the munitions and supplies stored at Concord's Rebel Farm arsenal. Revere reported to Dr. Warren that the longboats belonging to the British naval ships anchored in the harbor had been hauled out of the water for inspection and repairs. Then about midnight they had all been floated again and moored under the sterns of the big men-of-war. This, coupled with the known facts that General Gage had detached certain crack elements from the regiments earlier that day and had put them on special duty, spelled trouble for the patriots. These were the grenadier companies, composed of the biggest men in the army, who were Gage's heavy-duty troops. The other units on special duty were light infantry companies, the fleet footed men trained as flankers to a main force.

When the general took his troops out for conditioning marches he did not use long boats; he marched them across Boston Neck and into the country, or he sent them on the ferry north across the Charles River. But no sneak attack could be launched in this manner without alerting towns along the way.

Dr. Warren watched and waited.

Sunday morning, the sixteenth, Dr. Warren dispatched the hard riding, excellent horseman, Paul Revere, on his favorite duty, a quick gallop to Lexington to warn Sam Adams and John Hancock that General Gage might have in mind a lightning march from East Cambridge into Lexington to capture the two rebel leaders, and then sweep on to Concord to destroy the war supplies hidden there.

It was a serious threat. In the past several months the war stores had increased at the Farm. There were many muskets and cannon there, musket balls and cartridges, hundreds of barrels of gunpowder, reams of cartridge paper, spades, axes, medicine chests, tents, hogsheads of flour, pork, beef, salt, boxes of candles, wooden spoons, dishes, canteens, casks of wine and raisins, and dozens of other supplies for war. It would be a tremendous loss if the British got to the supplies.

On his way back to Boston, Revere wondered if the general would block the ferry and the Boston Neck at the same time as his thrust for Concord. It would seem a reasonable move to prevent any prior notice by a fast riding courier. Revere went to Charlestown on his way home. He looked up Colonel William Conant, a top Rebel leader in Charlestown and arranged with him to receive a signal from across the narrow Charles River as to how the general would be attacking. Revere would hoist one lantern in North Church tower if the troops were marching by land over Boston Neck, and two if they were going by small boat across the Back Bay and into Cambridge for a direct move toward Lexington. Revere said that after sending the signal he would try to get to Charlestown as well to help spread the alarm, but if he could not, the lanterns would tell the colonel what alarm to give to the population.

Nothing happened Monday except the manufacture of more and more rumors. Tuesday the weather cleared and turned bright and cold. As darkness approached the rumors were moving again, and odd bits of information turned up to make Gage's attack toward Concord the worst kept secret military operation in the history of mankind. Since many of the soldiers involved were billeted in Boston homes, it was impossible to keep the secret. One message was left at a house for a soldier that told him to be on the Boston Common by eight o'clock with a day's provisions and thirty-six rounds of ball and powder.

Each hour after sunset the tension seemed to mount, as new rumors and facts circulated among Boston's 15,000 persons. First came word that the troops would be moving, and it seemed that everyone knew that they would be going toward Concord to capture the supplies there and to pick up Adams and Hancock as well, on the way.

By ten o'clock that night some unknown messenger knocked on Paul Revere's door and summoned him to Dr. Warren's home, and shortly after that Paul Revere asked a friend to show the two lanterns in the tower at North Church to warn those in Charlestown about the coming of the British. The two lanterns signified that the troops would be crossing the Back Bay, probably landing near Cambridge.

Revere went at once to the river where he kept a boat and had a friend row him across to Charlestown where Colonel Conant and several others met him. They had seen the signals. Revere borrowed a horse from Deacon John Larkin and set off on his ride to warn the countryside. About the same time Dr. Warren sent another man around Boston Neck to spread the word toward Concord. He was William Dawes.

Early on the morning of April 18, Harriet and Robert had left the ferry at Charlestown and moved through the farming areas north and west, searching out more food for the Boston sick and needy. During the day they loaded the wagon half full and at six o'clock stopped in Lexington's Buckman's Tavern and Inn where they arranged for supper and rooms for the night. They ate and soon thereafter David came, as they had arranged a month before. The three of them sat in the common room away from the tavern and drank coffee and talked, warming themselves in front of the fire.

"How many trips have you taken now searching for food?" David asked them.

Harriet looked at Robert in question but he shook his head. "Maybe thirty wagon loads, maybe forty. After a dozen or so we lost track. But there is a continuing need until the blockade is lifted. I'm afraid someone is going to have to keep up such work all summer. Of course then we can send some of the people out to work on the farms and harvest their own food. It will be much easier for us then. But still there are two or three hundred who are old and sick and hurt so they can't even get out of their homes.

"You've heard the talk of war?" Robert asked suddenly. "Boston is filled with it. General Gage is about to move some of his troops somewhere and rumors are building on rumors."

"We've heard," David said. "Captain Parker sent word to stay close to our homes in case of a callup. Sam Adams and John Hancock are staying nearby and we have to defend them as well. We've changed our signals, too. Now it's two quick shots in a row, musket or pistol. That means for everyone to come running. I get the message from a farm two over from me. Then I saddle and take my long gun and ride pell-mell for the Meeting House.

"On my way in I saw Captain Parker outside the tavern pacing back and forth. He suggested that since I'm here I stay in town tonight, at least until two o'clock. He says something may be close to happening."

Harriet sighed. "If it has to be, it must. But I admit that the closer we come to actual armed hostilities, the less I'm liking it."

"Your Dr. McCallister will be in the very thick of it, won't he?" David asked.

She looked at him, and her face lost its concerned expression which was replaced by a controlled but anguished look of fear.

"Don't worry, they keep the doctors far back out of the fighting," David said. "They always did with the French and Indians. He won't have a thing to worry about, and neither will you."

"Thank you, thank you, David, for saying that. But I know that when men play with guns, people get hurt and killed. I guess that's one thing that every soldier and militiaman has to consider. Any time you hold a gun and someone else holds a gun and you're on opposite sides, anything can happen."

She turned away and dabbed at her eyes, then

took a deep breath. "I'm sorry, I usually don't let things get away from me that way."

David patted her shoulder and went and brought two big mugs of beer, and a glass of sherry for Harriet. "I didn't think to ask, are you a beer drinker now, Harriet?"

"No, David, I'm not. I've changed, but not that much."

"David, do you know why I asked you to meet us here tonight?"

"I have an idea, but tell me."

"Because we want you to come back home. We need you. The family needs you, the business needs you. We just want you to come back home. Nobody is going to be angry with you."

David moved over to the fireplace and threw another split log on the fire and stirred the coals. When he came back he was composed and facing Harriet.

"Big sister, I appreciate what you're saying, and your affection. We never have been a close family, but now I think I'm starting to understand a little more about what those words mean. I really don't think what we decide here tonight is going to have much effect on our future as a family. From the look in Captain Parker's eye, our company is going to be called out very soon, this week for sure, maybe even tonight, and when we go we will be fighting. I might be dead within twenty-four hours."

"Oh, no!"

"Oh, yes. You've been listening to the war

talk, the push for independence. It's everywhere. At first it was just the leaders like Father, and Dr. Warren and Sam Adams. But now it's everywhere. Even us farmers are talking about guns and war supplies and emplacements, and how many buttons down on a Redcoat's chest you shoot for the best results. This war, when it comes, will change our lives drastically. And it will come. Maybe not tonight, maybe not next week or next month, but it is coming. And I've been trained, I can shoot, so there's no doubt that when the time is ripe, I'll be in the fighting. Why should I pull up all my tent stakes and move right now, when I'll be leaving again very soon?''

He looked at both of them. ''Robert, what do you think about all this? Aren't we very close to a shooting war?''

''Yes, David. Extremely close. I don't see how the two sides can stay apart for more than another week, especially if Gage does send troops toward Concord. I think you should stay right here, it won't be long.''

Harriet looked from one to the other and she began to cry. Tears spilled down her cheeks, and David moved over and held her hand.

''Hey, don't worry, we'll be careful. We don't want to take a musket ball any more than you want us to.''

Robert agreed. ''Even if the war does start this coming month or next month, it will be a while before either of us could see any action.

We'd have to be reformed into new units, and then we'd need some unit training. Now, let's forget all about that and talk about something else. I know we're going to need a big pitcher of beer and some crackers. I think I'll bring back that whole bottle of sherry while I'm at it."

So they talked and talked, and it was nearly midnight when Harriet begged off, saying she had to get to bed.

"You're not starting to feel sick in the mornings, are you, Harriet?" Robert asked with a knowing grin.

She made a face at Robert. "Now, that is just none of your business, little brother, and I wouldn't tell you if I were."

They said good night and a short time later David shook hands with Robert and headed for his horse outside the tavern.

Just as he mounted he heard someone riding in fast from Boston Road and saw a man pull up at the Meeting House. David rode over to greet him, and saw his father's friend, Paul Revere.

"Where's Captain Parker?" Revere asked. "His wife said he was here."

"Let's try the tavern," David said. Indeed, Captain Parker was there, pacing in front of the fire. He spoke with Revere a moment, then the courier said he was off to Clark's house and hurried out the door.

Captain Parker shouted his orders plain and clear. "Alert the minutemen, call out the company. The British regulars have marched from

Boston with seven hundred men. They've crossed the Charles in longboats and are heading our way."

The belfry in front of the barn-like Meeting House rang with a series of two tolls, and in the distance David could hear many twin shot reports that would rouse the militia. There were some one hundred men in the company, but David had no idea how many would hear the call and respond.

David asked where he might get a weapon, and Captain Parker took him to the Meeting House and opened the magazine.

"Take over here, Rutledge. Give out a weapon, powder and ball to every man who needs it. Then have them report to the common. You come along, too."

By one o'clock there were ninety-five militiamen waiting on the green. The night had turned cold and men stamped their feet and rechecked their loads and primers. Robert had dressed and come down and brought out his long gun to stand with the Lexington militia.

Regulars, Marines? Grenadiers? The questions flew on the common. David and Robert talked in low tones near the Meeting House as they waited. Captain Parker had told them all he knew. Paul Revere and another man were spreading the word, arousing the towns, getting ready for the troops which were on the way to Concord where they were thought to be after the war stores, and to capture Mr. Adams and Mr.

Hancock, who had quietly faded out of the preacher's house and into the countryside.

Seven hundred regulars! The idea sent a shiver down Captain Parker's spine. His company could never repulse them. He had no orders what to do. Orders to oppose them with force and shot would have to come directly from Sam Adams. So what should he do? He looked over the Lexington Common, a triangle where the Boston Road came in, slanted to the right to Bedford and forked to the left to go to Concord six miles away. The roads formed a triangle of the Lexington Common. If he drew his men up on the green facing the Concord Road, but well in back of it, that could in no way be interpreted as challenging the right of the British to pass.

Captain Parker relaxed. He had no orders to fire, so it would be another eye-to-eye confrontation, and the British would march past throwing only insults at the non-uniformed militia.

By two a.m., his men were grumbling, and Captain Parker told them to wait. He had sent out six scouts on the road toward Boston to let him know of the approach of the British. No scouts had returned. He let the men go, telling those who lived close by to listen for the drum which would bring them back on the run. If they slept, it should be with their clothes and boots on and their muskets loaded and primed. The rest of the men took refuge in the warm interior of Buckman's tavern. There was more talking and worrying than drinking. The big hearth with its fire built up was the main attraction for the chilled militiamen.

While the Lexington militia waited, the British were having more than their share of troubles and delays. Colonel Francis Smith commanded the total force of seven hundred men being sent to seize the stores and the Rebel leaders. He was senior in command, but he was known as a grossly fat, slow thinking and usually late to everything kind of a man. Second in command was Major Pitcairn of the marines, an old line, highly intelligent and compassionate man.

After the usual precautions of secrecy, the men at last were loaded into the longboats, rowed quietly across the Charles and landed in a deserted section of Cambridge. There was good reason it was deserted; it was a long stretch of swampy land which the long boats couldn't work through. They off-loaded the men in knee deep water, and they waded ashore, wet, cold and angry. The troops waited on a dirt road until one a.m. for supplies to arrive. When they came most of the men threw them away since they had brought a day's provisions of their own. When they marched ahead they cut across an arm of land to maintain their secrecy and had to ford a wide body of water that turned out to be waist deep. The men's anger at their own officers increased.

By this time Colonel Smith realized he was far behind his schedule and sent Major Pitcairn ahead with six companies quick-stepping to secure the two bridges near Concord. His path lay through Lexington. Pitcairn was a careful soldier, and sent out advance scouts to lead the way and provide protection for his four hundred men. These scouts captured five of Captain Parker's six scouts, but the sixth one slipped away and gave the alarm.

When the British troops neared Lexington it was almost daylight, and the scout, Thaddeus Bowman, galloped into the Common and shouted at Captain Parker that the British were not more than half a mile behind him, four hundred of them with mounted officers.

Captain Parker called for the drummer to beat to arms. Men stumbled out of houses, the tavern and lofts. Soon seventy men assembled on the green and Captain Parker formed them up in a long file on the north end of the Lexington Common near the Bedford Road. The British would not have to cross the line to continue their march to Concord.

By the time the militia was in line, Robert Rutledge among them could see the first of the British troopers coming in from the Boston Road. They hesitated, then marched forward until the main body was between the Meeting House and Buckman's Tavern.

Harriet had been roused by the shouts from below and the galloping of horses. She jumped out of bed and dressed. As she looked out the window she saw Robert run from the Tavern and take his place in the militiamen's line. She saw it all from her second story window.

Harriet watched in shocked fascination and terror as the Redcoats continued down the road directly at the militia, avoiding the regular road to Concord in front of the Meeting House where they should have turned left. Instead, their officer guided them in back of the Meeting House and within sixty yards of Captain Parker's citizen-soldier formation.

When Captain Parker realized the regulars had continued their advance, he yelled at his men, ordering them to disperse. They began to fall back irregularly, searching for hiding places and protection. A few men stood steady, not moving. The British grenadiers gave a victory shout and an officer rode forward.

"Lay down your arms, you damned Rebels, or you will be dead men!" the officer shouted.

Almost on top of his shout came a command to "Fire!" and British muskets all along the line exploded. David ran backward, stumbled and fell, almost lost his musket, but got up and ran again. Now David heard the first shots, but felt no musket balls going past him. Robert had been at the far end of the line and quickly found shelter and protection behind a heavy farm wagon.

The first shots from the British were harmless, since they had been told to load with powder and wadding only and no ball. But the next volley slammed musket balls into the running militiamen.

Major Pitcairn rode into the men, shouting for a cease fire. He bellowed at them to stop shooting, that there had been no order to fire. No one knew who shouted the word, but the troops now on both sides were out of control. Fiercely Major Pitcairn screamed at his officers to control their men, to form them up and cease firing. He was embarrassed at the confusion and the lack of discipline that his troops had exhibited.

David turned to look at the British, but could see only a pall of smoke and hear more musket reports. He stopped a moment and at the same time felt his right leg blasted out from under him. David screamed in surprise and shock, and tumbled into a ditch and lay there, clutching at his thigh. A British grenadier ran up to him and looked at him for a moment. David saw the bayonet on the trooper's long Brown Bess musket still dripping with bright red blood.

The Britisher heard the call to reform and paused, looked back at David and hesitated just a moment more, then turned back and ran toward his unit. David saw him leave and felt the surge of pain flood into his brain and realized that he was going to faint.

Robert had not seen David fall. He held his position behind the wagon body and realized that he had not fired at the enemy. No one had ordered him to fire. He sighted in at one of the officers and fired, but he thought he hit only the horse. He wasn't sure how many of the men with him had fired. Robert leaned against the wagon, watching the Lobsterbacks forming up into units again. He saw the soldiers give a victory cheer and unleash a volley of fire into the air. Then they swung down the road toward Concord.

Robert looked out and watched the Redcoats vanish from the Common. He could see six or eight men who lay on the green, some of them were moving, some weren't. He waited a moment longer but heard no orders to move or assemble. A moment later he saw a woman running across the road from Buckman's Tavern, her long blue skirts flying. It was Harriet.

Harriet cried as she ran. She had a bedsheet in her arms and as she came to the first wounded man she knelt down beside him. Harriet had been shocked, angered and frightened by the sudden murderous volley of gunfire. She had stood in the window at Buckman's Tavern and screamed in disbelief as the hundreds of Lobsterbacks stood and fired at the militia. When the last shot sounded and the enemy had reformed and marched away, she had snatched the sheet from her bed and hurried downstairs.

The first man on the green had been shot in the chest. He looked up at her, thanked her with his eyes, but when he tried to speak, blood gushed out of his mouth, his eyes turned glassy and he died.

She stood, brushing away tears and ran to the next man, who had a musket ball through his arm. He had bled a lot already. Quickly she tore the sheet into strips, folded a piece over both sides of the arm where the ball had gone through and wrapped his arm with the long strip of cloth to keep the pads in place. She didn't know the man.

Harriet looked for someone else. She ran to a man who lay on his side, his throat had caught a musket ball and he bled a spurting stream of red. She tried to stop the blood. By that time Robert had run up and knelt beside her. They watched the man die, and could do nothing for him.

"That was Captain Parker, the company commander," Robert said.

They moved on, found four more dead, and patched up three others. Several of the dead had been bayoneted.

"Have you seen David?" she asked.

Robert shook his head. "He was in the middle of the line. I saw him just before the shooting started."

Two wounded men later, they found a man in a ditch, he was unconscious but breathing. It was David.

They stopped the flow of blood from his thigh, then bandaged it and found that the ball had gone in but had not come out. He would need a physician. Robert slapped David's face gently and brought him back to consciousness. They sat there, staring at each other for a moment.

"At least we're all still alive," David said, gritting through the pounding pain in his leg. He saw the bandage. "Go help the others, I'm fine now. Go help them!"

And they ran to find others who had been wounded. An hour later all of the injured were loaded in wagons and moved into the country, well off the roads. They knew the Britishers had marched the six miles to Concord and had run into intense Rebel fire and not been successful in destroying the war supplies.

The Rebels had stood and fought. The British were on their way back, and the Rebels were sniping and harassing them all the way.

Robert had taken David to the Kellogg farmhouse two miles out of Lexington where they put him on the couch and gathered around. Kate kissed him gently.

"We'll stay here until the British go back to Boston this afternoon," Robert said. "Then we'll go to Lexington and find out if there's a doctor who can help David. If there isn't, he'll have to go with us to Charlestown."

They sat and drank hot coffee and stared at each other.

"It has started," Robert said. "Our war for independence has begun and we won't stop until we have driven the British from our shores."

"Yes, it's begun," David said softly. "And God help us all."

Harriet looked at them both and smiled. "The British began it with another massacre. They killed eight good men back there and wounded ten more. They started this war of revolution, but we shall finish it! And when it is over, Massachusetts and all of the united Thirteen Colonies will be a free and independent nation."

"Amen," Kate said and they all cheered.

SOPHIE
Geoffrey Wagner

FROM RAGS...
Abandoned and abused, Sophie Daws had nothing to look forward to but a meager living on the streets of London. Her only assets were her vibrant spirit and remarkable beauty.

TO RICHES...
The influential Duke of Bourbon, stricken with Sophie's charms, transformed the saucy coquette into a court lady. Soon she rose to become one of the wealthiest, most influential women of her day, and one of the most famous courtesans of all time.

TO...
For more than a decade she held sway over France, but her power and beauty threatened to bring about the downfall of the only man she ever loved — the one who could make her the Queen of France.

PRICE: $2.95
0-505-51795-7
(cc: 50) 320 pp.

CATEGORY:
Historical Romance

SETTING: England
France.

AUTHOR'S HOME:
New York, N.Y.

Also by Geoffrey
Wagner: **Nicchia**
$2.75 0-505-51782-5
(cc: 50)

SOPHIE
GEOFFREY WAGNER

SEND TO: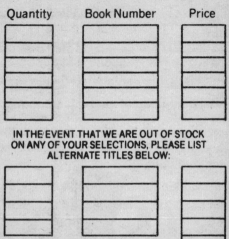

TOWER BOOKS
**P.O. Box 511, Murray Hill Station
New York, N.Y. 10156-0511**

PLEASE SEND ME THE FOLLOWING TITLES:

Quantity	Book Number	Price

**IN THE EVENT THAT WE ARE OUT OF STOCK
ON ANY OF YOUR SELECTIONS, PLEASE LIST
ALTERNATE TITLES BELOW:**

Postage/Handling
I enclose .....

FOR U.S. ORDERS, add 75¢ for the first book and 25¢ for each additional book to cover cost of postage and handling. Buy five or more copies and we will pay for shipping. Sorry, no. C.O.D.'s.

FOR ORDERS SENT OUTSIDE THE U.S.A., add $1.00 for the first book and 50¢ for each additional book. **PAY BY** foreign draft or money order drawn on a U.S. bank, payable in U.S. ($) dollars.

☐ Please send me a free catalog.

NAME _____
(Please print)

ADDRESS _____

CITY _____ **STATE** _____ **ZIP** _____
Allow Four Weeks for Delivery